SLAVE EXODUS

Unresisting, Alex allowed Amaarini to lead her forward, guiding her to the front of the pony cart, positioning her so that the broad, stiff leather band could be fastened about her tightly corseted waist, clipping the reins to either side of her bridle. Alex silently cursed the blinkers that hampered her vision so badly. Something was about to happen and, whatever it turned out to be, there was one thing of which Alex was certain: she was going to be at the centre of it.

'Is she wet, Boolik?' Amaarini demanded.

'No, not yet,' he reported. Amaarini's leering smile widened.

'All the better,' she rasped. 'Take her dry and let's hear her howl.'

Alex now began to struggle and squirm, redoubling her efforts as Boolik pressed the bulbous tip of his shaft against her orifice. Amaarini could restrain her impatience no longer. 'Take her!' she screamed. 'Now, Boolik! Fill her and watch her turn into a slut like all the others!'

By the same author:

SLAVE GENESIS

SLAVE EXODUS

Jennifer Jane Pope

This book is a work of fiction.
In real life, make sure you practise safe sex.

First published in 2000 by
Nexus
Thames Wharf Studios
Rainville Road
London W6 9HA

Typeset by TW Typesetting, Plymouth, Devon

Printed and bound by
Cox & Wyman Ltd, Reading, Berks

ISBN 0 352 33551 3

www.nexus-books.co.uk

Author's Preface

Slave Genesis, my first book in this series, has been variously described as adult science fiction, erotic science fiction, or simply as a fetishist's dream fantasy. I'm quite happy with any or all of those tags, but if you want to decide upon a definition, or category of your own, then do, please, be my guest. My only concern is that you enjoy the story as much as I am enjoying telling it.

In this, the second book, we meet again our heroes, heroines, villains and villainesses whom we left somewhat up in the air at the end of the first and the fate – or should that be 'fate worse than death'? – of the former police-woman Alex Gregory, now facing a life of servitude as a half-android pony girl, did not seem to be that much in the balance any longer.

However, your average Jennifer Jane Pope heroine owes more to the influence of Bob Bishop's Fanni Hall than she does to Pauline in her *Perils*, or to the whimpering, submissive maidens so beloved of Victorian and Edwardian writers of erotica and the feisty Alex will surely not be beaten that easily. Or will she? There is only one way to find out . . .

But, before you do, just a quick word or two about the concepts explored in these books. Genetically modified, android clone bodies into which human brains can be transplanted? A master species who may, or may not, have come from another planet? Life spans of four centuries, maybe more? Surely these are only visions of a future that, if it ever arrives, is still generations away.

Maybe so, and maybe some of the things I propose *will* never happen. After all, we still have yet to see Huxley's skimmers flitting passengers from one skyscraper top to the next and there is still no Transatlantic Tunnel, neither as described by Harry Harrison more than a quarter of a century ago, nor in any other form.

But, before you dismiss these possibilities out of hand and condemn them to the waste bin marked 'Miss Pope's more frenetic ramblings', please remember, among other things, Dolly the Sheep and, the next time you see a beautiful woman staring at you unblinkingly, ask yourself what date is *really* on her birth certificate.

Ask yourself, also, what price eternal life, or the next best thing to it, but meanwhile, do try to enjoy the life you already have. We're all a long time dead and this life ain't the rehearsal. In fact, the curtain is already well and truly up and the harness of fate is jingling over the bit of time . . .

If you have not read my first book in this series, *Slave Genesis*, or even if you have, and, as so many of us frequently do, have just sort of lost the plot, please read the following précis . . .

Jennifer Jane Pope

Prologue

The Shetland Isles, the most northerly part of the British Isles, remote, windswept and thinly populated, even among the larger islands, where the small police presence is occupied mainly in assisting the excise and navy patrols in detecting the drug smugglers who try to bring in their illicit cargoes by sea, via Scandinavia.

Outwardly, the island of Carigillie Craig, on the easternmost fringes of the Shetlands, is home to a respectable and expensive health farm, patronised by ultra-wealthy and often famous clients, but both it and its smaller neighbour, Ailsa Ness, hide a dark and sinister secret.

For nearly two centuries, both islands have been owned and controlled by a curious race of people, whose males can live up to four hundred years, but whose females die before they are thirty – even younger once they have given birth. But the leader of the colony, known to the outside world as Richard Major, and his right-hand man, Doctor Keith Lineker, have not wasted their time and have perfected the science of cloning and genetic modification to the extent that they are able to produce half-android, half-human host bodies – Jenny Anns – into which normal human brains can be transferred, and which can also live as long as their creators.

From the offspring of these clones, they can take DNA samples to produce further clones, into which the brains of their own females can be transplanted, offering them, too, extravagantly prolonged life expectancy.

Until now, the human brains for the Jenny Anns have been taken from women close to death – cancer patients, accident victims and even Jessica, whose original body was all but torn apart when an unexploded World War Two bomb finally detonated as she was walking home in 1951. After nearly fifty years in her stronger, fitter body, Jess is happy with her life as a pony girl, living in the underground stables complex on Ailsa and kept for the exclusive use of Andrew Lachan, billionaire tycoon, who ensures that when she is not serving him on his frequent visits to the island, she can enjoy a life of relative comfort and luxury, despite her ever-present bridle and harness.

The rest of the Jenny Anns are not so fortunate, for in return for their alleged salvation, they are expected to act as sex slaves for Ailsa's more discerning visitors. The reduced pain threshold of their bodies makes them ideal objects for the gratification of every imaginable lust and fetish, but most bear their crosses stoically, realising that there is no alternative and certainly no chance of escape.

One exception to this general air of acceptance is Tammy, but then Tammy is not like her sister J-As, for, until her original human body was washed up on the island after a storm wrecked one of the local trawlers, Tammy had been Tommy MacIntyre, a decidedly rugged and macho young fisherman, and the prospect of spending decade upon decade as the sexual plaything of a procession of warped masters and mistresses is too appalling to contemplate.

Meanwhile, a series of seemingly innocent and unconnected deaths elsewhere in the islands attracts the attention of Detective Sergeant Alex Gregory, local girl made good and still ambitious to do better. Why would an elderly man risk climbing on to the roof of his cottage to adjust a satellite dish that had been disconnected for a year? And why would a part-time coroner examining the bodies of the victims of a helicopter crash suddenly lose control of his car on a road known to be dangerous?

Detective Constable Geordie Walker, recently posted to the islands to keep him away from the threatened revenge of a crazed gangland boss he helped bring to justice, thinks that Alex is making too much of things, and their boss, Detective Inspector George Gillespie, approaching retirement and eager not to tread on too many wealthy or influential toes, agrees. Alex, however, is a lady not easily deterred.

She recruits the aid of her old friend and former fellow member of their university skydiving club, a local helicopter charter pilot, Rory Dalgleish, and makes a parachute descent on to Ailsa Ness under cover of darkness. Unfortunately for Alex, the island is about to receive other unwanted visitors, in the shape of Andrew Lachan, his former special services security adviser and a small team of hired mercenaries.

Unable to persuade Richard Major to sell him Jessie outright, Lachan is determined to abduct her to his highland farm retreat, but their seaborne landing attracts the attention of the island's own security men. In trying to evade the ensuing gun battle, Alex, who is still stunned from watching the human pony girls racing each other around the torchlit track at the farthest end of the island, slips and falls into a narrow ravine, breaking her back and paralysing her body completely.

When she comes round, it is to find that she, too, is now a Jenny Ann and expected to adapt to a lifestyle that is as completely alien to her as are the creatures who have inflicted this humiliation upon her. But if Alex is horrified at her expected new role, Andrew Lachan, the only survivor of the ill-fated kidnap attempt, has also awoken to find himself, like Tommy before him, now in a very sexy female body, sharing a stable with Jessie, the very reason for his coming here in the first place.

Alex's original body is removed to Carigillie Craig together with her parachute, and the scene is staged to make it appear that she had snapped her neck upon landing. Geordie, who knew that she was intending to land on Ailsa, not Carigillie, is instantly suspicious and suspects she has been murdered. However, despite Rory Dalgleish's assertions that Alex baled out over the smaller island, DI

Gillespie concludes there is no real proof of skulduggery and not even enough evidence to mount a thorough investigation.

Meanwhile, hundreds of miles to the southwest, the deaths of Andrew Lachan and some of his henchmen have been faked in an explosion aboard his luxury motor yacht, the *Jessica*. A former colleague of Geordie's, appointed to investigate the 'accident', is not entirely happy with the situation. Discovering a link between Lachan and Health-glow, the company supposedly running Carigillie, he telephones his old friend to see if he can throw any further light on things.

And now, read on . . .

One

The temperature in the subterranean stables complex was lower than usual this morning, but Alex Gregory knew only too well that the air that awaited her outside in the early post-dawn Shetlands autumn would be only a degree or two above freezing point and her near-naked condition would cause even the flesh of this new, artificially cloned body they had given her to shiver and sting.

She grunted, as the wide girth strap – in reality, it was more of a leather corset – was drawn tighter still by the young groom, whose youthful frame belied the strength in his arms and shoulders, and snorted through flared nostrils, as he slapped her playfully across her prominent buttocks. He stepped around in front of her, hefting one full breast in his upturned palm, and Alex, perched on the towering and humiliatingly hoof-shaped boots, glared down her nose at him.

The foul-tasting rubber-covered bit prevented coherent speech, but, even had it not been buckled so harshly between her stretched lips, protestations, she knew, would have been fruitless. Wherever they found this seemingly endless supply of new young tormentors to handle the pony girls in the stables, their characters never seemed to vary. Baby-faced they may have looked, but all of the grooms that Alex had encountered so far appeared to relish having so much feminine 'horse flesh' so helplessly in their charge.

'They' were the curious people who apparently ran the two bizarre islands out here in the wilds of the North Sea,

men and women with real names that were unpronounceable – Anglicised equivalents were substituted in everyday
use – and this latest addition to the stables staff appeared to
be one of them, the slightly elongated nose and hooded,
mildly reptilian eyes being a physical constant among them.

His name – the one used for both slaves and in the
presence of the constantly shifting stream of 'guests' who
availed themselves of their services – was Benjamin, though
he referred to himself as Benji as he talked to the girls while
harnessing them. His hair was dark, though not exactly
black, and his eyes were a curious blend: sometimes pale
amber, sometimes deep green.

He drew the left-breast harness in another notch,
causing Alex's already oversized orb to bulge even more
grotesquely, and flicked at the bell that hung from the
heavy ring that adorned the nipple.

'You're starting to look like a real pedigree mare now,
Jangles,' he grinned. Alex's already distorted features
twisted into an even more unattractive grimace at the use
of the pony name she had been given, a name made even
worse by the way in which her body had been adorned with
a glittering array of bells and brasses, so that every move
she made seemed to emphasise the fact that she had now,
in almost every way, become the embodiment of it.

'Yes'– Benji nodded, tightening the strapping around her
other breast, until its size and engorgement matched the
first – 'I reckon you could be another Jessie, given a bit
more training. Mind you,' he added, grabbing one side of
her bridle and tugging her head around and down, the stiff
leather collar about her throat digging into the tender flesh
beneath her chin, 'you've got a bit more spirit than Jess, as
anyone can see.

'Spirit ain't a bad thing, Jangles,' he continued, speaking
more softly now, 'but there's spirit and there's spirit, if you
know what I mean. Good spirit. Bad spirit.' He drew her
face closer to his own.

'Good spirit makes a pony run well, compete well,' he
said. 'Bad spirit causes disobedience. It's the bad spirit we
need to get out of you, Jangles.' Alex tried to avert her

6

eyes, but Benji simply tugged even harder at her bridle, twisting her neck around, the bit seemingly threatening to tear the side of her mouth, though she knew none of the grooms would risk such a disfiguring extravagance. She let out a plaintive whinny, horribly equine to her ears, though the high pain threshold of this new body was such that she was not truly suffering.

'OK, so we understand one another,' Benji sniggered, relaxing his grip and allowing her to return to an upright stance. He turned, picked up a long crop from the trestled stand to one side and swished it through the air, the braided leather whistling dangerously close to Alex's shoulder. Despite herself, she started back, which seemed to add to his amusement.

'Remember, Jangles,' he laughed, 'I do love that cute rump of yours when I've made it all pink and glowing, so let's have some proper discipline from you this morning. Now, stand and display and let's fit your tail and crotch harness. See?' As he spoke, Benji had turned and picked up another item from the stand, holding it up between them, like a trophy.

Alex swallowed, recognising the dildo as one of the largest the grooms used for training the pony girls. The only models larger were reserved for the really experienced girls, those who, like Jessie, had spent so long in this regime that trotting or cantering, while plugged with a twelve-inch phallus, had long since become just one more part of the day's routine.

Glumly, she eased her legs apart, adopting the required stance, and Benji reached down with his free hand, fingers sliding over her hairless mons, prising apart the swollen lips, probing for the little nubbin that they both knew would trigger instant lubrication, whether Alex liked it or not, so highly tuned was her body now to respond to certain stimuli. A few seconds later, the black monster slipped inside her, sliding upwards until its flanged base nestled snugly against her distorted outer labia, the rings from the piercings of which forced cruelly against them, drawing a low yelp from her throat.

7

The crotch belt was attached, its V-shaped front straps buckling on to the lower hem of the girth corset, the two thin leather fronds joining to produce a wider length in time to press the base of the dildo even further into Alex's softest flesh, passing beneath her and separating her buttocks, but not before the attached butt plug had been twisted home, holding the red and gold tail proudly out behind her.

'Nearly done,' Benji muttered, tightening the strap where it joined the rear of the girth, so that Alex's already high bottom cheeks were thrust higher still. He moved around in front again, clipping a heavy bell into position below her sex, a bell that later, if the mood took him, Alex knew could well be attached to the rings in her labia, using a cunning arrangement of clips that would also serve to hold the rubber phallus inside her, even though the crotch strap would need to be removed to effect the additional torture.

Now he checked her arms again, though there was little need, for in the three months since Alex had awoken in this hell, she had been, unlike some of the other girls here, kept permanently deprived of any real use of her upper limbs. Her hands had remained in curious leather mitten affairs, the tapering ends of which had been folded back and inwards, then fastened to the locking wrist straps to force her fingers into permanent fists. Not satisfied with this, whenever she was trained, exercised or put out for the benefit of guests, her arms were then folded double, caught up in laced, triangular pouches, so that they assumed the appearance of ridiculously stubby and totally useless chicken wings, but then drawn back by means of chains attached to rings at the elbows, until her breasts were forced forward and her shoulders pulled painfully backward.

Drawing a small step-up alongside her, Benji carefully took up the plumed headdress, mounted until he was slightly taller than Alex, and carefully attached it to the bridle harness, where it passed over the crown of her head, teasing what remained of her hair upwards until he was able to lace it around the plumage to form part of her crest.

'Right,' he said, not bothering to climb down yet. 'Let's see what you've learned, Jangles.' He pointed towards where the black and gold cart stood ready for her. 'Walk around the buggy twice, then get yourself between the shafts.'

Mournfully, head held erect by the stiff collar, aware that her distended flesh would now ripple at every step she took in the ridiculously high hoof boots, bells jangling at nipple, crotch and elbow, former Detective Sergeant Alexandra Gregory, a.k.a. Jangles the pony girl, moved to obey.

Acting Detective Sergeant Timothy Milburn Walker, a.k.a. Geordie to most of his colleagues outside his native Newcastle, regarded the trilling telephone receiver on his cluttered desk, pushed aside a stained coffee mug and a dog-eared sheaf of paperwork and stretched out a hand for the open packet of cigarettes on the window ledge to his left. He hesitated, fingers inches from the rumpled carton, sighed and reached for the handset.

'You took your bloody time answering.' Geordie recognised the slightly cultured tones of Detective Constable Colin Turner, despite the unusually poor quality of the connection. He guessed his one-time colleague was calling from a mobile. 'Don't tell me you've had an outbreak of sheep shagging and you're run off your wellies up there, eh?'

'Oh, fuck off, Colin,' Geordie said, but without any real malice. That was the trouble with tiredness, he reflected: it gave you little time for real emotions; things like phone calls just became a nuisance, especially when he had been fielding calls from Turner at weekly intervals ever since Alex Gregory's death on Carigillie Craig, and the man had still to produce one shred of tangible evidence that her demise had been anything more than a tragic accident.

'Well, and a merry Christmas to you, too, old boy,' Colin chuckled, between bursts of interference.

'There are still nearly four months to go,' Geordie said, reaching for the cigarettes again, 'and I don't suppose you'll be any nearer turning up anything worthwhile by then, either.' There was a short silence and for a moment Geordie thought the connection had been broken, but another crackle, followed by a loud hiss and Colin Turner's voice, suddenly came through loud and clear.

'That's where you could be wrong, old chap,' he said. 'Hang on, just let me pull over. I'm on top of a place called Butser Hill and there's a mast for these mobile johnnies not half a mile from here. Right, engines off, chocks in and all that.'

'Colin, you've never been in the RAF in your entire fucking life,' Geordie said, patiently.

'Ah, but the dear old grandfather was one of the few, old bean,' Turner retorted, quite unfazed. 'Family traditions, and all that. Now, where was I? Oh yes, hold fire a sec, there's a good chap.' There was another pause.

'Right, let's sort this paperwork into some sort of order. Now then, your man, Lachan.'

'He was *your* man,' Geordie reminded Turner. 'I never met him.'

'Me neither. If you recall, first I heard of him was when the coastguard started trying to fish bits of him and his boat out of the briny. I only got involved because his boat was registered at the Hamble down thisaways.'

'And he was supposed to have been a guest at the health farm place out on Carigillie,' Geordie agreed. 'Which was also where Alex Gregory died.'

The early morning air *had* been close to freezing point, the immediate effect, although the tugging reins prevented her from looking down to see for herself, being to arouse Alex's belled nipples to twin, hardened cones, sending a series of tiny tremors throughout her entire body.

It was the one thing that Alex hated above all else, the way in which this new body seemed to have been designed to work independently of her conscious mind. No matter how her psyche, her years of education and moral upbring-

10

ing might revolt against the indignities that these people continued to heap on her, something inside, something deeper even than subconscious thought, persisted in reacting at a level she could describe only as base, animal instinct.

And how they knew it, from the casually indifferent (at times) handlers through to those guests she had so far encountered. Yes, they knew, even if some of them might not quite understand, which was why, Alex assumed, they felt that they could treat her as if she were really nothing more than a pony, albeit a two-legged pony in a deliciously human, feminine body.

She trotted along the well-worn pathway towards the running circuit where she had first seen the pony girl races that fateful night. If she did not trot eagerly, she at least trotted with sufficient energy to persuade Benji that he had no need of either crop or whip, for while this new body could withstand and recover from levels of punishment that her original body most certainly could not have endured, the long driving whip in particular still stung and the crop, if laid on with sufficient enthusiasm, could make her buttocks feel as if they were on fire. Arms and hands useless, feet arched high on the heavy hoof boots, training weights in the thick soles making them drag at every step, lips curled back into a snarl about the tugging bit and blinkers focusing her vision into a narrow forward field, Alex turned towards the slowly rising sun, lowering her eyelids against its fierce glare.

Behind her, as she ran, dragging the grotesque little buggy and its youthful passenger, lay what had once been the real world. Somewhere back there, across a stretch of sea that now seemed as if it might as well be the width of an ocean, was an existence where people probably still remembered, even if they no longer mourned, a promising young policewoman whose life, according to the local papers, had to all intents and purposes ended when her parachute failed to open during an unauthorised attempt to land upon Carigillie Craig, which itself lay several miles from this place, Ailsa Ness, where the real Alex Gregory

11

had – or should have – died from a broken neck, as the result of a fall down a steep ravine, only to come back to life inside this taller, fitter, even more attractive body.

And to spend, if the man Lineker was to be believed, anything up to another three hundred or more years as she was now, bound, harnessed, chained and bitted, a fetish object to be used by anyone, man or woman, who could afford the price.

Had she been physically able to cry, tears would have trickled down on to those high, proud cheeks, only to be whipped away by the sharp wind, but that was one thing this new body would not allow. Yet, as her narrowed eyes beheld the monochrome vista that was another limitation of whatever science had gone into creating her new shell, Alex knew she was crying in her heart.

'Of course.' Colin Turner's voice became suddenly more sober. 'I *have* been doing my best at this end,' he said. 'No stone unturned, and all that. Bloody difficult following these paper trails, though. You should remember that yourself.'

'Yeah, but then I didn't have the benefit of a university education,' Geordie said. 'So, *have* you got any further?'

Andrew Lachan, a particularly wealthy Scots businessman, had met an untimely end a day after Alex Gregory's death, when his private motor cruiser, a luxurious and expensive piece of hardware called the *Jessica* had exploded in mysterious circumstances off the coast of Cornwall, as far away from the Shetland Isles as it was possible to be without leaving British coastal waters. Colin's original reason for contacting Geordie over the matter was that Lachan had, via a complex system of bank accounts, been paying substantial sums of money to a company called Healthglow, which owned Carigillie, the health farm situated on it and, as they had subsequently discovered, the neighbouring, even smaller, island of Ailsa Ness.

'It's all a matter of degrees,' Turner said. 'Been dotting I's, crossing T's and all that, checking on the finances of these health farm wallahs.'

12

'And?'

'And how many people did you say worked there?'

'Fifteen to twenty, depending upon the season, from the book work I was shown when we went out there,' Geordie said.

'And how many guests?'

'Around two dozen at the time. That was at the beginning of the summer, which is one of its busier times.'

'Quite,' Turner agreed. 'Shouldn't think the winter weather up there is all that healthy.'

'Very bracing, so I'm told,' Geordie returned. 'I'll let you know when I've survived my first winter up here.'

'*If* you survive,' Turner chortled. 'But let's get serious, old chum. From what you say, the total population of that bit of rock is somewhere around forty-five at best, say fifty tops, eh?'

'If what I was shown and told was accurate, yes.'

'Well, it certainly ties in with the accounts we've managed to dig out of Companies House.'

'And? Is there a "but" coming?' Geordie's policeman mind already knew that there was and Colin Turner knew that he would.

'There appears to be,' he replied, slowly. 'It's taken a while, but I've managed, through my own useful little sources, to track a few more accounts that can be linked with Healthglow, albeit the links are somewhat, shall we say, spurious.'

'Wouldn't stand up in court, you mean?'

'They would, ultimately, I'm sure. However, we need a reason to even get to court with them in the first place.'

'And are you any nearer finding a reason?' Geordie asked.

'Nearer, but not near enough,' Turner said. 'However, I do have a question you might like to consider.'

'I'm listening.'

'Of course you are. So, try this on for size. Your little island, in or out of the sun, has a maximum population of fifty for, say, half the year and let's say an average of thirty for the other half.'

13

'Seems a reasonable assumption. Go on.'

'Well, from the figures I have in my sweaty little palms at the moment, I should say that enough supplies are going there to support a population easily three times that number.'

'Figures can be misleading,' Geordie warned. 'All the health-food shite tends to cost an arm and a leg, don't forget.'

'So does a particularly fine brandy, old son,' Turner said. 'No, they're not importing rare vintages, that was just a f'rinstance, although they do seem to keep quite a good cellar up there, judging by this lot.

'No, I've got a particularly detailed victuals list here for the last eighteen months or so, and we're talking bulk, not cost. Enough chow to feed a small army, plus wines, spirits, luxury foods and so on – not healthy-eating stuff in my book, though much preferable to the old Turner palate.

'And there's more,' he said, pushing on before Geordie could gather himself for a reply. 'I've several invoices here for quite large quantities of leather, cured hides and stuff.'

'Coming up here to Carigillie?'

'Not directly, no. The stuff goes to a harness maker, not a million miles away from where I'm currently sitting. Traditional craft firm, by all accounts, making saddles, bridles, stuff for carts and carriages.'

'And then some of it gets sent up here?'

'Possibly, though there's no trail there yet,' Turner said. 'However, there's a trail back the other way. The place is actually owned by a Celia Butler, some sort of heiress, landowner, tycoon and one-time erotic fashion designer to the unwholesomely rich and idle fringes of a certain section of society.

'Doing a bit of backtracking, I see that Ms Butler is a frequent guest at Healthglow and that, while the various banking records show her as transferring a regular subscription to their account, she appears to be on a far more favourable rate than some of the other members there.

'Not only that, although it's early days as yet, my guess would be that a good auditor might just find that there's little or no trace of the leather materials that her place gets from the Healthglow route, at least not a financial one.'

'I see,' Geordie said, although in truth he didn't. 'So, you reckon she's trading finished horsy-type equipment in exchange for cheaper rates.'

'Maybe, but only if they run a fucking big riding school on that island. I've picked a few brains and the wise ones tell me that there's enough missing raw materials to outfit every nag in the Light Brigade and probably half of Custer's Seventh Cavalry to boot, no pun intended.'

'Well, if there were horses out on Carigillie, I never saw any sign of them,' Geordie grunted. He heard a low laugh from the other end of the line.

'No, I dare say you wouldn't have,' Turner said. 'Listen, old chum, you *can* get on to the Internet from the wilds up there, can't you?'

'Yes, why?'

'Well, grab a stub of good old-fashioned pencil and take down the following details. Have a surf, as they say, feast your peepers, educate the old brain box and then phone me back tonight. The bloody battery on this thing is about to go.'

15

Two

'So,' Richard Major said, leaning back in the huge leather reclining chair, 'you are now ready to test the new processors?' His companion, leaning against the heavy mantel shelf opposite him, nodded.

'It's now been three months since they were installed in the experimental subjects, so any potential malfunctions cannot be ascribed to the surgical processes,' he said. 'Not that I anticipate any malfunctions, Rekoli.'

Major smiled up at him. 'Nor I,' he said, tilting the glass to his lips. 'Your skill is beyond doubt, my old friend.'

'And your confidence appreciated,' Lineker smiled back.

'Remind me,' Major said. 'How many subjects, and which ones are they?'

'A total of ten now,' Lineker said. 'The fisherman, the policewoman, the Lachan idiot and our esteemed television star. However, I think it better that we leave Miss Charles for the time being, at least until we have had some experience with the others.'

'Wise, friend, wise,' said Major. 'No point in pushing our luck, as they say. The desirable Fiona is an ideal experimental subject, but we do not want to give her the slightest inkling as to what you did to her.'

'Of course,' Lineker concurred. 'While we now have six clones ready, it will be far more satisfying to conduct our final tests on the real lady. Much better to control a real media star than simply to substitute her with a tame pet.'

'Much better,' Major said, his features impassive as ever.

* * *

She had once been a young Scottish trawlerman named Tommy MacIntyre.

That much she knew. She remembered.

She remembered the night of the storm. She remembered the shipwreck. She remembered finally being washed up ashore on this island. She remembered what she had seen, the crazy scenes with human females being driven like animals, bridled, harnessed, racing with carts behind them, whipped on to greater efforts by the most bizarre drivers imaginable.

Like something out of a nightmare, Tommy had thought. Except that *this* was a real nightmare and now he was a she, and Tommy was now Tammy. And Tammy had joined those lithe female pony girls, racing with buggies at their heels, heavy hoof boots sparking on the cinder track, whips cracking across unprotected flesh, urging flagging limbs to greater efforts, breasts bouncing in flagrant rhythm, nipple bells returning their own taunting melody with every tormented stride.

'I'd kill myself, if I could.' Tammy kept her eyes lowered, avoiding those of her new stablemate.

'And let them find more unfortunates to take our place?' said Jangles. It was almost the first time Tammy had heard her speak, for the grooms had been keeping her firmly bitted, ever since her arrival in the stables, just a day or so after Tammy's own induction. Only when they had moved them in together, just a day earlier, had that infernal bit been removed and even then, only after several hours had the two even begun to exchange confidences.

'I'm beginning to think I must have gone mad,' Tammy said, deliberately keeping her voice to a mere whisper. 'I mean, look at me!' She nodded down with her chin, indicating her body, her arms still held immobile and useless by the two laced pouches.

'Aye, I know,' Jangles whispered back. 'It's the same for me.' Tammy's meticulously groomed eyebrows arched upwards.

'No fucking way!' she squeaked. 'You were born with tits, at least. I'm a fucking man, hinnie.'

17

'Not from where I'm standing!' For the first time in many long weeks, Alex Gregory found herself grinning. Mind you, she told herself, if ever there was a sign that she was really cracking, that was it. After all, what was there in this madhouse that . . .?

She looked across at the forlorn figure standing by the far bunk, the neck chain preventing her from moving far from it and permitting her just sufficient latitude to be able to lie down on the straw-filled mattress. No, that wasn't funny, not if the poor creature was telling the truth, and, no matter how grotesque and unlikely her story might sound, it was, in its own way, no worse than Alex's own.

'Sorry,' Alex said, shuffling along and perching on the end of her own bunk, trying to ignore the jangle of bells that now accompanied her every move. 'It's just that –'

'Aye, I know,' Tammy snapped back. 'It's bloody hard to believe that a fully functioning, male, heterosexual fisherman, capable o' swinging a hundred-pound basket o' bloody fish on to his shoulder, could possibly end up looking like this.' The nod was aimed at the prominent breasts that now adorned the front of the upper part of what, Alex had to admit, was a beautiful female body.

'Well, it may be hard,' she replied, quietly, 'but then I'm little better off. And by the way, Tammy, Tommy, whatever you're really called, for your information I wasn't born with tits. No woman is. They come later, unless you hadn't noticed. And my own – what *used* to be my own, anyway – weren't half the size of these obscenities.'

'Alex seemed to have some idea that this guy Major might have been the same guy who appears in various records concerning the islands, dating back . . . well, dating back into the last century, as it happens.' Even as he spoke, Geordie realised how foolish his words sounded and the expression on George Gillespie's craggy features told him that the DI thought exactly the same.

'You don't really believe that, do you?' he said, his soft highlands accent at odds with the hard glint in his eyes. Geordie shrugged.

'Does it matter what *I* think?' he said. 'OK, so she got a bit carried away. Presumably, there are plenty of families around these parts where the eldest son is named after his father – same where I come from, though in my case I was named after my grandfather. Whatever . . . the fact remains that there is definitely something not right about the set-up out there.'

'Except that neither you nor Sergeant Gregory, rest her soul, have, nor had, not the slightest shred of any evidence that might even justify another visit to Carigillie, let alone stand up in a court of law.'

'No.' Geordie turned away, staring out of the window, but not seeing the harbour, nor the gathering storm clouds beyond. 'No,' he repeated. 'I don't have a damned thing – unless you count a gut feeling. The same sort of gut feeling that Alex reckoned she had, only at the time I never believed it, either.'

'And now you do?' Detective Inspector Gillespie sat back, steepling his fingers and peering at Geordie over their tips. Geordie let out a loud sigh, shaking his head.

'Guv,' he said, at length, 'I'm not really sure what I think, feel, believe, or anything. All I know is that I *liked* Alex Gregory and that, despite the fact I knew she was a good copper, with a good record, I thought she was completely off the track on all this. If I'd known what she was intending, I'd have done everything within my power to stop her, but I didn't, so it's not worth beating my brains out over that.

'However, Colin Turner then comes back at me with this luxury yacht, cruiser, call it what you like, that gets blown up in circumstances that are, well, to say the least, not exactly kosher, and the late owner, a frequent visitor to the same island on which Alex supposedly broke her neck trying to parachute in at night, is spread over quite a large area of the Atlantic Ocean, in bits too small to identify.' He paused, drew in a breath and turned back to face his superior. 'And within twenty-four hours or so of Alex's death,' he finished.

'And was this Andrew Lachan on the island when Alex died?' Gillespie asked.

Geordie shrugged again. 'Who knows?' he countered. 'Not according to the book work we saw out there, I'll grant you, but then, if there was anything going on, would you expect his name to still be in the register?'

'Probably not,' Gillespie agreed, 'but then we're still dealing in maybes, aren't we? Your friend Turner may suspect that there's something suspicious about Lachan's death, but he hasn't got anything concrete, has he? No forensic evidence to prove a bomb, no known enemies, no nothing, apart from those radio fixes – and who's to say they were accurate?

'That *Jessica* could easily have been transmitting from exactly where the wreckage was found. A few miles is nothing, not given possible variations due to local weather conditions. No, I'm sorry laddie, we still have nothing.'

'What about this pony-girl stuff?' Geordie jabbed a finger at the pile of printouts he'd made from the various Internet sites Colin Turner had directed him to.

'What about it?' Gillespie demanded. 'We're grown men, Geordie. We know this sort of thing goes on, but murdering policewomen and blowing up boats is in a different league. This is all just people with slightly warped ideas and you can see from that lot it's all just a big game to the people involved. They aren't the sort to go around killing people.'

'Maybe not,' Geordie conceded. 'Maybe not the people involved in this end of things, anyway. But there are ties in here to a woman who was a frequent guest, member, whatever, at Carigillie and there's Dalgleish's aerial photographs, showing what could easily be some sort of race track on Ailsa. Is that all just coincidence?'

'I don't know any more than you do,' Gillespie snapped, slapping his palm down on the sheaf of papers. 'Which means we both know fuck all, so if you think I'm going to authorise an official return to either island, you can forget it.'

'And forget about Alex's death?'

'I didn't say that,' Gillespie almost snarled. 'Don't put words into my mouth, laddie, not if you want to stay around here beyond tonight.' He paused, stroking his chin. 'Alex's death,' he said at last, 'was a tragedy. The official line, given what we know for sure, was that it was an accident, caused by ... well, a misguided hunch, overeagerness, poor judgement ... whatever. That's the official line and, until I have anything concrete to the contrary, that's my line also.

'However,' he said, breathing heavily, 'if I thought there was any foul play involved, or rather that I could prove that there was, then I'd have the guts of whoever was responsible as laces for my granny's corsets.'

'So, you're not convinced it was an accident?'

'I didn't say that, either.' George Gillespie turned away, paced across his office, turned again and paced back to the desk. 'I'm due for retirement in another couple of years,' he said. 'I've spent almost my entire career up in this backwater, kept my nose clean, done a good job and earned myself a reputation as being a good, conscientious, level-headed copper.

'I can't afford to compromise any of that, Geordie, as I'm sure you'll appreciate.' He sniffed, noisily. 'However, seeing as how quiet we are here at the moment, should you choose to dedicate some of your spare time to probing for a few facts here and there, I wouldn't exactly be asking you for accurate diary dates, get me?'

Geordie nodded. 'And what if Colin Turner were to come up here for a few days?'

'Officially?'

Geordie shook his head. 'Not exactly,' he said. 'He's due a fortnight's leave and fancies a bit of fishing. He asked if I might put him up and maybe go out a few times with him.'

'And of course, you've got accumulated leave due you, too,' Gillespie pointed out. 'And our new bod arrives tomorrow, so once you've shown her the ropes, as long as you don't have a backlog of paperwork, what better time to take some of it?'

Geordie grinned, reached for his cigarettes, screwed up the nearly empty packet and tossed it out of the open window.

'My thoughts exactly, guv,' he said.

* * *

Jessie had seen much during her life. Two world wars, for a start, memories of troops marching off to the trenches when she had been a little girl, cinema newsreel footage of tanks clanking across a ravaged Europe, horrendous footage of skeletal survivors of the Nazi death camps, more footage of giant mushroom-shaped clouds of destruction over Hiroshima and Nagasaki and later, much later, television coverage of man's first step upon Earth's nearest celestial neighbour.

In between – and now only a jumbled series of stop-action memory clips – there had been the bomb blast, the unexploded German mine that had finally elected to detonate ten years later, injuring dozens and killing nine, a death toll that would have been at least one more, had not someone (Jessie still had no idea who) intervened to place her in the hands of Dr Lineker only hours before her original body would finally have given up the unequal struggle. Already past child-bearing age in her original existence, this new body, to all intents and purposes only half that age, had eventually brought forth a daughter, fathered by one of the males who held sway here in these islands, a daughter who was now herself nearly fifty years old, but who, like her mother, still looked no older than twenty-five.

And now, in the new millennium, nearly a century after her birth, Jessie was confused at last. For more than ninety years she had accepted her fate with a philosophical fatalism that bordered on the inane, happy to trade near death for even this life in which she spent the majority of her days in harness, bitted, blinkered, abused and used as a two-legged, bare-breasted, human equine, whose routine rarely varied between pulling a racing buggy and hours of near boredom in the luxury cell behind what was outwardly her stable stall, her only contact with the real world via the small television screen set high in the wall at the end of her bed.

Jessie the pony girl had known many masters and mistresses over the years, until finally she had come to love – no, worship – the man who had paid to make her his exclusive property, a man who had visited the island often, paying – as even Jessie understood it – a queen's ransom for the exclusivity of her services and a man who could, by his own admission, have afforded even ten times that amount.

Andrew. Andrew Lachan. Multimillionaire. Billionaire, even, from what little he had told her. He had driven her, ridden her, whipped her and loved her. He had even offered to buy her outright, but the people here had refused his money, even when he had upped the figures to unbelievable levels.

But Andrew Lachan was not a man to take no for an answer, whatever the circumstances. Looking across at her new stablemate, Jessie felt her eyes misting over and, if her body had been designed to allow it, she knew she would have cried as she regarded the cowed pony girl in her golden leather trappings, mouth silenced by the cruellest of training bits. Bambi, they called her.

Oh, why had Master Andrew been so foolish? Jessie did not understand a lot of things, despite what she had seen in her long life, but one thing she did know was that to try to take her away from this place by force was an act of total foolishness, a venture doomed to failure from the very start. These people were too cunning, too well prepared.

Too ruthless.

Bambi, they called the pony girl now. A mirror image, almost, of Jessie herself, a creature trapped in a body cloned from almost the same formula as the one in which Jessie had spent more than fifty years now and in which, whether she realised it or not yet, she was likely to spend at least another thirty decades, probably more.

Poor Bambi.

Poor Andrew.

Poor Andrew, with his consuming passion for pony girls. Poor Andrew, who would now be able to spend maybe three hundred years with his passion. Poor Andrew, thought Jessie.

Poor Andrew – who was now Bambi the pony girl himself. Or was that *her*self?

* * *

23

'Alex, why won't you call me by my real name?' Tammy looked as distressed and confused as she perpetually did. Alex looked across their joint stall and smiled at her.

'I'm sorry,' she said, shaking her head, 'but it's not easy thinking of you as a Tommy.' Tommy/Tammy stamped one steel-shod hoof boot on the stone floor and Alex would not have been surprised if the action had produced a shower of sparks.

'No harder than it is for me to think of you in a bloody police uniform,' Tammy snapped, sullenly. Alex snorted.

'There's a slight difference,' she said and immediately wished she hadn't. Tammy stiffened, but her attempt at defiance was somewhat spoiled by the way her changing attitude forced her already prominent breasts to thrust out even further.

'Look . . . Tommy,' Alex said, soothingly, 'we have to face a few facts here, whether we like it or not. Number one, we can't turn the clock back, so, what we see is what we get. Number two, right now we seem to have little option other than to go along with these weirdos, no matter how appalling that might seem.

'I don't know about you, but I have this survival instinct. Live to fight another day, and all that. Which is what, I suspect, we might not do if we try to put too many noses out of joint.'

'But why should they kill us?' Tammy whined, plaintively. The poor former fisherman was losing it by the day, Alex realised, but then that was hardly to be wondered at.

'Why shouldn't they?' she returned. She took a couple of steps forward, raising a useless, leather-mitted hand and placing it on her companion's shoulder. 'Listen, Tammy – I mean Tommy – they made these bodies they've given us. They appear to have made the bodies of several of our fellow stablemates, including that Jessie, so presumably they can make more and, presumably, at will.

'From what I've gathered so far, all they need are personalities to put into these bodies and so far they don't seem to have suffered much of a shortage. Some of their subjects – especially Jess – seem grateful for what's been

24

done to them, so grateful that they'll do anything and everything they're told.

'So, why should they go out of their way to keep a couple of rebels, eh?' Alex added. 'If we give them a hard time, then we know what will happen eventually. They'll use the whips and turn down our pain thresholds so it really bloody hurts. I've already had one demonstration of that, same as you have.

'So, we'll either end up giving in the hard way, or, if we can find a way to bear it – and I can't see myself putting up with too much of that – then they'll simply switch us off altogether. That Kelly girl told me they can reuse the bodies anyway.'

'Very bloody eco-friendly,' Tammy snarled. She raised her eyes, glaring at Alex. 'Well, they can do what they bloody want to me, I –'

'Exactly!' Alex snapped, cutting Tammy short in mid-sentence. 'That's *exactly* what they *can* do, Tammy. I mean, look what they've done already!'

'And so we give in, do we?'

'No.' Alex paused, breathing in deeply, or as deeply as the tight corset girth allowed. 'No,' she said, more quietly, 'we don't give in. We may let them think that's what we're doing, but we definitely don't give in. OK, we go with whatever they expect of us, no matter how distasteful that might be, but underneath we don't forget who or what we are.

'We wait, Tammy.' She half turned away, pursing her lips. 'We wait, we watch and we learn.'

'And then what?'

'I don't know,' Alex replied, her voice a hoarse whisper. 'Right now, I don't know. But,' she went on, nodding slowly, 'I do know that no plan is flawless and no person perfect. There'll be mistakes made, chances to be taken. And when the time comes, my beautiful little friend, it won't matter whether you're male or female, fish or fowl. We'll be ready to take advantage.'

'Yeah?' Tammy sighed, her splendid breasts rising and falling. 'You really think so?'

25

'I have to,' Alex said. 'I have to, otherwise I'd go fucking mad.'

Like the rest of the bastards here, she added, under her breath.

Amaarini Savanijuik stood before the bank of monitors, one gloved hand stroking her jaw absently. Tall, even without the additional height of her gleaming, thigh-length boots, hair piled high to enhance the effect, she had a presence that would have commanded any gathering, even without the skin-tight rubbery outfit and tightly laced corset that was now her habitual uniform.

Without turning away from the rows of screens, she spoke.

'Fascinating, Boolik,' she said, her full lips twitching slightly. 'Quite fascinating, don't you think?' The taller of her two male companions gave a slight shrug of his broad shoulders, his reptilian features twisting into a grimace. Boolik Gothar, head of security on both Carigillie Craig and Ailsa Ness, was a man who dealt solely in practicalities, and the finer points of what went on, especially here beneath the soil of the smaller island, Ailsa, frequently escaped him.

'If you say so, Amaarini,' he grunted. 'Personally, I find all humans to be very pathetic creatures indeed.'

'Of course you do,' Amaarini said, barely suppressing a laugh. 'You, Boolik, are a very uncomplicated being, which is why you are so good at what you do. However,' she added, maliciously, 'that has not, I note, prevented you from mating with the odd human.'

'At your suggestion,' Boolik snapped, though there was something too protesting about his tone.

'Of course,' Amaarini said, placatingly. 'All in the line of your duty, as we all appreciate. Tell me,' she added, 'what would your reaction be if I requested that you go down to the stables and mate with this human?' She jabbed a finger at the screen, indicating the passive figure of one of the two pony girls currently tethered just outside the stable they shared. Boolik shrugged again.

'What reaction would you expect?' he replied. 'She is no different from any of the others.'

'Except that "she" was a male in her original, human form,' Amaarini drawled.

'And?' Boolik said, quietly. 'Is that supposed to worry me?' He turned away, paced across the room and turned back again. 'These creatures are just that,' he said. 'They are creatures, created down in the laboratories, created in a form that is slightly more exaggerated than the body in which they were originally born. Created, I might add, to appeal to the human visitors on whom our colony largely depends for finance.

'Outwardly, these humans, either in their original form, or as the good doctor's Jenny Anns, are not so different from us, Amaarini, but that is where it ends. They are otherwise inferior to us in every way and, if it be deemed necessary, I will treat any one of them as another. Male, female – I do not recognise the difference.'

'Then you would happily go down there now and fuck our little Bambi, is that what you are saying?'

'Happily?' Boolik raised his eyebrows, emphasising the curious shape of his eyes. 'That is another matter, but, as you ask, yes, I would go down there and do whatever might be necessary, even to lowering myself down close to their base, animal instincts.'

'A noble sacrifice, Boolik,' Amaarini retorted. 'Very noble indeed. Of course, I do appreciate that there would be no gratification in such an act, not for one such as you.'

'Lady,' Boolik said, through clenched teeth, 'your sense of humour leaves much to be desired. Yes, I confess that there is a certain . . . something? . . . which I can enjoy from teaching these creatures their true station, but I would far rather take my pleasure with one of our own kind, preferably a female with whom I felt at least some semblance of symbiosis.'

'Of course, of course,' Amaarini said. 'Forgive me, Boolik, but teasing you is too easy.' She turned away from the screens at last. 'No,' she said, 'we'll leave such things to the grooms for now. They, at least, enjoy it and need no

27

urging. However, I may need your assistance on a little experiment I am planning.

'Our cute little Bambi, as you are aware, was, until a short while ago, the very singular Mr Andrew Lachan, and we also have little Tammy to consider. Both humans, both born male and both now looking like the woman of their previous dreams.

'Neither is coming to terms with "her" new identity, which is hardly surprising, even for humans. Therefore, we need a way of undermining their resolve, and I think I have one.'

'And my part in this?'

'Later, Boolik, later,' Amaarini smiled. 'For now, I think I shall just organise some different stabling arrangements, which I would like you to effect with the grooms. I do not wish either of them to experience another female presence just yet, you see.

'So, if you would be so good as to go below and give my instructions to Higgy, who is probably the best of the grooms to deal with this, I shall be pleased to entertain you to an excellent dinner in my quarters this evening.'

Three

Familiarity.

Familiarity breeds contempt, Tammy thought, as the groom, Higgy, continued tightening her harness straps. Well, these bastards are familiar enough, anyway.

She tensed, stifling a small gasp, as his fingers flicked across her shaven sex lips, drawing the crotch strap between her thighs, holding it in readiness as he reached for the inevitable dildo.

Total contempt, or total detachment? Was there a difference? The way in which the grooms handled their charges was both, their complete, apparent, nonreaction at the sight of so much near-naked female flesh was a form of contempt in itself. From her original male perspective, Tammy could not see how any red-blooded heterosexual man could remain unmoved by the sights that were a regular feature of life in the underground stables complex.

Stunning women – deliberately created in a variety of images that were guaranteed to arouse the opposite sex (and the same sex as well, as often as not) – were paraded in their leather tackle and gold and silver finery, breasts and buttocks bobbing and rippling, carefully oiled skins gleaming in the lights, rattling and jangling as they moved around on the hideous and nigh-impossible hoof boots, and yet the young males appointed to take care of and train them seemed largely impervious to their appeal and blatant availability.

At least, Tammy thought, they had done as far as she was concerned. Occasional grunts and squeals from other stalls bore testament to the fact that these outwardly immovable creatures were indeed subject to the frailties of human nature from time to time, especially in Higgy's own case.

But were they really human? Tammy mused, peering between her blinkers to where one of the youngest grooms, Jonas, was similarly preparing the filly, Bambi. *Damn them!* Tammy cursed, silently, the hard bit between her teeth preventing her from expressing her feelings out loud in any case. *Damn them to hell, they've got me even thinking like them now! She's not a filly, she's a woman.*

Though even that wasn't true, Tammy now knew, for Higgy had been at pains to point out that Bambi was little different from Tammy. Apparently – and Tammy had no reason to doubt the groom's word – Bambi, too, had been a man in her previous existence and apparently quite a rich and powerful man. Studying the other pony girl's reactions, Tammy wondered how she was coping with such a mind-numbing transition and, almost unthinkingly, parted her thighs to allow Higgy to slide the thick rubber shaft into her already moist sex.

'I can't believe you've been here as long as you claim and yet know so little about what's really going on here,' Alex protested to her new stallmate. Jessie, in full harness apart from her bit, which hung down below her chin, regarded her with the same frustrating air of unconcern.

'What is there to know?' she asked. 'I am well cared for, well fed and not treated too badly, overall. Both this stall and the room beyond are comfortable and warm and I am given generous recreation periods.'

'With colour TV, music, books,' Alex finished for her. 'Yes, I know, you've already said.' She sighed in total exasperation. 'I'm not even going to ask you whether it worries you that these perverts treat you like a bloody animal most of the time, as it obviously doesn't.'

'It's better than being dead,' Jessie replied, her fine features creasing into a semblance of a smile.

'That's only your opinion!' Alex snorted. 'Personally, I'm not so sure.'

'Unless you've ever been dead,' Jessie said, lowering herself carefully down into the straw and stretching her long legs out in front of her, 'you cannot make a valid judgement.'

'And you've *been* dead, I suppose?' Jessie's smile widened.

'Of course I haven't, but I was very close, as were you. In your case, I suppose, death may not have been an inevitability. Nowadays, from what I hear on the television, a broken neck, or back, is not necessarily fatal.

'However,' she continued, raising a mitted hand in Alex's direction, 'death itself may well have been preferable to the life you would have had, if you could call it life to be permanently confined to a wheelchair and unable to use either hands or legs. At least here we get to run and enjoy the open air.'

'And be used as a bloody sex toy by any bastard with enough money to pay our so-called masters for the privilege,' Alex snapped.

'Apparently that hasn't yet happened in your case,' Jessie said, closing her eyes. Alex paced across the small chamber, high boots dragging in the thick bed of straw.

'No, not yet,' she admitted. 'At least, no one's actually fucked me so far, though having a bloody great phallus stuffed in me front and back isn't much difference, not in my book. In any case, these damned grooms aren't exactly gentlemen when it comes to handling us. I've never had my damned tits pawed so frequently in all my life.'

'But they do us no harm,' Jessie said, languidly, 'and our bodies are designed to find such attentions agreeable.'

'Our *bodies*, maybe,' Alex said, only too aware of the truth of this statement. 'But there's still what's in here.' She raised a mitted hand of her own and tapped the side of her head. 'Don't you think I *hate* what their touches do to me?'

'It's something you'll get used to,' Jessie said, softly. 'I know I did.'

'Then maybe you're something I couldn't be!' Alex stormed. 'I know I'll never get used to it, let alone enjoy it the way you seem to.'

31

'Maybe not,' Jessie agreed, 'but then maybe they should have left you in a wheelchair for a few months.' She opened her large, dark eyes again, the smile gone now.

'I can remember before, you know,' she said. 'I can remember lying in a hospital bed, full of morphine, yet every nerve ending in my body still screaming for release. I would have pleaded with them for death, believe me, if I could have talked, but my vocal cords were shredded by a piece of shrapnel – and, in any case, our so-called society frowns upon such actions.

'I lay like that for days, waiting for death, hoping for death, ready to welcome it with open arms.' Jessie closed her eyes again, her expression reflecting the memories of her pain. 'I prayed to any and every deity for a release, any release, and then, one day, release came.

'All this,' she said, gesturing vaguely at her own near naked body, 'might not have been what I had in mind and it was a shock, as you should know, to wake up in a different body, but at least this body was pain-free and, although my initial reaction to what was expected of me was not far different from your own, I at least managed to rationalise things.

'I sat and asked myself one question. Given that there would be no release through death and that this existence, as you call it, was the only alternative to what I had, would I have elected this over what I was suffering?' The dark eyes were open again. 'There was only one answer,' she concluded, simply.

Being restabled with Bambi did not help Tammy's growing depression at all. Seeing what had allegedly once also been a man looking as feminine and desirable as Tammy now knew 'she' did herself simply added to the humiliation and desperation she felt and there was not even the opportunity to share thoughts and emotions, for both Jenny Anns were kept securely bitted whenever they were left alone, cruel bits that had thick rubber flanges attached to the beastly rods and that pressed down on to the tongue to render even the semicoherent efforts at speech completely useless.

32

Tammy had long since realised that the various accoutrements and harness straps, once fitted by the grooms, could not be removed without the aid of one of the keys that the young men kept on long chains about their necks. There were no implements with which to cut the tough leather, even on the rare occasions that the two prisoners' hands were left unencumbered, and no way in which it could be torn or ripped by any normal human strength.

The pair were left to lie on their respective straw beds, staring morosely at the bland stone ceiling of their stall, or else trying to doze, ears ever alert for the sound of approaching footsteps from outside, the irregular appearances of the grooms generally meaning the heaping on of even more indignities.

So far, they had stopped short of the ultimate degradation, but Tammy knew, in her heart of hearts, that it was only a matter of time, and the appearance of the cold-faced female they called Amaarini, and whom the guests apparently addressed as Amanda, followed by the even more severe looking security chief, Boolik, heralded the realisation of her worst fears.

'This one, first,' Amaarini said, jabbing a long finger at Bambi. Boolik stepped aside, making room for the two grooms, who pushed into the cramped stall and seized the hapless girl before she had chance to resist. Her arms were twisted cruelly behind her back and the leather retaining sheath was drawn up over them, leaving her totally incapable of defending herself.

The natural fighting instincts of Tommy the fisherman still remained within the body of Tammy and she leaped to her feet, backing against the wall, raising her already fist-shaped hands in an attitude of defiance. The security man swung around to face her, but Amaarini held up a cautioning hand.

'No, Boolik,' she said. 'These creatures have the new processors and now would seem as good a time as any to test their efficiency.' She unclipped a small, rectangular object from her wide belt and Tammy had just enough time to register that it looked not unlike a television remote control before the shock wave hit her. The bolt seemed to strike at the very small of her back, knocking her forward into the centre of the room, spine arched, a secondary wave of agony shooting out to the very tips of all four limbs.

As she lay in a convulsed heap, saliva drooling from her lips, Amaarini gave a cursory nod to the grooms. Higgy, the senior, stooped over the fallen pony girl, key in hand, and a moment later drew the saliva-soaked bit and flange from her numbed mouth. Then, aided by his colleague, he hauled her upright, steadying her while her arms were secured in the same manner as they had employed with Bambi, a method to which both unfortunates had now long grown accustomed.

'Well, the stun facility appears to work well,' Amaarini leered. She made some sort of adjustment to the hand control and pointed it at Bambi. A moment later, with a gurgled cry, Bambi also arched forward and only the intervention of Boolik prevented her from collapsing as Tammy had done.

'Excellent,' Amaarini cooed. 'There are individual control units for each of you and these master controls can be switched to operate on one girl at a time, or on all Jenny Anns present who have the new processor unit in their bodies.

'You bitch!' Tammy snarled, oblivious to any retribution her outburst might bring. 'You evil fucking –'
Amaarini raised the unit again, but this time there was no jolting surge. Instead, to Tammy's horror, she suddenly found that she no longer had a voice. Instead, as she struggled to speak, Amaarini thumbed the control device once more and, instead of speech, all Tammy's best efforts produced was a high-pitched whinnying sound, too equine in effect to evince anything but instant silence from the horrified pony girl.

'Now you even sound the part,' Amaarini laughed. 'A very clever development and a very useful one. It will eventually save us much work in monitoring you bitches around the guests. Now you can't let anything slip, even if you wanted to.

34

'Of course,' she added, 'the gags and bits will always have their aesthetic appeal, but from a point of view of security, this little toy is far more reliable, wouldn't you agree, Master Boolik?'

The security chief grunted, nodding. 'The sooner we have all the J-As upgraded, the better,' he said. He held out a hand. 'May I try that with the other one?'

Life, for Lulu, was a constant series of bewilderments. Not that it had ever really worried her that she had gone from being Laura Jane Meadows, a slightly angular and awkward research assistant with a regional television company, to being Lulu, type CB-Nine Jenny Ann, the generic nickname the masters gave to all the girls whom they had transferred into these new bodies.

This CB-Nine body was, after all, a very good body: slightly waifish and flat-chested, with close-cropped hair that never seemed to grow, yet a very healthy and robust body and one that attracted far more attention than the original, cancer-ridden body with which nature had originally endowed her. She had also long grown accustomed to the lack of a sense of smell and the monochrome vision and knew that, in time, if she proved herself worthy, even that latter inconvenience could be replaced by a basic colour vision. They had told her so and, whatever else they were, Lulu knew that they were not liars.

They didn't need to be.

Yet life here was still prone to confusion. The numbers thing, for a start, and then there were her memories. Not that she ever forgot anything – not completely, at least – but things never seemed to be in the same order each time she tried to recall them. Days became blurred and confused, times were all wrong and if it were not for her mentor – the latest was Julia – to tell her these things, Lulu would frequently not have known what she was supposed to be doing.

There had been a fault in the transfer, that much she did know. Someone had explained it to her last mentor, Catherine, who had explained it to Lulu in turn. Synopsis, that was it. No, synopsis was something you wrote, she remembered that now. Damn, what *was* the word? It was similar. Maybe it was synopsis after all.

Whatever, it was all to do with the way her brain was connected to this new body – not so new now, as she had been here for a long time, maybe even a year. Or ten. Numbers, numbers, numbers . . .

Something had gone wrong, anyway. Not something serious, not so long as you weren't worried about not being able to add two and two sometimes and make five. Or should that be six? It didn't matter, anyway. Lulu wrinkled her pert nose and grinned. At least she knew where she was supposed to be now.

It was here. Here in one of the robing cubicles at the end of the special guest quarters on the north side of the island. Curious, she knew all about north and south. And east and west. You could tell from the sun, once you were above ground. Not that these quarters were really above ground, but there were windows cut into the rock, which looked out, through screens of straggly shrub, towards the open sea, and they faced north, as they were perpetually in shadow.

'Time to get you ready, Lulu.' The door had opened noiselessly and the sound of Julia's voice started Lulu back to full awareness.

'Who is it today?' she asked. Julia, a head taller than Lulu normally and currently even taller, courtesy of the high-heeled boots she wore, gave her an almost apologetic smile.

'Master Eric, I'm afraid,' she said. Lulu shrugged.

'Oh well,' she said, 'at least he's very handsome.'

'And your threshold is on maximum today, isn't it?' Lulu pursed her lips and inclined her head.

'I suppose so,' she said. 'I reported to the station office as you told me and they put that box thing on the back of my neck.'

'That's OK, then,' Julia said. 'Master Eric is a bit too fond of the whip for my liking.'

'But he uses it mostly on Loin,' Lulu said. Her face brightened. 'I remember that,' she said, with an air of triumph. 'And Loin has the biggest cock I've ever seen.'

36

'Yes, I have seen it.' Julia grimaced. 'I'm surprised it hasn't split your little fanny in two before now.' Lulu's hand went down to her naked, shaven groin.

'Master Eric reckons I'm elastic,' she grinned, proudly. 'He reckons I could take a –'

'Shut up, Lulu!' Julia's tone was suddenly quite cold. 'Don't even think of such things. Master Eric is a dangerous individual, from what I've heard. He once told me that he'd personally killed around fifty people and ordered the deaths of hundreds more.'

'Oh.' Lulu looked even more confused than usual. She considered this statement for several seconds.

'But he wouldn't be allowed to kill us, surely,' she said, at last. 'The Masters wouldn't allow it.'

'Probably not,' Julia agreed. 'But enough of this nonsense. Let's get on with the job, shall we? Otherwise, if you keep him waiting, it won't just be you and Loin that Master Eric takes his whip to and my threshold isn't adjusted to maximum at the moment. C'mon, stand up and get over here.'

Obediently, Lulu sprang up and all but bounded to Julia's side. Completely naked as she was, her petite body and elfin features made her look like a teenager, the appearance of excessive youth deliberately created in her body type. In reality she was, as she sometimes remembered, in her mid-twenties, but an uninformed onlooker would never have guessed it.

'Full rubber enclosure, today,' Julia announced. She selected a pale-pink body suit from the nearest rack. The atmosphere in the room was heavy with the aroma of latex, Lulu knew, though she, of course, could detect no odours at all. She sometimes tried to think back, trying to recall the smell of rubber, but, aside from household gloves and bicycle inner tubes, she could not remember any intimate contact with the fabric in her earlier life.

She wondered how she might have reacted before, to the cool, slippery feeling as she eased her lower legs into the suit. Would she have relished its soft embrace as she did now? Later – quite soon, in fact – the coolness would be replaced by a sensation of generous, all-enveloping warmth, as her body heat built up inside the suit. A genuine latex suit would have been worse, she knew, for she had experienced one at first hand on several occasions, but lately they had taken to using a modified version, something that, Lulu had been told, had been specially developed for the exclusive use of the island, so that a completely enveloping, skin-tight suit could be worn for hours on end without too much discomfort and without the build-up of perspiration that was the inevitable result of too long spent inside a natural latex skin.

The generous dusting of the white powder that Julia applied to her body and limbs made it easier for Lulu to don the suit, but even so it was a painstaking process, for every last wrinkle and crease had to be smoothed out before the back zip was finally closed and locked at the neck. Failure to pay attention to such detail was regarded as a serious breach of discipline and the punishments for such oversights were many, varied and inevitably unpleasant.

There were twin, round openings, through which Julia carefully eased Lulu's budding mounds, the elastic grip of the suit fabric immediately squeezing them into greater prominence, causing the nipples to swell and harden. Julia smiled, and tweaked one of the stiffening cones between thumb and forefinger.

'Randy little minx,' she chided, though without malice. 'You can't bloody wait for it, can you?' Had she been able to, Lulu might have blushed at this teasing admonishment. Instead, she gave a sly smile and averted her eyes.

'I always try to please, you know that,' she said. 'After all, that's what we're here for, isn't it?'

'It's not for me to argue with that,' Julia said. She stooped, adjusting the slit opening so that it framed Lulu's swollen labia perfectly, then, on impulse, dipped her head and ran her tongue along the pink slit. She felt Lulu shudder at the intimate contact and immediately withdrew. One never knew when they were monitoring the cameras that were hidden everywhere across the island; a slight titillation was one thing, going too far with a slave before

38

she was delivered for her duties was something else. The guests preferred their subjects to arrive unsated.

The corset was white, severely boned and designed to lace down even Lulu's trim waist, so that by the time Julia had struggled to get the two halves together at the back, the little Jenny Ann's girth was no more than seventeen inches. The constriction, however, did not seem to bother the smaller girl overly and she immediately adjusted her breathing to the shallow pattern required in order to endure such restrictions on her lungs.

Lulu sat on a high stool, while Julia fitted her feet into the matching white boots, lacing them to the knee with precise care, knowing that a perfect, tight fit was essential if even Lulu was to be able to walk in such extreme heels. In fact, Julia knew, it was a matter of perverse pride in Lulu that she was one of the few Jenny Anns who could even stand in these ballerina boots, let alone walk in them, and it had taken, despite the innate strength of their J-A body, many months of practice and training to master the footwear.

The heels were towering, higher even than those that Julia wore, forcing the instep into an upright arch, so that the toes pointed straight down, cushioned inside a soft lining of the block toe, the pose and poise giving the name to the boots, for, once wearing them, the subject was forced to walk *en pointe* in the manner of a classical ballerina. A normal human body could not have endured such a torturous position for more than a few minutes at a time, but the raised pain threshold of Lulu's cloned body, together with the genetically modified strength of her leg muscles, allowed her to perform feats that no average female, nor even male, could have ever contemplated.

'Up and walk, please,' Julia commanded. Lulu did as instructed, mincing back and forth, confirming that the boots not only fitted properly, but that Julia's fitting had been precise. 'Comfortable?'

Lulu grinned. 'Of course,' she giggled. 'And taller, too.'

The mask now followed, an all-enveloping pink hood that matched the suit, enclosing face and head and fastening to the collar of the suit by means of a series of snap catches that could not be removed without the proper key. By the time Julia had finished locking them, apart from her crotch and breasts, all that was visible of Lulu were her eyes and lips, with two metal-rimmed apertures beneath her nostrils to permit air to enter via her nose when her mouth was gagged and sealed, as it soon would be.

Lulu turned and walked across to one of the long mirrors, pirouetting in front of the glass, admiring her reflection.

'I look like a candy floss,' she giggled. 'All pink and white.'

'And delicious enough to eat,' Julia muttered, half under her breath. 'Now, come back over here,' she instructed, in a normal voice. 'There's a wig to go with this and I have to stick it on, as you'll be going outside.'

'Outside?' Lulu's eyes widened behind the mask. 'Does that mean I'll be driving today?' Julia shrugged, picking up the long white wig with care.

'I don't know,' she said. 'Probably, judging from this outfit, but they haven't told me anything, except what to dress you in. Now, will you get here, otherwise none of us will be going anywhere except the punishment sector.'

The brutal demonstration of just how helpless they really were at the hands of their captors left Tammy feeling completely stunned and as near despair as she had been since first awakening in her new female body.

As if it were not already bad enough for a one-time macho young male to find himself trapped in a female shell, without the strength to resist a bunch of what were clearly depraved male captors, now even the females could exert total control over 'her', simply by flicking a few buttons, even to the extent of depriving her of the power of human speech and forcing her to sound like one of the creatures upon which this entire existence seemed to be based.

Still feeling numb, partly from the shock wave that Amaarini had triggered, but more so from the latest

40

revelations as to her true position, Tammy stumbled out into the main concourse, the younger groom leading her by the rein, bit once more replaced between her teeth. Ahead of them, the unfortunate Bambi could barely walk and only the combined efforts of Boolik and the senior groom, Higgy, got her as far as the curious stand that had been erected in the centre of the cavernous chamber.

As they drew closer, Tammy's mind cleared sufficiently for her to understand what the collection of tubular steel poles was for. In effect, it was a modern-day version of an old wooden pillory, a circular steel band on top of the central pole opening up to accept the neck, while two stubby poles projecting from just below this level terminated in smaller circlets, which were clearly to secure the wrists.

Two more short horizontals, fixed a few inches from the ground, formed a V-shape, which could be further adjusted, not just to lock the ankles of the victim, but also to force her legs as far apart as her captors required, a facility that was quickly demonstrated, using the bemused Bambi as the first model.

With her arms already helpless behind her back, the wrist manacles were surplus and only her neck needed securing, before the ankle hobbles were raised to the correct height, the steel bands locked about her boots and the twin arms cranked apart, so that the poor creature was forced to stand stooped over, straddle-legged and completely at the mercy of whatever fate was being planned for her.

'Neither of these two has yet been subjected to a racing plug,' Amaarini said, addressing the casual remark to Boolik. 'I've allowed the grooms to plug their butts from time to time, but otherwise they are both virgins. And you, my dear Boolik, may have the honour of deflowering the first one, seeing as how the bitch was responsible for the unfortunate deaths of your men.'

'I'd as soon just kill the swine,' Boolik snarled. 'One of those who died was of my own line, as you well know.'

'But Boolik, my dear fellow,' Amaarini drawled, 'if you were to kill the little slut, that would be it, wouldn't it? This

41

way is much better, I think. The powerful Andrew Lachan now no better than the pony girls he used to crave so much, lower even than the one he tried to abduct from here. Come, Boolik, you will need to be far more subtle if you are to play your full part here.'

The younger groom, who had moved in behind Bambi, now stepped back, holding up the crotch strap he had detached from her girth. 'See?' Amaarini smirked. 'The little slut stands there waiting for you, almost begging you to mate her.'

'Is she in season for mating?' Boolik asked, his hooded eyes betraying nothing. Amaarini shrugged.

'That isn't important,' she returned. 'Conception is not the important thing here. That can wait, as part of the overall programme. For now, Boolik, just take her virginity and make her squirm on the end of your rod, eh?' She flicked the small control unit in her hand and nodded to Higgy.

'Remove the bitch's bit,' she instructed. 'I want to hear her whinny as you ride her, Boolik. Her companion here,' she added, indicating Tammy, 'can watch and anticipate her own deflowering. I have just the right mate for her first ride and have even arranged a fat premium for the facility.'

She had seen this particular carriage only from a distance and then not properly. During the weeks Alex had spent in the stables, it had been kept at the far end of the concourse between the opposing rows of stalls, half covered by a large sheet, but now it stood in the centre, polished, gleaming and waiting.

Not one of the general racing buggies that were used in the pony-girl races, it was larger, longer and wider, designed, from the configuration of its central shaft and the two flanking bands, to be pulled by a pair, rather than a single girl. There was an upholstered seat in the rear, evidently for the comfort of two passengers, while at the front, a grotesque parody of a seat awaited an unfortunate driver. Seeing the curved bar and the rearing phallus, Alex averted her eyes.

Unresisting, she allowed Higgy to lead her forward, guiding her to the left-hand side of the shaft, positioning her so that the broad, stiff leather band could be attached about her tightly corseted waist, lifting the ends of one set of the traces and clipping the reins to either side of her bit. Another trace ended in a short, shiny metal bar, at the end of which were two more small clips, and somehow Alex was not surprised when Higgy lifted this and clipped it to the rings that hung from her distended nipples.

In all her weeks of training so far, Alex had never been subjected to this particular variation, but she did not need much imagination to understand that this particular rein could be far more useful for controlling a potentially errant pony girl than even those that ran from the bit in her mouth.

The blinkers hampered sideways vision, but, to her right, Alex was aware of Jessie being similarly harnessed to the other side of the shaft and, as a final refinement, a short chain was used to connect Jessie's left nipple ring to Alex's right, so that they would have to run with their upper bodies erect, shoulders almost touching. Alex closed her eyes, the heavy false lashes descending like twin curtains, trying to pretend that none of this was happening to her, but it was useless. The thick dildo – Higgy had selected one of the stoutest today – served as an ever-present reminder of her new status and the slightest movement was setting off tremors throughout her entire body that it was impossible to ignore.

Traces connected, the two grooms stepped back, looking at each other in silence, exchanging looks that made the blood run cold in Alex's veins. They were waiting for something, both men unusually tense. As she vainly attempted to suck back the saliva that was slowly dribbling from her bitted mouth, Alex's eyes darted back and forth and she silently cursed the blinkers that hampered her vision so badly.

Something was about to happen. She had no idea what it was, but it was plain, from the attitude of the grooms, that it was something out of the ordinary, even for this more than ordinary hellhole. And, whatever it turned out to be, there was one thing of which Alex was completely certain.

She was going to be at the centre of it.

The youngest groom, Jonas, joined Higgy and Sol to lead Tammy and Bambi back into their shared stall, Bambi stumbling heavily with every step, her eyes still closed in shame at what she had been forced to endure.

Mutely, eyes wide at the horror of it all, Tammy had witnessed every moment of her stablemate's humiliation, made even worse by the fact that the tall Boolik had exhibited an air of total detachment during the entire proceedings, other than that he had instructed the grooms to turn and face away before he started.

Then, while Amaarini looked on with undisguised relish and Tammy was forced to do the same, under pain of another jolt from the processor if she so much as lowered her gaze, the security man had opened the front of his leggings, exposing a flaccid male organ that had required some urging to rise to the occasion.

Eventually, however, he had achieved an erection that no normal male would have been ashamed of, holding it casually in one hand as he approached his waiting victim from behind.

'Is she wet, Boolik?' Amaarini demanded. He reached down and under with his free hand, probing for Bambi's gaping sex.

'No, not yet,' he reported. Amaarini's leering smile widened.

'All the better,' she rasped. 'Take her dry and let's hear her howl. She'll soon become wet enough anyway,' she assured him, as an afterthought.

Bambi now began to struggle and squirm, redoubling her efforts as Boolik pressed the bulbous tip of his shaft against her virgin orifice, but she must have known that it was all to no avail. Stooping slightly, Boolik began to force an entry, while Amaarini, her sloe eyes now gleaming with anticipation, was becoming visibly excited. Eventually, she could restrain her impatience no longer.

44

'Take her!' she screamed. 'Now, Boolik! Fill her and watch her turn into a slut like all the others!'

And, to Tammy's horror and disbelief, that was quickly what happened. Initially, as Boolik thrust deep inside her, Bambi's contorted face and whinnying cries of anguish left no room to doubt her own lack of compliance, but no sooner had the security chief begun to pump in and out of her than her expression and entire demeanour began to change.

Within seconds she was gasping and squealing, grinding her hips to his rhythm, the nipples on her dangling breasts swelling to hardened cones, her tongue lolling between quivering lips as her eyes rolled in an ecstasy she could neither control nor deny.

And, as she looked on in sheer horror and dread, Tammy's revulsion was made all the more awful in the certain knowledge that she, too, would soon be forced to undergo such a horrendous ordeal, yet an ordeal in which the carefully programmed physical responses in her new and hated body would betray her and reduce her to the same level of lust and deprivation as she was now being forced to witness from her stablemate.

In the stall once more, there was little conversation. Neither pony girl had yet had the power of human speech restored to her and the three grooms were clearly not in talkative moods, presumably because of the presence of Amaarini, whom even Boolik seemed to hold in awe.

'This one in red harness,' Amaarini said, striding into the already crowded stall and jabbing a finger at Bambi. 'Bring the other one along to one of the spare stalls,' she added, this time to Higgy.

'Master Eric has ordered the touring carriage for the afternoon and he wishes for a maid companion. I have arranged for a suitable costume to be sent down and I will join you when it arrives. Meantime, strip her and hose her down, but no nonsense, understand? She must remain intact for the moment.'

'Of course, miss,' Higgy said, smiling with what he evidently thought was complete innocence. 'Would I do

45

anything else?' Amaarini grimaced and aimed a sideswipe at the groom's head, which he only just managed to duck.

'Higgy,' she growled, turning back towards the open door, 'you are worse than the full human males. You would fuck the entrance to a rabbit warren, if it had hair round it!'

Peering down at her own smooth, hairless sex, Tammy guessed that, from what she had seen and heard of the senior groom, the hair would have been little more than an optional extra where Higgy was concerned. What was worse, it appeared that her own status of being 'off limits' to the grooms would soon be changing. Once Amaarini had extracted the maximum return for her current virginity, she, like the other pony girls, would become fair game.

As she shuffled round to follow Higgy out into the concourse once more, she could not stop herself from shivering uncontrollably.

Four

'It's very good of you to see me personally, Ms Butler.' Colin Turner held out his hand, which Celia Butler took in a firm grip. 'I appreciate you must have many calls on your time.'

'Not at all, Mr Marshall,' Celia drawled. She released her grip and turned away, almost spinning on the toes of her high-heeled knee-length boots. 'Never too busy to give my personal attention to a new and valued client.' She clacked across the parquet floor, the tight skirt straining with every step, to stand beside the imposing walnut desk that dominated the south-facing room and picked up the thin manila file that, apart from a complicated-looking telephone receiver, was the only thing that currently cluttered the inlaid green-leather surface.

'I've reread all your correspondence and your bank reference came back quite satisfactorily.' She smiled, catlike, and Colin nodded. The alias of Colin Marshall had been established for a few years now, as part of a long-term facility that enabled him to mix with the rich and famous without revealing his true vocation as a policeman. The account details he had supplied to Celia revealed a very healthy balance indeed, part of an inheritance that had landed in his lap while he was still a teenager.

'Of course,' Celia purred, 'I didn't really doubt your credentials, but you will appreciate our need for a little discretion.'

'Of course,' Colin echoed. 'I find it reassuring, Ms Butler.'

'You must call me Celia,' she said, brightly, her smile returning, wider than ever. 'And I shall call you Colin, unless you have any objections to that.' She regarded Colin's muscular frame and the expensive suit in which it was clad. 'I'm sure we shall become quite good friends.'

'I hope so,' Colin replied. He made an obvious gesture of checking the time on his Rolex wristwatch and was rewarded when Celia was unable to disguise her interest. 'However,' he went on, 'I do have another appointment later this afternoon and an hour's drive ahead of me, so would I seem too rude if I asked to get straight on with the business in hand?'

'Not at all, not at all,' Celia said. 'I quite understand. Now, let me see.' She flicked open the file and made a show of leafing through the few sheets of paper it contained, though Colin was pretty certain she knew exactly what was written on each of them.

'Harnesses and perhaps a small sulky,' she said, as if speaking to herself. 'But we have no details of the animal in question.' She looked up again. 'You *do* have a regular pony of your own?'

'Ah, yes, in a roundabout way,' Colin replied. 'She's, ahem, away temporarily – family commitments, you know, but I expect her to return within a week or two at the most.'

'I see. So just the one pony currently?'

'Yes, for the moment, anyway. There are other possibilities to be explored, but these things take time and have to be handled with a certain amount of tact and diplomacy.'

'Not to mention patience,' Celia added. 'Well, do you have the necessary measurements with you?'

'Well, not exactly,' Colin said. 'I mean, I thought these things were all adjustable and all that.'

'To an extent, yes,' Celia concurred, 'but here we deal in the finest-quality craftsmanship.' She nodded towards him. 'You would not even consider buying a suit off the peg for yourself, I presume?'

'No, of course not,' Colin said, adopting an indignant tone that was not entirely feigned. 'However, in my

48

previous, er, dealings, I have not had the option, if you understand my meaning.'

'Perfectly,' Celia said. 'Who have you dealt with previously?' Colin gave her two names he had gleaned from his Internet surfing; both were little more than general fetish-wear retailers and it was unlikely anyone would be able to check his story. However, he still covered such an eventuality.

'They have the advantage of being quite anonymous,' he added. 'Cash in the hand and no pack drill and all that. I must admit, I was initially a little cautious about furnishing you with my personal details.'

'Trust needs to be a two-way commodity,' Celia said. She closed the file and placed it carefully back on the desk. 'I have been servicing the needs of many wealthy and surprisingly well-known people for a good few years now,' she said, 'and I could not have been as successful if I did not do everything within my power to protect them.

'Now, perhaps you could give me an approximate idea of the size of the pony?' Colin paused, apparently thinking. He had already fixed a mental picture, that of a girl he had seen on one of the many websites he had trawled, but he did not want to appear too glib.

'About so tall,' he said, holding out his left hand, palm down, at a level just above his shoulder. 'Five nine, maybe five ten.'

Celia nodded, apparently approvingly. 'A nice tall pony. Very elegant and strong, too, I should imagine.'

'Well, I've nothing really to compare,' Colin said, 'but yes, I think so.'

'Bust, waist, hips?' Celia prompted. Colin appeared to consider again.

'About thirty-eight bust, I believe,' he said. 'D-cup, I think. Brandy is quite well endowed in that department.'

'Brandy, eh? Is she as spirited as the name might suggest?'

'Vintage,' Colin smirked, beginning to enjoy himself now. He regarded Celia Butler with interest. She appeared to be somewhere around the age of fifty, older than his usual tastes by far, yet more than just well preserved. She was still extremely attractive and, he reckoned, in her youth she would have been a total stunner.

'Girth? Waist, that is?'

'Well, I'm not completely certain,' Colin replied, slowly. 'She could be around a twenty-six or so, but she has a tendency to get a little flabby around the middle if she doesn't get sufficient exercise, and she *has* been away for a little while.'

'A little flab can soon be run off,' Celia laughed. 'From the flanks as well as the girth. Now, how about the hips?'

'Fairly average, I'd say,' Colin said. 'Her bottom is quite nice, but not too big. Can't be doing with great big arses, if you'll pardon the expression.'

'Let's assume around thirty-six then, shall we?' Celia suggested. 'So, thirty-eight D, twenty-six – we'll soon cinch it down to that anyway – thirty-six. Shoe size?' Here Colin was guessing, but as the girl in the picture was never going to figure in person, he also guessed it wouldn't matter and had worked out what he thought would be about right for a female of the proportions he had listed.

'Six and a half,' he said. 'That one I do know.'

'Splendid,' Celia said, reaching for the phone. 'I have a girl here who takes exactly that size and is not too far off in the other measurements. I'll just organise us some tea and arrange for Lisa to be brought to the viewing room.'

In the vacant stall, Higgy was quickly joined by a young groom Tammy had never seen before. His name, it quickly transpired, was Silas and there was some sort of family relationship between Higgy and him, although exactly what Tammy could not discern. From his features, soft and extremely youthful, he could not have been more than seventeen or eighteen years old, yet Tammy had already learned enough to appreciate that, in this strange world, appearances were deceptive more often than not. However, for the moment, Tammy had more pressing concerns than the likely age of the new arrival.

Quickly and efficiently, they stripped her, then cuffed her hands behind her back, before dragging her out and down to the farthest end of the main concourse, where the tiled area and the hose pipe awaited. Ignoring her inarticulate squeals of protest, they forced her to the floor with the high-pressure jet, laughing at her struggles and turning off the icy jet only when Tammy had been reduced to a shivering mound of glowing red flesh.

'Lovely tits,' Silas remarked, as Higgy pulled the un-resisting 'girl' to her feet. 'Nice arse, too,' he added. Higgy laughed and raised a finger in mock admonishment.

'Put it out of your head,' he said, thrusting Tammy back in the direction of the stall. 'This one isn't to be touched just yet, not by the likes of us, anyway. Mind you,' he went on, grasping a handful of Tammy's sodden hair and twisting it unnecessarily hard, 'if youse do a half-decent job today, I'll see to it that you get to screw her to your heart's content before the week's out.'

Silas skipped ahead, placing himself between Tammy and their ultimate destination. His smooth hands reached out, cupping her breasts, thumbs pressing against her nipples, which, to Tammy's chagrin, immediately began to harden.

'Perhaps just a little kiss?' he said. Tammy recoiled instantly and Higgy's reaction was very nearly as immediate.

'Get your hands off her, you stupid little bastard!' he snarled. 'I already told you, didn't I? Besides, you don't kiss a pony slut, you daft young idiot. Leastways,' he added, the grin returning to his face, 'not until you've taught her how to love you proper. Meantime, once I give the word, you just tup her when the fancy takes you. When she's ready to beg you, then you let her kiss you. It's a mark of respect, see?'

Whether Silas did see, or not, time was apparently pressing, for the two men wasted no more time in taking Tammy back into the empty stall, where they roughly towelled her dry and then dusted her entire body with what she assumed was talcum powder.

'Going to make you into a nice little snake maid,' Higgy announced, holding up the rubber body suit. 'Master Eric just loves his sluts in full rubber, so let's get this on you, eh?'

The rubbery fabric required a lot of patience and precision, trying to cling to Tammy's flesh despite the liberal coating of the powder, but Higgy in particular had obviously been confronted with this problem before and, after ten minutes or so of contortive struggling, Tammy eventually stood before them, clad from neck to toe in a second skin of pale blue, even to the tips of her slender fingers, just her nipples and her crotch protruding obscenely from strategically placed openings.

'Silas is right,' Higgy mused, fastening the collar band at the nape of her neck. 'You're very fuckable, gal, and that's a fact.' He reached around and took her right nipple between forefinger and thumb, chuckling at the instant response. 'Yes,' he said, nuzzling against the side of her face, 'whatever you was before, you'll learn different now. Young lad will enjoy you, and that's a fact, but Higgy gets first dibs down here, so when Master Eric has finished with you, you know what to expect.'

Tammy fought to ignore his words. After all, she thought, what did it matter? She had seen what Boolik had managed to reduce Bambi to and, regardless of the revulsion she now felt at what the groom was saying, she also knew that, when the time came, she would be helpless to resist, much as she was now helpless to ignore the urgings that his manipulation of her was generating deep inside.

Higgy's other hand dropped lower, cupping her denuded crotch, one finger stroking the tight opening like a feather.

'Less I'm much mistaken,' he murmured, 'this little hole is going to get seriously enlarged before the day is out. Master Eric will probably want to break you himself, but after that, well, it'll probably be Loin.

'Of course,' he went on, breaking the intimate contact, 'you won't know about Loin, will you? Well, Loin is Master Eric's slave. Master Eric treats him like a female slut most of the time, making him wear shoes even worse'n those you'll be wearing in a minute or two, but Loin is all man, I can tell you.

52

'That poor bastard has got the biggest cock anyone here has ever seen. Like a log, it is – that's why he's called Loin. Bigger'n a bloody elephant, I reckon. You'll be like a chicken on a spit, time he's through with you.'

Despite herself, Tammy let out a plaintive whinny and, for a second or two, she thought she detected a look of sympathy in Higgy's expression. His voice softened.

'Don't you worry, little princess,' he whispered. 'You get back here and old Higgy will take care of you. Then,' he added, his features contorting into a wicked grin, 'you can learn how to take care of old Higgy, eh?' He stepped back, turning to the younger groom.

'Stir yourself, you useless lump,' he said. 'Missy here needs some shoes, a corset and her nice new dress. No knickers, mind you. They'd just be a waste of time. Look,' he went on, as Silas held up the steel-coloured shoes. 'Just look at your pretty heels. Must be eight inches, at least.'

And Tammy looked, mouth agape, convinced that she would never be able to stand, let alone walk, in such devilish footwear, yet knowing that, regardless, within a short time that was exactly what she would be doing, walking, tottering, staggering even, towards a fate that was frequently described, by real women, as being worse than death and which, for her, who had formerly been Tommy MacIntyre the fisherman, would be worse than hell itself.

In the wide concourse that separated the two rows of stalls, Lulu saw that the large passenger carriage was already waiting for her, two pony girls harnessed to either side of the shaft, traces leading back and draped over the rail in front of the high driver's perch. Of the intended passenger or passengers, there was as yet no sign, but she presumed that Master Eric would be involved.

The two grooms stepped forward, taking Lulu from Julia without comment and leading her towards the vehicle, where, hanging from the front rail was a gag harness. Obediently, Lulu parted her lips as they drew the straps over her head, accepting the stubby, penis-shaped gag without protest, giving only a small grunt as the strap was pulled unnecessarily tight.

'Let's have you up, girlie,' Higgy said, grinning with anticipation. Lulu's eyes were riveted to the curving rubber phallus that sprang from the centre of the padded bar that comprised the driver's 'seat'; she was accustomed to such perches, for most of the racing buggies could be adapted to provide the optimum stimulation for their hapless drivers.

In the ballet-toed boots, it was impossible for her to mount the carriage unaided, but the grooms were well versed in their duties and quickly lifted her between them, each grasping the top of a slim thigh, spreading her to receive the waiting shaft, which slid into her with an ease that might have astonished an inexperienced onlooker. She barely moaned as her weight settled down on to the bar, and showed no reaction as they drew her booted feet down and locked them into waiting stirrups, thus removing any slight chance of Lulu being able to dismount herself.

The grooms now took her arms, forcing curiously padded mittens over her gloved hands, securing them by means of broad straps that locked about her wrists and then fixed back, via short chains, to either side of her corset, thus restricting the amount of movement available to her, while leaving just enough latitude for her to exert an element of pressure on the reins.

These were now connected to stout rings set into the tips of each mitten, snapped on with spring-loaded links, so that Lulu could not lose control of them, regardless of the situation. Ensuring that she was sitting in the standard, upright driving position, they adjusted the lengths of the various traces, removing unnecessary slack, and then, finally, satisfied that all was ready, the two young men stepped back and took up station on either side of the pony girls.

Trying not to be obvious, Lulu moved her head slightly from side to side, peering through the eye slits in her mask, trying to get an early sighting of Master Eric. She was not kept waiting for long, for, almost as though he had been watching the preparations from an unseen vantage point, Eric appeared from the direction of the tunnel that led back into the hillside, strutting with his usual, disdainful air, the shambling figure behind him looking as pathetic as Eric did powerful.

Lulu had never yet seen Loin's face properly. During previous encounters, he had either been kept hooded fully, a half-mask covering the top of his head, or else, on one occasion when he had been left unmasked, his features had been made up into such a grotesque parody of a woman, complete with huge, curly wig on his bald pate, that he would have been unrecognisable, even to someone who knew him well.

Today, his entire head was encased in a heavy, leather hood, the mouth and eye slits zipped closed; presumably, beneath the leather he would be gagged and, given Lulu's experience of Master Eric's particular penchants, his ears would also have been plugged and covered by muffling pads. Blind, deaf and dumb, and with his arms laced into a tight sheath behind his back, Loin was completely at the mercy of the man who held his leash, or of anyone else to whom Eric chose to give control of him.

He was, as ever when Lulu had seen him, a totally helpless, anonymous drone, but for one feature that was impossible to disguise in his usual state of near nakedness: the prodigious manhood, currently flaccid and laced into a leather sheath from which the leash to Eric's hand was connected, and yet still far larger than any Lulu had ever experienced before, could have belonged to only one person, and, as she was only too well aware, once aroused, it would achieve a length and girth that would put the phallus upon which she was currently impaled completely to shame.

With a small sigh, Lulu wriggled her slender hips, contracting her inner muscles on the inert rubber, already imagining what she was certain was still to come.

From the outside, the barn looked as though it had seen better days, which it undoubtedly had, but inside the impression was totally at odds with this. Walls had obviously been boarded and plastered, staging installed, lighting rigged and the floor paved with quarry tiles, about which were scattered several very expensive-looking and deeply upholstered sofas and chairs. Celia Butler led the way towards one of the central seats, indicated for Colin to sit and lowered herself alongside him, stretching out her long legs with languid confidence. She nodded towards the heavy curtains that covered what appeared to be the end wall.

'Lisa is blonde,' she said. 'You did not say what colouring your pony had.'

'Is it important?'

Celia afforded him one of her short laughs. 'Only if one is bothered with aesthetics,' she said. 'With a blonde pony, black tack is the best, in my opinion, although red runs it a close second, but with a brunette, especially one with dark skin colouring, one cannot beat white leather, and if the creature should actually be black, then white is an absolute must.'

'I see,' Colin said. He opted for innocence. 'So much to learn, Celia,' he said. 'I really hadn't given the matter that much consideration. Apparently your clients get more for their money than simple merchandise.'

'And I can see that you are a potential aficionado, my friend,' she replied. 'A little inexperienced, perhaps, but ever willing to learn and appreciate. I take it your pony isn't a blonde?'

'Well, actually, she is, sort of,' Colin said. 'I mean, she's not a blonde blonde, if you take my meaning, but she's definitely not a brunette.'

'Mousy,' Celia mouthed. 'Forgive my bluntness, but I think I know what you mean. But never mind, one can always give nature a helping hand. Bleach her white or make her a redhead, I would suggest. A man of your standing is entitled to expect a creature with outstanding features, wouldn't you agree?'

'Well ... yes, I suppose so,' Colin conceded. He appeared to consider the alternatives. 'Blonde, I think,' he

said, at length. 'Her skin tone isn't right for red hair.'
Alongside him, Celia chuckled and he regarded her with a
sideways, quizzical look.

'Mane, my dear,' she said. 'Always refer to it as their
mane. It can be styled to that effect, as you will shortly see.'
She half turned, looking over her shoulder, and spoke into
the gloom behind them.

'Margot, my dear, we're waiting,' she called out. 'Get the
silly mare out here now, please. I will not tolerate keeping
a master waiting.'

Finally, wearing a frilled and short-skirted latex dress in a
red as brilliant as the lurid blue catsuit that clung to her
every contour beneath it, Tammy could do nothing but
allow herself to be led back out into the concourse.

The stiff corset that she now wore beneath the dress was
compressing her waist to an extent that would have been
unbearable to a normal human body and even the Jenny Ann
body was suffering within its vicelike embrace. Her hands
had been left unhampered and unfettered, her arms required
to maintain even a semblance of balance on the cruel heels,
and, while she was still without a gag, such an addition
remained unnecessary, for her voice box continued not to
respond to the signals her brain was trying to send to it.

Higgy, holding on to her left elbow, guided her towards
the waiting carriage and the tall, well-muscled figure who
stood beside it. To *his* left, Amaarini, equally imposing in
her high boots, viewed the proceedings with an air of
detachment underlined by her folded-arms pose.

'Your virgin consort, Master Eric,' she announced,
mockingly. 'Such a sweet little thing, don't you think?'

Inside the skull-hugging hood and mask that had been
the final addition to her costume, Tammy knew she would
have been blushing, had this body permitted such a facility,
and was glad of the anonymity that the rubber face
afforded her, despite the lewd way in which the cloying
fabric forced her full lips into an inviting pout.

'You are certain that she *is* still virgin?' Eric said, from
behind his own mask. Amaarini simply laughed.

'Tighter than the proverbial drum, my friend,' she said. 'She was originally preserved intact by her family, but then that is another story.' Her erroneous explanation confirmed what Tammy had already suspected: whoever and whatever Eric and his fellow guest-visitors were, they were obviously ignorant as to the true nature of the human and supposedly female fodder with which they were constantly fed. Bitterly, as she was helped up on to the passenger seat of the carriage, she wondered what Master Eric's reaction might be if he knew just exactly what he was being offered today and then, with a shudder, realised that that was a question best left unanswered.

As she settled back against the thick upholstery, Tammy began to take stock of her surroundings, of the two harnessed pony girls who stood mutely on either side of the main shaft, of the candy-floss figure perched on the high driving seat at the front, and even of the macabre figure who stood tethered to the rear rail of the carriage. Even the leather sheath that currently held his male genitalia could not disguise the fact that this could only be Loin and Tammy was grateful that both he and his prodigious equipment were behind her and out of her line of sight.

The final addition to the party was now brought out and Tammy saw, with little surprise, that it was Bambi, now harnessed, as per Amaarini's instructions, in gleaming red leather, but, instead of being led forward to assist in the drawing of the vehicle, she was led to the rear of the carriage, her bridle rein knotted around the same rail to which Loin's tether was attached.

'Everything now to your satisfaction, Master Eric?' Amaarini stepped up alongside the carriage as Eric vaulted into the passenger seat next to Tammy. The leather-hooded head inclined towards her.

'Amanda,' he growled, 'your attention to detail is, as ever, beyond reproach.' He reached one hand across and patted Tammy's rubber-skinned thigh heavily. 'I shall, I am sure, thoroughly enjoy this little one and I can assure you that Loin will also be put to good use.'

Amaarini laughed. 'Then make sure your ponies are still capable of bringing you back,' she said. 'The spare mare,

Bambi, would make the best sport for him anyway, if I might be so bold as to offer a suggestion.'

'I'll bear your advice in mind,' Eric guffawed. 'Though the little wench up front also has a hot spot for the wretch, as I remember.' He leaned forward, tapping Lulu on the shoulder. 'Take us out, you little whore,' he said. 'Make these ponies earn their corn and I promise you Loin will give you your just deserts.' He sat back, wrapping a powerful arm about Tammy's shoulders, lifting one booted foot on to the bar that acted as a stabiliser for Lulu's driving seat.

'And you,' he said, placing his mouth close to her ear, 'will get far more than your deserts, that much I *can* promise you.'

Five

Despite Colin Turner's detailed directions, Geordie had quite a lot of trouble finding the late Andrew Lachan's Highlands estate. It was not just its remote location that was the problem, but rather the fact that the last ten miles of the approach could barely have been described as road and the cindered track frequently petered out altogether, leaving Geordie to painstakingly turn the car around and backtrack until he found where the correct route had branched off.

According to Colin's information, the estate covered several thousand acres, so the house itself, when Geordie finally came upon it, was something of a surprise, being neither large nor grandiose, just a simple, stone- and brick-built rectangle of two storeys, standing within a low stone-walled courtyard, within the bounds of which were a dilapidated barn and a long, narrow, single-storeyed brick building with the same dark slate roof.

As Geordie extricated himself from the car, the front door of the farmhouse opened and a tall, elegantly poised female, wearing a conservative, two-piece business suit in a deep blue, stepped out on to the uneven flagstoned surface. Locking the car door with exaggerated care, Geordie took advantage of the few seconds to study Sara Llewellyn-Smith and concluded that the grainy photograph that Colin had sent over the Internet did her no justice at all.

'I hope I haven't kept you waiting, Miss Llewellyn-Smith,' he said, striding towards her at last. The pert nose twitched in a gesture that could have been the beginning of a smile, but her expression remained neutral.

'Not at all, Sergeant,' she said. 'As I explained on the phone, I have been staying here for a few weeks, cataloguing various items for the executors. The place may not look much from the outside, but Mr Lachan has – had – collected together quite a few rare and valuable assets, many of which I believe have been in the family for several generations.'

She led the way inside and immediately Geordie was struck by the different ambience. Someone – Lachan himself, perhaps – had managed to lift the old farmhouse into something approximating the twentieth century, but without losing any of its important original features, including the huge, inglenook fireplace.

'The main computer is through here,' Sara said, pushing open a door that led into a small study and stepping briskly inside. Following her, Geordie noted the two walls lined with what were presumably very old books, the two heavy, leather-covered armchairs and the small, very old and undoubtedly very valuable desk upon which a computer terminal sat.

'Everything is up and running,' Sara said, fingers flicking over several keys, so that what looked like some sort of corporate logo appeared centre screen. 'However, I doubt you'll find anything of much use to you. The officers who came up from Glasgow copied everything, as did the London police at head office.

'In both cases, the material was the same, which is what I told them. Hardly surprising, seeing as how Mr Lachan's various offices are all networked to the same host server.'

'And you say there is nothing here concerning his, ah, personal interests?' Geordie said, sliding past her and slipping into the exquisitely carved chair.

'There's his diary, naturally,' Sara said, 'but that is nearly all business appointments. Here, let me show you.' She leaned forward, a discreet whiff of very expensive perfume wafting beneath Geordie's nostrils. Her fingers moved rapidly and the logo disappeared, to be replaced by what was clearly a diary page. Geordie took over and began scrolling through the screens.

'This entry here,' he said, pausing the screen and pointing. 'I presume HG refers to Healthglow?' He looked up and was rewarded with a curt nod. 'Mr Lachan appears to have frequented their establishment on a very regular basis.'

'Mr Lachan was a very busy and hard-working man,' Sara replied, her tone defensive. 'He liked to take any opportunity which arose to get away from the stresses and strains of business.'

'I'd have thought he could have done just that here,' Geordie retorted. 'Anywhere more remote than this place I couldn't imagine.'

'It was not my job to question my employer.'

'But you may just have wondered?'

'Not at all.' Geordie could feel the air between them suddenly bristling with electricity. 'As I said, it was none of my business. I was Mr Lachan's personal assistant in business matters only.'

'Of course.' Geordie let the reply hang there, the tone of it clearly hinting at scepticism, but if Sara caught it, she did not rise to the bait.

'Mr Lachan was a very good employer,' she said, simply. 'A hard man, yes, but a very fair one, too. He worked hard himself, as I have already said, and, naturally, he expected the same of everyone in the company, but we were all very well rewarded for our loyalty and application to our duties.'

'Presumably you would have met, or at least spoken to, most if not all of his business contacts?'

'Of course. My main duties concerned Mr Lachan's diary and schedules and I acted for him – in most cases – whenever he was absent.'

'And what about socially?' Geordie leaned back in the chair and looked up at her, noting how her eyes kept changing from amber to green. A trick of the light? Or was it an indication of mood swings. 'I mean,' he continued, 'with Mr Lachan being a bachelor, there must have been occasions when he entertained clients and their wives and would have needed a hostess.'

'Indeed,' Sara said. 'Many times. However,' she added, her full pink lips drawing into a tight line, 'any duties of that kind I was ever asked to carry out were carried out on a purely professional basis.'

'Naturally,' Geordie said. 'Whatever made you think I might be considering any other possibility?'

'Because,' Sara replied, tersely, 'you have bothered to come all this way in the first place. I have already spent many hours going through things, first with one police force and then with another. Your people have gone through all the company records in great depth and come up with nothing that should not be there.

'Someone seems to be looking for something which, in my opinion, they won't find. I understand, of course, that people make enemies in business, but Mr Lachan had a reputation for fair dealing and, in the eight years I worked for him, I can think of no one who would have reason to resent their treatment at his hands, let alone anyone who might want to kill him. The idea is preposterous!'

'You're probably right,' Geordie conceded, 'but there are still too many loose ends floating around out there, loose ends that could tie in to Mr Lachan, his death, this place and many other unexplained things. I'm a policeman, Miss Llewellyn-Smith, so I ask what some people might consider to be a lot of silly questions.

'That's because policing isn't as you see it on the telly. Stuff just doesn't fall into your lap, there aren't any lucky coincidences and, contrary to popular myth, neither do we have a supergrass in every pub, club and restaurant in the country.

'So we ask daft questions and we rely upon our instincts. Not that our instincts are infallible, but a few years on the job makes it a foolhardy copper who ignores them. A colleague of mine had good instincts. Either directly because of them, or indirectly, she's now dead.'

'I'm sorry.' Sara's expression remained bland. 'But I don't see what that has got to do with Mr Lachan. Or me, for that matter.'

'Neither do I,' Geordie said. 'Maybe nothing, but I can't yet say that for sure, so I keep probing.' He pushed the chair back and stood up. 'As you say, our people have already gone through this stuff, so I can get copies if I need to. What I'd like to do, meanwhile, is to take a general look around the place, if that's OK?'

'You've brought a warrant?'

'Do I need one?' For the first time, Sara smiled, displaying a row of small, even and very white teeth.

'If I said "yes", you'd only have to drive back and get one and then, after braving our local dirt tracks twice more, you would just be in a very bad mood, yes?'

'Probably.' Geordie grinned.

As soon as the pony-girl model, Lisa, was led up on to the low stage, Colin understood Celia's reference to a 'mane', for her bleached blonde hair had been shaved off on either side of her skull, leaving only a central strip, which was at once luxuriant and striking, for what remained was not only thick, but had been clearly treated with some sort of wax or gel, so that where it crossed the crown of the girl's head it stood up like a plume and then, where it cascaded down between her shoulders, it had been interwoven with red and black ribbons and flounced with her every step.

As the willowy, dark-skinned handler led Lisa into the spotlights, Colin felt his heart skip a beat, for none of the pictures he had seen on his computer screen could have prepared him for this sight in the flesh – and, apart from her singularly eccentric footwear, such blatantly naked flesh at that.

Lisa, he guessed, had to be nearer six feet tall than five feet nine and, although she was not heavily built, her entire body was finely toned, every sinew and muscle rippling beneath what appeared to be a fine coating of oil that gleamed and glistened beneath the shifting illuminations.

'One of the finest,' Celia whispered, her mouth close to Colin's ear. 'Unfortunately, however, only a part-timer. The silly child still harbours dreams of becoming a television actress.' Which, Colin thought, given the right casting, Lisa certainly could have been, for the face above the incredible body and beneath the fantastic hairstyle was truly beautiful.

'At the moment,' Celia continued, 'she has a small role in a science-fiction series, so the mane is not a problem. I just hope she doesn't get offered a part in a period drama – it would be such a waste. Mind you, there are always wigs. Lisa dear, step down here and let Master Colin see your hooves, please.'

Her face totally impassive, the girl descended the short drop to the main floor and swayed easily across to where Colin sat, apparently completely at ease on the towering heels of her footwear. As she moved, the sound her feet made on the hard flooring was sharp and resonating and, peering closer, he realised that the wide hoof-shaped soles were actually shod with metal.

'Very impressive,' he breathed, quietly. 'And expensive, too, I shouldn't wonder.' Celia mentioned a figure in the hundreds of pounds and Colin resisted the temptation to whistle in astonishment.

'And these are available in different colours?' was his only visible reaction. Celia nodded.

'Black is always the most popular,' she said, 'but they also come in red and white and we can make any other colour to order. A dappled brown is very popular, especially among masters who prefer their ponies to be dressed in authentic colours. There are body suits to match, naturally.'

'Naturally,' Colin said. He smiled encouragingly at Lisa, who simply stared back at him, unreacting. 'I should imagine that Lisa would look quite stunning as a dappled mare.'

'Indeed she does,' Celia said. 'In fact,' she added, as if on the spur of the moment, 'perhaps you should see her as such. Margot can prepare her, while we retire to the guest lounge for a little while. I dare say I can interest you in a glass of champagne – vintage, of course.'

Six

Tammy's watershed came only too soon, as she had feared it would.

Under Lulu's expert guidance, the two new pony girls performed to Master Eric's obvious satisfaction and he instructed the diminutive driver to canter them around the network of pathways that crisscrossed the otherwise uneven terrain that was Ailsa Ness. The carriage bowled along at a steady pace, Loin and Bambi lumbering in its wake, unable to do anything but follow where their traces led them, Loin struggling in the ridiculously high heels in which he had been shod, Bambi rapidly beginning to feel the effects of the heavily weighted hoof boots.

They continued in this manner for about an hour, whereupon Eric became bored. He kicked gently at Lulu's rump.

'Rein 'em in over in that clearing,' he instructed. Obediently, Lulu guided her two charges over on to the grassy expanse to the right of the track and pulled hard back on the traces. Eric turned to Tammy.

'I hope you've enjoyed the fresh air, my dear,' he said, his tone mocking. 'And now, here seems as good a place as any in which to dispose of the burden of your virginity.' He regarded her, grinning as he saw her eyes widen.

'Well,' he said, swinging his legs over the side of the carriage, 'it'd have to happen, sooner or later.' He jumped down, moved around the rear of the carriage, stepping easily over the dangling tethers that held Loin and Bambi to its rear rail, and came around alongside Tammy.

'Let's have you down, then,' he said, reaching up to her. For a brief instant, she considered trying to resist. After all, there were really only the two of them, for the two pony girls, Lulu and the hapless Loin and Bambi were all held in their various straps and chains, but one look down into those eyes was enough to convince Tammy that not only would such a course of action prove fruitless, it would also lead to the sort of retribution she could only imagine in her worst nightmares.

Lifting her down with ease, Eric deposited Tammy on the stony grass and turned back to Lulu.

'Keep the nags steady, girl,' he instructed. He looked her up and down. 'Comfortable?' he added. Lulu knew it was pointless to say otherwise. Mutely, she nodded, eliciting a wide grin from him.

'That's a good girl,' he sniggered. 'You just stay that way until Loin is ready for you. Mind,' he went on, 'the bastard has a bit of a stretching exercise to take care of before that, eh?'

He took Tammy by the arm, leading her across to where a long-ago-fallen tree lay in a disfigured tangle of stunted trunk and branch stumps.

'Your bridal bed, sweetness,' Eric said, pointing to the gnarled and lichen-stained wood. Tammy closed her eyes, trying to blot out every memory that remained within her confused head, but she knew it was no good. Her every instinct cried out for resistance; there were just the two of them, after all, but, when she opened her eyes and looked again, she knew that nothing she could do would prevent the inevitable.

She walked to the fallen trunk, turned and looked back at the man who was to be the instrument of her final degradation. Slowly, she lowered herself, settling her rubber-covered rump on to a section of the tree that had long since been stripped of its original bark and then, with calm deliberation, reached down and raised the frilled hem of her skirt.

Peering through the slits in her mask, she parted her lips and let out a low, animal keening sound, wishing that she still had the power of speech, wanting to tell this animal that this was not a surrender, but rather a soulless acceptance that sheer physicality could not be resisted.

Leaning backwards, slowly she spread her thighs, reaching down with one rubber-clad hand to part the sex lips similarly, knowing that even the slightest stimulation would trigger the responses that would help her through the coming ordeal, staring resolutely at the impressive organ that Eric was even now unveiling, all too aware that, when the beast had had his way with her, there was an even greater trial to come.

As Master Eric moved in to claim his prize, she looked beyond him, seeing the featureless, unseeing head of Loin, deliberately not seeing what lay in readiness for her, remembering what Alex had said.

And, as Eric's rampant manhood began to prise her apart, Tammy began to recite the mantra in her head.

One day, one day soon. One day, one day soon.

One day.

Soon.

Soon.

And stars exploded as the body they had given her betrayed her, as she had known it would.

The guest room was situated at the far end of the barn from the dais where Lisa had first been displayed. It contained a well-stocked bar and more comfortable seats, and had several large television screens set around the walls, though these were currently dead. Affecting an air of nonchalance he did not feel, Colin accepted the chilled champagne. As promised, it was a good vintage and he reflected that Celia Butler's business must be more than just good if this was how she treated even a prospective buyer.

Their conversation remained mostly innocuous. Celia enquired as to what line of business Colin was in and he replied simply that he had no need to work, having been left a large sum of money by his grandfather, a statement that was actually perfectly true.

'I must confess that I do find life just a trifle unchalleng- ing at times,' he said, airily. 'I suppose that's why I have adopted a few new, er, interests, as it were.'

'Training a full-time pony girl brings its own challenges,' Celia said, 'but then, as I understand it, your pony isn't actually full-time?'

'Not yet,' Colin agreed, 'though I'm working on it.'

'Perhaps you might like to consider sending her here for some professional training?' Celia suggested. 'Or even coming with her yourself? Our facilities are excellent and my senior handlers have trained almost as many masters in the correct disciplines as they have trained their mounts. The fees are not negligible,' she admitted, 'but we have never yet had a dissatisfied client.'

'It would certainly be worth considering,' Colin agreed. 'I'll give it some serious thought, I promise.'

By the time they returned to the main area, Margot had already returned with Lisa, the statuesque girl now clad from neck to toe in a figure-hugging latex suit, dappled as promised, and now wearing a pair of hoof boots that blended perfectly with its colouring. With a start, Colin saw that there were two small openings through which her ringed nipples protruded as two stiffened cones, and a further, ovoid opening that left her denuded sex clearly displayed. Pulse quickening, he realised that she looked even more exposed and vulnerable than when he had first seen her naked from the knees up.

'Perhaps you would like to see the very top end of our range?' Celia suggested. 'We have special dressage har- nesses, most impracticable for everyday use, but wonderful for displaying a pony on formal occasions.'

'I'm in your hands,' Colin said. 'You are, after all, the expert.'

'Splendid,' Celia enthused. She nodded to the sultry handler. 'Full gold display, Margot,' she said, simply. 'And bring Stella in to see to Lisa's make-up, if you would.'

Stella proved to be a stocky woman in her mid to late thirties, brown-haired, relatively plain, but clearly fit and strong and probably, Colin guessed, not someone to be trifled with. However, her immediate talents seemed to lie in the way she handled the contents of the box she brought with her and, while Margot began fitting the gold girth corset, she went to work on Lisa's face.

The pony girl's eyes were soon rimmed with black, after which her eyelids were painted a sparkling gold. Heavy false lashes in the same metallic colour were then glued into place and her lips glossed to match. Meantime, Margot was adjusting the girth straps and compressing her already trim waist to almost impossible proportions, although, from Lisa's lack of reaction, Colin assumed that she was more than used to such stringent treatment.

Mutely, she now held out each arm in turn, for Margot to draw up their length a pair of curious, full-length leather mittens, each of which was laced so tightly as to mould itself to the contours of the limb. Leaning forward with genuine interest, Colin saw that the tapered ends enclosing the hands and fingers effectively rendered them useless, a situation emphasised when Margot bent each fist double in turn, threading a wrist strap through the ring at the tip and tightening it to produce a rigid fist.

'Already, as you can see,' Celia said, turning to Colin, 'she is unable to remove anything herself. Even with the arms left free she cannot untie laces or unbuckle straps. Of course, the arms are not usually left free anyway and there are a number of ways they can be further secured, as you will shortly see. Basic pouch first, please, Margot,' she added, addressing her instructions to the handler.

The woman nodded and quickly produced what at first looked to Colin like a gold leather shopping bag, but he quickly realised his mistake. Folding Lisa's arms behind her back, the forearms horizontal and parallel with each other, Margot drew the soft leather pouch over them, using what Colin had assumed to be handles, but were, in fact, adjustable straps, placing them over the helpless girl's shoulders, crossing them over her prominent breasts and drawing them back to reattach them to each side of the pouch, preventing it from slipping off and further drawing the captive arms in tightly against Lisa's back. The overall effect, apart from rendering her as helpless as Colin could imagine it was possible to be, was to drag her shoulders back and force her to thrust her chest out even further.

'A proud pony already,' Celia commented, 'but we shall make her prouder still. Bridle her now, Margot, please.' The handler was quick to comply. Deftly, she threw the apparent tangle of gold straps over the top of Lisa's head and within seconds had drawn the various components into their correct positions.

Leather bands encircled forehead, chin and crown, and another strap descended to the bridge of the nose, dividing there into two thinner straps that ran down either cheek until they met up with the chin strap at the jawline. Where each strap passed the corner of the mouth was set a stout, gold-plated ring, whose purpose became quickly apparent.

Deft fingers attached either end of the bit to these rings, prising apart the teeth so that the thick rubber rod was pulled far back inside the mouth, dragging the lips back into a grimace and rendering any coherent speech impossible. Having silenced her charge, Margot turned her about, taking a firm hold on yet another strap that hung loosely down from the crown of the bridle, threading it through a buckle at the top of the girth corset and tightening it mercilessly until Lisa's head was drawn cruelly back, whereupon the ensemble was completed by the addition of a broad, studded collar, so that even if the taut strap had been released, it would have been almost impossible for the pony girl to return her head to a normal position.

'You may add the final touch yourself, if you wish,' Celia said, nudging Colin's elbow. He turned his head, slowly, and was unable to contain his gasp of surprise. In her hand, rotating it gently, Celia held a long, curved, golden rubber dildo.

Before them, without waiting to be told, Lisa shuffled her hoofed feet apart, spreading her thighs and her exposed sex, the pink inner flesh glistening invitingly . . .

A cursory look around the farmhouse itself revealed nothing, which did not surprise Geordie. Of the four bedrooms, only one showed signs of recent occupation, that being used by Sara Llewellyn-Smith during her stay. One other, the largest, still contained a few personal effects and articles of clothing that Sara confirmed had belonged to her late employer, but nothing there was of interest.

Not quite sure what it was he was searching for, Geordie nevertheless switched his attentions to the outbuildings. The large barn, the roof of which showed signs of repair work carried out within the past few months, was his first target. Inside, the pale sunlight streamed through the open doors, illuminating a wall rack that contained a variety of wooden and metal implements, but closer inspection showed them to be nothing more than farm tools, and all of them had seen much better days.

To one side stood a neat stack of metal drums, which, Sara informed him, held diesel fuel for the generator that stood in a lean-to at the rear of the farmhouse, and there were several gas bottles, which were apparently used in portable heaters to supplement the two open fireplaces that were still functional, which, Geordie presumed, were the reason for the high stack of cut logs that occupied a large area at the other end of the barn.

It all looked perfectly normal.

Except . . .

At the farthest end from the doorway, where the light from outside barely penetrated, something had been covered over by a large, plastic tarpaulin. Stepping closer, blinking in an effort to accustom his eyes to the gloom, Geordie reached out a hand and grasped the sheet.

'Any idea what this is?' Behind him, he heard Sara take a few steps nearer his back.

'Some sort of old farm cart, I think,' she said. 'I had a quick look under the cover, but I didn't think it was of much interest. Probably been here since the year dot.'

'I don't think so,' Geordie said, softly, drawing the tarpaulin further aside. 'Let's have a proper look. Ah, yes, it's a cart all right – some sort of buggy. And I don't think it's anywhere near as old as you seemed to believe. Here, let me get this thing off and see if we can't pull it over by the door a bit.'

Rolling the plastic away, he discarded it in an untidy heap, then bent and hefted one of the twin shafts that jutted from the front of the little vehicle. It came up easily and, as Geordie dragged it around, the buggy moved easily on well-greased wheels.

'If this isn't modern,' he said, dragging it across to the pool of sunlight by the doorway, 'then someone has at least spent a bit of time renovating it. See, all this paintwork is still quite fresh and the brass fittings have been polished up in the past few months.'

'Maybe Mr Lachan was intending to use it,' Sara suggested. Geordie coughed, clearing his throat.

'That'd be my bet, too,' he said. 'Yes, this'd be about the right size.' He peered closer at the raised, single seat, running his hands over the padded upholstery. The plastic tarpaulin and the mild summer air had combined to keep it virtually as new as it had been when it had been made, which, in Geordie's estimation, could not have been more than three or four months earlier.

'Actually, it seems a bit on the small side,' Sara said, moving closer for a better view. 'It's the sort of thing you see at seaside fairs – you know, kiddie rides, being pulled by a Shetland pony.'

'Yeah,' Geordie said. 'A Shetland pony. That's exactly what I was thinking. Mr Lachan interested in ponies, was he?'

'He never said so,' Sara replied. 'But then –'

'But then you never pried into his personal likes and dislikes,' Geordie finished for her. 'Yeah, you said. Well, this little beauty certainly hasn't been in here too long, so maybe he was planning to get himself some livestock, eh? Would he have asked you to take care of that sort of transaction?'

'He might,' Sara admitted. 'He hadn't said anything up to . . .'

Her voice trailed off and she turned away, but not before Geordie had caught the gleam of a tear in the corner of her eye. Sara Llewellyn-Smith may well have been telling the truth about the purely business nature of her relationship

73

with the late Andrew Lachan, but it was obvious she had truly cared for the man.

'I understand,' Geordie said, quietly. He heard her sniff. 'And I'm sorry to have to come here and pry about, but, if your boss's death was anything other than an accident, surely you'd want us to find out and get to the people responsible?'

'That goes without saying,' she muttered, trying, apparently, to regain her normal icy composure. 'But I don't see what ponies and pony carts have to do with anything.'

'I should hope you don't,' Geordie said, but he mumbled the statement quietly to himself. Clearer, he changed tack slightly.

'If Mr Lachan *was* intending to bring in either horses or ponies, where would he keep them? This place is a bit big and draughty for livestock in the winter, I'd have thought.'

'The stables, I expect,' Sara replied. 'The building across the yard – it used to be a stable block, from the look of it.' She turned towards the open air, anticipating Geordie's next move. 'Come to think of it,' she added, 'it looks like someone has been doing some refurbishment work in there recently. The inside walls have all been painted, at least.'

The outer stable door had been completely replaced during the summer, Geordie realised as he lifted the latch and swung the two halves open together. Not only that, but someone had gone to the trouble of running an electricity supply from the main house and the fittings were all modern. He flicked along the bank of switches just inside the door and a series of fluorescent tubes began to flicker into life, revealing a main concourse area, which ran along the front of the building like a wide corridor, off which were a series of inner stall doors, all with their bottom sections bolted closed and their top sections open and hooked back.

White emulsion gleamed from the masonry and the woodwork showed signs of having been sanded down and stained around the same time the walls had been painted. The smell of new paint and varnish still hung in the air. Geordie stepped forward, leaned over the first stall door

74

and looked inside. The rectangular cubicle was empty, save for a small bale of straw that stood in the farthest corner and an empty, broken wooden crate.

A quick inspection of the second stall revealed exactly the same, except that this time the crate seemed to be in better repair. The third stall held no crate, but there were several bales of straw, which occupied half the cramped floor space. It was the fourth and final stall that was most interesting. Geordie reached down for the bolt and opened the lower door.

'There must be some kind of switch in here,' he muttered, as his bulk immediately blocked most of the light from outside. 'Ah, yes, here we are.' There was a metallic click and a small, low-powered lamp in the ceiling started to glow and steadily brighten.

'Well, what have we here?' Geordie stepped inside the stall and moved over to the right-hand wall, to which had been affixed a rack of timber slats, from which projected several dowel pegs. Hanging down from these were a variety of what were clearly whips and crops, plus several hanks of new-looking rope. Turning, he addressed Sara over his shoulder.

'I thought you said you didn't know whether Lachan had an interest in horses,' he said, sharply.

Sara shrugged her elegant shoulders. 'To be honest, Sergeant Walker,' she said, resignedly, 'I didn't even take a proper look at whatever this little lot is supposed to be.'

'Well, take a look now,' Geordie invited her, stepping aside. 'You sound like the kind of girl who's seen the inside of a riding stable before now.'

'One shouldn't look for stereotypes,' she retorted, but nevertheless moved forward and reached out for one of the crops. 'Yes,' she said, 'this is definitely new. See,' she said, flexing the braided leather between her hands, 'it's far too stiff. It's been oiled, right enough, but it needs a lot more work. If you cut across a horse's quarters with this as it is at the moment, it could damage the flesh.'

'Needs to be more supple, I presume,' Geordie prompted.

'A *lot* more supple,' Sara confirmed. She reached out again. 'Ah, now this is better.' She took down a second crop and swished it through the air, striking the rack with a report that sounded like a pistol shot inside the confined space. 'This is a lot older, for a start. See how flattened and worn the braiding is.'

'And how old would you guess it to be?'

Another shrug. 'Depends upon how much usage it's had,' she said. 'Five years, maybe – more likely ten. It's been well looked after.' She held it up for his closer inspection and he saw how the well-oiled leather shone, even in the dimmish light.

'So, if this was Lachan's, he's been into riding for a good few years?' Geordie grinned.

'*If* it was his,' Sara snapped. 'One can buy these things second-hand, you know!'

'I expect one can,' Geordie agreed. 'Especially if one knows where to look. Recognise any of these other bits and pieces?'

'Not as such,' Sara said, studying the rack. 'I mean, I can guess what they all are, but I hadn't seen them before I came in here a few weeks ago and, as I said, I didn't really give them a second glance then. This, for instance,' she added, 'is a bull whip.'

'And would that be used on a horse?' Her eyebrows shot upwards.

'Good heavens, no!' she exclaimed. 'I can't imagine what anyone would need such an awful thing for. Look at the way the tip is split into three and look at the little weights on each thong. Ugh! This would cut any animal to ribbons!' She replaced the coiled whip with evident disgust and turned away back towards the corridor.

'Whatever these things are doing here and whoever brought them here, I can't see that it's at all relevant,' she said. 'For all we know, Mr Lachan may have found the stuff here and simply been renovating it.'

'Yes, of course,' Geordie said, following her out and pushing the lower door together after him. 'As you say, they tell us nothing.' *Nothing we don't know already*, he added, under his breath.

'Is there anything else you'd like to see?' Sara said, when they were once again out in the bright autumn sunlight. 'Only today is my last day here for the present and I really should be making a start back before too long. The nights are beginning to draw in now and you've seen the roads around here.'

'Yes, I have that,' Geordie said. 'Those tracks make ten miles seem like thirty.'

'I'd have said fifty,' Sara said, 'but then I suppose all times and distances are relative.'

'Yeah.' Geordie stopped, turning back towards the stable block, squinting against the lowering sun. 'Yes, distance is all a matter of perception at times,' he said. 'Tell me, Miss Llewellyn-Smith, how long would you say that stable building was?'

'Pardon?' Sara narrowed her eyes and looked at Geordie curiously. He nodded towards the building.

'How long from one end to the other?' he persisted. 'Forty feet? Fifty feet?'

'I'd say nearer sixty,' Sara said, confidently. 'Not far off the length of a cricket pitch.'

'And I'd say you're right.'

'I know I'm right,' Sara retorted, testily, 'but I still don't see – Oh!' She stopped suddenly, mouth open. Geordie's expression was midway between a smile and a glare.

'Exactly,' he said, softly. 'The little area by the door is maybe ten or twelve feet wide, then there are the four stalls, each around eight feet wide. That makes a total of around forty-five feet maximum, and that building is, as you so rightly say, at least sixty feet long. C'mon, hen, I'm going to take another look inside.'

Seven

Loin.

Blindly, the wretched creature heaved away at Tammy, his huge shaft ploughing into her with every rhythmic lunge, forcing her thighs so wide that she thought she would be rent in two, yet triggering lightning bolts that she could not ignore, even if she barely understood them.

No longer Tommy, she lifted her legs, wrapping her ankles about him, dragging him into her, though he needed no such urging. Through the gag beneath the leather hood that blinded him from knowing with whom he copulated, she heard him gasp and groan, as she, in turn, squealed and whinnied, driven to a peak of abandon she had never realised could exist.

Loin.

Blind. Blindly obedient. Machine-like.

Beneath the tirade of his master's whip, unseeing, unhearing, unspeaking, Loin finally unleashed in Tammy a storm far greater even than that which had once nearly killed, and finally delivered to a fate worse than drowning, a poor creature that was now driven to a precipice of lust that once, what now seemed years ago, a poor yet proud fisherman would have found impossible to believe could ever have existed.

The room, once someone had realised it had to be there, was not difficult to find. The false wall was actually timbered, with a mock stone cladding fixed to it on the inside, so that a casual observer would have assumed that it was, indeed, the end of the block, but rapping on it with the knuckles produced a telltale hollow sound and it did not take Geordie long to realise that the wooden whip rack was actually concealing a door. After a few seconds of experimental probing, one of the slats moved, there was a click and that entire section of the wall swung open. A few more seconds groping about and Geordie's fingers found the light switch.

'Ye gods!' he gasped, as the tube lights flickered into life. 'Now this *is* interesting.' He moved inside, Sara almost stumbling over him in her haste to follow.

'Crikey!' she gasped. 'What on earth . . .?' For fully half a minute they stood together in silence, taking in the bizarre display. One wall was almost completely covered with leather tack and bridles of every imaginable colour; there were chains with manacles hanging from hooks, long boots that either laced up or buckled – or both – all with the most astonishing-looking heels; and what could only be described as a collection of leather corsets was laid out on a small trestle table.

But most incredible of all were the two female figures that stood in the centre of the chamber, and it had been a few seconds before Geordie had realised that they were not actually real women, but very realistic mannequins, decked out as he had seen several girls presented in the various websites he had visited at Colin's behest.

The 'girl' on the left had been harnessed in gleaming black leather, complete with blinkers and bit, the huge heels, shaped, as were those on the other boots in the room, to roughly resemble hooves, raising her to a height of well over six feet. Her silent companion, just a little shorter, due to the slightly lower heels of her footwear, had been favoured with a similar rig in red leather, but with the lower half of her face encased in an intricate arrangement that gave her features a decidedly equine appearance.

Sara finally found her voice.

'I don't understand,' she breathed, huskily. 'What exactly are they supposed to be?' Geordie stifled a harsh laugh.

79

'Can't you guess?' he said. He took half a step forward and pointed to the nearer dummy. 'These are your Shetland ponies, Miss Llewellyn-Smith. At least,' he added, 'this is what the real thing is supposed to look like.'

'But it's – it's –' Words seemed to fail her and Geordie came to her rescue.

'I'm afraid, my old lovely,' he said, his accent thicker than usual, 'that this isn't exactly a surprise to me. It would appear that your late boss was a bit of an enthusiast over what's apparently known as pony girls.'

'What? Dressing dummies up in harnesses?' Geordie refused to meet her gaze.

'The dummies are – or were – only temporary, would be my guess,' he said. He nodded towards the far end of the room, where a solid timber bed had been secured to both floor and wall, a neatly packaged bedding roll sitting atop the bare, rubber-covered mattress. 'This place was being kitted out for use by a real live pony girl. I reckon.'

His eye caught the glimmer of something lying at the feet of the red-harnessed mannequin and he stooped forward to retrieve it. The chain did not appear to have broken, but closer examination revealed that the small catch would not properly close. Geordie turned it over on the palm of his hand, the fingers of the other tracing the carefully worked lettering.

'And I'd also bet a few bob,' he said, breathing deeply, 'that her name was Jessica.'

'Like the cruiser,' Sara said, her voice barely more than a whisper. Geordie weighed the gold identity pendant carefully.

'Yeah,' he said. '*Just* like the cruiser.' He turned, pocketing his trophy. 'I'll give you a receipt for this,' he said, pushing past Sara towards the previously hidden door.

'I still don't understand,' Sara protested. Geordie grunted.

'I'm not sure I do, either,' he confessed. 'But if that computer in the house can access the Internet, I'll try to throw a little light on the subject. I'd . . . well, I'd rather not explain it myself.'

'That much I *can* understand,' Sara said, the nervousness in her forced laugh betraying her emotions.

'All I now need,' Ramon Valerez said, silkily, 'is a definite delivery date.' He reached out and pushed the leather-bound case across the desk, flicking the lid closed and hiding the case's glittering contents. Opposite him, Richard Major remained totally unmoved.

'It will be soon, Ramon,' he said. He placed a hand on top of the case and moved it back towards Ramon, albeit that the movement was all but imperceptible. 'This is not necessary yet, as I have told you. Payment upon delivery, that was our agreement.'

'Surely, Ricardo,' Ramon smirked. 'But time is money, in my business as in any other. My people thought that perhaps a small incentive . . .?'

'Ramon!' Major laughed, removing his hand and returning it to rest upon the other, which, in turn, lay easily on the edge of his desk. 'What is it with you people? Yes, I understand your inherent mistrust – that is the nature of your business – but surely you must, by now, have formed a better opinion of us here.

'Yes, I could take your money and deliver you a consignment, but I prefer to wait just the little while longer it will take in order for me to be certain that the quality of that consignment is up to what you need. Our relationship would be in jeopardy if I did anything less.'

Valerez nodded, but he made no effort to retrieve the case and the diamonds it contained. 'I understand, Ricardo,' he said, 'and I appreciate that you are a man of honour, but how much longer must we wait? Take this as, shall we say, seed capital. If it helps you speed up the project, that is to the advantage of us both, but give me a date, please.'

'Ramon,' Major said, evenly, 'it is not a question of the money. We have more than adequate resources to fund this project and it *is* very near to completion now. We have the prototype Jenny Anns here and subject to a full evaluation. So far, the results are excellent, but we have yet to subject any of them to proper testing.

'That is about to start, I give you my word; and then, when Keith's preliminary figures are borne out, as I am convinced they will be, work can commence on producing a full batch for shipment. Trust me, Ramon, you will have your girls within a matter of weeks, complete with the trainers necessary to turn them into the beasts of burden you need for that terrain.

'Mind you,' he added, finally pushing the case back across the desktop, 'there is a part of me that considers it a waste. These girls are the epitome of every male fantasy.'

'Which I know only too well,' Ramon smirked. 'However, the girls you provide for us are worth far more in the role for which we need them. The mountain trails at home are steep and uneven. Four-legged beasts frequently end up in the bottom of ravines and our normal two-legged carriers ... well, they simply cannot be trusted, as I explained before now.

'Neither are they in any way strong enough for what is required,' he continued, 'whereas the Jenny Anns, capable, with adjustments, of withstanding extremes of cold, pain and anything else they might need to confront, they are the real answer.

'Each girl can carry fifty kilos with ease and travel fifty kilometres in any twenty-four-hour period, even through our mountain passes. And, if they ever should be apprehended, they can say nothing. There is only the one problem.'

'Which would only arise if ever one of the girls were to die and her body fall into the hands of the authorities,' Major said. 'But fear not, my impatient friend. Keith is already working on that, which is yet another reason for patience. By the time he has finished, the girls you have will never survive capture in a state which would enable the medical people to discover the truth about them.'

'You people are very thorough, Ricardo,' Ramon grinned. He tapped the lid of the case. 'And I trust you, something I could not say about many people I have dealt with, I promise. So ... keep these. They are nothing in the overall picture, when all is said and done. I want – I *need* my pony girls and I am relying on you to deliver them.

Lineker has begun work on the Indian girls we brought this time, I presume?'

'He has,' Major confirmed. 'It is too early, of course, for quantified test results, but he tells me that his initial analyses are more than promising. If you have the facility ready on schedule, I think we can safely say that it will, within a few weeks of activation, be producing as many creatures as you could possibly need. The girls we send you from here will be as nothing.'

'Except as role models,' Ramon grinned. 'Our local mountain girls are, to say the least, a little slow. Not that any beast of burden needs inordinate levels of intelligence, but it would be preferable if we could at least re-create something of what you have achieved here. The nights in the mountains are, after all, long and cold.'

'As they can be here,' Major concurred, with a slow smile, 'especially during the winter months.'

The scenes she had seen on the computer screen should have been horrifying, but they had been far more than that. The policeman had been out of his depth, that much Sara had gleaned even from the time they had entered Andrew's secret chamber and he had sought to cover his confusion by thrusting the digital images under her nose, expecting her to be horrified, frightened, appalled.

And Sara knew that she should have been all of those things and more and knew even more so that the problem she now had stemmed not from her being so, but from quite the opposite.

After he left, she had sat there, in Andrew's private study, that final image frozen on the computer screen, staring at it, but not seeing it any more, the images that were racing through her head far more vivid than anything that a bunch of pixels could ever hope to conjure up. At last, with the early-evening sky already darkening beyond the picture window, she rose, standing on legs that trembled with uncertainty and apprehension, holding on to the side of the desk, not willing to trust herself to limbs that could betray her uncertainty with such traitorous ease.

The door to the hidden chamber stood open, as they had left it, the lights still burning inside. For several minutes, Sara stood in the entrance, transfixed by the sight of the two bizarrely garbed figures, the blood pounding in her temples, her breathing shallow and rapid. The air inside the building was cool, yet small beads of perspiration broke on her forehead and the palms of her hands felt clammy.

Finally, she seemed to come to a decision, but it was a choice that was not consciously made and, as if in a trance, Sara stepped inside, fingers reaching blindly for the clasp on the hem of her skirt.

Quite why Dr Lineker seemed to have taken a particular shine to her, Helen had no idea and she did not particularly care, for his continued patronage assured her of a far easier life than that afforded to most of her Jenny Ann compatriots and, as the weeks rolled on, she had begun to consider her status as that of a favoured concubine.

True, she still spent the majority of her time in the small, cell-like room deep beneath the hillside at the far end of the island, but more and more now she found herself living in Lineker's private quarters, both here on Ailsa Ness and also, since three weeks previously, in his picturesque cottage on the larger island of Carigillie Craig.

Her new role also exempted her from some of the more extreme costumes, including the rigorous corseting that gave the Jenny Anns their stiff and narrow-waisted postures that the guests seemed to idealise. Instead, Lineker favoured loose gowns, ankle-length, flowing creations made from the synthetic fabric that was more and more being utilised in place of the less practical latex, but which resembled it in every way except its ability to permit the skin to breathe.

The doctor did seem to share the guests' penchant for ridiculously high heels, but the ankles of this body, combined with its higher pain, or 'discomfort', threshold, made this only a minor inconvenience and Helen was well aware of what such extreme footwear did for the aesthetic appeal of her legs.

She stretched these legs now, reclining on the heavily padded couch, making no attempt to pull the folds of her dress, which had ridden up her thigh, down below her shapely knees. On the far side of the room, seated in the small bay window, overlooking the rocky cove below, Lineker seemed engrossed in his own thoughts, but Helen had come to know him better than that now.

'Master,' she said, softly. He looked up immediately, his curiously reptilian features softening. 'Master,' she repeated, now sure of his attention, 'you seem to be preoccupied this morning. Have I done anything to offend you?'

His thin lips twisted into a smile, for they both knew that, if she were to offend him, he could as easily have her whipped as bother to discuss the matter with her.

'You know different to that, my dear,' he said. He sat back, turning slightly in the upright chair, reaching up with one hand to brush the straggling hair back across his head. 'There are just so many things for me to consider,' he said. 'So many different things, my little dear. I should like to be able to talk more of them,' he went on. 'You, above all the others, might just comprehend, but it is all so complicated.'

'I should be honoured for my master to confide in me.' Helen had not been slow in learning the sort of etiquette that was expected of her, nor the fact that Keith Lineker's ego could be easily massaged by the right amount of pandering. She made her eyes wide, running her tongue along her upper lip.

'I know I am just an ignorant slave,' she continued, 'but if there was even the smallest thing I could do . . .' She allowed her offer to hang in the air, but, when Lineker did not respond, continued in the same, soft voice.

'I know how much I owe to you, Master,' she said. 'At first, admittedly, it was difficult to adjust to my new situation, but then you would understand that without my telling you. Now, of course, I have no doubts. You gave me renewed life and I can do no less than to offer that life to you.'

'As I said, Helen,' Lineker mused, 'there is something about you that seems to be sadly lacking in the majority of

85

your peers. I think it is a matter of intelligence, no more, no less. Tell me, Helen, do you understand why it is so necessary for you to bear my offspring?'

She eased herself upright, deliberately adopting a posture that spoke of earnestness and even eagerness. 'I *think* so, Master,' she said. 'Our baby – *your* baby, that is – will provide the basis for a host body for your youngest natural daughter.'

'And it doesn't worry you that I need the tissue samples from this baby to ensure the continued survival of my daughter?'

'There is no way that it could,' Helen said. 'Neither should it. After all, but for you, I would now be dead and, if this body you have created for me can be of any service to you, well then, could I find it in me to deny it? No, Master, my body is yours, my life is yours. You must do with it as you will.' She eased the dress fabric up to her hip and smiled across at him.

'Master?' He regarded her, without expression. 'Master,' she persisted, 'may I lie with you? My belly is empty and yearns to be filled.'

Lineker stood up, turning to stare out of the window. For several seconds, he stood in silence. Then, without turning, he spoke.

'Later, Helen,' he murmured. 'Later, I promise, but for now, there are matters even more pressing that require my attention.'

Eight

Mary Three.

She knew that she had once been Mary McLeod, but Mary McLeod would have been dead a long time ago now, body eaten away by the insidious cancer that had been her hereditary prize.

'Was that to your satisfaction, Master?' She sat back on her haunches, peering down through bleary eyes at the youthful figure beneath her. Joshua Willingford III stretched, sighed and opened his own eyes, gazing up at her with a peaceful smile.

'Wonderful, Mary,' he sighed, reaching lazily for one nipple. Mary shivered in delight, twitching and involuntarily swivelling her hips, an action that brought an immediate response from the young man, whose still-rampant organ was yet buried deeply within her.

'Vixen,' he laughed. 'Foxy lady in leather. Sheesh, how I love you, you little slut.' Mary giggled and even that referred response brought an instant response from Joshua. He reached out with both hands, grasping her about the waist, and lifted her from him, setting her down again across his thighs, so that his organ rested between them.

'I want to savour you, Mary,' he breathed, smiling. 'I keep trying to tell you, there's no rush. There need never be a rush, not ever again.' He raised himself on one elbow and gazed at her, earnestly. Just say the word, Leather Mary,' he said. 'Just say the word and you can come away from here with me. Come away from here now, today.'

Mary shifted her weight backwards, her knees cramped in the high, tight leather boots, placing her hands about her tightly corseted waist, the corset leather for Joshua, rather than the normal rubber, for that was what Joshua paid them for and Joshua could afford to pay for what he wanted.

Most of the guests preferred either the rubber or the synthetic substitute that the island people had perfected, but not Joshua. Slave or not, Mary had to be clad in black leather, even to the half-mask hood that covered the top portion of her head. Even to the long, tightly laced gloves.

On Ailsa, money talked.

But money, even Joshua's inherited fortune, would talk to deaf ears when it came to one thing, that much Mary knew. No matter how much the young millionaire offered of his late father's fortune, one thing was certain. Mary Three, once Mary McLeod, now living beyond the time that nature and fate had once decreed, Mary Three, Jenny Ann type CB-Fourteen, could never leave the island.

For this was her fate now and, as she bent forward over her eager suitor, grinding the nub of her clitoris against the stem of his throbbing shaft, it might have been beyond her powers to prevent a tear or two falling upon his muscular chest.

Except that Jenny Anns did not cry.

Jenny Anns *could* not cry.

Naked now, Sara stood again, studying the two figures, her eyes occasionally flicking across to where the bewildering array of other leather accoutrements hung from the wall. The evening air was growing colder by the minute, but she no longer felt it and now she had stopped the trembling that had earlier beset her.

Without realising that she had moved, she found herself standing by the trestle table, holding a wide leather corset in her hands, some inner part of her brain taking in the details, working out the intricacies. Slowly, she began to wrap it around her, adjusting the height until the top of the busk sat beneath her breasts, as, she could see from the mannequins, was required.

88

One by one, she slipped the metal catches together, closing the front of the garment, sucking in her breath as the cool, stout leather began compressing her waist, and then, peering at the two silent figures, she twisted and turned, adjusting the buckles at either side, tightening the sheath even further, until her breathing was coming in short, shallow gasps, and she began to feel as though the two halves of her body were entirely separate entities, the top half seemingly floating without the support of the lower.

Turning back to the rack and walking slowly, it was as if she had suddenly become weightless and her legs seemed to have developed a will of their own. She reached out and took down one of the black pairs of boots, turning them over and then turning again herself, placing them carefully on the trestle top, examining the detail with which they had been crafted.

With slow deliberation, Sara drew the long zip down the inside, pushing aside the row of tiny straps that were intended to buckle over it once the boot was in place. Bending forward with extreme difficulty, she peered inside the boot, pushing a hand down to feel the way in which the sole had been designed to hold the foot as though it were perched on a high stiletto heel. The leather was smooth and unblemished and her touch told her that it had been moulded to the very contours of a foot arched into such an extreme position.

She took the right boot in her two hands, lowering it until the heavy, hoof-shaped sole was resting on the stone floor, and carefully pushed her foot down into it. Her warm flesh slid in easily – evidently, whoever the boots had been originally made for took the same shoe size as she did.

The zip purred upwards, closing the boot almost to the top of her thigh, and she began fastening the securing straps, barely able to reach the lower ones and realising now that it would have been more practical to have put on the boots before the corset. Not worth altering it now, she thought, and reached for the second boot. Five minutes later it was done and she stood, perched, breathing hoarsely, a sheen of moisture covering her shoulders and breasts. Once more, she studied the two mannequins and returned her attention to the rack of straps, trying to identify the curiously shaped piece that covered their crotches. She examined several that appeared to be the right shape, but discarded them when she saw what was attached to them. Then, finally, she walked across to the black-clad model and fumbled for the buckles that held it to the bottom of the corset. As it came away in her hands, Sara gasped, for not only did this piece of harness also have the same, large, phallus-shaped object attached to it, but the mannequin was equipped with a very realistic vagina into which it had been inserted.

For several seconds, Sara stood transfixed, the Y-shaped strap dangling from her hands, until slowly a curious expression began to form on her lovely face. Her tongue flicked along her top lip and, with as deep a breath as she could manage, she shuffled her heavy shod feet apart and brought the tip of the rubber shaft up against her now moist sex.

With a little groan, she pressed it home, the tapered tip parting her unresisting outer lips, forcing an entry beyond the inner and then sliding into her rapidly lubricating tunnel, until its full length was embedded deep within her, filling her as no human organ had ever done before. Clenching her muscles to grip the invader, she quickly began buckling the retaining strap into place, drawing it as tightly as she could manage without actually cutting herself in two.

Straightening up, she brought her thighs together and heard, as if the sound had come from someone else, a small, quavering cry. Suddenly she stopped, peering down at herself, as if realising, for the first time, what she was doing. For a few seconds, a wave of doubt threatened to engulf her, until a small voice from within began to mutter to her consciousness.

If this was what he'd wanted, why not? He can't see you now, anyway. So why shouldn't you? These things were obviously meant for his whore, whoever she was. Jessica.

Yes, Jessica. Sara closed her eyes and tried to imagine Jessica. Did she look like these lifeless mannequins? Did she look like Sara herself?

Her inner muscles spasmed around the rubber dildo, sending small shock waves up and down her spine.

What does it matter what she looked like? She's not here. He's not here. There's just you. You and your memories. Everything else is gone – everything but these things.

These beautiful things . . .

There was no way she could possibly put on those curious little triangular leather sheaths that held the arms on one of the models, nor even the rectangular sheaths that caught up the arms of the other behind its back, but they both appeared to also be wearing long gloves that sheathed their arms and Sara quickly found a pair that laced up to the shoulder, while leaving fingers and thumbs exposed.

Working one-handed, she found that the laces presented a challenge, but a strange sense of determination and purpose had overtaken her now and, setting her jaw, she began working patiently up the length of the first arm. The process of fitting both arms took nearly half an hour, but time had long since ceased to exist for her. In the coolness of the secret room, apart from the harsh sound as the air hissed in and out of her nostrils, the only other noise to disturb the heavy silence was the occasional metallic scraping as Sara shuffled her steel-shod feet.

At last the intricate challenge was completed and, with a loud sigh, she let her arms fall to her sides, swallowing several times as she tried to lubricate her dry throat.

'Well, Andrew,' she said, speaking out loud, her voice echoing in the empty space, 'how do I look? Is *this* how you'd have liked *me*, too? Would you have been just a bit more interested if I'd come to work like this?' She blinked, trying to ignore the tears that were misting her eyes.

'What did you pay her, Andrew? How many thousands? How many others were there? Was this the only way you could face your women, eh? Well, don't I make a good pony girl too?'

She looked back at the silent mannequins. There was still one other thing missing and she quickly found what

91

she needed from the rack. However, sorting out the tangle of straps was something else and it was a minute or two before she understood how the bridle fitted. She drew the various straps into position, tightening them where necessary, using the mannequins as a guide, until only one thing remained to be done.

'You bastard, Andrew Lachan,' she whispered, and then thrust the thick, padded rubber bit into her own mouth, clipping it to the rings to either side of her lips and biting into it with a ferocity she had never known before.

Again, she stood motionless for an age, breasts rising and falling, heart pounding steadily in her chest. She should, she knew, feel stupid, and quite why she had garbed herself so she could not say, but what she was now feeling was quite different. Anger, yes, revulsion, yes. Frustration and a sort of despair, also. There was an emptiness inside her now, a feeling of loss that gnawed at her insides and she snorted, her distorted lips vibrating against the rubber that forced them apart.

You wanted a pony girl here, Andrew. Well, take a look at your new pony girl now. Did Jessica have anything I don't have, eh? Wouldn't you just love to come back and drive me now, you swine? Well, this is for you, you poor sad bastard.

And for me, too.

She turned, walking unsteadily towards the door and the outer rooms, moving into the corridor that led to the outside world, hips swaying as she fought to master the steepling boots, metal rasping on stone as she moved towards the dark evening that lay outside, the sound changing as she stepped on to the cinder-strewn mud and grass, heading towards the five-barred gate that opened on to the empty hills beyond . . .

'How'd it go at your end?' Geordie propped the mobile phone between shoulder and ear and reached across to the glove compartment for a fresh packet of cigarettes. 'Any progress?'

'You wouldn't believe me if I told you,' Colin said, but nevertheless proceeded to give Geordie an edited version of the events at Celia Butler's farm.

'Sounds like it was some of her wares we found up here,' Geordie said, when he was through. 'Unfortunately, however, it proves nothing. If consenting adults want to play horsy, so long as they don't do anything in public that could contravene the various decency laws, then we can't stop 'em.'

'True enough,' Colin agreed. 'But I'd still like to push it a bit further with the Butler woman.'

'Not to mention the gorgeous blonde horse girl, eh?'

'Pony girl, old boy,' Colin corrected. 'Must get the terminology right. Listen,' he continued, his tone becoming more serious, 'it would help if you could find anything at Lachan's, anything at all, that gives us a definite tie-in to the Butler operation. Maybe we could use it to apply a bit of pressure. Madame Celia is a pretty cool customer and the world finding out about her predilections probably wouldn't worry her one jot, but her prized customers might not like being associated with someone who was under investigation, if you get my drift.'

'I get it all right,' Geordie said, 'but I don't hold out much hope.'

'The secretary bird couldn't tell you anything more, then?'

'She was as surprised as I was when we found the hidden stable room,' Geordie said. 'I could be wrong, but I'm pretty convinced she hadn't the faintest idea of what Lachan got up to in his private life. She just isn't the type.'

'Never put any faith in types myself,' Colin chuckled. 'Still waters and all that. Press her a bit harder.'

'I'll do my best,' Geordie said. 'Maybe I'll nip back over there. I'm only at the end of the track to the estate. The gorgeous Sara claimed she had to get away a bit sharpish, but no car's come past me and there's no other way out that I know of. Maybe she just wanted rid of me, so an unexpected quick return – who knows? All the same, I reckon our best chance is with your end. You say this Butler sort has invited you back to stay?'

'Oh, yes,' Colin said. 'Problem is, I'm supposed to take my little pony girl with me and I don't happen to have one

93

handy. Don't suppose you have any willing volunteers up your end of the country?'

Geordie let out a loud snort. 'You'd have had more chance of getting Alex Gregory to play pony girl than you would with any of the women we've got in this division,' he said. 'You'd be better off putting an ad in the *Sunday Sport*.'

Money, so the saying goes, cannot buy happiness, but Ramon had spent half a lifetime in an effort to prove that wrong. The other half of his life had been spent in earning the money necessary to obtain that proof, starting in a gutter in one of the lesser-known South American cities and, by a mixture of cunning and ruthlessness, rising like the proverbial rocket to become one of the most feared men in even the dangerous and nefarious circles in which he now moved.

It is often said of successful men, if generally not to their faces, that they achieved their status by climbing on the backs of others. In the case of Ramon Valerez, it was frequently said, by those who had watched his spiralling career, that the backs on which he had risen generally had knives thrust in them first. That, too, of course, was never said to his face and never even too loudly, for Ramon Valerez appeared to have ears everywhere.

Rich enough, by the early nineties, never to have to worry about money again, he nevertheless remained driven by the same ambition that had brought him thus far, the burning lust for absolute power refusing to loosen its grip. Besides, as he knew only too well, there were certain things from which you could not retire, for such a move would be construed as weakness and the slightest sign of weakness would bring the wolves baying.

His trips across the ocean to the tiny haven of Ailsa Ness were therefore as fleeting as they were frequent, small slices of relaxation cut from the cake before the other diners realised they were gone, so that, by the time the greater table was being cleared, Ramon was once again back at its head.

Ailsa was the one place where Ramon could relax his otherwise habitual vigilance, leaving even his regular entourage of minders on the larger neighbour, Carigillie, from where they could monitor both the underground, undersea tunnel that connected the two Shetland outposts and the sea and air approaches. Meanwhile, their lord and master was free to indulge some of his more extreme tastes.

There was always the meal first – three, four and even five courses, served by mute, masked maids, shuffling in and out of the room in their jingling chains, only the flickering of their eyes betraying their near humanity.

And there was always the special guest, tightly corseted, so that she could eat only like a sparrow, also masked and clad from toe to crown in yet more gleaming rubber, perched, when she rose from the table, on the highest heels imaginable, so that she was forced to tiptoe about the room in the tiniest of steps.

It was supposed to be a different girl every time and generally, it seemed to Ramon, the arrangement was honoured, though his hosts knew as well as he did himself that it would have been impossible to know otherwise. In truth, Ramon did not much care, though it amused him to think that the anonymous, ladylike rubber mannequin who shared his table on one evening might be one of the shambling, anonymous maids who waited upon it on his next visit.

On this particular night, her name was Molly, though Ramon insisted upon addressing her as Lady Margaret throughout. She was, he had been told, a type AA-Ten, which meant, in layman's terms, that she was very tall, strongly built and with particularly prominent breasts and buttocks. Her hair was of a blonde colour so pale as to be almost translucent and, in accordance with Ramon's instructions, it had been put up into a high ponytail and drawn through a circular opening in the crown of her helmet, so that it cascaded down beyond her shoulders as a contrasting frame for the shiny black face.

Blonde was Ramon's favourite colour, for it was rare to find fair hair – unless it was dyed – where he came from. Of course, there *were* European women at home, but they

95

were generally the wives and daughters of men too powerful for even Ramon to risk antagonising. Even he needed to cultivate support wherever possible and he knew that his particular proclivities would not go very far in that direction.

Besides, Ailsa was so much simpler, not expensive by his standards, and now had the added bonus of becoming a sound business investment. He took a perverse pride in being the only outsider to share the secret of the Jenny Ann project with Major and his people, for it had taken many years to win their trust. Even then, he knew, it was only the promise of his financial support that had swayed the issue, huge injections of cash to push forward a programme that had, to Ramon, more than the one obvious advantage.

At first, of course, he had had no idea about the true nature of the girls who served here. Subservient, strong, durable, particularly those who ran regularly as pony girls.

'They'd make excellent pack horses,' he had once joked to Richard Major and, for what Ramon had in mind, there was not a creature born more fitted to the precipitous mountain trails that were often too narrow even for the sure-footed mules that were usually employed for transporting Ramon's stock-in-trade.

When he finally realised what these girls really were, it was even better and, as he told Lineker, their technology, using the sturdy Andean Indian girls as seed material, could produce a never-ending supply of even stronger slaves, bred not for the bedroom nor the pony circuit, but for the pack and the most arduous conditions imaginable.

He pushed his dining chair back from the table, picked up a fresh napkin and wiped his lips. Like his dinner guest, he was heavily masked, so that only eyes and mouth remained visible. It was how Ramon liked it best – he could not see her face and she could not see his. Faces were not what he wanted to see. There were too many faces in the world. Faces could not be trusted and some should not be remembered.

Faces were disturbing. Particularly dead faces.

Particularly in his dreams.

Nine

Alone in the darkness, Sara ran and ran, oblivious to the weight of the hoof boots, teeth clenched around the hard rubber bit as her full breasts bounced against her ribs in time with the rhythm of her loping stride.

Time.

It no longer meant anything.

Stars. A half-moon. A velvet blanket overhead and the smell of heather and grass.

Freedom – the freedom to run and run, a wild creature loose with no boundaries, no fences, no rules. Sara cantered to a halt, shaking her head.

There should be rules. There *ought* to be rules. A pony needed discipline, order. Rules. A pony needed a master.

Suddenly, there were tears in her eyes and the night air felt cold against her clammy flesh. Half blinded, Sara turned, stumbling in the heavy boots, grabbing blindly for support from the straggling bushes beside the rough pathway. She sobbed through the bit, fingers scrabbling to release it from the bridle, desperate to spit out the foul-tasting rubber.

And then she understood and a wave of panic rose up to engulf her, for the clips refused to respond to her frantic efforts. Blindly, she reached behind her neck, grasping at the buckles that held the bridle harness, somehow only half surprised when the thick leather refused to release.

She sank to her knees on the soft ground, gloved hands covering her eyes, a stifled wail rising into the night sky as she realised what she had done. Eyes still closed, she tugged at the various buckles, the result ever the same, the darkness preventing her from seeing the truth for herself, yet all the time knowing it for what it was.

Damn them!

She had trapped herself with her own curiosity and passion, for there was no escaping the inescapable and the harness into which she had so willingly put herself was exactly that – inescapable.

Molly shifted her position imperceptibly, trying to ease the cramping corset and the high busk that cut into the flesh beneath her breasts, even through the protective skin of the rubbery suit. Politely, she refused a further chocolate, knowing, as she knew Master Ramon did too, that eating while wearing such a restrictive outfit was a special kind of torture, particularly for a girl who, under normal circumstances, boasted a healthy appetite.

'Perhaps you need to take more exercise, my dear Lady Margaret?' Having waited upon Ramon's table on several previous occasions, Molly knew exactly what was hidden behind that remark and she had seen so many others suffer before her. In the adjoining room, the cycling machine would be waiting, complete with its special saddle. Alongside it, newly made up with silken rubber sheets and pillows, the huge four-poster bed was also prepared, but there would be much to endure before the enigmatic Ramon took her to it.

'As Your Lordship sees fit,' she replied, demurely. She had rehearsed the script thoroughly, knowing that she was not permitted to address him by his name, even though others might. The ritual had to be perfect and any mistakes on Molly's part would earn a punishment far worse than the inscrutable figure opposite was likely to impose.

Slowly, Molly stood up, the long, rubberised skirts rustling about her booted ankles, the puffed oversleeves of the dress awkward and cumbersome.

'Would My Lord have any particular form of exercise in mind?' More ritualising, and she wondered whether he was aware that she knew what was really coming. She sighed to herself, stepping away from the table, watching, waiting. Ramon rose in his turn, unhurried, assured, stretching languidly, so that the dark latex of his body suit rippled and seemed to dance under the flickering light from above.

Fleetingly, his hand dropped, brushing against his crotch, and, whether it was a deliberate gesture or not, Molly's eyes were drawn to the tightly swathed bulge of his maleness, obvious beneath the stretched fabric, even in its semitumescent state.

'A gentle ride, perhaps,' he said, his thin lips twitching as he spoke. He stepped towards her, holding out his hand for her to take. 'I have a special treat for you, My Lady,' he went on, steering her towards the connecting door. 'And some particularly interesting scenery.'

'You look like you could do with some help.' Geordie stood in the outer doorway of the stable, regarding the pathetic figure with complete detachment. He had seen only the last few minutes of her ordeal and he understood little, if anything, of it; but one thing was beyond dispute: why ever Sara Llewellyn-Smith had chosen to garb herself in the outlandish leather costume, she was now unable to remove it, despite her best efforts.

At the sound of his voice, she stopped struggling with the clips on the side of her face, turning to him, eyes huge and round with the horror of her discovery. Face ashen, she backed away, feet stumbling in the heavy boots, until she was pressed hard against the far wall, alongside the laden harness rack. Geordie held up one hand in a gesture of pacification.

'Take it easy, lass,' he said, softly, making no effort to close the gap between them. 'Just calm down and let me have a closer look. There must be a trick to those catches and panicking won't help any.'

For long seconds they faced each other across the width of the silent room and then, as if only just realising, Sara raised her gloved hands to cover her naked breasts. She jerked her head slightly and tried to speak, but nothing intelligible escaped past the bit. Geordie took half a pace, raising his other hand to join the first.

'Look,' he said, 'I don't know what's going on here and, unless it directly concerns my investigation, I don't really care. You want to go playing horses in the middle of the night, that's your affair, but I need to talk to you again, and from where I'm standing, I don't reckon you're in exactly the condition for that to happen, OK? Now, are you stuck in that stuff?'

There was a brief pause and then Sara nodded her head, lowering her eyes to avoid his gaze. Still Geordie made no further move towards her, instead studying the picture she presented. Regardless of the bizarre harness equipment, or maybe because of it, he tried not to ask himself the direct question – Sara Llewellyn-Smith was all woman, and quite a woman at that.

'Come over here, then,' Geordie instructed. Another short delay, but they both knew she had no other option, and finally, head still down, she shuffled towards him.

'Bugger,' he said, in little more than a whisper. It needed only a cursory examination to realise the problem. The catches, clips and buckles were not stuck: rather, each piece was cunningly designed to conceal the fact that, once fitted, it locked into place to prevent the wearer removing it. Already Geordie was getting the picture in his mind and it removed any suspicion from it that Sara had indeed known about this secret room beforehand.

He didn't understand it himself, but clearly she had been intrigued with what they had discovered here and had returned after his departure and then been tempted into trying on some of the gear herself, not realising that she was trapping herself in a stout leather bondage from which she would be unable to escape unaided.

Calmly, Geordie explained the situation to her, felt her stiffen and heard the strangled little cry in the back of her throat. He laid a soothing hand on one bare shoulder, his own flesh now as damp as hers.

'Easy,' he said. 'Whatever the problem, we'll have you out of this lot quick enough. If it comes to it, there must

100

be something around the place I can use to cut through some of these straps. Mind you,' he added, more to himself, 'this is strong leather. No, hang on a minute – what's this?'

He took one of the bit links between finger and thumb, turning it slightly to reveal a tiny hole in the metal of one of the clip sections. It was not quite perfectly round and there was a slight distortion from a true oval shape. Sara's eyes flickered up and sideways and he smiled down at her, though the high boots meant that the difference between their heights was considerably less than it had been when they had first met.

'This looks like some sort of keyhole,' he explained to her. 'Now, all we have to do is look around here for a key that will fit it.' Which proved to be easier said than done and, ten minutes' fruitless searching later, they still had not found anything that looked remotely as if it might unlock the various connections.

'The house,' Geordie said, at last. 'Lachan's study. Wherever he might normally keep the key, I'd bet he kept a spare, for emergencies. And this,' he added, turning towards the doorway, 'qualifies as an emergency in my book.'

The screen had been erected across one wall of the room, immediately in front of the exercise cycle. As she entered behind Ramon, Molly saw that the picture was currently frozen, showing a gently winding lane ahead and hills in the distance, visible through clumps of sparse Highland trees.

The machine itself was not so very unlike the machines that were kept in the gymnasium, part of the exercise regime that ensured peak fitness for all the Jenny Anns on Ailsa, but there was at once one, obvious difference. In place of the regular saddle, a padded bar had been fitted, from which rose a thick phallus, already glistening with a lubricant and waiting for her like a silent sentry.

Wordlessly, Ramon guided her to stand beside the contraption, turning her around so that he could begin the

101

laborious task of unlacing the back of her bodice. He worked slowly, clearly savouring every moment, until eventually the top of the dress fell loosely from her shoulders and he was able to draw the puffed sleeves from her arms, leaving them clad in the tight underskin that was part of the suit that encased her entire body.

Fingers now worked at the waistband, loosening, unclipping, and then the skirt, too, was falling, hissing down her black sheathed legs to form a voluminous puddle about her booted ankles. Taking his proffered hand, she stepped clear of the fabric with as much dignity as she could muster and, for several long seconds, he stood back, admiring her body, every curve and sinew as obvious as if she had been naked, the two hardened cones of her nipples projecting grossly through the strategically placed openings.

'Excellent,' he said, eventually. He placed his hands about her corseted waist, trying to make fingers and thumbs meet, but even the tight lacing Molly was enduring had been unable to reduce her span quite that far.

'As I thought,' he muttered. 'Too much fat.' Molly could barely stop herself from laughing out loud at this, for even without the corset she had a waistline as trim and flat as any she had ever seen. With an effort, however, she controlled herself, knowing that laughter now would be regarded as unforgivable. One hand went down to the tops of her thighs.

'Spread,' he said, simply. Obediently, Molly shuffled her feet wider and his fingers quickly found the zip, drawing it forward so that the rubber skin parted to reveal her hairless sex. 'And now to mount you,' he said, turning her to face the cycle.

As the dildo slid into her, Molly squirmed and wriggled, trying to settle herself into as comfortable a position as was possible, given the nature of her seat. The shaft was thick, but it really wasn't too uncomfortable, she told herself, as Ramon busied himself placing her feet on to the pedals and buckling over the straps that would keep them there. Of course, as she well knew from similar experiences and the tales of others, the act of pedalling would force her hips to rotate and the friction thus generated would produce problems of its own – not necessarily unpleasant problems, she reflected, as long as a girl didn't mind pedalling herself to one orgasm after another while a masked stranger looked on.

He moved behind her now, attaching a strap that would prevent her lifting herself clear of the phallus saddle, then once again came to the front, guiding her hands to the handlebar grips and attaching manacles on short chains that allowed her just sufficient scope to operate the small gear lever and what appeared to be a handbrake, something else that the machines in the gym did not have.

Finally, from somewhere on the front of the frame, he drew out two long, thin cables, the ends of which terminated in small, metallic, circular clips. With practised ease, he attached them, one to each of her nipples, snapping them shut on their springs to trap the engorged flesh and distort it even further.

'I shall now explain the rules to you, Lady Margaret,' Ramon drawled, stepping back between screen and machine. Crouched forward, Molly peered up at him, breasts rising and falling.

'Everything is set for a journey of precisely eighteen miles and you have exactly one hour in which to complete it.' He smiled down at her. 'From that, as I am sure you can work out for yourself, you will need to maintain an average speed of eighteen miles per hour. Of course, with varying gradients, bends and other hazards, your speed will vary greatly.'

He stooped forward and picked up a small black box, pointing it down to the front of the machine stand.

'Once you start,' he continued, 'everything will work automatically, but this control enables me to demonstrate your cycle's unique features. On the downhill sections, you will easily be able to reach speeds in excess of thirty miles an hour.' His smile widened.

'However,' he said, 'whenever you exceed twenty-eight miles per hour, this will happen.' He pressed something on the hand control and instantly Molly's eyes and mouth

103

shot wide open, for the thick shaft inside her seemed suddenly to have taken on a life of its own. It bucked, shook, pulsed and a series of tiny shocks seared through her tender inner flesh.

'Aaaahhhh!' She could not prevent herself and only the sudden cessation prevented her from achieving the fastest orgasm she had ever experienced. She slumped forward, gasping for air.

'Of course,' Ramon chuckled, 'there are some who might prefer to ride that way, not that I would advocate it. Half a mile of that and I doubt whether even your constitution would enable you to reach the finishing line. So, a little prudence is required, especially as you will not really enjoy yourself if your speed drops below twelve miles per hour. In that case, this is what will happen.'

Again he triggered the device in his hand, but this time the sensations it produced were totally different and in no way pleasurable. A bolt of fire seemed to shoot up from Molly's loins, striking into her chest with a ferocity that took the breath from her even more quickly than the pleasure shocks had done.

She ground her teeth in agony, wishing that he had gagged her, for she was unable to prevent the tiny squeal of agony that tore its way past her lips.

'Below twelve miles per hour, you will receive similar shocks at twenty-second intervals,' Ramon was saying. 'And furthermore, if you should fail to complete the course in the allotted time, you will be left to endure the same punishment for a further thirty minutes. Now, are you ready to begin?' He stepped to one side and Molly nodded, glumly.

'The screen, of course,' he added, poised to press the button that would signal the start, 'will show you the road ahead at all times. Do try not to come off the road, Lady Margaret. I can assure you that the consequences of that would be far worse than anything I have demonstrated thus far.'

Geordie's hunch proved correct: he found the peculiar little key in the top drawer of the study desk and quickly used

104

it to unlock and detach the bit, drawing it from a grateful Sara's spittle-flecked lips. With a solemn gesture, he offered both bit and key to her, but she made no move to take them.

'I – I'd like to try to explain,' she said, swallowing hard. 'I don't really know what came over me, you see, but I just kept thinking, after you'd gone –'

'You don't need to justify anything to me,' Geordie said, half turning away from her. The sight of her ample breasts, slowly rising and falling in their leather webbing, was now beginning to have some unwanted effects on him, seriously prejudicing his usually calm approach to the job. 'I'll just go through and put a kettle on, while you finish getting yourself sorted out. We can talk when you've got some clothes on.'

'No.' A slim hand, the long, well-manicured fingers protruding from the glistening leather that sheathed the rest of the limb as far as the shoulder, closed over his wrist, though the grip remained loose, almost apologetic.

'No,' Sara repeated. She gave him a defiant stare as he turned back to face her. 'I have to talk now, while I'm still . . . while I'm still like this,' she said, her voice husky and halting. 'I need to try to understand this myself, you see.' She released his arm, turned and walked across to stand in front of one of the bookcases.

'Look at me,' she said, spreading her arms sideways. 'Go on, take a good look, Sergeant. What do you see, eh? Nothing else left for me to hide like this, is there? Well, *what* do you see?'

'Well . . .' Geordie hesitated, wondering just exactly what the right words were in this sort of situation, or if, indeed, there *were* any right words. Sara saved him further embarrassment.

'I'll tell you what you see,' she said. 'You're looking at a stupid, frustrated female, one who is old enough to know better, yet let the thought of a man, to whom she had devoted several years of completely faithful service, playing sick games with some perverted little tart, get through to her, even though the man in question has been dead for three months.'

'You were in love with your late employer?' Sara looked down at the carpet again.

'Yes,' she said, simply. 'I was in love with Andrew, though I doubt he ever realised it and he certainly never did anything to take advantage of the situation, even if he had understood it. He was always the perfect gentleman, always businesslike. In fact,' she added, stifling a harsh laugh, 'I'd have described him as a totally cold fish.' She looked up again.

'Until this afternoon,' she said, 'if you'd tried to tell me about . . . about all this, I'd have called you a liar. I just couldn't believe it of him. Then all that stuff you showed me on the computer, on the Internet. And when you left I just sat in here, thinking, my head going round and round in circles.'

'So you thought you'd try to find out for yourself what it felt like?' Geordie suggested.

'I suppose that just about sums it up,' Sara said. She was making no effort to cover herself and Geordie realised that only a thin strip of leather was covering the fullest extent of her modesty and that even that was now starting to fail in its task, for the lips of her sex were puffed out, bulging to either side of it. He raised his gaze again, but Sara had already seen him staring.

'Yes,' she said, nodding her head, 'it's quite sick, isn't it? I mean, what sort of woman pushes a huge rubber cock inside her, eh? And what sort of woman lets a man do it *to* her?'

'I really couldn't say,' Geordie muttered. He turned, heading for the window to open it, suddenly needing a cigarette like he'd never needed one in his life before.

'I can see I'm embarrassing you,' Sara laughed. 'Well, I've embarrassed myself, so why not? But I'll tell you something, Sergeant Walker, though I'm not sure I understand it. When I was out there, just now, wearing all this stuff and just running, I felt something I've never felt before. I felt completely *free*, completely at one with myself. Yes, I was imagining myself pulling that cart thing, with Andrew sitting there, probably flicking me with one of those long whips, maybe shouting at me to go faster.

'It was like being drunk, Sergeant,' she continued, as Geordie finally got the window open. 'And yet everything was so clear at the same time. I wanted him to be back here and, yes, I'd have been his pony girl whenever he wanted.'

'It looked to me as if it was supposed to be a full-time position,' Geordie said. 'Under that sacking stuff by the bed down there was a small television set and on the outside wall I saw a bracket that looked as if it were intended for a satellite dish. Your Mr Lachan was preparing that stable stall for a long-stay tenant, I'd say.'

'Tell me,' Sara said. 'Tell me honestly. Do you know who she was?'

Geordie lit his cigarette, inhaled deeply and blew a stream of smoke towards the open window. 'No,' he said, turning back to face her. 'No, I don't have the faintest idea. I was going to ask you the same question, but I take it you'd give me the same answer I just gave you.'

'Yes.' Sara paused, pursing her lips. 'I've been thinking about it, but there just aren't any candidates. So far as I know, Andrew had no female friends – no male friends, either, in case that's what you might be thinking.'

'Not to judge from those dummies down there,' Geordie retorted. 'They were most definitely female. Anyway,' he said, drawing on the cigarette again, 'wouldn't you be more comfortable with some clothes on?' Sara let out a little snort and stepped across to the corner of the desk, picking up the bit from where it had been discarded.

'I don't know what I feel any more,' she mused, turning the rubber cylinder over in her hands. 'I thought I knew myself once. OK, maybe I was a bit of a sad case, trailing around after a man who obviously didn't feel about me the way I felt about him, but I at least thought I was happy enough. I suppose I was really getting to be a frustrated old maid – that's what I'd have become ultimately, anyway. No, before you ask, I'm no innocent virgin, but there haven't been any men in my life since I started working for Andrew.'

'I wouldn't be so bloody ungallant as to ask that sort of question, I can assure you,' Geordie said, but Sara's only reaction to this was to burst out laughing. He raised a quizzical eyebrow and she finally managed to control her mirth.

'Ungallant!' she exclaimed. 'Oh, what a lovely quaint expression. You stand there and talk about being ungallant, and I'm standing here with a rubber cock up my cunt, bare-arsed and bare tits, looking like I don't know what. Ha! Ungallant indeed.

'Listen, Mr Detective,' she went on, fiercely, 'I don't care about ungallant.' She brandished the rubber bit in his face. 'You know what I want? I want what I never had with Andrew. I want to have someone put this – this thing – back into my mouth and take me down and hitch me up to that fucking cart contraption and drive me all over the estate.

'Yes, I can see that shocks you, but I'm through lying to myself. Let's face it, it's done me damn all good for years, so why keep up the pretence? Yes, I realised out there I'd have let Andrew Lachan do to me whatever it was he was planning to do to whoever it was he was planning to bring here, but I also realised something else, too. I'd probably let any man do it to me now, just to get that same feeling back again!'

Geordie's eyebrow rose even higher, the other one mirroring it. '*Any* man?' he asked. The smile on Sara's face reminded him of the Mona Lisa. Holding the bit by one of the connecting rings, she let it dangle like a short pendulum.

'Fancy a pony girl, Mr Policeman?' she asked. 'A nice, sweet little pony girl of your very own?'

Geordie cleared his throat noisily and put the cigarette to his lips in an effort to cover his confusion. 'I don't think so,' he managed, at last. 'I don't really have a . . . a need, as it were.' He paused, blinking as the smoke curled into his eyes. 'However,' he said, thoughtfully, 'I know a man who might.'

Ten

'Fifty-seven minutes and thirty-four seconds,' Ramon said. 'You are clearly a lot fitter than you looked, Lady Margaret.'

Slumped over the handlebars of the infernal cycling machine, Molly felt anything but fit. She had managed to stay above the minimum speed limit apart from two brief occasions, the agonising jolts from the deep-seated dildo more than sufficient encouragement to strain tired leg muscles for even greater efforts, but the downhill stretches had nearly proved her undoing each time she came to one.

Without a speedometer to gauge her acceleration, she frequently passed beyond the upper speed limit, whereupon the instant sensual assault made it almost impossible to retain any real degree of control. The last time, she knew, she would have lost it completely, had not the eventual intervention of a short upward gradient allowed her sufficient respite in which to regain something approaching her senses.

Sweat-soaked, even though the catsuit she wore was not authentic latex, she fell into Ramon's arms when he finally lifted her from the saddle. Tenderly, he lifted her chin and his lips met hers.

'Poor Lady,' he crooned. 'Poor exhausted Lady Margaret.' He turned, moving to the bed, and carefully lowered her on to it, spreading her thighs wide. Blearily, she looked up at him, her eyes refusing to focus correctly, a phenomenon she had not experienced in all the years she had spent in this body.

'Master,' she croaked. 'I need a drink – please.' With an easy spring, Ramon was on the bed himself, straddling her tiny waist, fumbling at the crotch of his own rubberised leggings.

'Of course you do,' he said, softly, 'and a nice long drink you shall have.'

Even travelling nonstop and sharing the driving between them, Geordie and Sara did not reach Colin Turner's hotel until mid-afternoon and they were both feeling pretty jaded by the time they got to the rooms he had booked for them. Nevertheless, taking only enough time to shower and change, Geordie met Colin in the restaurant by four o'clock.

'I'd never have thought it of the delectable Miss Llewellyn-Smith,' Colin chortled, after the waiter had taken their orders and returned with drinks. 'She struck me as very much Miss Tin Drawers.'

'I didn't realise you'd actually met her,' Geordie said, surprised. 'You never said.'

'Wasn't really time,' Colin apologised. 'The bloody battery on the mobile was going again. I must get it looked at, damned useless thing. Anyway,' he continued, scratching the side of his nose with a well-manicured fingernail, 'I did meet her – in Lachan's London office, a couple of days after the explosion that killed him. I'm surprised she never mentioned it to you, or else she's just forgotten my name.'

'I'm not entirely sure I told her your name,' Geordie confessed, 'not your full name, anyway. All I said was that we were looking into this pony-girl thing that her boss was obviously involved with, just in case that had anything to do with his death. I told her you'd been to see this Butler woman and she'd invited you back to stay for a day or two, but that you were supposed to provide your own pony.'

'Makes a change from "bring a bottle", you've got to give it that!' Colin quipped. 'So, did she take much persuading?'

Quickly, Geordie related the events of the previous evening, leaving out any direct reference to the proposition

110

Sara had made him, or to the fact that he had politely declined it. When he had finished, Colin let out an appreciative whistle.

'Well, I'll be ...' He sat back, the fingernail once more busy on the side of his nose. 'So, Miss Tin Drawers fancies herself as a pony, does she? It's tempting, but it could be a bit dodgy.'

'Not if you play it right. There was a satellite phone link at the estate and Lachan's computer had Internet access, so we copied off and printed a few bits and pieces before we came away. Sara's had her nose into them, doing a bit of studying on the way down here – when she wasn't driving or napping, that is.'

'Yeah, but these people are real connoisseurs,' Colin pointed out. 'They'll smell a fake a mile off.'

'I don't reckon to that, bonnie lad,' Geordie said. 'Listen, you've already told the Butler woman you're both pretty raw newcomers anyway, so she won't be expecting much. All you need to do is turn up with Sara and a couple of bits and pieces of harness stuff, then open your wallet and start treating her to a few quality additions. If you get to stay there for the weekend, you should get plenty of time to sniff around.'

'Trouble is, old beanbag,' Colin said, sombrely, 'I ain't convinced I'm going to find anything relevant. I mean, I may learn a few things I never knew before, but what these people get up to hardly constitutes a breach of the law. And I can't see my guv'nors reimbursing me for a whole set of pony-girl tack, can you?'

'Well, like you say,' Geordie smirked, 'just put it down to experience. You get to have the lovely Sara as your own personal pony and, as for the gear, there's no need to go mad. You can bloody well afford it yourself, anyway.'

'Oh, can I indeed?' Colin retorted. 'Have you seen the sort of prices this bint is charging for her stuff?'

'A lot less than that suit you're wearing, I expect,' Geordie replied. 'And I never thought I'd live to see the day when you complained about paying for quality.'

* * *

111

It was always a relief to get out from the claustrophobic subterranean complex that included the stables, especially when there were no onerous duties involved, but Bambi hated the way the grooms treated them just as if they had been real ponies, keeping them bitted and blinkered, arms sheathed helplessly across their backs, long-tether reins leading from their harnesses to wooden stakes driven deep into the ground.

They were expected, Higgy informed them, to keep on the move, loosening muscles that might become cramped with too much inactivity, occasionally performing a short routine of high stepping, which brought the knees up as high as the hampering boots would permit, an exercise that was supposed to strengthen the joints and improve endurance.

Having tethered Tammy and Jangles near the path leading down to the rocky cove via which Bambi, when still Andrew, had led the abortive raid to kidnap Jessie, Higgy led the one-time business magnate some distance away, stopping just short of the woods and tying off the long leather rein to a gnarled root.

'This should be far enough, pretty one,' the groom said, fumbling with his belt buckle. He saw the look of horror in Bambi's eyes and laughed. 'Well, did you expect to keep on with the special treatment, eh?' he sneered. 'Listen, pretty girl, you've been broken, so now you're fair game. Part of the grooms' perks, you are.'

He dropped his leather breeches about his ankles and kicked them clear, lifting his rough shirt to reveal that he was wearing no underwear and that his shaft was already responding to the stimulus of hand and eye. With his free hand, he reached out and dragged Bambi closer. She felt his warm breath on her cheek and the heat of his organ as it brushed against the top of her thigh.

'Seniority counts here, pretty pony,' he whispered, hoarsely. 'So good old Higgy gets first crack at you, now the masters have done their bit. The other lads then get their turns, as the fancy takes them, which it usually does all too often. 'Spect a couple of 'em will be out to you before dusk, even though it's not strictly allowed to fuck fillies in the open, but then this time of year we ain't likely to see any guests outside this late in the afternoon. Now, little Bambi, let's have those lovely legs wider, shall we?'

He had removed the girth strap while he spoke, sliding out the hateful dildo that Bambi had been forced to endure since her ordeal at the hands of Boolik the previous day. He held it up, holding it beneath her nose.

'That's *your* musk, that is,' he chuckled. 'First time you've ever smelled yourself, I reckon. Well, it'll not be the last, that's for sure.'

She knew she should struggle, even if only to make some token show of resistance, but it would only prolong her ordeal and delay the inevitable by just the briefest of times, for Higgy, as Bambi well knew, was far stronger even than he looked and was quite capable of administering a thrashing that would be painful, even for this body.

She relaxed, letting him enter her and thrust upwards, filling her warm tunnel to the hilt, trying not to acknowledge the sensations that his slow, pumping action were already triggering. Instead, she closed her eyes and tried to remember when it had been different, when it had been Andrew in charge and Jessie, his dear Jessie, who had been the willing, compliant recipient of *his* favours.

And he tried to pretend that the whinnying, gargling screams that were now filling the air were Jessie's and not Bambi's, for Bambi was really Andrew, wasn't she? And Andrew could never . . .

Could she?

'I'm not at all sure about this.' Colin Turner dropped the sheaf of papers on to the bed of Sara's hotel room and walked across to the minibar. 'I mean,' he said, over his shoulder, 'it's one thing to go up there pretending I've got some filly – no pun intended, by the way – who I'm intending to fit out with a load of this Butler wench's tack, but quite another to actually take the supposed pony girl in there with me, especially when we've hardly met.'

'From what Sergeant Walker told me on the way down here,' Sara said, before Geordie could muster any reply, 'I

113

thought you were a man of many talents and, forgive me if I'm wrong, but isn't there something more than just Andrew Lachan's death involved here? Something about a female colleague in the Shetlands, I think you said?'

'She was my sergeant up there,' Geordie confirmed, 'and, as I started to tell you earlier, she was found dead on Carigillie Craig, around the last time your late boss was supposed to be visiting the place. However, she told me she was going to the other island, Ailsa Ness.'

'But you can't prove it?' Sara said.

Geordie shook his head. 'No, we can't prove anything and we don't even know we actually have anything to prove. It's just good old-fashioned copper's gut feeling. Colin has it concerning Lachan's death and I have it over Alex's. Taken separately, you could say we were both maybe placing too much faith in our hunches, but there's the Healthglow link all the way through this and Healthglow ain't quite what it's supposed to be, or I'm a Dutchman.'

'And you think this Butler woman is supplying all her pony-girl equipment to this Healthglow crowd, is that it?' Sara asked. She had been holding a glass of brandy in her slender hands for several minutes, but as yet had made no attempt to drink it.

'We *think* that's what's happening,' Colin confirmed, 'but we can't be a hundred per cent on that, either. And,' he went on, 'even if she is, as far as I know that isn't a crime. 'Tain't even that unusual, either, not if you believe all the Internet stuff.'

'So why would anyone want to kill either your sergeant or Andrew?' Sara persisted. 'I can see that certain people, including Mr Lachan himself, might be a bit worried about their involvement becoming public knowledge, but if anyone was thinking of blackmailing him, surely it would be self-defeating to kill him?'

'It would, certainly,' Colin agreed. 'Like I said, we don't even know where to start looking at this thing from. The company books show nothing and Geordie here has been all over both islands up there in the wilderness.'

114

'Not *all* over,' Geordie corrected him. 'They didn't try to keep us away from anything, but old George Gillespie was a bit wary of putting any size twelves on delicate toes. There were a couple of well-known names staying on Carigillie.'

'But you did get a reasonable look around, didn't you?' Colin said.

'Yeah, sure, we got the full Cook's tour, but then they'd have had enough time to hide anything they didn't want us to see.'

'So the Butler woman is your only new lead,' Sara said, 'and, if any of us want to get any further with this, that's the next logical step.' She spoke quietly, yet with a firm authority, and Geordie could imagine what an excellent right hand she had afforded Andrew Lachan. What he couldn't imagine was her exposing that side of herself that he had seen the previous evening, not to a whole crowd of strangers.

Except, he realised, with a sudden lucidity, it would be the fact that they were strangers that would make it easier for her and she certainly didn't seem to have any last-minute qualms now they had come so far.

'Well, it's up to you,' Colin said, shaking his head. 'I'll do my best to play my part, but the real pressure will be on you. I've seen the sort of things they expect those girls to wear.'

'So has your friend here,' Sara said, a slow smile spreading across her exquisite features, 'and I was the one wearing them at the time.'

'I'm still not happy about using a civilian,' Colin persisted. Geordie started to guffaw, but checked himself.

'You reckon you're gonna find a female PC who'd do it instead?' he asked. 'Anyway, you great Hooray Henry, this is hardly an official line of enquiry, is it? I'm on leave and you haven't exactly been up front with your lords and masters about what you've been up to.'

'As long as I don't go overboard on the overtime, they don't really care,' Colin yawned. He gulped down a mouthful of whisky and wiped his mouth with the back of his hand. 'So, we go play neddies with Ms Butler and her pals, yes?'

'Unless you've got a better idea,' Sara said, standing up and placing the untouched drink on the window ledge. She nodded towards the heavy case that she and Geordie had brought with them from the farm in Scotland.

'Perhaps one of you would be gentleman enough to move that through into the bathroom,' she suggested. Colin raised one quizzical brow. 'I'm going to change into something a little less comfortable,' she explained, seeing his lack of comprehension. 'If I'm going to be your pony girl for the weekend, then the sooner you get used to seeing me in the role, the better. If you go all bug-eyed the first time over the weekend, someone will realise it's all just an act.'

Geordie coughed, stood up and turned towards the door.

'I think I'll go and get myself a pint,' he suggested, but Sara merely smiled and shook her head.

'No,' she said, firmly, 'I want you to stay, too. It's nothing you haven't seen already and you can show friend Colin here how the key thing works. It was bad enough when I thought I was stuck like that back up there, without getting myself in the same fix in a room in a busy hotel. Just make sure that door's locked and get the case into the other room, will you?'

Even from a distance of around two hundred yards, Alex could see quite plainly what was happening to Bambi. The groom, Higgy, was at last able to exercise his unwritten rights, now that the poor creature had lost the virginity that had come with her new body.

Alex shuddered and turned away from the spectacle. Higgy was clearly in no hurry and she knew from bitter experience that he could make this sort of ordeal last interminably. He seemed to take a perverse delight in seeing how many orgasms he could induce in each of his charges, apparently not fully understanding that every Jenny Ann's body was programmed to react to even the

116

mildest sexual stimulus, and the fact that he could have a pony girl writhing and moaning for an hour or more at a time owed nothing to any prowess or expertise on his part.

Out to graze. Alex walked slowly across the uneven grass, staring down at the ground, occasionally kicking at it with her heavy hooves, wishing that she dared to kick the grooms in the same way. Such a rebellious act, she knew, would be both pointless and masochistic. Even if she did manage to inflict any damage, they would repay her for it tenfold and she had witnessed an errant girl being whipped, only a week or two after her arrival here.

Out to graze.

Some hope, she reflected, morosely. Even if she had fancied eating grass, the thick bit and gagging flange that filled her mouth made such an act impossible. Further over the island, in the other area used for exercising the pony girls, there were two small drinking fountains, fed, apparently, by underground springs and operable, even when wearing the cumbersome hooves, by means of a foot level, the water jets spurting out at about chest height.

These fountains were supposed to be for the ponies, but even drinking was a messy and inefficient business while bitted. Grimly, Alex wondered how real horses managed it and then instantly chided herself for such stupidity. Real horses, after all, had mouths and faces far better adapted for wearing a bit with the minimum of inconvenience.

She stopped before the tether pulled her up short, turned and began pacing back the way she had come, struggling to keep herself from looking back towards Higgy and Bambi. Get a grip, she told herself, fiercely. You have to stay focused.

But focused on what? She came to a halt again, closing her eyes. From the very first moment Alex had refused to be cowed or broken, refused to accept the horror of what was happening to her, the awfulness of what they intended to turn her into, convinced that ultimately, regardless of what they did, she would find a way to escape, but the days kept passing and still they had not offered her the faintest glimmer of hope.

Time was becoming difficult to gauge. She had tried to keep a count in her head, but she could no longer be sure of the accuracy of her mental record. The angle of the sun in the sky suggested early autumn, probably mid-September, which meant she had been here for three months now, but could that be right?

Three months?

Three months and still no plan, not even a half-formed idea? But what could she possibly do? Angrily, she flexed her arm muscles, but as usual the leather pouch held her rigidly. She grunted against the bit in bitter frustration. They were just too efficient, their methods tried, trusted and seemingly infallible.

Maybe, just maybe, if they ever transferred her to the general maid and bedroom services, she might get a break – the girls she had seen in those roles were not subjected to the same strict bondage that was inflicted on the inhabit-ants of the stables complex, after all – but so far they showed no signs of expecting her to be anything but this bizarre parody of a beast of burden.

She opened her eyes again. Ahead of her, though at least fifty yards away, she saw Tammy pacing up and down in the aimless way that was their only choice when it came to what the grooms referred to as recreational exercise. Alex shook her head. Poor Tammy. On top of everything that Alex had to suffer, Tammy had to endure the knowledge that she had once – and not so long ago, either – been a man.

Now she – and Alex found it hard to think of Tammy as anything but a she, even though she could vaguely remember Tommy MacIntyre as he had been – was being forced to undergo the worst of horrors, with the promise of even more to come.

Out to graze. Pony girls who could not eat grass – out to graze. The situation was as farcical as it was horrific and yet, to listen to Jessie, they were supposed to feel grateful for their situation! Miserably, Alex stared down at herself, down through the valley between the obscene orbs with their pierced and belled nipples, down past the forcibly

118

flattened stomach, to where the thick leather strap descended between her thighs, holding in place the constant reminder of her completely helpless status.

Who in their right mind would feel grateful for this, she asked herself. Who could ever take any pleasure out of being turned into an object of carnal lust and desire?

Eleven

'She is certainly a very beautiful filly, Mr Marshall,' Celia
Butler said, addressing herself to Colin Turner as though
Sara were not in the room with them. 'What do you call
her?'

'Her name is Sara.' Colin smiled and shrugged. 'That's
what I call her as well. Should she have a different name?'
Celia mirrored his gesture.

'If you're her master,' she said, 'then that decision is
yours alone, though I would suggest that Sara is maybe
more a girl's name than a pony's name.'

'What would you suggest?' Celia considered for a few
moments. Sara, meanwhile, still wearing the simple white
cotton dress and tailored blue jacket in which she had travelled
from the hotel, stood mutely. Even in the short time she had
had available to study the various documents they had printed
from the Internet sites, she had learned enough to know what
was expected of her. Even though she was not yet in harness,
the mere fact of their arrival at Celia's farm signified that she
was already expected to be 'in character', or else not yet exist.

'Ultimately,' Celia said, at length, 'I think the choice of
name should be yours, Mr Marshall. Yes, I could make
suggestions, but I have always found that the name is best
given by someone who knows the pony well, as it should
be appropriate, if not to a physical attribute, then perhaps
to a character trait.'

'I see,' Colin said, genuinely bemused. 'Well, as I told
you the other day, we are both new to all this and, to be

120

truthful, we haven't even known each other that long. We met through – well, let's just say it was a convenient contact route.'

'Of course.' Celia nodded, knowingly. 'And you have suitable facilities available, I presume?'

'I own a piece of land,' Colin replied, truthfully. 'There's a lake and licensed fishing rights in season, some arable farmland that I lease to a local farm co-operative, a fair-sized orchard and a few acres of woodland. The house is very secluded and there are tracks through the woods, which are fenced off securely.'

'It sounds admirable,' Celia said. 'And do you have a stables building?' Colin forced an apologetic sigh.

'There *is* a building,' he explained, 'but it hasn't been used for a good many years and I'm not sure it would be viable to repair it.'

'I quite understand,' Celia said, taking him by the arm and guiding him towards the small bar that now stood to one side of the huge barn in which he had watched the blonde Lisa being turned into a human pony. 'However, not to worry. I can recommend a very good man who would build you a single stall unit from new, quite large enough for one pony girl, unless you wish to make her a permanent fixture, that is. He is very reasonable – you'd be surprised.'

'Oh, it's not the money,' Colin said. He half turned, trying to catch Sara's eye, but she remained steadfastly looking straight ahead of her, almost unblinking. 'No,' he continued, as Celia moved behind the bar herself, 'the money isn't a bother. I'd happily knock the old block down and rebuild a new one the same size. It's just that I'd assumed that the stabling requirements for a pony girl would be somewhat different from the more traditional facilities.'

Celia laughed, lifting an empty glass to a brandy optic. 'Not so different as you might think, Mr Marshall,' she assured him, with the completely confident air of the lifelong expert. 'A degree of warmth, as few draughts as possible, a little additional padding beneath the straw in the sleeping area and troughs for eating and drinking. The latter can be substituted by a very clever tap arrangement that makes it possible for the pony to get herself a drink while wearing her bit and full harness. I will show you examples later, if you like.'

She handed a generous measure of the neat spirit to Colin, who took it with a nod of thanks.

'I presume you would like one of my grooms to prepare your filly, while we relax a little and forget about the outside world? I have other guests arriving shortly, but they are all regulars and will take their ponies directly to the main stables before changing in the house itself.'

'Well, if it wouldn't be too much trouble,' Colin agreed. He turned again to see if there was any reaction from Sara herself, but the elegant blonde continued to act as if she were blind and deaf. 'We have brought a few of her things with us,' he continued, turning back to Celia. 'There's a case in the car. I could go and fetch it.'

'No need.' Celia waved a dismissive hand. 'Let Margot have your keys when she gets here, but it might be a good idea to fit out your filly with our tack from the word go, just so you get a better idea of what she could look like. Leave it to Margot to decide if it's worth using any of your own equipment, though you did tell me that most of it had been bought from fairly, uh, inexpensive outlets?'

'The word "inexpensive" is relative, as I'm beginning to discover.' Colin twisted his features into a rueful smile. 'However, as you say, Ms Butler, one gets what one pays for. So, yes, if you'd like to hand Sara over to Margot, that would be fine by me.' He wished he could get even half a minute alone with Sara, just to be sure that she was still up to this, but even to suggest anything that would create the opportunity would, Colin knew, be liable to raise suspicions. Instead, he raised his glass in a toast.

'To Blondie!' he cried and, when Celia regarded him blankly, he nodded towards Sara. 'I thought that would make a good name for Sara,' he explained.

Celia furrowed her high brow. 'Ah,' she said. 'I see.' She held her own glass lightly between elegant fingers, the long, blood-red nails reflecting dancing patterns into the amber liquid.

Colin's own expression became questioning. 'Is there a problem?'

Celia's look became rueful. 'Not a problem,' she said, though not with conviction. 'It's just that we do already have a pony here for the weekend by that name and, well, he's a colt.'

'Eh?' Colin was genuinely astonished. 'You mean he's a fella?'

Celia nodded. 'Of course,' she said. 'We don't limit our ponies to females only, Mr Marshall. In this day and age that might be construed as sexual discrimination.'

Few things ever disturbed Lulu's almost perpetual state of acquiescence, but this evening had been uncommonly distasteful. Alone in her room at last, she stripped herself while the bath was running and examined herself in front of the mirror, twisting and turning, horrified at the vivid patterns that he had created on her back and buttocks.

Lulu was used to the whip, the crop and the cane, but not like this. The hooded figure, indistinguishable from so many others she had encountered during her time here, had been like a wild animal, lashing at her helpless body with such ferocity that two of the canes had splintered.

And then, finally, as she had hung, screaming silently through the gag, he had simply turned away, broken the final rod over his knee and walked out of the room, leaving her for the duty mentor to release an hour later.

Stiffly, every fibre screaming, she lowered herself into the water, stretching herself slowly and shuddering as the heat began to permeate her tortured flesh.

'Bastard!' she hissed, through pain-clenched teeth. 'Bloody bastard!'

Who he was, she had no idea and, although his hood preserved his anonymity, Lulu was certain she had not encountered him before. The guests here were a strange lot – even she was aware of that – but few of them were genuinely cruel to the Jenny Anns. Offhand, casual,

123

dismissive, yes, but it was rare to find one who acted as savagely as this monster.

Heightened pain thresholds or not, Lulu desperately hoped she would never see him again.

It was, Geordie knew, going to be a long vigil, but it was not the first such observation he had tackled and would not be the last, and he had come well prepared, apart from the flask of coffee and the tiny camping stove and kettle.

Experience and routine – and part of his routine was that the boot of his car acted as a permanent repository for a number of useful tools and implements that he had acquired during his years of service, including several rather expensive items of equipment that were souvenirs of his posting to the Met, which the London force, with its legendary lack of attention to the finer details, had apparently forgotten were in his possession.

The camera and binoculars were the major prizes, both designed for night work and, between them, probably worth more than Geordie's car itself. The laptop computer and the satellite phone uplink unit had been even more expensive when they were first acquired, but now were becoming commonplace and, as a consequence, much cheaper. Geordie's set-up, by current comparison, was antiquated and slow, but it functioned well enough for his purposes and – he grinned to himself in the darkness of the car's interior – would serve to help pass the boring hours that any stakeout inevitably involved.

His encounter with Sara, much to his surprise, had sparked in him an interest that he needed to investigate further and the material they had taken from the Internet so far was, so far as he could tell, little more than the very tip of the iceberg. The subject of pony girls was not one he would previously have found interesting, but then, he was man enough to admit to himself, he hadn't even known that it existed until a few days ago.

Now, not only were there countless thousands of pages and images to explore, there was the memory of Sara herself, although Geordie still found it not just difficult to understand, but almost impossible to believe, the way she had acted. In a matter of minutes, she had changed from the cool and aloof executive into what he could only describe as a slavering animal: it was as if putting on all that leather stuff and those amazing boots had acted as a switch, shutting down the Sara Llewellyn-Smith part of her brain and activating something that lurked on a far more primordial level.

He operated the electric window, took out a cigarette and lit it, letting the thin stream of smoke billow out into the dark night beyond, while his gaze travelled down to the distant lights that marked Celia Butler's property. It had taken him ten minutes to remove and reposition enough branches from the screen of bushes behind which he had parked the car, so that he could be confident that no one down there on the farm would be able to see the vehicle, while at the same time he would afford himself an uninterrupted view of the buildings and yard.

Quite what he was waiting to see, he had no idea, but then that was par for the course and frequently such operations as this proved fruitless. Colin and Sara, inside the farm itself, were far more likely to come up with something, but it never hurt to be thorough. Besides, he thought, smiling again, he could as easily surf the Internet here as he could in a stuffy hotel room, which was exactly what he would have been doing if he had waited behind for the weekend.

The statuesque female groom, Margot, led Sara out into the night air and across an empty, rectangular courtyard, towards a long and much lower building on the far side. She opened the outer door, stepped away and motioned for Sara to walk ahead of her, apparently not considering it necessary to speak.

Inside, a broad corridor led both left and right, off which, at regular intervals, led what Sara realised, from the split doors that divided them off, were stalls. Margot jabbed a finger to indicate left and they continued to walk until they came to the sixth door, the top section of which stood open and clipped back to the wall. With a monosyllabic command, Margot halted Sara before it, pushed her brusquely clear and swung open the lower door section.

'Inside,' she said, tersely. 'And get stripped off. I'm just going to the tack room and I expect to see you naked by the time I get back with your stuff.'

The stall was quite cramped, the floor area maybe ten feet by eight or nine. The horses that had originally been quartered here had not been spoiled for space, she thought, but then she remembered what she had overheard of the conversation between Colin and the hard-faced Butler woman and understood. These stables had not been built for four-legged equines; the brickwork looked old, it was true, but there was no way the building had originally been designed to house the sort of horses one usually found in these circumstances.

Originally a country girl herself, Sara Llewellyn-Smith had ridden regularly as a girl and had been thrown from enough hunters to appreciate the size of the beasts. No, old or not, these were stables built specifically for human pony girls and the realisation came as more than a slight shock to her. Somehow, because she had seen the pictures and read the stories on the Internet, she had just assumed that human pony girls were a modern phenomenon, but on this evidence, it was clear that it had been going on for a very long time.

For several seconds, she stood just inside the door, sniffing the air, taking in the mixed odours of leather and straw, her mind wandering back to her childhood and her teenage years and to Marsh, the stepfather who had come into their lives a year after the death of her own dear father.

At least ten years younger than Sara's mother, who had been besotted with him, he had been sweetness itself with Sara and her elder sister Emma whenever anyone was around, but brusque and even harsh, especially with Sara, once there were no witnesses, meting out severe punishments for the most ridiculously trivial misdemeanours.

As she stood there, eyes half closed, Sara could remember that Sunday now, as vividly as if it had been the weekend before, though it had to be sixteen years – half her lifetime – ago now.

She had been mucking out the stables – the four of them had continued to live in the large house that had been in Daddy's family for nearly two centuries – as a punishment for allegedly chipping an Edwardian vase in the hallway, a vase that had been slightly damaged for as long as Sara could remember.

Marsh, however, had been immovable.

'If you want your allowance at the end of the month,' he said, 'then you can work for it.' And he had dispatched her to the stables with instructions to clean out the six stalls while the horses were grazing in the paddock.

It was a task that would normally have taken Sara no more than two hours, but the night before she had sneaked out, climbing down the ivy from her bedroom window, and gone to the river. There had been no secret assignation involved: at sixteen, Sara still tended to regard boys – at least the boys she knew – as being a complete waste of floor space. Instead, she had walked along the riverbank in the light of the full moon, simply enjoying the solitude and tranquillity that she seemed always to crave.

Not returning until shortly before dawn, she had therefore had only two hours' sleep, before being rudely roused by Marsh and confronted with her alleged 'crime'. Consequently, after half an hour of raking out soiled straw, she made the mistake of sitting down in the corner of the third stall, where she had immediately fallen asleep.

Her wristwatch told her that she had remained asleep for over three hours and, with a guilty start, she had leaped up and set about completing her punishment task, finishing, eventually, well after midday. Still heavy-eyed and now exhausted by her exertions, she had slumped down in the end stall and promptly dropped into a deep sleep once again.

As she lay on fresh, clean straw, this time Sara's slumber lasted even longer and might have continued, but for the noises from the first stall – the one that was normally used just for storage – that finally disturbed her. Sitting up, she checked the time and cocked her head on one side, listening to the unfamiliar sounds, at first thinking that it might be a puppy that had wandered into the building and become trapped.

With a heavy sigh, Sara hauled herself upright, rubbed her eyes blearily and stepped out into the wide passageway that ran along the front of the stalls. She paused again, listening keenly. The whimpering was much louder now and it was definitely coming from the first stall, just inside the outer door, which was now closed, although Sara definitely remembered leaving it latched open.

However, the source was no puppy.

For several seconds, Sara stood in the doorway to the end stall, mouth and eyes open in silent, speechless astonishment at the tableau before her, unable to believe the evidence of her own eyes.

Her sister, Emma, stood transfixed against the rear wall of the chamber, transfixed by the leather straps that held her arms stretched wide to two of the old iron rings set in the stonework. Her legs were similarly spread, held by lengths of cord that were knotted about her slender ankles and tied off, one to the bottom of a broken feeding trough, the other to a crate that held an assortment of old ironmongery.

She was naked from the waist down and her cotton blouse had also been pulled open, revealing the fact that she habitually did not wear a brassiere. Not that her nudity was fully visible from where Sara stood, for in front of her, thrusting powerfully upwards between her legs, his power-ful hands kneading Emma's unresisting breasts, was the figure, unmistakable even from the rear, of their stepfather, Marsh.

At last, Sara managed to break free from her trance, but the shriek of horror that tore from her throat seemed to come unbidden and she was still unable to move her feet, unable to run, unable even to lift her hands in her own defence when he drew himself free of Emma, spinning around, face contorted with a mixture of guilt and fury.

Cursing incoherently, he grabbed at Sara, seizing her wrists and dragging her out and along the passageway, hurling her bodily back into the stall from which she had just come. There, hanging on a wall hook, were several thin lengths of leather, broken pieces of harness and lunging reins. He grabbed one strand and, twisting her arms cruelly behind her back, used it to lash her wrists together, throwing her into the straw and using a second length to bind her ankles.

He stood up, stepping back, his eyes roving about the walls, apparently seeking something else. Eventually, his gaze lighted upon a broader strap, a section of a bridle that had become worn out and replaced, but not yet discarded. Snatching it in one hand, he tore a strip of cleaning rag from an adjoining hook. Balling it into a wad, he forced it between Sara's teeth and used the strap, buckling it about her head, to keep it there.

Breathing heavily now, he stepped back to the doorway, apparently oblivious to the fact that the front of his trousers had remained gaping open throughout and that his organ still thrust upwards in a bulging and rampant erection. He glared down at the helpless Sara and then, without a word, turned and was gone, leaving her whimpering and terrified in the corner of the stall.

Some time later, Emma had come to release her, but before freeing her wrists, her sister had crouched alongside her, trying to explain in hesitant, broken sentences. Little of what she said made any sense to Sara, in her traumatised state, but she was just about able to comprehend that what Marsh had been doing to her was not without her consent and that she had been a more than willing participant in the activities Sara had witnessed.

'Please, Sassie,' she had begged, using the family's pet name for Sara, 'please, don't say anything. Mummy would be so distraught if she knew and it'll never happen again, I swear it!'

Whether Emma kept to that promise or not, Sara never did discover, for a week later she was dispatched to an exclusive all-girl college in Norfolk, from where she finally ended up in an even more exclusive finishing school in Switzerland, but she knew that what Emma said about their mother was true and so kept Emma and Marsh's awful secret thereafter, although, as she grew older and more independent, she never missed an opportunity to make the hateful man squirm whenever she did see him, which was as seldom as she could make it.

Now, as the pictures faded and she came back to the present, Sara began to understand something about herself that she had kept buried, right up until Geordie Walker's fateful discovery of the hidden stable room . . .

Twelve

Tammy stood in front of the tall mirror, staring at the image she now presented, relieved to be out of the stables, yet knowing that this latest transformation did not bode well for her.

There had been no warning. The two grooms had entered her stall early that morning, stripped her without ceremony and dragged her out to be hoscd down. They had then simply cuffed her wrists behind her back, thrown a rough blanket around her shoulders, and deposited her on a bench at the far end of the stable concourse.

She had sat there for what had seemed like hours, but afterwards she realised that it had not really been that long before the two mentors came for her. She recognised Julia immediately, but the second female was of a type she had not previously encountered: short, stocky, dark and with eyes that spoke of a Middle Eastern origin.

'Who's a lucky girl then?' Julia greeted her. 'Come on, move yourself, silly. There's a nice room waiting for you up top and a fabulous new wardrobe. I don't know what you've done, but someone obviously likes you around here.'

The room was, without question, more than 'nice' and, after the months spent in the stables, it seemed like a palace, beautifully furnished and thickly carpeted, but Tammy had learned more than enough in her short time on the island to know that all was never as it seemed here. If they were moving her into these luxurious surroundings, then they had a purpose and she also knew that she was unlikely to appreciate it.

However, if she had learned one lesson from the stables, it was that it was pointless to protest, even less so to resist. She allowed them to guide her to the stool in front of the ornately carved dressing table and sat obediently at Julia's behest.

'No need to look so worried, lovey,' Julia said. She opened the box that was sitting in front of the mirror, revealing a comprehensive make-up kit. 'This is promotion, believe me. You don't get a place like this easily, I can tell you.'

'And there's no such thing as a free lunch,' Tammy retorted. 'Where's the catch?' Julia stroked her shoulder.

'Oh, Tammy,' she said, 'what are we to do with you? I know it must be hard for you, but you won't help yourself by getting all moody. I tried to tell you before, what's done is done, so we might as well make the best of things. Whatever you been before, things are different now, so just relax and try to enjoy yourself. Look here, this is all quality stuff.' She indicated the make-up. 'There are girls out there who would have to work for six months to afford this lot.'

'But I'm not a girl,' Tammy growled.

Julia pointed to the mirror and laughed. 'No?' she said. 'Well, excuse me, but that says different. OK, I can understand your problem, but then we've all had to face something similar. We were all once something different, but now we're something better.'

'That's easy for you to say,' Tammy snapped. 'I was quite happy the way I was.'

'Yes, well that's as maybe,' Julia said, 'but we can't turn the clock back, can we? Now, tell me you're going to be a good girl while I see to your face. Otherwise we'll have to bring in a frame and strap you to it.'

Tammy conceded to the inevitable. 'OK,' she sighed, 'I'll sit here and be a good little girl, if that's what you want. You'll do whatever anyway, won't you?'

'There's sensible,' Julia's companion said, speaking for the first time. Tommy recognised her accent as Welsh, the lyrical, singsong intonation unmistakable. 'And you don't know how bloody lucky you are,' she added, with a note of bitterness in her voice. 'Try spending forty years in this body and you'll know what it means to be underprivileged. Bloody drone, that's all I am and that's a fact.'

'You know that's not true, Megs,' Julia told her. 'And they have promised you a transposition.'

'Yeah, for the past twenty years,' the other woman riposted. 'All I ever hear is, "Just be patient and it'll all be sorted out" and what happens? Bloody nothing, that's what. There's always excuses, yet they can take some bloody macho Jock and give him a body I'd die for. It's just so unfair.'

Julia brushed aside this minor tirade and addressed her attentions to Tammy once more. For nearly an hour, she worked patiently and, although Tammy would never have admitted it, the result she achieved was quite stunning. Except that Tammy did not want to look stunning, as she had already learned that to do so carried the sort of penalties she did not want to incur.

'Paris, eat your heart out,' Julia said, brushing an errant lock of hair back into place. 'My God, Tammy, you could earn a fortune as a fashion model.'

'Well, pardon me if I don't let that go to my head,' Tammy grunted, though secretly she could not tear her eyes away from her reflection. With an effort, she shook herself mentally. They weren't going to get to her, no matter what they did. This – this *thing* in the mirror was not her, not *him*, more to the point. And yet, she knew, it was. Whatever, whoever, she had once been, this perfect confection that stared back at her so sullenly was now the truth. Had she been able to, she knew she would have cried.

'Right,' Julia said, 'come and see your new wardrobe.' And there was no denying that they had spared little expense. Not that Tammy was, nor had Tommy ever been, a fashion expert, but there were certain things that screamed quality in any field and the clothing Julia revealed when she opened the doors to the long closet did exactly that.

133

'If I'm supposed to be impressed, then fair enough,' Tammy said, 'but don't expect me to be grateful.' Julia took out a long, dark-blue evening gown and held it up. The velvet-like material seemed to have a depth beyond that of any simple fabric and its surface danced like a thousand rivers in the moonlight.

'But isn't this just too fantastic?' she breathed, clearly overwhelmed by the garment. 'Look at it, Tammy. The rest of us only ever get to wear rubber stuff and leather, never anything like this.'

'Yes, it's beautiful,' Tammy conceded. 'But why for me?'

Julia's expression changed, darkening somewhat. She passed the dress to Meg, took Tammy's elbow and guided her to the edge of the bed. 'Listen,' she pleaded, earnestly. 'I'm not supposed to even know about this myself, let alone tell you, but it's only fair, I suppose.' She looked deeply into Tammy's face before continuing. 'You,' she said, eventually, 'have been specially selected.

'These people – the masters and mistresses – gave us new bodies, as you know, but we're not just here for the obvious and neither was this science of theirs developed just to provide a steady stream of whatever you might like to call it for a bunch of rich perverts. We're part of a programme to help them continue their race. I listen to what gets said around here, even though I never let anyone realise I'm that interested. We – us Jenny Anns, as they call us – some of us, anyway, we're supposed to provide two things. Well, one thing really.

'We're here to give them children, children they can also use to manufacture more cloned hosts that their own females can transfer into, otherwise they'd die at a ridiculously early age. I don't really understand the half of it, but that's what all this is really supposed to be about.'

'You can't be serious!' Tammy gasped. 'They don't intend –'

Julia nodded. 'Yes,' she said, levelly, 'that's exactly what they do intend. Your reproductive cycle will be reactivated and you will be mated.'

'And all this stuff,' Tammy said, waving a hand towards the wardrobe, 'is supposed to make me feel better about it?'

'Not exactly,' Meg cut in. 'You'd as best tell the silly cow, Jules,' she added. Tammy looked from one to the other.

'Tell me what?' she demanded.

'My God!' Colin's lower jaw dropped and he could not disguise his utter astonishment at the transformation Margot had effected with Sara. The tall groom swayed towards him, Sara's lead rein twisted nonchalantly around her left wrist, a wicked-looking riding crop dangling, by a leather loop, from her right.

'Meet Sassie, Master Colin,' she announced, silkily. 'Apparently that was what they called her when she was younger and it seemed more appropriate than the name you've been calling her. I trust you approve.' Whether she meant of the name, or of the way Sara/Sassie now looked, Colin could only guess and he was not disposed to ask.

'Quite stunning,' Celia said, appearing at his elbow and indeed he could not dispute her choice of words, for stunning was the only way to describe the fantastic creature who now confronted him.

She had been dressed – poured might have been a more accurate description – into what appeared to be a latex body suit. It was mostly cream in colour but with piebald patches, and the long boots, with their towering hoof-shaped heels, had been coloured to match. The leather of her harness shone scarlet, the lights from above twinkling on a myriad gold studs and fittings, buckles and brasses.

The leather girth corset had been drawn in so tightly that it seemed Sara's waist must surely snap in two, and how she was managing to breathe in it Colin could not imagine, especially with the thick bit now cruelly distorting her crimson lips. Her blonde hair had been drawn up and back, pulled through a short leather tube set in the bridle harness where it crisscrossed the crown of her head, so that it now flowed down her back in a rippling mane and her eyes had been lavishly made up with red and gold shadow, matching red and gold false eyelashes completing the effect.

135

From the neck downwards, only her breasts remained uncovered, protruding through circular apertures in the pony suit and tightly tethered about their bases by a complicated leather harness that was attached both to the girth and to the high, studded collar that forced her to walk with head held uncommonly erect.

Her nipples, which appeared swollen and hard, had been encircled by tight clips, from each of which dangled a tiny golden bell and between which had been fastened a slender gold chain that swayed with her slightest movement, as did the two bells that now hung from her pierced earlobes. And, from the tightly drawn leather gusset strap, which Colin rightly concluded was the only thing covering her sex, another, larger bell swung in time with its smaller counterparts.

'She still doesn't walk well,' Margot said, in a tone that suggested she was more than willing to correct that fault – and quickly. 'But she has good legs, excellent flanks and a long neck. All things considered, she is not a bad animal.' Colin cringed at this last remark, but Margot's seeming refusal to consider her a human being did not seem to affect Sara.

She stood proudly erect, chest rising and falling in shallow movements, staring directly ahead of her, only the occasional flicker of the outrageous eyelashes proving that those finely chiselled features were actually animate. Despite himself, Colin felt a hungry stirring in his loins and began to understand just what it was that made these people tick.

Thirteen

The girl's name was unpronounceable to most Westerners, so her captors had renamed her Samba, a tribute to the natural rhythm and grace she displayed when she danced, whatever the music. Her companion, who she learned had come from a village some seventy miles from her own, they had called Gypsy, on account of the huge, limpid pools that were her eyes and the unexpected bursts of temper she displayed when annoyed.

Samba was uneducated, but not unintelligent, and she had been quick to pick up the languages – first Spanish, a dialect of which was spoken in her own village anyway, as a second language, and now the curious English, although the mixture of accents and dialects she had encountered thus far were more than confusing.

Gypsy, she realised, was dim, even by the standards of those mountain villagers Samba had encountered back in her native South America, and refused even to speak Spanish, so that Samba was forced to communicate with her in the broken tongue that was all that survived of the aboriginal language in her own, lowlands village.

Lying on the low pallet that had served as her bed in the weeks since they had both been brought here, Samba looked across the narrow, caged area that she shared with Gypsy, to where the other girl lay on her own bed, flat on her back, mouth wide open and snoring loudly. Pig, she thought. Bloody barbarian pig. The sow even ate with her hands, tearing at the meat they were given and ignoring

137

most of the vegetables, gravy dripping down her jaws and spilling on to the thin white smock that had been their uniform during their stay in this strange place.

Samba had no real idea where they were, just that it had taken many days' journey to get here, days spent hooded and blindfolded in trucks or in a confined, windowless space that rocked and swayed alarmingly. One of the guards had tried to explain to her, but his Spanish was worse than her own and the only word she really understood was that meaning ship. She had seen pictures of ships, of course, but had never even seen the sea in real life and had never imagined that a journey over it could be so terrible.

Except, as one of the Spanish-speaking crewmen explained to her during the final stages of the voyage, their journey had not been over the sea, but under it, in a special ship called a submarine. The thought had horrified Samba and she had cried herself to sleep.

Eventually, they had been brought ashore again, once more hooded, so that they could not see their surroundings, the awful-smelling leather being removed only when they were once more inside – this time, if the sign language of the strange woman in the white clothing was to be believed, actually under the ground. Samba could picture the huge caves her father had shown her in the mountains above their village, but this place was nothing like them. She was reminded, instead, of the mission hospital, where her grandmother had taken her as a girl and the doctor had splinted and set the leg she had broken falling from a tree by the river.

But why these people would want to bring her to a hospital now she could not understand, for there was nothing wrong with her and the damaged leg had mended without a trace inside a few weeks. She had tried questioning them, but they either did not understand her, or else they pretended they did not, regarding her with blank faces, or sympathetic smiles.

And so she had simply listened, talking instead to the two young men who came daily to take Gypsy and her out

138

for a long walk in the fresh air, where the smell of salt hung as heavily as did that of the mountain mists at home and where, between the trees and the precipitous hillsides, she could see the green and blue shimmer that she knew was the sea under which they had come to this place.

The two guards, as she thought of them, were named Sol and Jonas and their real job, they tried to explain, making frantic gestures and bobbing up and down, seemed to be to do with horses. They made grooming motions and mimed driving a cart, and then Jonas had mimed something unmistakable in any culture, but which, Samba thought, no sane man would ever really consider, so she assumed she had misunderstood his meaning.

How much that was true she discovered a few days later, when the grooms led them through the stables area and they saw for themselves the true nature of their charges, pale-skinned human females kept in harnesses and bridles, mouths filled with cruel bits, tiny chariot carts waiting for them to draw and whips waiting to encourage any who dared to slack. Samba had been horrified, but Sol and Jonas had just laughed at her expressions and returned both girls to their cage again, where Samba lay that night, shivering despite the warmth, unable to sleep, in terror that she might soon end up as one of those poor girl ponies herself.

Nothing she now wore, as Sara knew from bittersweet experience, could be removed without a key and the help of someone else, but it appeared that these people were not satisfied with even that state of helplessness, for, as soon as Margot had led her back to the stable building, she quickly fitted thick leather mitts over her hands, doubling them over into useless fists and then snapping on steel links that held her wrists tightly to either side of her girth.

Sara had never before felt so thoroughly vulnerable, not even when she had lain trussed hand and foot in the stables at home, yet strangely the sensation did not trouble her at all. She stood motionless, while Margot clipped the large blinkers to either side of the harness that enclosed her head, and did not flinch, even when the woman ran an appreciative hand over her latex-sheathed hip. The groom seemed pleased.

'Untrained you may be, Sassie,' she smiled, 'but you're a natural thoroughbred, if ever I saw one.' Her hand moved across and down, pressing lightly against the gusset strap where it covered Sara's crotch and the tiny triangle of fair pubic hair that was all Margot and her clippers had left her. She pressed harder, forcing the embedded dildo even deeper, and Sara let out an involuntary groan.

'We need to find you a tail now, I think,' Margot whispered, her face close to Sara's. 'And a nice plug to remind you it's there.'

Unable to see the gusset strap herself, Sara realised the fiendish ingenuity of its design only when Margot inserted the thin rubber shaft through the appropriate hole in it and continued to push until Sara relaxed her sphincter muscles to allow it to enter her. When it was fully home, she felt Margot twisting it half a turn and realised that the motion had somehow locked the wicked probe to the strap itself and that no amount of straining on her own part could now expel it, nor rid her of the fabulous, multicoloured tail that was affixed to it.

'I didn't want to show you to your master all in one go,' Margot smirked. 'I like to keep back the odd surprise. But he'll see that tail now when he climbs up into his seat to drive you, so make sure you wag it well, pony slut.'

Sara closed her eyes and bit hard into the toughened rubber, but it was to no avail. With a horribly equine-sounding squeal, she yielded helplessly to the wave of orgasm that swept, like a raging tornado, through her entire body.

The three figures stood on the gantry, looking down at the evenly spaced rows of steel and plastic sarcophagi, and, for several minutes, there was complete silence, save for the low hum of the hidden machinery that supported the newly developing life forms they studied through the misted perspex lids.

'How long now?' Ramon was the first to break the spell. Keith Lineker half turned towards him, but his gaze remained fixed on the fruits of his labours, the ghost of a smile playing upon his lips.

'Another two days for sections A and B, four days for D and E,' he replied. 'The nursery section has been enlarged since last week and extra auxiliaries briefed in their duties. All twenty will be ready for implanting in another two weeks, once we've had time to check out their various functions.'

'I'm impressed,' Ramon said. 'Twenty new lives from the two I brought you.'

'And as many more from them as you wish,' Richard Major reminded him. 'According to Dr Lineker, both girls were very healthy specimens.'

'Very healthy,' Lineker confirmed. 'However, with the second batch, I have taken the liberty of a little experimentation. I have added in from the DNA samples I have cloned from previous donors. The young fisherman had a very strong physique, which was what enabled him to survive the wreck of his ship, and then there is Jessie, whose host body type has proven one of the most suitable for arduous tasks.

'Your Indian girls are very sturdy and their evolution makes them eminently suited for the climatic conditions where you will be using these new creatures, but I fancy they can be made stronger still and a little less stunted in their appearance. It will be interesting to compare the performances of both batches, I think.'

'Ever the scientist, eh, Doctor?' Ramon's top lip curled into a harsh smile. 'Well, if it makes for stronger ponies with longer staying power, so much the better. I shall ensure that you get your figures regularly. And the facilities back there should be ready quite soon, anyway,' he added. 'Tell me, do you intend to bring extra DNA stock with you still?'

Lineker nodded. 'Frozen samples,' he said, 'and the raw materials, too. I have selected a number of existing subjects to bring over with me, as that will not only give me the benefit of fresh samples, it will also open up the possibility of starting a breeding programme with some of your local ethnic male population.'

'It would be useful if you could produce male versions of these creatures,' Ramon nodded. 'If not, it would be, perhaps, a viable alternative to begin a natural breeding programme.'

'It would be interesting, from a scientific point of view,' Lineker agreed. He turned away from the rail, placing a hand on Ramon's arm. 'Unfortunately,' he added, 'the resultant offspring will be of little use to you for many years. As you know, they take as long to reach adulthood as do any other human offspring, whereas my Jenny Ann hosts reach maturity in weeks, rather than years.'

Sara had expected that she would be hitched up to a pony cart out in the yard between the stables, the barn and the house, but to her surprise and consternation, when Margot finally led her out into the open air once again, there was the unmistakable silhouette of a horse box waiting there, the ribbed tailboard already lowered.

'Up you go, Sassie, there's a good girl.' Margot emphasised her instruction with a casual flick of the riding crop. It was not a hard blow, but it landed across one buttock cheek with such expertly directed accuracy that Sara leaped forward without thinking and was almost prepared to run up the ramp to avoid another stinging cut. Margot followed her into the van's interior.

'Don't worry,' she said. 'Your master will follow on in one of the cars. You didn't think we did the serious stuff here, did you? Far too near the main road and far too open. No, you're going to Mistress Celia's special training stables.' She pressed Sara back against one side of the vehicle and drew two stout straps over her shoulders, crossing them between her breasts and then buckling them tightly to stanchions set at waist level.

'It's not too far,' she said, stooping lower to buckle a second and third strap about each of Sara's booted thighs. 'Takes less than half an hour, but we can't have you falling

142

about in here, can we?' She drew further straps over each instep, trapping Sara's hoofed feet firmly to the floor and, if Sara had felt helpless before, now she felt as if she had been encased in immovable steel.

From outside the van came the clatter of more hooves and two more pony girls were herded up into the interior, backed against the wall opposite Sara and similarly secured by another pair of female grooms, who did not even so much as glance at Sara. Completing their tasks with stunning efficiency, they were gone again, almost before Sara had time to take in their appearances.

'One more for this box,' Margot called out into the darkness. A muffled voice replied and Margot laughed. 'Yeah, OK,' she called back. 'It'll keep him nice and hard.'

To Sara's astonishment, the fourth pony was a male. Beneath all the tack and with the same bit and blinkers as the girls wore, it was difficult to make out his features clearly, especially as the interior light was very dim, but he appeared to be in his early twenties, dark haired – whether the ponytail mane was real or an extension Sara could not tell – and strongly muscled.

Like the girls, his body was sheathed in gleaming rubber, in his case black, with a white stripe leading from his chin to his waist. His face had been carefully made up with a black foundation, leaving a white blaze from his forehead to his chin, and there was a large, silver ring set through his septum.

Again, exactly the same as with the females, his waist had been cinched impossibly tight and he wore thigh-length boots to which his hooves were attached. However, where the girls' genitalia were covered by the broad gusset strap, his very erect manhood had been laced into a black leather sheath, the ring in the top of which had been attached to a thin chain to keep it upright and close to his abdomen.

In the near darkness, Sara saw his eyes flicker, his head turning so that, hampered by the blinkers, he could look at her. She felt herself redden, for despite the disfiguring bit and bridle, there was no mistaking the expression on his face and she was glad that none of them could speak, for she knew she would have betrayed herself all too easily.

'This is Nomad, Sassie,' Margot said. She reached down, seized the sheathed column and squeezed it. Nomad gave no indication of pain, but Sara winced involuntarily. 'Nomad is a wilful beast,' Margot went on, as his groom completed the task of securing him for the journey.

'He used to be a proper stallion, but we normally keep him in this gelding rig. One day, I suspect, his mistress may want to have him gelded properly. Not this fine shaft, of course, but those two useless appendages hanging beneath it. That way he can still get it up, but it can't do any damage, the way it once did to his mistress's daughter.'

Sara felt an icy hand gripping at her stomach and shuddered in her unyielding bondage. The casual indifference with which Margot treated such a subject and the obvious fact that she actually meant what she was saying was more frightening than anything Sara would have thought possible.

She gritted her teeth about the foul bit and stared steadfastly at the girl opposite her and, for the first time, she began to regret agreeing to become such a willing participant in this sinister charade. Before it was over, she suspected, she was likely to regret it even more.

The corset was satin, frilled with lace at the hem and the cups, dainty and feminine in appearance, but, as Tammy was laced into it, she realised that appearances in this case were deceptive, for the frothy confection hid a boning that produced as severe an effect as did any of the leather pony girths.

'Why bother?' she gasped, as Julia tied off the laces. 'If I'm just being turned into a glorified brood mare, then why doesn't he just get on with it?'

'Because Master Richard insists on certain standards and protocols,' Julia said. 'You are to become his concubine, the next step down from a wife, although I don't think he's ever actually had a wife. He will want to show you off to his most important guests and you must be dressed and act accordingly.'

'And, being able to turn my voice off at the flick of a switch,' Tammy muttered, 'he doesn't have to worry about me opening my mouth and telling his guests just exactly what goes on down here?'

'I'm afraid,' Julia smiled, sadly, 'that your voice will be kept deactivated during any periods of contact with the guests.'

'And won't they find that just a wee bit strange?'

'In this place?' Meg laughed, raucously. 'You can't be serious, surely? If the lord and master takes it upon himself to select a mute companion, who the hell do you think is going to question that? From what I remember of the outside world, most men would give their right arm for a wife who couldn't speak.'

Julia backed Tammy over to the dressing-table seat and began drawing the silky stockings up her legs, fastening them to the array of garters that dangled from the hem of her corset.

'These are not real silk,' she said. 'Actually, I'm not sure what they're made of, but they're very hard-wearing and almost impossible to rip, let alone ladder. They'd be worth a small fortune on the open market.'

'That's all this place is anyway,' Tammy sulked, as she stood to step into the brief thong that Meg held out for her. 'It's a bloody flesh market, that's all. We're just here to provide the filling for people who can't digest real relationships.'

'Very profound, I'm sure,' Meg said, tugging the elasticated garment around Tammy's hips. 'But I never was very big on philosophy and when you've been raped and beaten by a couple of drunken ex-miners and left for dead, it gives you a different slant on things, I can tell you.'

'Now,' Julia said, selecting a pair of white, high-heeled court shoes, complete with delicate ankle straps, from the bottom of the closet, 'you may find these a bit hard going at first. There's no ankle support as there is in the boots, so it would be sensible to practise walking in them a bit beforehand.'

'I thought our bodies were supposed to be tougher than normal,' Tammy challenged.

Julia nodded. 'Of course they are, and that includes our ankles, otherwise we'd never manage to walk in half the footwear we're expected to. But just take a look at these heels, you silly girl: they're at least eight inches high and you'll barely be able to get more than your toes on the ground.'

The accuracy of her prediction was quickly proved and, with her feet arched into the incredible shoes, Tammy found she could hardly balance at first. Standing precariously, she tried her first step and only Meg's quick intervention prevented her from falling headlong.

'This is bloody ridiculous,' Tammy stormed. She slumped back down on to the seat, lifted her right leg on to her left knee and reached for the shoe.

'I shouldn't bother even trying,' Julia said, seeing what she was about to do. 'The straps lock on and, even though they might not look much, I can assure you they're virtually unbreakable. You won't even cut through them with a knife.'

'But I can't possibly walk in these!' Tammy wailed. 'Please, there must be some with lower heels.'

'Not for you, my girl,' Meg rejoined. 'His Lordship has a penchant for heels, the higher the better, so the sooner you get practising, the better. Now, hold out your arms and let's get these gloves on you.'

'And then we can see to your dress,' Julia added. 'Plus there's some beautiful jewellery.'

Tammy's shoulders slumped in defeat. 'Well,' she said, 'pardon me if I don't get all excited.'

146

Fourteen

Three months in the stables had taught Alex that the appearance of the haughty Amaarini rarely boded anything other than trouble for someone, and her mere presence created a tension among the pony girls that did not dissipate until she had settled upon the object of her current displeasure.

On this occasion, that object was Alex.

'My staff tell me you are being less than co-operative, Jangles,' she said, dominating the doorway of Alex's stall. 'I had hoped that stabling you with Jessica might have taught you some better habits, but it appears not. Your timings on the practice runs are abysmal, your bearing, other than when you are in full harness and cannot do otherwise, is slothful and your entire manner is resentful, even to attempting to corrupt your stablemate.'

'And did you really expect anything else?' Alex snarled. She was, as ever, in harness and bridle, but her bit had earlier been removed to enable her to eat and her mitted hands hung free, if useless, at her sides. She stood against the back wall of the stall and faced Amaarini defiantly.

'This is precisely what I mean,' Amaarini continued, smoothly. 'We give you a splendid new body – save your life, probably – and all you can think about is rebellion. Escape, too, I shouldn't wonder, even though you've been told, time and again, that that is impossible. The weight of your hooves alone would drag you under, assuming you

147

ever got as far as the water, and then there are vicious currents, as I'm sure you must be aware.'

'At least I'd be out of this place,' Alex snapped. 'I'd rather be dead than suffer any more of these indignities.'

'Death is such a final solution,' Amaarini sighed. 'If you'd ever been truly faced with the choice, as I once was, perhaps you might appreciate your situation more.'

'Well, exactly!' Alex laughed, but without mirth. 'You had a choice; I didn't. On balance, I'd have preferred it if you'd left me to die.'

'But you might not have died,' Amaarini pointed out. 'Broken necks are not always fatal, though Dr Lineker assures me that, in your case, you would have been paralysed from the neck down.'

'Better than being paralysed from the neck up!' Amaarini shook her head, her eyes narrowing. 'And don't think anything you can do will ever change the way I feel,' Alex continued, bravely. 'Oh, yes, you might make me grovel and beg and you might have given me a body that responds to things that would normally make me cringe, but you won't change what's inside here.' She raised one mitt and tapped the side of her head. 'You may make me act like the rest of these poor bitches,' she added, 'but you'll never make another Jessie out of me.'

Amaarini gave a tiny snort of laughter. 'That, my dear little Jangles,' she said, 'sounds like a challenge. And I can never resist a challenge. I think we'll make a pony out of you yet.'

'There's no cause for alarm, Mr Marshall,' Celia Butler said. 'I should, perhaps, have explained better beforehand, but it's all quite logical, if you think about it. This address is fairly well known, especially in the pony circles and, while it's one thing to demonstrate various stock items here, it's quite another when we come to the proper training and racing days. That's why I keep my second establishment.'

'But how far away is it?' Colin protested. 'I mean, a chap ought to know where he's going.' He tried to play up to his best Hooray Henry image, not wanting to appear too inquisitive at such an early stage in the operation. It was imperative to act the rich and slightly vacuous dilettante, a role that he had used to great effect in the past.

'Less than twenty miles from here,' Celia assured him, 'but the roads between are less than ideal, so it usually takes anything up to a quarter of an hour. The last five or six miles are along something little better than a mud track,' she added, by way of further explanation. Which sounded, Colin thought, rather similar to Geordie's description of Andrew Lachan's Highlands estate.

'Well, I suppose you know best, dear lady,' he said, affably. 'Mind you,' he added, with a forced laugh, 'I'll have to watch out for the jolly old suspension on that jalopy of mine. My mechanic chappie tells me there's more rust than metal underneath.'

'I shouldn't worry about your suspension, Mr Marshall,' Celia said, silkily. 'We provide the transport. The Range Rovers are waiting outside as we speak. And, when we get there,' Celia added, taking Colin's arm, 'we really must find you something more suitable to wear. Savile Row is scarcely appropriate for the stable yard.'

Geordie steered the car carefully into the wide field gateway, switched off the lights and cursed. Leaving the engine ticking over, he opened the door and climbed out of the car, his eyes scanning the darkened skyline, but it was useless.

Away to the right he could see the yellowing lights of the small village he had passed through just before leaving the second of the two A roads they had taken, but of the little convoy he had been following there was no sign at all.

He had watched through the night glasses as the two horse boxes were loaded with their human cargo, recognising Sara as one of the four figures to be herded into the second vehicle, even at that distance. He had had even less trouble identifying Colin, and the woman who had accompanied him out to one of the Range Rovers was, he assumed, Celia Butler.

149

There had been several other women and two men, all dressed in clothing that suggested that they were stable hands or grooms, and the entire party, he calculated, numbered more than twenty. As the vehicles moved out of the farmyard, Geordie had been forced to wait to see the direction they were heading in before he could risk turning on his own lights, and, by the time he had reached the road via the circuitous lane by which he had originally gained his hilltop vantage point, the convoy was some way ahead.

He had caught up with it again on the first main road, having seen which way their headlights turned at the junction, but had been forced to stay well back, for there was little traffic about and he did not want to alert them to the possibility that they were being followed.

It had been a calculated risk and one that had been sound enough until they left the second A road, whereupon Geordie initially missed the fact that they had turned off and was forced to make an abrupt U-turn to get back to the junction down which he had seen the last taillights disappearing.

Shortly afterwards, the trees on either side grew denser and then they were driving in deep forest. He had seen the lights ahead as he crested a small hill, lost them again as the road dipped down and, by the time the road climbed again, there was no sign of them.

He walked over to the five-barred gate, climbing up on to the middle rung for a better vantage point, but it did not help. Either they were driving without lights – madness on these lanes – or they had already stopped somewhere. Or maybe the trees away to the left were simply too dense for light to penetrate.

Geordie cursed again, jumped down on to the hardened mud and fumbled in his pocket for his cigarettes and lighter. As he blew out the first stream of smoke, he was already thinking furiously, but he knew that there was little he could do immediately.

He could drive back and forth and around and around on these narrow tracks and lanes, but, after this amount of time, any lights he might see would be inconclusive. There were, after all, bound to be quite a few farms in the area, plus odd cottages, and he couldn't just barge in anywhere without a good reason.

He made himself think calmly.

Colin had clearly gone with them voluntarily. He had appeared to be chatting to his female companion and no one had forced him to get into the Range Rover. Sara had been trussed neatly in her pony-girl costume, but then so had the seven others, including the three males, so it was safe enough to assume that this was all just part of their little pantomime.

So, clearly they had all simply been moving to another venue, presumably somewhere even more secluded than Celia's farm premises. It was, after all, Geordie had to admit, not so very far from so-called civilisation and, if they were intending any outdoor activities, they would want to be somewhere where the likelihood of being accidentally overlooked was as small as possible.

There was a reasonable-scale road atlas in the glove compartment, but it would be unlikely to give Geordie the sort of information he needed. The smallest detail it showed would be no smaller than a small village and he needed something that would indicate the position of individual buildings.

The local police station, wherever that might be, would probably have something suitable, but that might require explanations he didn't really want to give. Country coppers tended to be a nosy bunch, as Geordie knew from experience, and the fewer people who knew about this particular little adventure, the better – at least for the time being.

On the other hand, he argued with himself, where else could he find something that would show him what he was looking for? He already knew the sort of place they would most likely be heading for: remote, private, well away from anything that might attract unexpected visitors – a place very like Andrew Lachan's estate, for example.

But out here, in the dark, in an area he knew nothing about, he didn't even know where to start looking. He

151

climbed back into the car, closed the door and wound down the window, and it was then that he remembered the computer on the back seat and the box of electronic gadgetry in the boot.

The pain was, in truth, now not very great, just a mild discomfort as the various healing injections and sprays began to take effect, but it was made worse by the knowledge of why it had been inflicted upon her and the bushy tail that now sprouted from the upper cleft in her buttocks was worse than anything Alex had imagined these monsters capable of.

Amaarini had performed the surgery herself, taking great pleasure in explaining to Alex how, while she was not a regular member of Lineker's team, she had been amusing herself by developing this technique and how the tail had been developed so that the cell cluster from which it sprouted matched the DNA of the particular recipient – in this case, Alex.

'Just a tiny incision and a little laser grafting,' Amaarini said, as she worked away, while Alex, spread-eagled face down on the operating table, remained conscious throughout, a local anaesthetic numbing her system to any possible pain at this stage.

'The drugs we will give you will ensure that there is no chance of rejection and, in a few days, your tail will be a part of you, growing as naturally as the hair on your head.' She stepped back and the white-coated female assistant moved in to begin sealing the wound, using a device that resembled a penlight torch.

'Ideally, Jangles,' Amaarini said, walking around the table and stooping to look into Alex's eyes, 'I'd like to develop a technique to give you a proper pony face, too. Maybe then you'd be a little more appreciative.

'It's more than possible we can do that, too, but in the meantime there are other alternatives, as you are about to find out. Then,' she continued, standing erect once more, 'I shall take personal charge of you for a while, train you myself and run you until you beg me to stop. Except you won't be able to beg, pony girl, because your voice is turned off now and it will stay off until I can see an improvement in your behaviour for myself.' She turned to the nurse.

'Once you've finished with her, have her sent back, but to a separate stall, and tell Higgy to prepare her for me. He already knows what I want and has everything in readiness.'

Lying helpless on the table, Alex fumed in enforced silence, but at the same time there was another emotion beginning to rise up and take the place of the anger she had felt during all these weeks.

Fear.

Fifteen

Quite how they had managed it, Colin had no idea. It could have been in the car, or it could have been something in his drink earlier, but, whatever it was, the result was the same. He could remember the Range Rover bumping over the uneven approach road from Celia's farm and then turning on to a properly made-up country road, but after that, nothing.

Nothing until now and, as his head slowly cleared and vision began to return, he knew they were in some sort of trouble. Despite his carefully rehearsed act, something had gone wrong and the Butler woman and her cohorts had clearly decided to act.

And how they had acted!

Blinking in disbelief, Colin stared along the length of his supine form and came jolting back to full awareness. With a startled gasp, he tried to sit up, but was immediately jolted back and almost choked by the thick leather collar that encircled his throat and was, he quickly realised, connected to some sort of restrictive chain or cord behind his neck.

And, in the next second or two, he saw and understood the full extent of what they had done to him while he was unconscious. Even as he took in the details, the overall effect was unmistakable, for he was now dressed in the full paraphernalia of a pony boy, exactly as the two other males he had seen being taken out into the yard, just before their departure.

The long boots, the brown latex body suit, rib-crushing girth, bridle straps encircling his head and long leather sleeve mitts holding his arms rigidly to his sides. The only thing that was missing was a bit: presumably his captors had not wanted him to choke while unconscious, but they *had* laced his penis into a leather sheath and, astonishingly, it seemed to be in a state of full erection.

Fighting back the initial urge to panic and struggle, Colin tried to relax his muscles, then flexed them to test his bondage, even though he already knew that they would not have left him any chance to wriggle free of it.

'We pride ourselves on making quality merchandise, Mr Marshall.' Celia Butler's voice came from behind his head and, as he tried, unsuccessfully, to crane his neck around to see her, Colin guessed that she must have been standing in the room all the time, waiting for him to come round and, he was sure, eager to crow.

But what had they done wrong? How had they been rumbled so quickly?

'Quality, Mr Marshall,' Celia repeated, walking slowly around into his field of vision. Despite his predicament, Colin barely managed to suppress a gasp of awe at the sight of her, for since the last time he had seen her, sitting next to him in the back of the Range Rover, she had changed completely. In place of the immaculately tailored designer clothes – skirt, blouse, jacket and court shoes – she now wore a costume that was as outlandishly bizarre, in its own way, as anything Colin had so far seen in the pony outfits.

He was lying on a low divan bench, but she was standing far enough back from him so that he could just about see her feet, which were now encased in gleaming red boots, laced to the knee, above which she wore what appeared to be jodhpurs of soft white kid. The sleeveless shirt was also of white kid and, set against this and matching the colour of her boots, she had laced herself into a polished leather waist cincher as severe as anything Colin had seen among the pony girths.

A studded red choker and a curious, studded red leather mask, which covered the entire top half of her face, giving it a sinister appearance which the glittering eyes did nothing to dispel, and shoulder-length leather gloves, again in the same vivid crimson, completed an image that, with the six-inch heels to add to her already impressive height and bearing, had been meticulously cultivated to create an air of complete dominance and power.

'As I said, Mr Marshall,' she said, holding up a pair of calf-length pony boots, 'one cannot better quality. I presume you recognise these.' Colin peered up at the boots. They were no different from several pairs he had now seen in the past few days.

'Boots,' he said, simply. 'Hoof boots.'

'*My* hoof boots,' Celia snarled. Colin looked at her blankly, for he could not conceive of the haughty figure before him, nor even the Celia Butler he had originally met, allowing herself to be turned into a submissive pony girl.

'*Your* boots?' he said. 'I'm sorry, I don't understand. Listen, there's been some sort of mistake here. Why don't you just let me up from here? I'm sure we can resolve this.'

'I'm sure we can,' Celia sneered. She waved the boots again. 'I'm sure you can explain to me why these boots were in the case in your car – together with several other items that were made in my workshops. Correct me if I'm wrong, Mr Marshall, but you did tell me that the equipment you had so far purchased for Sassie was cheap and inferior.'

'Well, yes,' Colin said, thinking furiously and trying to ignore the pounding that had suddenly started up inside his head. He wanted to kick himself for being so stupid as to bring any of the pony paraphernalia from Lachan's. If Celia Butler was supplying the stuff to Healthglow, then it made sense that she had also supplied the stuff Geordie had discovered in the hidden stable room.

And if Celia's products were so exclusive, it stood to reason that she, or one of her minions, might well recognise it for what it was. A sudden idea occurred to him and he grabbed at it, as a drowning man grabs at even the smallest piece of driftwood.

'Most of our equipment *is* cheap,' he agreed, 'which is why I would never have insulted you by bringing it here. The things from the car were simply the few pieces of any quality and they were a gift from a friend – a friend who originally introduced me to this, er, interest.'

'He must have been a very good friend indeed,' Celia retorted. 'The things Margot took from your car would have a total cost in excess of three thousand pounds.'

'They were more in the way of a long-term loan,' Colin said. His brain was still scrambling feverishly and he wondered if they had questioned Sara yet and, if and when they did, how she would react and what she might tell them. He decided to go for broke.

'Unfortunately,' he went on, 'my friend is no longer with us. He was killed in a tragic boating accident, back at the beginning of this summer, so I have been unable to return the stuff he loaned me. In fact,' he added, 'there were a lot of other things at his private home, so I imagine he must have been a regular client of yours, as it was all of the same high quality. His name was Lachan,' he finished, watching what he could see of her features for any reaction.

'Andrew Lachan?' Colin tried to nod, but the stiff collar made the gesture all but impossible. 'I see,' Celia said and her mouth twisted slightly. 'Yes, I knew him and you're right, he did order a lot of things from us. Might one ask how exactly you knew him?'

'Business, social, you know the way these things go,' Colin said, noncommittally. 'Look, this really is all so unnecessary, I assure you.'

'I think I'll be the judge of what is or isn't necessary,' Celia snapped. 'In the meantime, what about the girl?'

'What *about* her?'

'Where did you meet her, eh? For someone who purports to be a complete beginner at all this, you seem to have been remarkably fortunate in finding such a natural.' Colin hesitated, wondering just how far to go, but realised that the more of the truth he could use, the better it would be. With luck, if they did question Sara, she would catch on to what he was trying to do.

'Look,' he said, 'I'll be perfectly honest with you. Sara – Sassie – used to work for Andy Lachan; in fact, she still works for the company. She wasn't my original pony girl at all and she didn't even know about Andy's interests. However, as you have seen, she seems to have a particular talent and, when she stumbled upon the truth, well – you've seen her. You be the judge. You can ask her yourself, if you don't believe me,' he added, hoping that she wouldn't.

Celia's lips formed into her distinctive, twisted smile. 'I'm sure that Sassie will tell me whatever it was you told her to say beforehand,' she said.

'Why would I tell her anything beforehand?' Colin protested. 'I didn't know you'd recognise those things, did I? Listen, if I'd realised where Andy had bought them from in the first place, I'd have been only too happy to have said as much. But I wasn't going to mention his name without knowing that you already knew about him. OK, so he's dead, but there's such a thing as his memory – and his reputation.'

'I can appreciate discretion,' Celia murmured. 'However, I shall be making further enquiries and I shall certainly question Sassie.'

'OK, fine,' Colin said. 'Make all the enquiries you like, talk to Sassie, whatever. But please, can you let me out of this little lot?'

'Certainly not,' she snapped, the smile becoming more like a grimace. 'We can't have you running around the place loose, not till I'm sure of your pedigree. Besides, it doesn't hurt for a prospective pony master to understand the lot of the pony and I frequently suggest a few hours of role reversal for novices. We don't just train the ponies here, Mr Marshall,' she leered. 'We also train their masters and, as I said, you will become a better master if you understand how it feels to be in harness.'

'You can't be serious!' Colin exclaimed. 'You can't just keep me like this!'

'And why not?' Celia retorted. 'Twenty-four hours should be enough, providing you respond correctly. After that, you can start taking control of your own pony – so long as my enquiries provide satisfactory answers, of course.'

'This is bloody ridiculous!' Colin stormed. He was beginning to get very worried now, originally unable to believe that the woman meant what she was proposing, but rapidly beginning to understand that she did.

'Ridiculous or not, Mr Marshall,' Celia replied, coolly, 'that is exactly how it will be and you are not exactly in a position to argue, are you? Therefore, I suggest that you just lie there quietly and in a while I'll send Margot in to fit your bit. Meantime, I must consider a suitable pony name for you.'

It had not taken Sara very long to realise that something had gone wrong. When the horse box finally lurched to a halt, her three companions in the rear were quickly unfastened and taken out into the darkness, but there was no sign of Margot and no indication that any of the other grooms was about to release her. Instead, she was left for what seemed an age, strapped rigidly to the inside of the van, unable to move anything other than her head.

Fighting down the feeling of panic, she forced herself to breathe slowly, clearing her head and considering the possibilities. Was this a test of her nerve? Were they out there watching, testing her to see how she reacted to being left in such a helpless position?

Had they simply kidnapped her? Was that it? Did Colin really know that she had been moved, or was he even now sitting back there in the huge barn area, happily sipping cocktails or whatever with the Butler woman, completely oblivious to her fate?

But that had to be ridiculous, she told herself. How would they explain her disappearance to him? Or would they simply . . .?

She shook her head, refusing to contemplate any such possibility. People just didn't act in such a way, after all. But then people didn't usually dress other people up as ponies and use a whip on them and neither, in what she had once thought of as the normal world, did people willingly consent to being dressed up and treated in that way anyway.

Damn it, she thought. This was crazy. *She* was crazy. Whatever had possessed her in the first place? She closed her eyes, not wanting to probe that route too deeply. Not that it mattered now: she was here, trapped in the role she had thought would be so exciting, miles from anywhere she knew and totally at the mercy of people who were –

What? What were they? The two policemen seemed to think that all this might have some connection with Andrew's death. It seemed unlikely to Sara, but then finding the stable room had been a complete shock, too. And if there was a connection, how much danger was she now in herself?

Before she had time to consider this line of thought further, the sound of boots on gravel heralded the arrival, finally, of Margot. The tall groom stepped up into the interior and took up a position immediately in front of Sara. However, instead of starting to undo the straps that held her to the body of the vehicle, she reached out, unclipped the bit at either side and wrenched it from Sara's mouth.

'Time for a little chat, pony girl,' she snapped. The crop was still swinging from her wrist and Sara's eyes were drawn to it like magnets. 'For a start, Sassie, I want to know your full name.' Sara opted for playing the innocent, still unsure whether this might not be just another test.

'My name is Sassie, mistress,' she replied, demurely, lowering her eyes. 'You named me Sassie.' Margot's reaction was swift and uncompromising. With one swift lunge, she captured Sara's left nipple between the thumb and forefinger of her right hand and twisted it viciously. Sara let out a shrill screech of pain.

'Don't get fucking smart with me, pony girl,' Margot hissed. 'I meant your real name. Sara what?' Blinking away tears of pain, Sara told her.

'And you worked for a man named Andrew?' Sara drew in as deep a breath as her tightly corseted waist allowed.

How they knew was unimportant, but they clearly knew. She nodded.

'Andrew Lachan, yes,' she whispered. Margot pursed her lips.

'And what was his relationship with your so-called current master?'

'Relationship?' Sara repeated. 'I don't think there was one.'

'According to Mr Marshall there was.' Sara was still furiously trying to think and to gain time.

'My master wouldn't lie,' she said simply, and earned another tweak of her tender flesh for her pains, though this time it was not quite so savage. 'I mean,' she gasped, swallowing hard, 'I think they knew each other, but I'm not certain how well.'

'Well enough, it seems,' Margot retorted. 'And how long did you play pony for this Lachan?' Sara decided to risk the truth, reasoning that they could check certain things anyway.

'I never did,' she replied. 'Master Colin is my first master.' She breathed deeply again. 'I never even knew about him, not until after he was dead.'

'So, how did you come to have Master Colin as your master?'

'It was – it was all a bit confused,' Sara replied. 'He – well, he will tell you himself.' Margot swung the crop around her wrist, catching it deftly in her hand.

'Oh no,' she leered, swishing the braid through the air. 'You're going to tell me, my dear Sassie.'

Sixteen

Alex might have tried to resist, regardless of the consequences and without realising the full horror of what was planned for her, but Higgy entered her new stall accompanied by one of the younger grooms, Sol, and the lad was holding one of the remote-control units, one that was tuned to her particular cyber-electronics. With a smile of triumph, he pointed the device at her and pressed one of the buttons and immediately a numbness flooded throughout Alex's entire body.

She could still stand, but no longer could she move her limbs of her own volition, reduced to the state of a helpless mannequin, as the two grooms set about carrying out Amaarini's instructions.

They began by removing her bridle and harness, then carried her across to the low bunk and laid her on it, stripping off her boots to leave her completely naked. Sol then produced a spray can and began coating her legs with its contents, holding them clear of the thin rubber mattress. Alex, meanwhile, could feel nothing of this, but Higgy was at pains to explain.

'We've got a nice new pony suit for you, Jangles,' he said. 'The stuff it's made of lets your skin breathe, so you can keep it on indefinitely. The stuff Sol is putting on you makes it like it's part of your own flesh – no wrinkles and no little bulges. Very pretty effect, as you'll see.'

And see Alex did, though she would never have used the word pretty to describe the result. Once the stretchy leggings were in place, they hauled her upright once more and Sol continued spraying the rest of her body, the two men easing up the suit in stages, until finally she was sealed in it from neck to toe.

The fabric was almost pure white with just a few small grey and black flecks in it, and the new boots that were now put on to her legs were coloured to match, so that her pale body was in stark contrast to the gleaming black hooves. Only her nipples and crotch remained uncovered now, while her new tail projected through a strategically placed slit and Higgy nodded, approvingly.

'That'll keep you warm, as well,' he said. 'Weather's starting to turn out there now, so you'll be glad of it eventually. Right, harness her up, Sol.'

They replaced the body harness they had taken from her, but Alex was sure that Higgy now tightened the girth even more severely. Her arms were laced back into the restrictive sleeves, her hands strapped back into fists, and then the two limbs were fastened together at her back, forearm to forearm, before the regulation leather pouch was drawn up over them and locked into place.

'Seems a shame to have to do the rest of this,' Higgy muttered. 'But then orders are orders and you ain't the first pony who needed to learn this way.' He began pulling a stretchy hood over the top of her head, drawing the fabric down until it covered her entire face, tucking it into place under the collar of the body suit and smoothing it carefully to remove any ripples.

'For some reason,' he said, tugging at the rubbery mask until the various apertures were in the correct places and the two soft tubes had been inserted into her nostrils, 'I've been told not to use the spray under this one. Maybe she wants to be able to change it without too much bother. There, that's about it.'

Alex stared out at him, the clear plastic lenses over each eye giving a slightly distorted perspective to her vision, air hissing in and out through the nose tubes, sounding horribly loud inside her head. Meanwhile, behind her, Sol was drawing her hair out through a small opening in the crown of the hood, a slow process, but one with which he persevered, until her blonde mane was once more cascading down between her shoulders.

Now, at last, Sol triggered the control, returning sensation and movement to Alex's body, though not the power of speech. Her lips, however, were now sensitive enough to feel the stiffened rim that encircled the mouth opening and the purpose of this quickly became apparent.

Before she could even think of resisting it, Higgy thrust a wide, soft tube into her mouth, a tube that he then locked to the stiff gasket with a simple twisting motion. Had she still possessed the reflex, Alex felt sure she would have gagged on the awful thing, but as it was, she just stood there, jaws distended and mouth completely full.

'There's a tube through the middle for water and liquidised fodder,' Higgy told her, 'but don't worry, it all works automatically. When Her Ladyship wants to feed you, you'll feed, whether you wants to or not.'

'Her Ladyship may decide not to feed the ungrateful little mare!' Both grooms jumped visibly at the sound of Amaarini's voice and Higgy's face was the picture of guilt, but the tall woman seemed more interested in Alex than in his disrespectful reference to herself.

'Well, Jangles,' she said, 'I see you're nearly a complete pony now. Just your pony face to fit and then I have a nice new bridle for you. Get her finished, please Higgy,' she added. 'I fancy a nice little buggy ride before dawn. The air is so much more stimulating during the hours of darkness.'

It had taken Geordie nearly two hours of dedicated Internet surfing, the laptop computer perched on his knees in the confines of the back seat, and he had been on the verge of abandoning his search when he had finally hit on the sort of site he had been looking for.

With a sigh of relief, he began scrolling down the menu of Ordnance Survey maps, first narrowing the field to the appropriate region and then, at the fourth attempt, bringing up the first map that covered the area he wanted. He studied the screen intensely, making mental calculations of time and distance, and eventually concluded that there were a total of nine sectional maps covering the likely area of search.

Ignoring his body's growing demands for more nicotine, he methodically brought up each map in turn and downloaded it to the hard drive, then disconnected the phone link and sat back to stretch his cramped knees. The engine was still running, providing electrical power to the computer's ailing batteries, and he said a mental thank-you to whatever force had prompted him to top up the fuel tank earlier in the day. Even so, the tank had dropped to a little over half full and he knew he would be faced with the necessity to fill it again before too long.

Even without a close study, it was already obvious that the search could be a lengthy one and, a further hour on, he now had a list of more than twenty possible sites and the ninth map still to evaluate in detail.

'Probably a waste of time anyway,' he muttered to himself, reaching into the glove compartment for a fresh packet of cigarettes. Outside, beneath the driver's window, the ridged mud of the gateway approach was already littered with butts.

'If I do manage to find the right place,' he told the computer screen, 'they'll probably have left and gone back again anyway. I should have stayed put and waited.'

But, whether it was just natural curiosity, or perhaps some deep-rooted instinct, a little voice kept telling him that he had made the right choice. Now, all he had to do was find the right place.

'He's some sort of policeman,' Margot said. She slipped the loop off her wrist and tossed the crop on to the coffee table. 'The girl *is* an employee of Lachan's company – she was his personal assistant for several years – and she certainly never knew anything about his interests outside of work, but she definitely is raw.

'Apparently, Marshall's colleague – his real name is Turner, by the way – went up to Lachan's place in

Scotland and started poking around. Lachan had been putting together some sort of stable, though she doesn't know who for. Apparently the stall was in some sort of secret room.

'Anyway, little Sassie seems to have got a bit turned on by the thought of being someone's pony and, when friend Turner wanted a volunteer to come with him for this weekend, she practically jumped at the chance.'

'But what would the police want with our operation?' Celia demanded. She had been pacing up and down, the sound of her needle-sharp heels muffled by the thick carpet. 'Or is there something else?'

'It's not us,' Margot assured her. 'Not directly, anyway. It would seem that Turner has been investigating the circumstances of Lachan's death. The girl wasn't too clear on the finer points, but apparently he's attached to some sort of department that keeps an eye on the rich and powerful and there was something about the way Lachan's boat blew up that his bosses weren't happy with.'

'And somehow,' Celia mused, pausing in her stride, 'they've discovered that Lachan bought stuff from us? So why not? No . . .' She paused, stroking her chin. 'No, they wouldn't just come in and be up front with us, would they?'

'Not if they thought that anything to do with Lachan's death might be linked to us, no,' Margot agreed. 'Well, we both know that whatever happened to Lachan has got bugger all to do with either of us, or this place.'

'Of course it hasn't,' Celia said. 'If Lachan's death was anything but an accident, I doubt it had anything to do with anything other than his business. The police could go through this place, the farm and even the flat in Chelsea and they'd find nothing we aren't already advertising quite openly in certain quarters.'

'So, do we just tell him that, Turner I mean, and throw the pair of them out?'

'Not just yet,' Celia said. 'For a start, there's the girl.' She nodded down at the crop on the table. 'How energetically did you use that on her?' Margot shrugged.

166

'Only as much as I had to,' she said. 'She's got a few stripes on her backside, under the suit, I should think, but nothing that will be showing in a day or so.'

'And where is she now?'

'In a nice safe stall, in C block,' Margot replied. 'I gave her a shot of mild tranquilliser and left her to sleep. What about Turner?'

'Downstairs in the cellar,' Celia said. 'He's safe enough for the moment, but we have to work out what to do with the pair of them.'

'There's not much we *can* do with them, surely.'

'Well, we certainly can't do anything that would harm them,' Celia agreed. 'However, we could keep them here long enough to convince Turner that we aren't the sort of people to get mixed up in suspicious deaths – and, at the same time, we could gather ourselves a little insurance.'

'Insurance?'

Celia nodded, smiling to herself. 'We don't know much about our Mr Turner, of course,' she mused, 'but my guess would be that, if he's a policeman, he wouldn't take too well to his colleagues seeing him as he is now. A few photographs, a little video recording or two – that should do to keep him from being too eager to bring our names into it.

'I think we'll keep them both for a few days' intensive training and then present them with a souvenir record of their stay, don't you? You can handle him and I'll take the girl. There's something about dear Sassie that I find most appealing.'

Margot smiled back at her. 'Sometimes, Mother,' she said, 'I wonder how you ever had me!'

Logic dictated the order in which to investigate the likely sites to which Celia might have taken Colin and Sara, and Geordie passed a further hour of darkness, using the small flashlight to make notes and plot a route that would save the optimum amount of time.

He decided against remaining in the gateway until dawn – most farmers were up and working at such unearthly hours and he didn't want to attract any unnecessary

167

attention just yet, in case his quarry was closer than he thought. He checked the fuel gauge, flicked on the headlights and turned around, heading steadily back the way he had come.

He drove for six miles before coming to the small service station he remembered passing during the evening pursuit, and cursed again when he saw that it was not twenty-four-hour. He pulled on to the deserted forecourt, consulted his road atlas and came to a decision.

With some two gallons, plus the reserve in the tank, he could easily make it across to the motorway, from where it was a matter of some ten miles to where the map indicated a proper service station. He checked his watch: that would take maybe forty-five minutes, a hot snack and fresh coffee another half an hour and there would still be three hours before first light, plenty of time to take a nap on the back seat and start heading back before dawn, and still probably an hour or more before this godforsaken little place reopened.

At daylight, he would begin his search, stomach and tank replenished, fresh coffee in his flask and an additional two packets of cigarettes to support his already dwindling reserves. He reached out with his left hand, flipped the radio into life and changed station until he found one that was playing a well-known soft-rock track.

'Tally-ho!' he chuckled to himself, thrusting the gear lever into first, and then, as the car moved forward and he turned back on to the deserted road, he laughed out loud. 'Giddy-up, Neddy!' he cried and accelerated away in a screech of tortured rubber. Colin, he thought, would have been proud of him.

The stall was far smaller than the one Andrew Lachan had been preparing for his unknown pony girl in the Highlands and Sara felt almost claustrophobic when Margot finally closed the door on her, leaving just the dim ceiling lamp for illumination.

She had thought of struggling when Margot freed her arms to fit them into the tight leather pouch behind her back, but the groom was very powerful and the threat of the whip remained constant, the braided crop ever swinging from the tall woman's wrist. The opportunity for resistance was quickly gone and now, with a short chain tethering her high collar to a shoulder-high hook in the wall, Sara was again completely helpless.

Her initial panic subsided slowly and with its demise came a new feeling, akin to the sensations she had experienced while running out on the moor that first evening, yet more acute now, for the illusion was more than that. Then she had simply imagined herself totally in the power of another, whereas now, until they decided otherwise, she was forced to remain as a pony girl, the bit between her distended lips a constant reminder of that fact.

The neck chain was too short – probably deliberately so, Sara guessed – to allow her to sit, let alone lie on the straw, but she managed to prop herself against the corner walls, taking at least some of the strain off her tortured feet. Sleep was impossible, but she did, eventually, drift into a semiconscious reverie, in which images of a girl came flitting in and out of her imagination.

The girl was blonde, but her hair was unlike any Sara had ever seen on a human head before, continuing to sprout from her neck and from between her shoulder blades, so that it billowed behind her as she ran, almost blending with the magnificent tail that sprouted from between the cleft in her magnificent buttocks.

Her eyes were wide and her nostrils flared, as she loped easily over the undulating ground, the small cart bouncing along behind her, the faceless driver standing, hauling on her reins and cracking his long whip above her head as he urged her to even greater efforts.

'Yes, I think you could become quite sensational, Sassie.' The sound of Celia Butler's cultured voice jerked Sara back to the present and the reality of the cramped stable room. Her eyes flew open and she began to blush, wondering if the moaning sounds had been made out loud, or had merely been part of her vision.

Celia was dressed even more exotically than Sara herself, the studded and sequinned mask and headdress topped with a luxuriant plume of red and black feathers, the tight corset emphasising the swell of her hips in the jodhpurs and the swell of her magnificent breasts inside the straining white kid shirt. Sara peered at her from beneath the heavy curtain of the false eyelashes Margot had glued over her own.

'But I hear you've been a very naughty filly,' Celia continued. She stepped inside the stall and moved closer, until she stood only a foot or so from where Sara was chained. 'Margot has told me all about it and I have spoken severely to the man who called himself your master.' Her lips curled into a sneering smile.

'Master indeed!' she snapped. 'A bumbling amateur. I doubt he'd have appreciated what he might have had with you.' She reached out with one gloved hand and gently hefted Sara's left breast, as if weighing it. 'Of course, by the time he leaves here, he'll know more about pony training than he ever bargained for, but I still doubt he'll ever deserve a magnificent pedigree like you, Sassie.

'Does he know how much this excites you, eh?' she asked. The gleaming eyes, peering through the almond-shaped apertures in her mask, seemed suddenly to soften. 'Does he know, Sassie?' she repeated. 'Or haven't you even been able to admit it to yourself yet?' Sara continued to regard her impassively, trying not even to blink, but Celia had only just begun and there was something about the way she spoke that seemed to be reaching down into Sara's very soul.

'It's true, isn't it?' Celia went on. 'Somehow you know you were meant for the harness, don't you? What did it feel like the first time, my pretty filly, eh? What does it feel like now? Yes, I can see that it excites you to be so powerless, to be so much in the hands of others. See, these show the truth that your face tries to hide.' Gently, she began to rub Sara's engorged nipples with her thumbs and then suddenly, without warning, bent forward and kissed each one in turn, drawing the hardened cone into her mouth each time and sucking gently upon it.

'Beautiful,' she breathed, standing upright again. 'Perhaps we should have them properly pierced and ringed before we send you back. Would you like that, Sassie? Permanent rings with my brand tags on them? Would you like to be my very own little pony, you sweet thing?' One hand went down and pressed against the crotch strap, pressing deeper the dildo it held in place, persisting with the pressure until Sara could no longer stand it.

She closed her eyes with a groan and shuddered, her muscles stiffening. Immediately, the hand was removed.

'You don't even need a man,' Celia whispered. 'None of us do. You can have the cock all day long, as you have now, a cock that never fails to gratify, never betrays you and never, never wanders. Do you like your cock, Sassie?' She pressed against the strap again and, helplessly, Sara nodded, though she continued to keep her eyes firmly closed. She felt Celia's warm breath upon her cheek.

'My little pony,' she whispered. 'Only not so little, eh, Sassie? Oh, but these are magnificent specimens.' She stepped back again and this time weighed both Sara's breasts, one upon each palm. 'I can't wait to see these bouncing along.' She released the two globes and flicked at the nipple bells with her forefingers. Sara shuddered again at the sound and slowly opened her eyes. The masked face was impassive now.

'I think you will enjoy being my pony, Sassie,' Celia said. Automatically, Sara felt herself nodding, telling herself it was the only thing she could do under the circumstances, yet knowing that she might have done so even if there had been an alternative. 'We shall see, though,' Celia continued, 'whether you have what it takes.'

She stepped forward, unclipped the tether chain from Sara's collar, then followed this by unlocking and withdrawing her bit. She raised one cautionary finger and made a soft, shushing noise.

'No talking,' she warned. 'Ponies never talk and they have tongues and mouths for only one purpose. Kneel, pony girl.' With great difficulty, Sara managed to drop to her knees and would have toppled forward had Celia not been expecting this and put out her hands to steady her shoulders. Sara winced as the tight leather of the boots dug

171

into the backs of her knees and knew she would be unable to rise again unaided.

Level with her eyes, Celia was fumbling at the crotch of her jodhpurs, fingers pulling at fastenings, until she was able to draw apart the soft white kid, revealing when she did her shaven and swollen sex, the deeper pink slit already glistening with anticipation.

'Come, my little pony,' she whispered, one hand grasping at the top of the bridle harness and drawing Sara's face closer, so that she could smell the deep musk and almost taste the bittersweet juices. 'Come lap at my trough, little Sassie, and show your mistress what an obedient pony slut you are.'

Seventeen

Not even in her worst nightmares could Alex have anticipated what Amaarini meant when she referred to her 'pony face' and, even when they showed her in the long mirror, she could still scarcely believe what they had done to her, for her features now bore no human resemblance and the face and head that now confronted her were most unmistakably equine. As the horrendous contraption was fitted to her, Alex gathered from their conversation that she was not the first errant pony girl to wear one of these punishment devices, but the knowledge hardly consoled her as she fought back the waves of claustrophobia that swept over her.

At last, as the straps and laces were adjusted and the eye holes settled in line with the perspex lenses on the inner helmet, Alex began to regain some measure of self-control, though it was, she realised sourly, the only control she now retained and, with her own head imprisoned in the long-nosed horse head, she could not even communicate with facial expressions. Worse still, the layers over her ears were badly affecting her hearing and everything about her sounded fuzzy and indistinct.

It took Higgy a few minutes to complete the task of connecting the open mouth to the tube in her own mouth, after which came the final fitting of her new bridle, similar to her original one, excepting that the straps were aligned to the new contours, and the bit, which fitted inside the gaping mouth and over the lolling, rubber tongue, had no direct contact with her own mouth.

However, either the original designer of the head, or perhaps Amaarini herself, more recently, had overcome the problem of the driver needing a method of conveying his or her instructions, by the simple expedient of continuing the reins through rings on either end of the bit and running them downwards to connect with the rings in Alex's nipples.

Now, a simple tug meant that she either turned her head in the direction indicated, or else her nipple and entire breast would be painfully distended, the pain surmounting even her heightened tolerance of it.

'Well, pony face,' Amaarini sneered, 'you've got your new tail and now you've got your new head and that's the way you'll stay until I'm satisfied you've learned your lessons.' Her voice boomed inside Alex's head and she realised that the thick padding over her ears must contain speakers. Peering through the twin layers of lenses, she saw the small microphone that rose from a clip on Amaarini's tunic.

'And meantime, unless I say otherwise, the only voice you will hear will be mine. The grooms will tend to your basic needs, but you will no longer be exercised by anyone but myself. Before long, dear little Jangles, the only world you know will be me.

'Now, time flies, as ever, and I have a nice new buggy for you to draw. The technicians have only just finished assembling it and I am eager to try the new features it incorporates.'

There was nothing else to do but wait. Houdini himself would have been hard-pressed to escape from his situation, Colin reflected, grimly. Celia Butler's assertions about the quality of her merchandise were not overstated in any way: everything about the pony harnesses spoke of attention to detail – and durability.

The long sleeves into which his arms had been laced would have left little enough scope for flexibility of the elbows, even without the additional links that held them to the sides of the excruciatingly tight girth, so that the collar

174

and chain that were designed to keep him from sitting upright were very nearly superfluous. Rising from his current horizontal position would have required a great deal of strength, balance and determination and even had he managed that, Colin realised, he could not have hoped to get too far very quickly.

His legs had been left free, but that freedom was only relative. True, there were no shackles or straps to secure them to the divan, but the long boots had been laced on as tightly as the arm sheaths, so that bending the knees was all but impossible and, when he tried raising his feet from the thin mattress, he quickly appreciated the near unbelievable weight of the hoof-shaped soles – or, rather, he didn't.

And it was not just the weights in those soles that would hamper any attempt at escape. Incredibly, the insides of the boots had been sculpted in precisely the same fashion as those he had seen on the girls, elevating the heel in the manner of a vampish stiletto shoe, so that, when he finally was allowed to stand upright, he would be poised on near tiptoe. He would not, Colin thought, make a very elegant pony!

Behind his head, he heard the door open once again and he waited for Celia to walk around in front of him. However, the figure that came into his restricted field of vision was not Celia, but Margot, and the expression on her face did not bode well. For a few seconds she simply stood looking down at him and then, with a movement too practised and swift for Colin to react, she swivelled the dangling crop into her grasp and brought it hissing downwards.

It exploded on the mattress, millimetres from Colin's hip, with a loud report that made him gasp and jump. Margot simply smiled, but it was not a pleasant smile.

'Scared, Mr Turner?' The smile widened and became, if it were possible, even more malicious. 'Oh yes,' she said, detecting the telltale reaction in his eyes, 'we know all about you now. Well, maybe not *all* about you, but enough for now. Dear little Sassie was only too eager to talk, once I'd demonstrated the alternatives.'

175

'Where is Sara now?' Colin demanded. 'What have you done to her?' Margot leaned over him, moving her face closer to his.

'To be perfectly frank, Mr Turner,' she purred, 'I haven't really done anything I wouldn't have done anyway. You supposedly brought her here for training, so I just started that with a slightly firmer hand than usual, you might say. Oh, don't worry,' she continued, 'she hasn't come to any great harm. Nor will she, so long as we all finally come to an understanding.'

'What sort of understanding?'

'The sort of understanding that leaves us free of further police harassment,' Margot said, straightening up once more. 'Whatever you might have thought to the contrary, Andrew Lachan's death had nothing to do with any of us. You need to understand, Mr Turner, that in our particular field of expertise, we ask little of our clients – guests, my mother prefers to call them – other than their ability to pay.

'You may not believe me, but I can assure you that I knew very little of Lachan's business, nor his background. My mother – that's Celia, in case you hadn't realised – knew him a little better, but even she confined her dealings with him to just the one specialised field.

'If there was something to his death, it is not our concern and neither would it have been linked to us in any way.'

'If what you say is true,' Colin said, keeping his tone reasonable, 'then all this is totally unnecessary and can only serve to bring you trouble you don't need. However, if you release me now and are prepared to answer a few questions, I'd be prepared to overlook what's happened – put it down to a sort of misunderstanding, as it were.'

The crop slashed down again, landing even closer than before, and Colin flinched. Margot merely laughed at his discomfiture.

'Oh no, Mr Turner,' she said. 'We need better assurances than that. As for questions, well, I shall be the one doing the asking. You came here for training, though perhaps not of the sort I have in mind for you.

'Oh, you won't come to any real harm either,' she said, nonchalantly. 'Nothing that won't fade long before the memories of this weekend do, to say nothing of the photographs.' She flexed the crop between her hands.

'By the time you do leave here,' she continued, 'you will know exactly how a pony boy or girl is expected to behave. I intend to give you the benefit of my great experience for the most intensive few days' training possible, at the end of which you will be presented with a comprehensive video and photographic record of your stay here.

'Who else that record is presented to will depend upon you.' She leaned closer again. 'And who knows,' she added, her voice a hoarse whisper, 'you may even decide to come back for more.'

'Don't hold your breath,' Colin grated. 'I'm not that sick.' Margot extended the crop, flicking the tip against his leather-sheathed erection. Colin winced, willing the thing to subside, but it had remained steadfastly rigid ever since he had awakened here.

'You may surprise yourself,' Margot said. 'And you wouldn't be the first. A few days with this thing stood up like a flagpole and no relief for it and you'll be begging me.' Colin tried to ignore this remark, but it wasn't easy, for her words seemed to confirm a suspicion that had been forming in his mind. Apart from the knockout drug, it seemed almost certain that they had introduced some other chemical into his system: nothing else he could think of could have accounted for his persistent arousal.

'Where's Sara now?' he demanded. Still she smiled.

'Oh, little Sassie is in safe hands,' she said. 'It would appear my mother has taken quite a shine to her. She, too, may get more out of this weekend than she bargained for. Now, I have to go and prepare your stall, Plodder.' She started moving towards the door as she spoke, but paused to flick his chest with the crop.

'That will be your name from now on,' she said. 'Plodder the plod. Yes, I think you'll make a good Plodder. Nothing racy or stylish, but you seem to have been built for stamina. A good workhorse, Plodder, that's what you are and, by God, I'm going to make you work!'

Alex had been taken out throughout the night before, for the grooms frequently exercised any pony girl who had not been recently run in the hours before dawn, but never before had she felt as wretched as she did now.

The pony suit did keep the chill air at bay, it was true, but the head was heavy and cumbersome and even the new collar that Amaarini fitted around her neck did little to alleviate the discomfort it caused.

Amaarini, if she appreciated this, showed no sign of sympathy: on the contrary, she seemed determined to honour the promise she had made earlier, whipping Alex on to greater and greater efforts, forcing her to run at such a pace that even the headlights, one of the new features on her buggy of which she had boasted, seemed woefully inadequate insurance against Alex's stumbling over some unseen obstacle.

At last, as the first grey fingers of the new day began to appear in the east, Amaarini hauled back on the reins, eliciting a muffled squeal from Alex, while at the same time her booming command to halt slammed painfully through Alex's reeling head. Behind her, Alex felt the weight of the cart shift as Amaarini stepped down, and a moment later her shadowy, distorted outline came into the narrow field of vision between the blinkers.

'Well, you're fit enough, Jangles,' she sneered, 'and you seem to be getting the idea. Shame that we've had to take such extreme measures with you, but I'm confident we shan't have to do it again. A month like this and you won't be in a hurry to repeat the experience.'

Alex stared out at her, horrified. A month! The woman could not be serious. Even these two hours – if indeed it had been that long – had seemed to last for ever and the prospect of remaining in the anonymous pony outfit for one minute longer than necessary appalled her. Amaarini stretched out a hand and patted the side of Alex's inanimate muzzle.

'You didn't think this would just be for a day or two, did you?' she taunted. 'Not after the insubordination you displayed. No, you are far too wilful, far too proud. I suppose it's the training you had in your old job, but we've dealt with worse.' She seized one of the loose reins and jerked Alex's nipple cruelly.

'You'll be only too glad to get back to the way you were,' she said, 'and I don't mean playing policewoman, either. No, you'll never be anything but a pony girl from now on. It just depends on whether you want to stay as a horse face, or not.

'From now on, Jangles, everything you do will be reported to me and every show of dissent will earn you an additional day like this, as well as a sound thrashing. And it doesn't worry me how long you take to learn, either. I have all the time in the world.' She stroked the head between the widely spaced eyes.

'Now,' she said, turning her head towards the approaching day, 'the dawn is upon us and I have other duties to attend to, but then so do you. We'll just take a nice brisk canter back to the stables and you can thank Higgy properly for all the trouble he's taken over your splendid new appearance.'

Alone in her inner sanctum, Jessie sat staring at the television screen, although she paid little attention to the programme it was showing. She could not concentrate and the things her new stablemate had said to her refused to go away.

Everything Jessie had come to accept and believe in told her that Jangles was wrong. After all, these people had given them all new life and had cared for them ever since, so it was surely only right that she should repay that debt in the only way possible. It wasn't even as though she had been asked to do anything she hadn't enjoyed, especially during the time she had been Master Andrew's personal favourite, but Master Andrew was gone now and, in his place, there was a mirror image of herself, the reluctant and surly Bambi.

Amaarini had told her – delighted in telling her – that Bambi had once been Master Andrew, but how was that possible? Master Andrew had been strong, powerful, and he had promised her a life even better than this, so why would he turn himself into a reflection of herself?

Once, things had been clear for Jessie, but now there were too many confusions, too many contradictions. Jangles – Alex, as she insisted her name was – was unlike any of the other stable inmates. Alex was bitter, angry, determined. Everyone knew there was no way off the island and none of the other girls even considered escape as an option, but Alex . . . Alex had made up her mind and Alex had said so many hurtful things to her.

Alex had told her that she was a glorified whore and Jessie knew that was not right. She rose, her harness jingling softly as she moved across the small room, scooping up the television control between her useless hands, pressing the red 'off' button with her nose and dropping the device into the small easy chair.

Her heart ached for Master Andrew. Things had been so much easier with him. He had explained everything so simply and Jessie had known, beyond doubt, that she was his and that he had loved her deeply. But now he was gone – where, she knew not, but Amaarini had told her that he would never return. Jessie wanted to cry, but she had not been able to cry for so many years.

And, unable to cry, Jessie turned her thoughts full circle.

They had taken him from her. She had no idea how, nor why, but Alex was right – they, *they,* had taken her beloved master from her and reduced her once again to the status of general pony girl, pawed at, whipped, mistreated, insulted and by creatures who were not fit to lace the boots of the man she had worshipped.

And, in that moment, Jessie came to a decision. She was not sure why, any more than she was any longer sure of anything, but a small voice from within would not let her rest. She had, she was only too well aware, already lived far beyond a reasonable span and even further beyond the time that the bomb would have left her, and so, she reasoned, life now owed her nothing.

There was still a good deal of thinking to do, she knew, but the important things were now clear in her mind. Without Master Andrew, she no longer cared whether she lived or died. There would never be another like him and her daily routine now served only to emphasise that point.

She had, she realised now, reached the end.

And she would, she resolved, do whatever was necessary to help her stablemate, Alex.

If ever the opportunity arose.

Eighteen

The search was taking even longer than Geordie had feared, roads that were shown on even the computer map almost disappearing at times and at best little more than dirt tracks for the most part.

On a crest above the fourth possible site, he switched off the engine, reached for the thermos flask and poured himself a cup of coffee. Like the first three possibilities, this was another dead end: just a simple, two-storey stone cottage, a couple of small shed buildings and a greenhouse with several broken panes – nowhere to hide two horse boxes and a couple of large Range Rovers – and the only sign of life, during the ten minutes he had been watching the place, a small child and a rather scruffy mongrel dog.

Visiting all the prospective targets was going to take all day at this rate and only then if he was lucky, but there was no other option than to just keep going, ticking the places off, one after the other. He told himself he was probably only being paranoid anyway and that they could all, by now, be back at Celia's original address, but somehow he knew that wasn't the case.

Colin and Sara's visit had been planned as a weekend-long affair, so, wherever they had been taken, it was logical that was where they would remain for the duration. And they'd probably be quite all right there. Colin was an experienced officer and very resourceful, and Sara . . .

Well, Geordie mused, unless he was no judge at all, Sara was very likely to be enjoying every minute of her 'enforced' stay. If the way she had reacted in Scotland and again in her hotel room was anything to go by, then by now she was probably at boiling point. Geordie had barely recognised her during the few seconds between her being led from the stables and loaded into the horse box.

Even with the powerful night glasses, the figure that the woman had led across the yard bore very little resemblance even to the pony-girl version of Sara he had seen twice before. The grey-green picture had not done their efforts justice, but even so, Geordie could see that someone had gone to a lot of trouble with her exotic make-up, turning her into something that he suspected she would really relish being . . .

Sara's head was beginning to spin. Lack of sleep and food, combined with Celia's continued ministrations, had left her weak and exhausted, so that she could now barely stand in the steepling hoof boots. Celia, however, seemed inexhaustible and now she had even more strenuous intentions towards her victim.

'You are a very pretty pony indeed,' she said, securing Sara's bit once again, 'but you are obviously nowhere near fit enough. Therefore,' she continued, taking up the slack in the loose reins and wrapping it around her fist, 'we must see to it that you get the proper exercise.

'As a general view, Margot would see to it that your master put you through your paces, under her strict guidance of course, but the circumstances here are just a little different from usual, aren't they, my pet?' She patted Sara's cheek and turned to lead her out into the yard.

'Your so-called master has enough to worry about, without you,' she continued, as Sara stumbled awkwardly in her wake, 'and Margot has her hands full enough with him, so I shall be delighted to continue your training myself.'

Sara barely heard her, nor was she really aware of being hitched up to the shafts of the little buggy cart. The dildo was now back inside her and every movement made its presence all the more insistent, the carefully sculpted nodes doing the work for which they had been designed, so that Sara found herself teetering on the verge of orgasm, despite her zombie-like state. Vaguely, she knew that the moment she started to run, or even to trot, her body would surrender again, her willpower swept aside, as it had been so many times already.

But that, as Celia had told her, was what being a pony girl was all about, surely. A pony girl existed only to serve her master or mistress, to work, to please and, if she was obedient, to be pleasured as and when her master or mistress decided. A pony girl had no mind of her own, no self-determination, no choice and, in surrendering herself to the harness, Sara had become Sassie and thus surrendered the individuality that only a human could possess.

Celia moved around in front of her and began fondling her breasts, pinching gently at her nipples and smiling at her facial contortions and the tiny gasps of desire that forced their way past the bit gag.

'Poor Sassie,' she crooned. 'so, so confused and hot, but so willing and beautiful. You deserve a mistress who will appreciate your qualities, not a ham-fisted master who will work you into the ground and then just use you as a simple pleasure receptacle.

'I think I should like to make you mine, little Sassie,' she sighed and stretched forward and planted a tiny kiss on the tip of Sara's nose. Sara stared back at her, through glazed eyes, unable to believe that she could respond like this to and with another woman, a tiny part of her brain trying to tell her that it was wrong, yet every tactile sense and response screaming the lie to this. She felt a bead of saliva begin to trickle down on to her chin, but she no longer even felt embarrassment at this helpless, animal response.

How could she, that other voice kept saying. There was no blame, no shame. Her mistress would care for her and her mistress would make all the decisions. She was Sassie, harnessed and bitted, mute and mutant, a creature of pleasure – a creature of nature. She felt Celia climbing up into the seat behind her and gave a tiny yelp as the very tip of her driving whip flicked across her unprotected rump.

'Hup now!' Celia called, shaking out the traces. 'Walk on, girl. Walk on.'

'Whoa there, horse face!' Amaarini jerked savagely back on the reins. The bit in Alex's artificial mouth jammed in the rubber jaws, but the thin leather lines snatched viciously at her ringed nipples, eliciting a high-pitched whinny of pain. Alex felt the cart behind her lurch and, a moment later, Amaarini appeared in front of her.

'I imagine you're beginning to regret your attitude now, pony,' she sneered. 'If you could talk, I expect you would be ready to beg for clemency, but of course you cannot talk, can you? Of course not. Everyone knows that ponies can't talk.'

They had stopped just outside the entrance to the underground stables complex and the sun was just beginning to climb above the horizon, but the air remained crisp and Alex's breath came in clouds of vapour, adding, she realised, miserably, to the effect Amaarini had striven so hard to achieve.

'Well,' Amaarini said, sourly, 'I have work to attend to, so I shall have to leave you for the moment. I have promised your services to Higgy, not that he would usually bother waiting for my permission anyway, but he is also somewhat busy for the next hour or so.' She moved back alongside Alex and began unhitching her girth from the shafts of the cart.

'Therefore,' she continued, 'I have arranged for something that will both keep you out of trouble meantime, and teach you a valuable lesson.' She reached up, seized Alex's bridle and spitefully jerked her head around. 'There,' she said, pointing. 'Just the thing for a pony slut.' She stooped down and quickly unbuckled the crotch strap that ran between Alex's thighs, pulling it aside and withdrawing the rubber plug that had been worrying at her for the past two hours.

Alex peered through the double lenses, trying to focus on the object of Amaarini's attention. It appeared to resemble a small vaulting horse and it had been placed on

185

the grass a few feet to one side of the entrance. Built of rough timber, the narrow top had been padded with leather and from its centre rose a huge, curving phallus, gleaming darkly against the low sunlight, its height and girth dwarfing the dildo that Amaarini had just taken from her.

'Now,' Amaarini said, her tone dripping malice, 'let's see how eager you are to minimise your punishment.' She nodded towards the waiting structure. 'You can work out what to do, I'm sure,' she said, starting to laugh. Alex hesitated, staring at the huge shaft.

'Go on, horse face!' Amaarini urged her and slapped her hard across the buttocks to emphasise the order. 'Get your sluttish legs spread and squat on that! It's about all you're worth at the moment.'

With a groan of resignation, Alex began to move forward. To impale herself upon this fearsome weapon was an awful prospect, but the alternatives, she knew, would be far worse. Besides, she reasoned, they had already brought her so low, what did one more humiliation count for? She shuffled across to the end of the block, splaying her stride so that she could straddle it, but, as she did so, she realised that the gruesome head and the stiff neck collar prevented her from seeing her intended target.

Instead, she was forced to lower herself gradually, waiting until she felt the cold tip of the hard rubber pressing against the opening in her pony suit and then, to her shame and chagrin, she had to start wriggling her hips, rotating her pelvis, blindly seeking the correct position. She made several hopeless attempts, each one drawing a loud guffaw from the watching Amaarini, and then, as she was beginning to think that the challenge was impossible, suddenly the conical tip slipped into position, prising apart her warm entrance and nestling, waiting, threatening.

Desperate to succeed now, Alex uttered a wail of surrender and let her weight drop down, squealing in a mixture of horror and unexpected lust as the thick member thrust up into her. And, as she settled her weight on to the padded surface, the now familiar shock waves began to detonate once more. Without thinking, she began to raise and lower herself, but Amaarini had other plans for her.

'Stop that, you little animal!' she roared and her crop scythed through the air, slashing across Alex's shoulders. Alex howled in pain and anger. 'Settle yourself, you stupid pony. This isn't for your benefit, it's for your education!'

She stepped up alongside Alex, stooped and seized her left ankle, dragging it up and back and forcing her to bend her booted knee painfully. From the side of the box structure hung a thin strap and, a moment later, it had been employed to secure the limb so that Alex's heavy hoof hung several inches clear of the ground. Moving quickly around to the other side of her, she repeated the operation on Alex's right ankle and then stepped back, nodding with evident satisfaction.

'Well, you can pleasure yourself all you want now, pony girl,' she leered. 'Get yourself nice and ready for Higgy, whenever he finally gets around to you. That's about all you're good for now, isn't it?' She bent closer, hissing like a snake.

'Maybe you'll learn from this, you worthless little bitch,' she said. 'And maybe you'll realise that it doesn't matter what you once were, out in that world out there. Here, you're nothing but a slave, a commodity. Without us, you'd be even worse off. No one asked you to come poking around here, but then that's what you and your kind are all about.

'You're all worthless, the whole lot of you. Call yourselves civilised? You don't understand the meaning of the word. Sit there, horse face, like the animal you are and enjoy your thoughts. Give yourself what pleasure you can and wait for that oaf, Higgy. He's little better than you are, if the truth be told, but at least he appreciates when he's well off. So will you, eventually, dear little Jangles.' She straightened up and stood back, towering over Alex.

'Yes.' She nodded. 'So will you.' She turned and headed towards the entrance to the stables and, just before she closed down the radio link to the speakers over Alex's ears, she loosed off one parting shot.

'Animal whore!'

Alex closed her eyes once more and fought against the instincts that were threatening to prove her insult to be the truth.

Nineteen

Geordie leaned against the side of the car, cigarette dangling from his mouth, and carefully crossed off the next address on his list. This one made number ten and still no sign. He peered through the gap in the hedge, only half listening to the raucous beat that was coming from the huge transistor radio that was perched atop the cab of the tractor, watching the hunched back of the muscular youth who was currently engrossed under its raised bonnet.

Another working farm, albeit one where the work involved probably raised barely a subsistence living, but then that was the way things were going these past few years. The days of the small farm were numbered, and the numbers, Geordie reflected, were not high. He sighed, tucked the notebook into his jacket pocket, and eased himself back behind the wheel.

Colin had long since passed the stage of embarrassment. The permanent erection and his near nakedness paled into insignificance when compared with Margot and her whip, for the statuesque young woman seemed to take great delight in employing the lash at the slightest provocation.

Harnessed tightly between the shafts of a curious-looking cart, bent almost double by the tight straps and chains, he had been forced to run – if the shambling, awkward gait could be called running – for he knew not how long now, with Margot perched behind him on the high driver's seat, shouting encouragement that she reinforced with a liberal and energetic application of the lash.

'Run, Plodder, you lazy beast!' seemed to be her war cry. 'Pick up those hooves, you useless bloody animal! Hup! Hup!'

And then she had hauled him to a halt, jumping down and coming around to twist his head sideways, her fist wrapped around his bridle, her face glowing with a mixture of excitement and cruelty. With her other hand, she reached under him, grasping his leather-sheathed erection, and laughed, close to his ear.

'Won't go down, will it, Plodder?' she taunted him. 'Know why? 'Cause mumsie hates men and she's given you a little something to keep your little cockie nice and hard. Drives you wild, doesn't it, little man? Want to put it somewhere nice and warm, don't you? Eh?

'Well, even that won't help you, 'cause you won't even be able to come. Oh, you'll want to and you'll even think you're about to, but it won't happen,' she chuckled, gleefully. 'Don't believe me? OK, let's show you, shall we?' And she proceeded to release Colin from the shafts, though not from the rest of the bondage that kept him so helpless. She swished the crop across his buttocks and even the rubber skin did not lessen the searing band of fire that exploded within them. He leaped forward, even the bit unable to stifle his howl of anguish.

Margot waved the crop menacingly and pointed it towards the muddy ground.

'Get on the floor, Plodder!' she snarled. 'Go on, you animal. Get down there, on your back!' With his arms trussed uselessly behind him, Colin struggled to obey, dropping first to his knees, then on to his side and, finally, rolling over to stare up at her. She stalked over, standing astride his prone body, the tip of the crop flicking at the leather tube that held his masculinity.

'Hopeless,' she sighed. 'Totally hopeless – and you thought you could be a master.' She crouched over him and he shivered, knowing he was helpless to resist, terrified of her, yet at the same time stunned by the power of her beauty.

'And now,' she said, laying the crop aside and concentrating on the laces that secured the sheath, 'it's time for a small lesson in humility. My dear mother prefers softer flesh, whereas I appreciate the firmer approach. And this,' she said, drawing the leather sleeve clear and discarding it carelessly, 'is about as firm as flesh gets.'

Her gloved fingers closed about his shaft and he moaned as she drew down the flesh, exposing the distended purple crown and squeezing firmly, so that the already tortured flesh became translucent, the blue-black veins rising to the surface in a throbbing web.

'One of us,' she said, her free hand pulling at the crotch of her breeches, 'is going to enjoy this.' She eased herself forward, her warm, wet orifice descending upon his trapped penis like a starving hyena. It gaped, yawed and in an instant was devouring its prey. With a grunt of satisfaction, Margot let her weight drop, her full buttocks smacking against the taut flesh of his upper thighs. She leaned over, stared into his eyes and grinned.

'Fuck you, Plodder!' she breathed. 'And that's what I'm going to keep doing, over and over again, till you squeal for release. And guess what,' she said, lifting herself slightly and then impaling herself violently once more. 'You can't do anything about this, can you? You can't come, you can't go soft and you can't escape. You're just a prick with hooves, Plodder, dear. My prick.' She ground her hips and groaned, softly.

'My prick, Plodder,' she said again and Colin, trapped helplessly beneath her, felt her entire body begin to shudder and convulse.

'Give 'em some exercise, that's what she told me,' Jonas said. He turned to his fellow groom and grinned. 'She even said I could harness 'em up and get 'em pulling a buggy,' he added. Sol frowned. He stared through the bars at the two dark-skinned girls and shook his head.

'Why bother?' he said. 'They're much too small to be ponies and it always takes so long to get 'em into harness. Just put 'em on leashes and let's take 'em across to the woods.'

'Fancy 'em, do you?' Jonas laughed. He pointed to Samba, who continued to sit, cross-legged, in the corner of the cage. Her huge dark eyes regarded him stoically, her finely chiselled features as impassive as ever. 'Bet you'd prefer this one,' he challenged. Sol considered the girl, then shrugged.

'Not fussy,' he replied. 'They've both got nice tits, though I reckon they'll both be all saggy in another couple of years. They ought to wear something to support them nice juicy melons.'

'I've got something to support 'em,' Jonas sniggered, making an expansive gesture with his hands. 'Lovely little things they are, and no mistake. And I reckon they'd look sweet in harness.'

'You would,' Sol retorted. 'But I've got to get back for the mid-shift, so I can't be doing with all that nonsense. Let's just get 'em collared and take them walkies.'

'Which one do you want, then?' Jonas persisted. Sol nodded at Samba.

'I'll take her,' he said and crooked his finger, beckoning her to the bars. For a moment or so, she continued to stare at him, but then, with a seeming lack of effort, she rose easily to her feet and glided across, grasping the steel in her hands and pressing her face against the cage. He leaned forward, forming his lips into a *moue*, and she immediately aped his gesture. Sol began to snicker and she laughed back at him.

'Reckon she fancies you, too,' Jonas said. He drew the key from his belt and unlocked the narrow gate. Samba remained at the bars, but her companion, the one they called Gypsy, slid backwards on her buttocks, pressing herself against the solid steel wall that formed the back of the cage. Jonas shrugged, turned away and collected the first collar and leash from the small trolley he had brought in with them.

'Here, little puppy bitch,' he called, softly, stepping inside the cramped area. He opened up the collar, offering it to Gypsy, who remained huddled in a defensive ball, her eyes slitted as she watched his approach. Jonas shook his head. 'C'mon, puppy girl,' he said, good-naturedly, 'it's

192

walkies time and then I'm going to show you a nice new form of exercise.' He saw her rounded breasts moving under the thin shift and licked his lips.

'C'mon now,' he encouraged her. 'You may not speak the language, but you know what you've got to do. Or you will do,' he added, 'by the time I'm through with you.'

'Gotcha!' Geordie switched off the engine and sat back, a satisfied grin on his tired features. Millhouse Farm, the fourteenth name on his list, a cluster of early Victorian farm buildings and the ruins of an even earlier structure that had once been, he could see, the water mill after which the farm had taken its name. The river that had originally provided its motive power was now little more than a shallow stream and tangled undergrowth spread down from the banks and across the mud that had once, presumably, been part of the river bed.

Two broken-down brick piers and a solitary, badly rotted post were all that remained of the bridge that doubtless carried the narrow track beyond the farm itself and, if the map were to be believed, on through three miles of woodland, to a small hamlet that rejoiced in the name of Gregory's Bottom, and then further still to where the main trunk road linked the southern Home Counties with the beginnings of the West Country.

Geordie, however, was more interested in the farm itself, the old barn and the unmistakable lines of the two horse boxes that were parked behind it, invisible from the track road itself, but, from the angle from which Geordie had approached this neighbouring hilltop, in plain view. Under normal circumstances, as they had obviously accounted for, the distance from this vantage point to the farmyard itself was such that, in the unlikely event of anyone taking the trouble to climb to this remote spot, they would have seen nothing to excite their interest, but, as Geordie focused the high-powered binoculars, he was able to examine the scene in sharp detail.

He grunted with satisfaction when he spotted one of the Range Rovers hidden among the trees, just back from the

approach road a good half-mile from the farm, congratu-
lating himself on the caution that had prompted him not
to make a direct approach. There was only one figure
sitting in the vehicle, presumably a lone lookout, and,
probably, in radio or telephone contact with the house
itself. As a further precaution, a length of sturdy tree trunk
had been placed across the track, placed in a position that
was meant to suggest it had simply fallen there, but a
cursory examination showed that this particular piece of
woodland debris had been dead for a good few years.

'Not keen on visitors, obviously,' Geordie muttered to
himself, but it was no more than he had anticipated. Celia
Butler and her friends would not want any accidental
tourists stumbling upon their playground unexpectedly,
not if the scenes in the yard were typical of the games they
liked to play.

Geordie studied the scene through the binoculars, open-
mouthed. With Sara, he had looked at and even copied off
a wide selection of photographs, but now, seeing it in the
flesh, even after his brief encounter with Sara in harness, it
was difficult to believe.

There were four pony girls and one male, his harness
and accoutrements almost identical to those of his female
counterparts. At first glance, they appeared to be naked
beneath the leather webbing, but, on closer inspection,
Geordie saw that they were all wearing skin-tight body
suits, fabric that clung to their flesh and yet somehow
made them appear all the more naked.

Their features were largely obscured by intricate bridles,
bits and blinkers, as Sara's had been when he had watched
her being herded aboard the horse box the previous
evening, yet Geordie was certain that she was not among
the women down there now. Novice or not, there had been
something about her bearing that made her completely
distinctive, whereas the four who were being put through
their paces below were, apart from the obvious, not
particularly notable.

Neither were the crew who were handling them, Geordie
noted. One overweight, balding and obviously middle-aged

male, one slightly younger, but even more overweight, a scrawny woman with an untidy urchin-cut hairstyle and a tall, thin, chinless type, who, Geordie could well imagine, probably spent most of his life behind a desk in the city.

'Sad bastards,' he mouthed. 'Wonder what you're all running away from.'

And then he saw her, the tall, commanding figure of the woman he had seen leading Sara into the van just a few hours earlier. The steepling heels and thick, platformed soles of her boots made her appear even more commanding, but even without them, he guessed, she must have been around six feet tall. He remembered Colin's account of his first visit to Celia's other premises and nodded, grinning to himself.

'So, you have to be Margot,' he whispered. 'Well, our Sara is quite something, but then you're something else. Way-ay, man, but you're some woman.'

He tracked her across the yard, zooming in with the binoculars until she all but filled the frame, and so mesmerised was he by her sheer presence, she had reached the cart that stood at the end of the barn before he gave any attention to the creature she was leading. When he did, his jaw dropped even further.

'What the –' He jerked the glasses away, wiped his eyes with the back of his hand, blinked and looked again, but there was no mistake. 'Ye gods!' he breathed, unable to take his eyes off the spectacle for a second time. 'I don't believe it!'

Tammy was almost beginning to wish she was back in the stables. At least there, she thought, she had learned what to expect and it was somehow easier that they mistreated this body that she had grown to hate so much, whereas now, it appeared, the hated shell was to be glorified, pampered, adorned and then . . .

And then it didn't bear thinking about. She ran a gloved hand over the flat contours of her stomach, her fingers defining the boning of the strict corset beneath the thin layer of rubbery fabric that was the dress she now wore.

She closed her eyes, trying to visualise how that same stomach would look and feel just a few months from now, but it was not something she really wanted to even think about.

Pregnant? A baby? She shook her head and bit her lip. No, it couldn't happen, surely, not to her. Whatever they had done, she knew she wasn't a woman, not inside. Slowly, she turned, opening her eyes to stare at the image in the mirror, not wanting to believe, not any more than she had wanted to believe so many other things these past three months, yet knowing that what she saw was now the truth.

The woman who confronted her was beautiful, as she had been throughout the entire summer, but now she was both beautiful and elegant, tall – the spindly heels exaggerated her height – and desirable beyond a doubt. The strapless dress hugged her every contour, covering everything, yet hiding nothing, stopping a bare inch short of the ankle straps that kept her tortured feet imprisoned within the impossible shoes, the silvery blue fabric rippling and dancing, reflecting the lights in a myriad hues whenever she so much as breathed. She made a stunning picture, Tammy knew, but that knowledge served only to deepen her misery, for the woman in the mirror, though she might easily have been the woman that Tommy MacIntyre might once have wanted, was most certainly not the woman he wanted to be.

There were tracks through the woods, but they were uneven, deeply ridged mud beset with tufts of coarse grass, and progress was necessarily slow as a result. Celia, it seemed, was quite content for Sara to simply walk, for even with its sprung-steel suspension, the little buggy in which she sat bounced and lurched alarmingly at times. She could, Sara reflected, as she plodded on, have chosen somewhere better suited for her chosen sport, but then this place had undoubtedly been selected as much for its remoteness and privacy as any other factor.

At last, Celia hauled back on the reins, calling for Sara to stop. Gratefully, she came obediently to a halt, breathing hard now, despite the slow pace, for the combined weight of the cart and its passenger still required a lot of effort to keep moving. The shafts shuddered, dipped and rose, almost throwing Sara off balance, and then Celia was standing before her, unfastening the bit and pulling it from her mouth.

'You've done well, Sassie,' she smiled. 'Have you enjoyed our little outing?' Sara nodded, unsure whether she was expected to speak or not. Celia reached out and patted her cheek.

'You are well suited to the harness,' she said. 'You wear it well – and proudly. Do you feel proud, pony girl?'

'I – I'm not sure ... mistress,' Sara mumbled. Her mouth still felt misshapen and awkward. 'Should a pony girl feel proud?'

Celia smiled again. 'Of course she should,' she said. 'She should feel proud that her mistress feels proud of her.'

'Then ... then I *am* proud, mistress,' Sara whispered. 'And ... and I feel good,' she added, blushing. 'I don't know why, but I do.'

'You feel good, Sassie,' Celia told her, gently, 'because you are finally finding your true self. It's a long time since I saw anyone as suited to the harness as you are.'

'Even – even Jessie?' Sara ventured, saying the name before she could stop herself.

Celia's eyes narrowed. 'Jessie?' she repeated. 'What do you know of Jessie?'

'There was a brooch, a name tag, whatever,' Sara replied, cautiously. 'It was in the stable that Mr Lachan was preparing.' Celia's expression relaxed again.

'Ah,' she sighed, 'I see.'

'You *knew* her ... mistress?' Sara added, rapidly. Celia shook her head.

'No, my dear Sassie, I didn't know her,' she replied. 'I have seen her, yes, but only from a distance. Your former employer guarded his territory well?'

'His territory?'

'Jessie,' Celia explained. 'I – I can't really tell you the full details,' she continued, 'but Jessie was – how can I say this?

197

– Andrew Lachan's personal pony girl. He never owned her as such –' She paused, her forehead creasing into lines of concentration. 'Oh, I just can't explain it properly, not yet, but Jessie was Lachan's favourite. He paid for her services, but she belonged to someone else. Not that the someone else ever availed himself of those services, I might add.' She shook her head and gave out a forced laugh.

'It's all far too complex for you to understand,' she said. 'Maybe one day, my pet. Who knows, you might even get to meet her. Would you like that?'

'I – I'm not sure.' Sara hesitated. 'Is she beautiful?' Celia laughed and her fingers stretched out and lightly brushed Sara's breast.

'Are you jealous, Sassie?'

'Should I be? He was only ever my employer. There was nothing between us.'

'No,' Celia agreed. 'But maybe, if he'd seen you as I'm seeing you now, maybe then there might have been.'

Samba had spent enough of her childhood without the luxury of shoes not to be at all inconvenienced by having to walk barefoot across the grass, despite the unevenness of the surface and the frequent stones that projected from the mud. The soles of her small, brown feet were nearly as tough as the leather of the collar that had been locked about her neck and her diminutive stature hid a body strength that would have surprised many.

Sol looked back over his shoulder at her and tugged impatiently at the leash, seemingly oblivious to the fact that moving quickly with her hands cuffed behind her back was unwise. Stubbornly, she refused to increase her pace, ignoring his urgings, and eventually he stopped and walked back to her.

'What's up with you, you stupid bitch?' he snapped, irritably. Samba's English was still very basic, but the tone of his voice and the expression on his face spoke a common language.

'Hands,' she said, simply, rattling her chained wrists the best she could. 'No hands.' Sol looked at her, shaking his head.

'Of course no hands,' he said, speaking slowly. 'Hands chained. Keep you good girl.' Slowly, Samba smiled up at him.

'You not want Samba bad girl?' she said, seductively. 'Samba be bad girl sometime.' Sol stared back at her and then the light of comprehension dawned in his eyes.

'Oh, yes,' he said. 'Yes, Samba can be bad girl. Samba want to be bad girl with Sol?' By way of reply, she sidled closer to him, pressing her pert breasts against his sleeveless leather jerkin and rubbing herself against him in a manner that needed no words of explanation. She heard him take a sharp breath and then his hands were in her hair, fingers twining, and bending back her head, though not cruelly.

'Yes,' he whispered, 'I bet you'd make a good bad girl.' His fingers disengaged and a single finger descended to trace a line across her pouting lips. Samba reacted instantly, opening her mouth into a round O and enacting a mime that was completely unambiguous. Sol's face creased into the widest grin yet.

'I reckon so, too,' he said and his hand was now on her left breast, massaging it through the thin fabric of her shift. He turned his head, looking from side to side. Of Jonas and Gypsy there was now no sign and if there were any other grooms or guests out exercising the stable inmates, Sol knew they would be away over beyond the trees to his right, either at the racetrack oval or on the more even roadway leading to it. He looked down into Samba's face again.

'C'mon, shortie,' he said, quite kindly, 'let's go this way. I know a nice little clearing where we won't be disturbed.' Samba continued to peer up at him, her expression now bland. She rattled the manacles again.

'Hands?' she said. Sol hesitated and then nodded.

'OK,' he agreed, turning her around and fumbling for the key in his belt pouch. 'But they have to be cuffed in front of you, at least, until I get you somewhere private. They'd have my bollocks for earrings, otherwise.'

'Bollocks?' Samba repeated, childlike. Sol grunted, drawing her arms around in front of her, placing her hands, palms outward, against his crotch, while at the same time snapping the loose manacle back around her free wrist.

'Yeah,' he grinned. 'Bollocks. I'll explain later, but I don't think you need that much telling, do you?'

Twenty

Appearances, Geordie knew only too well from bitter experience, could be deceptive and those same bitter experiences had also taught him not to act without at least some thought beforehand.

Therefore, for an hour, he sat on the bonnet of the car, observing the scene in the valley below, chain-smoking and drinking the two cans of lager he had persuaded the young service-station attendant to sell him out of licensing hours sometime before dawn that morning.

So far, since arriving here, he had seen no sign of Sara, but that, he knew, probably meant nothing. The likelihood was that she was still inside one of the buildings down there, though there was also the chance that she had left the immediate vicinity before his eventual arrival. The idea – the original scenario, at least – had been that Colin would bring her to Celia for a weekend of intensive training, training that would also include himself.

However, neither Colin nor Geordie had envisaged that Colin's training would take the form it was currently taking. Knowing Colin as he did, Geordie could never have imagined his voluntarily going into something that would include his current treatment. Playing the role of master to the apparently willing Sara was one thing – allowing himself to be turned into a human pony was quite something else.

The fair-haired amazon appeared to be sparing him little, Geordie saw, following their progress through the binoculars. The crop she wielded looked to be a vicious weapon, but, although she wielded it frequently, whether it was more *for* effect than *having* an effect he was too far away to be sure. She certainly appeared to be making Colin hop about, but then Geordie had no way of telling how much of that was simply pantomime.

One thing he could be sure of, he reasoned, eventually: he couldn't be sure of anything, not stuck up here on this windswept hill. If he wanted to be certain of anything – which he did – he would need to get closer to the action.

He considered the overall situation.

For a start, there was only one of him, but then that also had positive advantages. One person could move about a lot more easily than could several people and, initially, this was only a reconnaissance situation, after all, so numbers didn't count.

Except that he had no way of knowing exactly how many of them there were down below. There was the lookout in the half-hidden car by the roadblock – male or female he couldn't be sure – and there were the nine or ten people he had seen in the yard, or passing through it. There was also Celia Butler, who, although she hadn't yet put in an appearance, Geordie was certain must be on the premises.

So how many others were there that he hadn't yet seen?

The two horse boxes had carried four human ponies each, plus a driver and a passenger in the front. The two Range Rovers had carried eight people between them that he had been able to count for certain and there was also an elderly Austin van parked under the trees to the left of the main farmhouse. That could have been there for weeks, but he had to consider the possibility that there was at least a driver still somewhere about.

So, eight 'ponies' and nine, maybe ten, others. The ponies didn't count for his immediate purposes. They all seemed to be securely harnessed and wearing gags, or bits, so they would not be a problem. It was the ten others who warranted careful consideration.

Geordie raised the glasses and began counting again . . .

* * *

Bad dreams came in two varieties, Colin thought: those you woke up from and those you didn't, and this one certainly fitted into the latter category.

Exhausted now, every muscle in his body screaming out for relief, he stood between the shafts of the cart, sweating profusely inside the pony suit, wondering just how much further the blonde bitch, Margot, thought she could push him. His calf muscles, tortured by the extreme height of the hoof boots, were threatening to knot into agonising cramps now, forcing him to keep stamping his feet – as per Margot's instructions – which, he knew only too well, served only to emphasise the equine picture she had so cunningly contrived.

'Ah, Plodder,' she said, when she finally returned from a lengthy conversation with one of the other drivers on the far side of the yard, 'how I wish I could keep you for a month. I'd get rid of all the flab and give you real muscle tone.' She slapped his hip. 'Because,' she went on, 'when all's said and done, you do have the makings of an excellent pony boy.' She flicked at his still-erect organ, the tip of her crop slapping against the leather that sheathed it.

'And this,' she laughed, 'shows great potential.' She moved alongside him and began busying herself with the metal clips that secured his girth corset to the shafts. 'In fact,' she said, 'I think it's about time we explored its potential properly. Not that you'll enjoy it much, I'm afraid, poor nag. But I think I've earned a little recreation of my own, don't you?'

'That's it, my little lovely,' Sol said, lowering Samba gently on to the springy heather patch. He sank down beside her, sitting and smiling down into her upturned eyes. 'That's nice and comfortable now, isn't it?'

Samba stared back at him, only her eyes animated. She understood only the isolated word or phrase, but she knew well enough what he intended. Brazenly, she lowered her shackled hands to the hem of her shift and drew it up over her stomach, spreading her legs to reveal the swollen lips of her sex.

'You fuck?' She had heard the word so many times back home and it was one that apparently transcended many language barriers. She extended one finger, parting the puffy labia, gently massaging the swollen bud that lay just within, the slim digit already glistening with her juices. Sol grinned and nodded.

'Oh yes,' he breathed. 'I fuck all right.' He was already fumbling for the clips and buckles that secured his breeches and had soon wriggled free of them, kicking the garment aside, so that he was naked from the waist down. Her hands sought and found his semierect organ, urging and coaxing, though it needed little bidding. Instantly, it began to respond.

'Oooh!' Samba grinned, coquettishly. 'Biggie big!' Sol snorted, trying not to laugh.

'Yeah!' he said. 'Biggie big, you betcha.' He rolled over, raising himself on one elbow, his other hand grasping his now rigid organ and forced his knees between hers. Obligingly, Samba parted her legs even further and now his grin threatened to split his features in two.

'You really want this fuckie-fuckie, don't you, titch?' he said. Samba said nothing, but her hips rose towards him, her hampered hands clawing to guide him into her. With a strangled cry, Sol thrust home, amazed at how easily her apparently slight body accommodated his full length. Instantly, she wrapped her legs around his back, her heels digging into him, drawing him deeper still.

'Fuckie!' she gasped and he groaned as he felt the walls of her tunnel contract fiercely about his throbbing shaft. 'Sol fuckie Samba!' she cried and began humping up and down with a vigour that almost unseated him.

'Whoa!' he gasped. 'Easy there now. No rush, little 'un. No rush. Where's the fire, eh?'

Margot, it seemed, was an advocate of outdoor sports. She led the unresisting Colin away from the cart, away from the yard and away from its other occupants, guiding him around behind the barn and along a narrow track into the trees. It was all he could do now to remain upright, the

204

heavy boots with their steel horseshoes dragging awkwardly across the rutted surface, stray branches whipping at his shoulders as they moved deeper into the woods.

At last, they came to a small clearing, an area perhaps twenty feet across, where the ground appeared more even beneath its thick carpet of lush grass.

'This should do nicely, Plodder,' Margot announced. She stopped, turned back to Colin and began reeling in the lead rein, dragging him towards her. 'We've exercised your legs,' she said, 'so now we'll exercise a different muscle, eh? Let's have you down, then.'

She jerked suddenly on the leather leash, at the same time extending one leg, so that Colin was sent sprawling helplessly, landing first on his side and then rolling over on to his back, where he lay gasping, looking up at her as she stood over him.

'You should try to look happier,' Margot taunted him. 'After all, when I've finished with you, there are at least another four females here and that's not counting the pony girls.' She saw the look of surprise in his eyes and sniggered like a small girl.

'Oh yes, Plodder, my brave steed,' she said. 'You're going to service them all before the day's out. That stuff my dear mother shot into you lasts for hours and makes Viagra seem like Junior Aspirin, I promise you. God knows what it is, or where she gets it from, but it certainly works.

'You should count yourself lucky,' she continued, bending down over him and tugging at the straps that secured the sheath around his penis. I thought all men considered themselves to be studs and that's just what you're going to be.' She pulled the leather sleeve clear and tossed it aside, her gloved fingers grasping his burgeoning shaft. Involuntarily, Colin gasped.

'Feels nice, does it, Plodder?' she teased, manipulating him slowly. 'Bet you feel like you could come like a bloody fountain, don't you? Well, that isn't going to happen, I promise. Whatever this stuff is, it just keeps you hard – it doesn't let you actually come.

'Oh, you'll feel like you're about to explode, but you won't get any relief, not for a long time. We don't do these things for the benefit of our ponies, after all. This thing is for my pleasure, not yours.' She waggled his erect penis, forcing a groan from between his lips.

'Now,' she said, releasing her grip and standing up again, 'just you lie there. I shan't keep you long.' Within seconds, she had stripped herself naked from the waist down, kicking aside boots, breeches and the ridiculously tiny triangle that was her panties, then planted herself above Colin once again, legs spread wide, deliberately displaying herself to him. Despite his predicament, he felt his pulse beginning to quicken and knew that his manhood would have been ready for her even without the insidious drug they had given him.

'It's hungry for you, Plodder,' she whispered, hoarsely. 'My little mouth is longing for something to fill it. Would you like to fill it for me, Plodder?' Without stopping to think, Colin nodded.

'Well,' she said, smiling crookedly down at him, 'so you shall.' She dropped to her knees, spreading herself even wider, easing her body forward until the gaping lips were immediately above his throbbing shaft. Once again, she took it in her hand, coaxing it as if she thought she could make it yet bigger, then offering it up to herself and rubbing the straining purple helmet against the moistness of her sex.

She sighed, closing her eyes, and continued to use him as another woman might use a dildo, rubbing herself with him, titillating herself, squirming slightly so that the very tip of him just began to penetrate her and then pulling away again. This time, they groaned in unison and Colin tried desperately to thrust upwards, but she simply lifted herself out of his range and twisted his eager flesh spitefully. He moaned again, though this time as much in pain as in pleasure.

'Not yet, Plodder,' she breathed, half opening her eyes. 'You forget that you're only an animal, a beast of burden. You do nothing until I tell you. Lie still!'

206

Again she commenced the torturous routine, rocking herself back and forth, using him to stimulate her, yet refusing him the entry he so badly craved. She paused, leaning forward, until her face was only inches from his, her tongue flicking along her top lip.

'This is what is really meant by cock-teasing, Plodder,' she hissed, through teeth that were now clenching in paroxysms of lust. 'A man can be driven mad this way, wouldn't you say?' Had he been able to speak, Colin would have said so, but with the bit stifling any chance of coherent speech, he simply whimpered and tried to nod. His actions seemed to please Margot.

'I can be cruel,' she said, 'but not that cruel – not today. Here, Plodder, stable your stallion!' And with a cry that was part shriek, part howl of triumph, she bore down with all her weight, driving the breath from him and impaling herself fully, the howl dissipating into a long, drawn-out whine and her entire body already convulsing in an advanced state of orgasm.

Gasping from his exertions, Sol rolled to his left, his hands grasping Samba's hips and pulling her with him, so that now she was atop him, knees bent and straddling him, his entire length still buried deep inside her hot little maw.

Reaching up, he clawed at the flimsy shift, his fingernails ripping the fabric easily, exposing her budding, youthful breasts with their pinkish brown tips, highlighted against the coffee brown of the rest of her flesh. He reached for them, pinching and twisting, rolling them between forefinger and thumb, and she cried out delightedly, wriggling and squirming and thrusting down further, so that pubic bone ground against pubic bone.

Sol looked up at her, but she was not looking back at him, for her eyes were closed, her face screwed into contortions of pure, animal lust, her mouth hanging open and her tongue lolling between her gaping lips.

'Oh yes!' he gasped, jerking his hips upwards to reciprocate her downward thrusts. Dimly, he realised that he should slow down, hold her still, savour the warmth of her and extend his own enjoyment, for he knew that his self-control was close to being lost, but then, he thought vaguely, as the tide began to well up, this was just the first time. They had hours ahead of them yet.

Hours and hours.

And that was just today.

Twenty-One

Slowly, Margot rose, Colin's slippery shaft sliding out of her to fall back flat against his stomach, where it bobbed and bounced ludicrously, still throbbing with the need to be satisfied, a need he knew would continue for hours yet and with no prospect of being fulfilled.

'Not bad, Plodder,' Margot said. She regained her feet, legs still spread wide and shuffled backwards until she was standing over his feet. With one hand, she explored her gaping sex, withdrawing it again and displaying the glistening fingers.

'Dirty pony!' she rasped. 'Just look at what you've done to me.' The smile that played across her lips reminded Colin of a cat that had just finished devouring its latest catch.

'I can't put my panties back on like this,' she said, putting a distasteful expression on her features now. 'It would ruin the silk. No, this will never do, Plodder.' She reached forward and down, grabbing up the reins she had discarded earlier, yanking on them viciously, so that Colin's head was jerked off the ground.

'Up!' she commanded. 'Up and let's have that bit out, so you can use that tongue to clean up your mess. Come on, Plodder, get up, you lazy nag, or I'll have the skin off your arse!'

Samba sat back, her shoulders becoming limp, as her small body continued to tremble through the final stages of orgasm. Every muscle in her body suddenly relaxed and the stone fell from between useless fingers. Slowly, she opened her eyes and watched as it rolled from Sol's chest to bounce a few inches across the grass and heather and sucked a deep breath into her heaving chest.

It was not a large stone – little more than a pebble, in fact – small enough that Sol had not seen it when she had scooped it into her hand, clenching it in her fist to hide its presence. No, it was just a tiny piece of rounded rock, smaller than an egg.

But much harder and large enough if used efficiently.

Samba had seen her father stun wild dogs with stones no bigger; two of them had even regained consciousness eventually, dragging themselves away into the bushes with tails limp, heads and spirits cowed.

She sighed and looked down at the unconscious figure beneath her, feeling his warm penis already shrinking inside her. She furrowed her brow and stared at his chest, holding her own breath until she detected the slight rise and fall of his chest cavity, for she had not wanted to kill him, not if it could be avoided.

No, it was all right, she could see now. He was still breathing, though the lump on his left temple was continuing to swell and would be a painful reminder for some days, she suspected. Not that *she* intended to be around when he finally woke up, for she suspected he would leave her with even more painful reminders if she were.

She eased herself back and rolled clear of him, springing to a standing position with practised grace, but then collapsing back on to her knees as her oxygen-starved leg muscles gave way beneath her. She swore, softly, rolling again into a sitting position, and reached out with her fettered hands to massage her circulation back into life.

Finally, when she was sure the strength had returned to her limbs, she stood again, though this time a little more carefully, and then stood for a few seconds more, wriggling her toes and stamping her feet until she was certain the cramps would not return. Sol remained motionless and, as she turned to his discarded breeches and belt, Samba could not help but smile slightly.

She looked back at the recumbent groom and, as her fingers closed around the keys in his belt pouch, she nodded, recalling something she had heard once from a European truck driver, whose vehicle had clattered into their village, only to grind to a screaming, steaming halt and remain there for several days until another truck brought both the parts and the mechanic needed to fix it.

'Well fucked!' she said and, as she began unlocking the first manacle, and felt the first warm juices surrender to gravity and begin to trickle on to her upper thighs, Samba began to giggle.

Crouching low, Geordie carefully parted the branches of the bush, peering ahead and listening keenly. The voices were much closer now, but it was still difficult to pinpoint them, or to be sure just how far away they still were.

It had taken him more than an hour to get this far, scrambling down the blind side of the hill and then skirting in a wide circle, so that he approached the farmyard from an oblique angle, keeping the screen of trees and dense undergrowth between himself and the buildings. Inside his old camouflage jacket, which had lived in the boot of the car for nearly a year since its last airing, he was beginning to feel uncomfortably hot, his efforts working up quite a sweat, but, more than the physical discomfort, he was beginning to feel distinctly uneasy about the way this unofficial operation was turning out.

The sensible course of action, he knew, would be to take out the mobile phone, call up the local nick and ask for a couple of cars to give him back-up. The fact that there was no real evidence, no actual crime, as such, was immaterial. From what he had seen – and he had used the camera, with its telephoto lens, to capture the proof – he would be justified in assuming that a fellow officer was in jeopardy, but then there would be questions afterwards that neither he, nor Colin in particular, would want to answer and Geordie also knew that Colin would never forgive him if those particular photographs ever became common knowledge, even within the confines of the police force.

Another option would be to simply march in, frontal assault, brandishing his warrant card, and simply bluff it. After all, whatever else these people might be, he had no evidence to suggest that they were really dangerous. A few overweight white-collar types and a small handful of fetish freaks, that was all they were. There had been no sign of any weapons – unless one counted the whips and crops – and nothing to suggest any true violence or coercion, so the likelihood was that they would simply fold, hand over Colin and Sara, and be grateful that no further action would ensue.

Except . . .

Except the whole idea had been to get both Colin and Sara in on the inside, to win the trust of this weird bunch and enable Colin to snoop around for anything that might connect Celia Butler with Andrew Lachan, or, more particularly, with the events leading to his death and, despite Colin's apparent current situation, nothing had so far happened to suggest that the plan had been compromised.

Yes, Colin was at present being led around the place like a show pony, which had not been envisaged, but then who was to say that was a significant setback? These people, after all, were hardly normal – at least not by any definition Geordie was prepared to apply – and he had no idea of what had transpired since Colin and Sara's arrival at the first farm.

Maybe Colin was just going along with whatever it was the Butler woman had proposed, still trying to win that confidence, trying to be 'one of them' and still biding his time. On the other hand, from what Geordie had seen from the hilltop, his former colleague had not looked to be exactly in charge of the situation.

As for Sara, there was still no sign of her. So what was he to do, Geordie asked himself. He sank down on to his haunches, pulled out his cigarette packet and lit up, all the time listening and watching, while still trying to order his thoughts.

It was his call now, there was no getting away from it. Did he just continue to wait and suppose that their plan was still valid, or did he pre-empt everything now and try to call a halt to what was happening? And what if the sight of his warrant card failed to impress them? Weapons or not, they outnumbered him heavily and the fact that half their number was female hardly seemed to matter.

The Butler woman looked capable of being a handful anyway, and, as for the amazonian blonde who had led Colin off into the trees, she looked as if she probably chewed four-inch nails as snacks, regardless of how stunningly sexy she appeared.

Geordie checked his watch, calculating the hours between now and darkness falling. Night was the most powerful ally of the attacking force, as every military manual was only too quick to stress. Under its cover, he could hope to do more than he was likely to achieve in broad daylight, but dusk was still nearly three hours away and a lot could go wrong in that time.

He blew out a stream of smoke, sat back in the soft grass and tried to come to a decision. It could all be just so much harmless fun, or it could be something far more sinister – but which was it?

For the first time in a very long time, Geordie Walker found himself stuck for an answer, but he did remember one piece of advice from his training days: when in doubt, do nothing, unless there is a third party whose life or wellbeing is being obviously threatened. So, he asked himself, was Colin's or Sara's life or wellbeing currently under immediate threat?

The only people who could answer that question, he told himself, were Colin and Sara themselves.

'OK, then,' he said quietly, 'so where the fuck are you both?'

But there was, he also knew, only one way to answer that particular question. Stubbing out the half-smoked cigarette under his heel, he peered through the branches again, took the best fix he could on the voices and began to move away to his right, mentally crossing his fingers that he had made the correct choice and trying very hard not to tread on anything that would make a sudden noise.

Twenty-Two

The expression on Gypsy's brown face was one of sheer terror, whereas Jonas's features, as he lay now at her feet, were frozen into a mask of total surprise, his eyes still wide open, despite the fact that the branch with which Samba had hit him had rendered him instantly unconscious.

Letting the branch drop from her fingers, Samba knelt beside him, feeling his neck and nodding when she found a pulse there. If killing him had been necessary, then she knew she would have had little compunction, but death, as she well knew from experience, was a pretty permanent condition and one that she did not relish inflicting unnecessarily. She looked up at Gypsy, who was still leaning against the tree, tunic hitched about her waist and legs agape, and pointed at the recumbent groom.

'Well fucked,' she giggled, but Gypsy's existence had clearly been less colourful than her own and she failed to see the joke. With a dismissive shake of her head, Samba sprang to her feet again and jabbed a finger at Gypsy's nakedness. Stumbling over the almost forgotten dialect, she kept her instructions simple.

'Cover yourself,' she snapped. 'Not harlot. Him and other force us, but no shame. Come. We go.'

Gypsy hesitated for a few seconds, her eyes wide and glazed still, but at last she seemed to comprehend and eased the thin fabric down over her hips.

'Where go?' she asked, shakily. 'Where go? Him!' She pointed at Jonas. 'Big trouble for you! Where other one

214

go?' Samba grinned, considered a possible translation and realised that, even supposing there was an accurate translation, her knowledge of the hills language didn't extend to it. Instead, she reverted to the Anglo-Saxon original, though she would not have known of its derivation.

'Him too,' she said and made a swishing motion with her arm. 'Him well fucked, likewise. Sleep big, like this one. Now come!' She grabbed Gypsy's arm and hauled her away from the tree against which Jonas had been taking his pleasure with her. Not that she was going to admit as much to this doltish mountain slut, but she really had no idea of what to do next. The key she had taken from Sol opened Gypsy's manacles easily enough and they were, for a short time at least, not under direct supervision – but that was as far as her forward planning had taken her.

However, one thing she was sure of. Standing here in this second clearing, with Sol unconscious and likely to come round at any time in the first clearing just a matter of yards away, was not wise. Where to head for ultimately might require some consideration, but for the moment, anywhere but here was eminently preferable. She nodded towards the trees to the north of the grassy space.

'Come,' she said, leading the way. 'We go hide. Then we go far again and find priest man, or doctor. But different doctor,' she added, feeling Gypsy stiffen at the mention. 'Not bad doctor like other one, but like mission man.'

'You are a very beautiful woman,' Amaarini said. Tammy eyed her neutrally, sensing that she was trying to bait her. 'Yes,' the statuesque trainer nodded, stepping closer, 'you are very beautiful and Julia and Megan have done well preparing you.'

'From what I've seen and heard,' Tammy replied, grateful that her voice had been restored to her, albeit temporarily, 'there are at least another two or three here identical to me, so why was I chosen?'

'A fair question,' Amaarini replied. 'No doubt you suspect it is just a little quirk on our part, having fun at your expense because you were once male, eh?'

215

'Aye, something like that,' Tammy said, sullenly. She wished the long rubbery dress did not hobble her legs so effectively. Amaarini was bigger and more powerful than she was in her female body now, but Tammy doubted the big woman had had 'his' previous experience of Saturday-night bar-room brawling and a well-directed kick, especially from a foot wearing such wicked heels, could disable an opponent far bigger even than she was.

'Well, my pretty one,' Amaarini said, evenly, 'I'm afraid to have to disillusion you in that regard. Yes, part of the reason for your being the chosen consort is to do with your previous life, but it was not made with any vindictiveness in mind.'

'Should I be pleased to hear that?' Tammy retorted.

'Quite frankly,' Amaarini said, 'I couldn't care less what pleases or displeases you. As far as I'm concerned, your species is an inferior creation and, as a Jenny Ann now, you may be better off physically, but you are little more than a useful resource.

'I'm not certain just how much you understand, so I shall briefly explain the situation. Our people – my people – are far more advanced than yours in every way imaginable, but centuries away from our original home led to a problem. Our males live several of your life spans, but our females seldom live past thirty of your years, and even less once we give birth to an offspring.

'As a result, Dr Lineker, as you know him, and his team developed a complex method of producing new host bodies, into which we could be transferred, much as you were transferred. There was, however, a small problem.

'If the doctor transferred us into a host cloned from our own line of DNA, that host would live no longer than an original body, whereas the clones produced from human DNA lived several times longer than their original donors.

'A few attempts were made to transfer a few of our number into these human clones, but there were factors that caused the host to reject the brain within hours and no way of producing any chemical agent to prevent this.

'However, when some of our males interbred, either with human females in their original state, or with the cloned

216

Jay-Ays, DNA samples from the resultant hybrid infants produced hosts that accepted the transfers, those hosts cloned from the clones, as it were, living much longer and therefore proving more satisfactory.'

'So you intend to use me as some sort of brood mare to produce a bairn for you to make more clones from?' Tammy managed to hold her temper and disguise her disgust with some difficulty. 'But why me in particular? You don't even know that the reproductive bits of this body work.'

'Oh, they'll work all right,' Amaarini assured her. 'They work in all of you, once they're reactivated. Of course, we keep your reproductive cycles dormant when we have no need of fresh stock – otherwise we would have unwanted infants screaming the place down – but a simple injection has always served to awaken them when required.

'And in your case, even that step has been made redundant. The cybertechnology that connects your brain with the rest of your new body has been steadily modified over the years. Now, not only can we switch your voice off and on at will, we can control almost all your bodily functions using the same control system.'

'Ah, so the fact you can turn me on and off is the reason I've been selected for this . . . this . . . dubious honour?'

'Oh, far from it,' Amaarini assured her. 'There are quite a few who can be controlled similarly now, but, apart from sweet little Bambi, they were all females originally. And, despite the obvious feminine attributes of your delightful-looking body, your brain will still contain strands of DNA that are male.

'You see,' she continued, smiling maliciously, 'the doctor has never managed to clone from a human male body, at least not to produce a male host that was capable of surviving beyond a week or two. This means that we cannot extend the lives of our males without placing them, too, into female host bodies when they near the end of their normal life span.'

'You didn't seem to worry about putting me into a female body,' Tammy snapped. 'But then I'm just some sort of commodity, aren't I?'

'Well, precisely,' Amaarini said, easily. 'And we do have some of our males now in female hosts, rather than risk losing their years of accumulated knowledge and experience. However, it may well be possible to use your future offspring to make that necessity a thing of the past.'

'So I get to be the Bride of Frankenstein,' Tammy muttered. She shook her head, but then another thought struck her. 'Tell me,' she said, "cause there's one little question that springs to mind.'

'And what might that be?'

'You refer to us as humans,' Tammy said, choosing her words carefully now, 'and to yourselves as being a much older race. So where did you people – your people – come from originally? Have you been lying low for hundreds of years?'

'In a manner of speaking, yes,' Amaarini replied, 'though there is never any need for us to lie that low. We are – outwardly at least – so very similar to you and most of us, while still in our original bodies, are frequently taken as having some sort of Eastern ancestry.'

'More like bloody snakes,' Tammy said, but Amaarini ignored the insult.

'As for where we came from, it would be a waste of my time and yours for me to try to explain. Our forefathers came here a very long time ago now, from a place so far away that it would be almost impossible for your minds to comprehend.'

'I see,' Tammy said. 'So you *are* bloody aliens?' And somehow that knowledge did not surprise her as a similar revelation might once have surprised Tommy MacIntyre.

'A properly designed harness and bridle frames and enhances true natural beauty,' Margot said, softly. She ran the fingers of her right hand gently down Sara's cheek, then leaned forward and kissed her delicately on her distended lips, her tongue flicking between them to caress the bit.

'And you make such a perfectly pretty pony, Sassie,' she whispered, her other hand sliding up over the tight corset girth, fingers spreading to cup one breast. Sara felt her legs beginning to tremble once again, but made no effort to pull away.

'Such softness should not be wasted on some brute of a man.' Margot smiled. 'No man could possibly hope to appreciate what you really are. My mother taught me that lesson very early on in my life.' She paused, seemingly hesitating, and then appeared to come to a decision. In a trice, she had removed the bit again, shaking off the coating of spittle. Sara swallowed, gratefully, licking her lips.

'I should keep you bitted all the time,' Margot said. 'You look so pretty with your nice bit in, but it does have its disadvantages. Come.' She took Sara's pouched arm and steered her towards the straw-filled mattress in the far corner of the stall, guiding her down on to it and then stretching out alongside her.

'You've never made love to a woman, have you?' she said, raising herself on one elbow, so that she was looking directly down into Sara's face. Sara shook her head.

'No . . . mistress,' she added. 'Not until today.'

'Ah, but that wasn't making love,' Margot said. 'Not properly making love.' She patted the crotch strap between Sara's legs. 'For a start, you've got that great big thing in there, haven't you? That's just a pony reminder, Sassie dear, something to help you realise that you don't need a man for anything. Tell me, is it comfortable?'

'Comfortable?' Sara stared up at her, surprised at such a question, but, as she made to say more, it suddenly occurred to her that it maybe wasn't such a stupid thing to ask after all. Initially, when the massive-looking phallus had been eased into her, while it had not hurt as such, there had been no way of ignoring its presence, whereas now, after several hours with it in place, she had almost come to be able to forget it was there.

'It's not . . . uncomfortable,' she replied, cautiously, wondering whether this odd female might suddenly take it into her head to replace it with an even larger model. 'But must I wear it all the time?'

'As a pony girl, yes,' Margot answered, kindly, 'except for certain circumstances.' Circumstances, Sara reflected grimly, that did not include the need to relieve herself, for she had twice now been forced to urinate while standing with her legs splayed, the golden trickle spraying out to either side of the strap and drenching the rubbery pony suit. Fortunately, the fabric appeared to be completely waterproof and the splatterings had quickly evaporated, but the memory of her embarrassment was not so easy to be rid of.

'Tonight, Sassie dearest,' Margot continued, once again fondling Sara's breasts, 'you shall have rid of the thing, if you tell me you would like to come to my bed.'

'Yes, I should like that.' The words were out of her mouth before Sara realised what she was saying, but it was too late to retract them now, even if she had wanted to, and she could not honestly say that she did. 'Yes,' she repeated, in a hoarse whisper, 'I think I *should* like that.'

'I thought perhaps you might,' Margot said. 'It will be better than sleeping down here in all this straw, though you mustn't think that it will be a regular occurrence. It will do you good to spend a few nights in a proper stable.'

'A few nights?' Sara's eyes widened in alarm. 'But I thought I was only going to stay here for the weekend.' Margot pouted her lips and kissed the tip of Sara's nose.

'You can leave now, if you really want to,' she replied. 'Your policeman friend will be kept here for another day or so, just until Mother has enough material to be fairly sure he won't go causing trouble for us, but there's no real reason for you to stay.'

Sara struggled to sit up, but Margot pushed her firmly back on to the straw.

'Do you want to leave, Sassie?' she demanded. For several seconds, Sara considered this proposition.

'If I stayed for a while,' she said, at last, 'could I have my arms free? My shoulders are starting to ache and I can't do anything for myself.'

'But that's how it should be,' Margot smirked. 'I'll do everything for you that I think is necessary. No, your harness and bridle stay on, even in the bedroom. The bit and this,' she added, patting the hidden dildo, 'can be optional, but we can't have a pony girl running around unharnessed, can we?'

'No, I suppose not,' Sara muttered. 'So, if I stay, then I stay as I am now, near enough?'

'That's right, my sweet. Just as you are – my very own, adorable pony girl.' She paused, studying Sara's face, looking deeply into her eyes.

'So?' she prompted. 'What's it to be? Go? Or stay?' Sara sighed deeply, the corset cutting into the tender flesh beneath her flattened bosom, and tried to ease the position of her legs. All she succeeded in doing was reminding herself what was trapped between them, strapped inside her until Margot decided otherwise. Closing her eyes, she sighed again.

'Stay,' she said, surrendering to the inevitable and opening her mouth to receive the bit that had magically reappeared in Margot's hand.

Twenty-Three

It seemed, Geordie thought, that Celia Butler relied mostly upon the remoteness of this, her second establishment, for its security, although the farmyard quadrangle itself did have a wall running between the various buildings that faced on to it and the wall had been more recently topped with a barbed-wire fence. The uneven grassy area outside that perimeter, which provided the most space for their games, was, however, completely unprotected and he was able to work his way quite close to the various scenes of action without encountering any alarms, trips or wires.

Pressed against the trunk of a tree and relying on the screen of wild undergrowth as camouflage, Geordie stood for over half an hour, watching and listening. Away to his right, some fifty yards distant, but near enough for him to be able to hear Celia's distinctive voice, he could see that Colin was being put through his paces in no uncertain terms, but then the same could be said of the two pony girls and the other male who were also in this same area.

Quite what they all got out of this, Geordie kept telling himself, he didn't know, but the growing bulge in his trousers, as he watched the breasts bouncing and jingling on the trotting girls, was hard to ignore, let alone explain.

The various handlers, male and female, appeared to be dressed in various parodies of riding outfits, the fabrics mostly either silk or rubber, judging by the way they reflected the sunlight. All wore boots with elevated heels – wicked-looking stilettos in the case of the women and more solid, almost Cuban heels in the case of the two men. Both men and one of the women wore masks that covered the majority of their features, while a second woman wore a highwayman-style mask that covered just the area between her brow and cheeks, though still obscuring enough to effectively conceal her identity.

And when, after about fifteen minutes, a third man appeared from within the farmyard, this time wearing a hood that covered his head entirely, the germ of an idea began to form itself in Geordie's mind, for this man, who strutted arrogantly from one girl to another, giving orders even to the handlers, could have been anybody and, Geordie thought, as a battered-looking Range Rover lurched into view from the general direction of the main road, it was a fair bet that there would be others beyond that fence, at least by nightfall, just like him.

The concept of an island was completely alien to Samba. The sea, in her limited experience in her native country, had been something that was a long way off, something that ran along the edge of the land and beyond which were other worlds, more large areas of land where different peoples lived. The idea that the sea could surround an area of land so apparently small as this one came as a rude shock to her and she still could not quite bring herself to believe the truth.

Eventually, dragging a reluctant Gypsy with her, she had scaled the steep hill that dominated one end of the land, climbing to within a few metres of the jagged peak, from where, crouching among the scrawny bushes that somehow clung to the rocky slope, she was able to gain an unobstructed view on three sides. A few more minutes spent scrambling to the far side of the hill confirmed her worst fears – this tiny scrap of land was bounded by water in all directions and the nearest alternative land was a smudgy outline very nearly on the horizon.

'Well fucked,' she muttered to herself and ignored Gypsy's questioning look. She raised a warning hand when the other girl opened her mouth to speak and squatted down on her haunches, fiercely racking her brain for alternatives, not that there seemed to be many.

Men used things called boats to cross the sea. Samba remembered seeing pictures in books and hearing talk back in the village, but she had never seen one in real life; and, as she scanned the sea with keen eyes, it did not seem to her that that situation was about to change. On the other hand, she reasoned, the two of them had been brought here in some sort of boat and presumably these people also came and went at intervals.

For a start, she was certain, they had to bring food by boat. From what she could see of the island – which was most of it from her high vantage point – they grew no crops. Not, she thought, running her fingers through the thin, pale soil, that this place would support much of anything. Even the soil in the mountains above her village was better than this stuff.

She raised her eyes, looking towards the west and the steadily dipping sun. It would be dark in another two hours. She had no watch and could not tell the time properly anyway, but Samba knew exactly how long an hour was and two of them would see the end of the sun for the day.

Darkness.

Darkness could be scary, especially to a little girl, but darkness could also be an ally, as it was to the hunters and to the village men who went foraging for supplies in the logging camps beyond the next village. Little girls feared the night, but bigger girls learned to move through it like ghosts themselves. She nodded and turned to her companion, who had seated herself, cross-legged, her chin cradled in her hands, eyes closed.

'We wait,' she said, firmly. 'Wait darkness. Then find boat. Must have boat and go home.'

Gypsy nodded, but Samba doubted that she had understood. Not that it mattered either way, she thought, and settled herself back into a more comfortable position.

'This will be something of a new experience for you.' Amaarini kept a firm hold on Tammy's elbow as she

224

guided her down the corridor leading to the stables. 'And it may serve to help you appreciate what you are being offered,' she added, acidly. 'I should imagine that you've spent sufficient time down here in harness not to want to repeat the situation. Or did you enjoy being a lowly pony girl?'

'How could anyone possibly enjoy *that*?' Tammy snarled.

Amaarini gave a short laugh. 'Many do,' she asserted, 'though your circumstances were a little individual, it has to be admitted. No, Tammy, you would never have been ideal material, but then that was always part of the challenge and there are quite a few of our guests who would have willingly paid treble for your services, had we ever dared let them know the truth about you.'

'And now I'm supposed to feel gratitude?' Tammy retorted. 'And just because you've taken me out of the stable, dressed me in a load of tarty finery and told me I'm expected to have some freak baby?'

'What you feel,' Amaarini replied, 'is of absolutely no concern to me, I assure you. What will be will be, regardless. Whether you decide to co-operate or not, it will happen, that much I can promise. Meantime, part of my duties is to ensure that you receive some basic coaching.

'Our leader is a very special being, as are we all, in different ways. But he is the leader and entitled to the respect and loyalty that his position demands. And that,' she continued, her tone suddenly very hard, 'includes having a consort worthy of him.' She stopped, turning abruptly, and seized Tammy's nipples through the stretched fabric of the dress.

'You may hate these,' she hissed, 'but don't flatter yourself that they will mean even *that* to him.' She pulled her right hand away and snapped her fingers in front of Tammy's startled eyes. 'Rekoli will do with you whatever is necessary, but do not, even for one second, think that you are worthy of him, or even that he would care about you.

'What you will learn is merely enough to satisfy appearances. You will be with him in the presence of human

225

guests and it is only fitting that you should fulfil their expectations. The consort is required to attain certain standards, so attain them you shall. Starting,' she sneered, 'with learning how to drive a pony-girl cart, for it would be demeaning for your lord and master to have to drive you. Do you understand this?'

'I think so,' Tammy replied. 'I'm supposed to play the dutiful little wifey, yes? And what if I don't?'

In answer, Amaarini reached inside the pouch hanging from her belt and withdrew the all-too-familiar remote-control unit.

'I think,' she said, 'that you can probably work that out for yourself. However,' she added, returning the unit into the pouch with exaggerated deliberation, 'anything you might think you could imagine would be as nothing to the reality. The life of the most humble pony girl would seem like paradise, compared with what I shall inflict upon you if you fail in this.'

The life of a humble pony boy had long since lost its appeal for Colin, despite the fact that Celia seemed capable of bringing him to the point of more orgasms in an hour than he had previously experienced in any one month. But then that was the problem – he was merely coming to the brink and not, as Celia had promised him, actually coming in reality. How much more of this exquisite torture he could endure he had no idea, except that he knew it could not be very much.

'Such a proud cock, Plodder,' Celia taunted him, caressing his erection with both hands, but in a way that seemed to indicate her complete detachment from it. 'So hard, so shiny, and so big – and look at all the pretty blue veins on it.' Without warning, she gripped him fiercely, her nails digging into the tender flesh and her wrist twisting spitefully. Colin gasped through the gagging bit and his knees started to buckle.

'All men are so useless,' Celia sneered. 'This just goes to prove that, if there is a god, then she must be a woman. Only a woman would have the sense to place a man's

226

testicles on the outside and at such a convenient height for punishment.' She twisted again and Colin groaned in genuine agony.

The mother, he thought, was ten times worse than the daughter. At least Margot seemed capable of appreciating his organ for what it offered, whereas Celia appeared to take its state of constant rigidity as an invitation for attention of a totally different kind.

'By the time I've finished with you, Mr Policeman,' she growled, maintaining her grip, 'you'll never want to come within fifty miles of me, or this place, ever again. Oh, I'll let you come before you finally leave here, have no fear of that. But, when you do, it won't be inside some nice warm, obliging little cunt.

'Oh no, my Plodder. You'll be masturbated in front of an audience, filmed on digital video in full, glorious Technicolor, coming like a fountain in Trafalgar Square. And afterwards, compliments of the house, I'll give you a digital-disc copy of the entire event, so you can watch the highlights in the privacy of your own bedroom and consider how your colleagues might receive any number of the other copies I'll have tucked away in readiness.'

Samba crouched in the bushes, staring at the sight just a few yards from her, quite unable to understand what she was seeing.

Her experience of white, European women was limited, it was true, but one thing she was sure of, they were not supposed to be treated like this. For that matter, even the lowest native slut would not be subjected to such humiliation. Mules, after all, were mules and humans were humans.

But this woman was attired with all the trappings of a packhorse: heavy leather harness, blinkers, reins and even a tail. The head, Samba realised, had been strapped over her own, hiding her features and creating the equine effect, but for what reason she could not imagine.

Maybe, she thought, they had no horses here; perhaps the climate did not suit them, for it was, after all, so very different from home. But to use a woman for such a menial chore? No, surely even these people could not consider that acceptable. There had to be something here that she did not understand. Maybe it was a religious ceremony, a ritual dedicated to some sort of god.

Crouching lower still, Samba waited and watched, watching in particular the other two females, one of whom she recognised, though the other, the smaller one, was a total stranger to her. The taller woman, the one they called Amaarini, who seemed to hold a position of some respect and authority, was most definitely in charge of the situation here, striding most purposefully towards the horse-faced woman and the cart, while her companion struggled in her wake, her ability to walk hampered by a long skirt that Samba could see was far too tight-fitting to be practical.

She could not even get herself up into the cart unaided, and Amaarini had to half lift her on to the driving seat, then climbed easily into the space next to her, thanks to her own far more suitable attire of leggings and boots. The first woman took up the leather traces uncertainly – from the expression on her face, Samba guessed that she was a reluctant participant in all this – and took the long driving whip that Amaarini handed her with obvious distaste.

'I can't use this,' she said, shaking her head. 'It shouldn't be necessary.'

'But it most certainly is necessary, Tammy,' Amaarini countered, 'and you will not only use it, you will learn to use it properly. You have felt its kiss yourself, so you will appreciate how the whip can focus the attention of even the most stubborn pony girl. Just use the very tip, there, between the shoulder blades.

'You need not lash her hard, not at first,' she added, 'but, if she does not respond suitably, then you will be expected to increase your own efforts until she gets the message.'

'But she's just one pony girl to draw this carriage with two of us in,' Tammy protested.

'So she will appreciate it much better when she is again one of a pair,' Amaarini said. 'She has been a lazy, reluctant mare so far, so a taste of reality will do her no harm at all. Now, walk her on, or I'll have you strung up and whipped.'

And, as Samba watched in horrified awe, the girl Tammy flicked the long whip towards the shoulders of the anonymous pony girl and shook out the reins, and the hapless creature leaned into her task. Slowly, the large spoked wheels of the buggy began to turn and, with a final lurch over an uneven tuft, the unlikely trio were on their way, bells, brasses and buckles clattering and jingling in the night air.

The barbed wire proved little hindrance. The side cutters that Geordie carried in his toolkit in the boot of the car were of high quality and sharp and the twisted metal strands offered virtually no resistance. In a matter of seconds, he had opened up a gap more than large enough for him to slither over the stone wall and drop to the ground in the deep shadows afforded by the end wall of the barn.

With darkness had come a bank of clouds from the southwest, obscuring both stars and moon, though Geordie had no idea what sort of moon was due that night, nor even what time it was scheduled to rise. He thought back, trying to remember the previous evening, but there had been too many other things on his mind at that time and there had been cloud about then, too, so far as he could recall.

Not that the moon should matter, he told himself. He needed to get inside at least one of these buildings, where he was sure to be seen eventually. The trick was to be seen and not noticed – at least not noticed as an intruder.

Immediately across the yard from the barn, separated by a good thirty yards of gravelled open space, stood the main house. It was old and very unimpressive, but it seemed to be quite large. Geordie counted the windows he could see from where he was and guessed that there were at least six bedrooms on the first floor and what appeared to be another three rooms in the attic above it. Of the nine upper windows on this side of the building, there were lights burning in five of them, but his attention was drawn to one of the darkened rooms, the window of which stood immediately above a small lean-to ground-floor extension at the furthest end of the structure.

There was even what appeared to be a water butt, perfectly placed for Geordie's purpose, and the old-fashioned sash-construction windows would have catches that were child's play to someone of his experience. All he had to do was get from where he was to where that barrel was and that, he reflected, ducking deeper into his dark corner as a door opened opposite, framing a dark silhouette against the light within, was not quite such a simple matter.

Inside the tunnel leading down through the stable area, the overhead lights had been dimmed and Samba moved carefully, anxious not to make any noise; at the same time her ears keened for any sounds that would warn her that someone was approaching from the opposite direction.

Earlier, the two grooms had led Gypsy and her outside via a different route, but the door to that tunnel, cunningly hidden behind a movable outcrop of bushes, had been closed behind them and there was no sign of a keyhole or handle on the outside, leaving this entrance, from which Samba had watched both the weird pony woman and Amaarini and her pupil driver emerge just after dusk.

Samba's first instinct had been to remain outside in the open air, but her stomach was gnawing away inside and Gypsy, too, had begun to complain that she was hungry. Hunger was not an unknown experience to either of them, but then neither was the feeling of weakness that generally accompanied it after a little while, and Samba knew they would both need all their strength if they were to stand a chance of getting away from this place.

In her own country, there were roots and berries that could be eaten to stave off the effects of genuine starvation, but here, as she had already noted, the vegetation was poor and the dangers of eating any plant she did not recognise had been drummed into her as a child. Which left them with only one option. Or, rather, it left Samba with only one option, for the terrified Gypsy had made it clear, especially from her sign and body language, that nothing was going to induce her to go back underground.

Leaving her companion some little way into the woods at the foot of the hillside, Samba returned alone, lying in the patch of undergrowth nearest the wide doorway and watching it for several minutes before finally venturing closer.

So far, there had been no further signs of life and everything seemed quiet within, but that, she realised, could change without warning and the little cart, with its pony girl and passengers, might also return at any minute.

She reached the end of the tunnel and saw that the gradient levelled out into a wide, high-ceilinged chamber that looked as though it had been carved out of the solid rock by hand, for the angles were all too regular for the cavern to have been formed by natural forces. Breathing slowly, Samba crouched down, peering into the half-light, her sharp eyes searching for any movement.

She saw the rows of doors set along either side of the main area, recognising their split construction from the stables she had known at home. At the same time, she saw the collection of carts, carriages and buggies drawn up along the end wall, to the left of where she now was, and realised that, like the one she had seen outside earlier, their size indicated that they were not intended to be drawn by four-legged creatures.

She sucked in a deep breath, her heart beating faster now, for she realised there was more danger in this place than even she had thought before. These people – the doctors and the nurses in whose charge they had been since their arrival, and now the two men who had taken them outside and ravished them with such nonchalance – were clearly evil. At first, their actions had simply confused Samba, but now she thought she was beginning to understand. Somehow, it seemed, they were able to use their medicine to turn girls into dumb animals. For what purpose precisely and just how it was done, Samba had no idea, but one thing now she thought she was certain of. If they did not get away from here, she and Gypsy would very soon be living in these stables and wearing harnesses and awful horse-head hoods like the poor girl outside.

Still in a crouch, she scuttled towards the parked carriages, eager to take advantage of what cover they offered and to use them until she could get to the far side and the first stable door. It was risky, she could not deny, but the alternative was to try to get from this end of the stable area to the darkened tunnel entrance that led off from the furthest end and the distance between her and it seemed very great indeed.

Besides, she reasoned, they would have to feed the girls they kept stabled here and it was unlikely that their diet would be the same as that of a real horse, so the silent stalls offered the best chance of a food source. It all depended upon none of the inmates raising the alarm, but if they all had their heads and faces encumbered like the first girl, the chances of their not being able to make too much noise were definitely in her favour and, she thought, smiling grimly to herself, as her fingers closed around the thick iron latch ring, they might not even realise that she was not supposed to be here in the first place.

Twenty-Four

'I'm afraid Mother insists that you take part in the evening's entertainment, Sassie,' Margot said. She stood in the doorway of Sara's stall, legs astride, boots firmly planted, her hands on her broad hips. As she scrambled to her feet, Sara saw that the tight-fitting jodhpurs were now gone, in their place a short, pleated, leather skirt and gleaming black stockings.

'And I'm also afraid that you have excited just a little male interest,' Margot continued, stepping inside and reaching up to untie Sara's bridle rein from the iron hook set in the wall above her head. 'So, our little assignation is going to have to wait.' She wrapped the leather traces about her fist and pulled Sara towards her.

'I'm just a little surprised that she has given in to their pressure,' she said, her tone betraying a hint of bitterness, 'but she says she has one or two rather special guests here this evening and she doesn't want to risk offending any of them by refusing.' Margot sighed and shook her head.

'You do know what that means, I suppose,' she said. Sara stared at her, eyes round, wanting not to have her suspicions confirmed. Margot's next sigh was even heavier.

'It means,' she said, speaking very slowly, 'that you are going to get what we call "covered" this evening and by any bloody male out there who takes a fancy to you, not to mention their bloody male ponies.' Sara swallowed hard and let out a little gasp. Margot pulled a face.

'Well,' she said, 'at least it might make you appreciate me even more, by the time they're through with you!'

It had quickly become very hot and uncomfortable inside the rubber horse mask, but worse still, because of the way the outer eye apertures were positioned wide on either side, Alex found that her field of vision was very restricted, with a blind spot dead ahead of her and the blinkers reducing the remaining peripheral vision badly. As a result, she was now very dependent upon the commands issued via the traces attached to her bit by her driver, and the fact that the reins were in the hands of the inexperienced Tammy did little to inspire confidence.

In addition, Amaarini had left the sound receptor system switched off, so that any noises that did penetrate the ear-muffling pads inside the head mask were distant and vague; to all intents and purposes, Alex was now running deaf, as well as virtually blind.

The experience was even more surreal than just being on the island in a different body, for the night was dark, with no signs of other human life along the route to the oval track where she had first seen the bizarre pony-girl races. It was as if she were running in her own world, with even the weight of the carriage seeming to melt behind her, the only sounds the snort of her breathing through the long nostril tubes and the steady thump-thump of her heart against her ribcage.

Only one of the lighted bedrooms seemed to be currently in use. Geordie stood outside the door, listening to the muffled sounds of giggling coming from within. At the end of the passageway, a staircase led both down and up, with more noises filtering from the lower level. He moved cautiously to the banister rail and peered downwards, but all he could see was the lower landing, which was as deserted as the stairway itself.

For a few seconds, he paused, considering his options. The ground floor was a no-go as things stood, but there were several rooms unoccupied on this first floor, still to be checked out, plus at least three more above, but someone could appear here at any moment. He raised his eyes, studying the upper section of stairwell, and made a decision.

'There's been a slight change of plan, Sassie dear,' Margot announced, when she finally returned to Sara's stall. 'Don't look so worried – with luck, we may be able to save you from the attentions of all those nasty, sweaty men out there. By the time this deer hunt is finished, they'll probably have forgotten all about you, or else they'll be too tired.

'These things can sometimes go on all night, you see,' she continued. 'And after a little while, if it gets too tedious, I can slip away and drive you back here. No one will know we've gone. Everything gets very confusing out there in the darkness, which is supposed to be half the fun.

'I'll just have to make sure I don't actually catch a doe tonight, though I must confess that one of the new candidates is almost as pretty as you are. They'll be preparing them in the barn shortly, so I thought I'd take you along and let you see it for yourself.

'Who knows, you might fancy being the quarry yourself next time. That would make you a proper little deer, wouldn't it my dear?'

The first two closets were filled with an assortment of rubber and leather female costumes, but the third was far more promising. This end room in the loft, unlike the first three Geordie had tried, which had contained little of interest, appeared to be some sort of wardrobe department, the entire width of the gable-end wall lined with deep closets and lower units stretching along either side beneath the eaves.

The mixture of aromas was far headier than he had anticipated, the air heavy with the smell of latex, hides and something else which he could not quite place. Although no expert, Geordie reckoned that the combined cost of everything up here probably exceeded the value of the building itself.

For a full minute, he stood in the centre of the room, debating the wisdom of his original idea, now he was confronted with it as a practicality, but there didn't seem to be a more likely alternative available at short notice. He stepped forward, selected a pair of leather breeches and what appeared to be a rubber shirt, both in black, and, feeling slightly foolish, began to fumble with the buckle of his belt.

The main area of the barn was a hive of activity when Margot led Sara back inside. There were two other pony girls already there, both tethered against the far wall, away from the main action, where they stood docilely watching the proceedings. After a few seconds' indecision, Margot led her over to join them.

'The girls down the end are the does,' she explained, waving vaguely to where about a dozen people were crowded around six females who stood out from the rest by virtue of the dazzling, fluorescent colours of the latex body suits into which they appeared to have been poured. Pink, blue, green, yellow, orange and lilac, they were as distinctive from each other as they were from the generally black- or red-clad majority.

As Sara watched, fascinated, she saw each of them being fitted with boots similar to the ones she wore herself, except that these versions did not appear to have any support under the heels. Instead, the instep arched up and over, giving the appearance of a far more streamlined hoof of the kind one might have expected to see on a deer, though how anyone could walk in them was beyond Sara. The design meant that the wearer would have to keep her weight forward, on to toes tortured into an impossible position; failure to do so would surely result in her toppling backwards, ending up, presumably, in a very ungainly heap.

These six creatures, however, appeared to have little difficulty in mastering the ridiculous contraptions, although moving about on the relatively even surface inside the barn would not present the sort of problem that the rough ground beyond the yard would surely create. It would be interesting, Sara mused, to finally see them running, for, although the unsupported heels would doubtless be a severe handicap, the girls all looked more than just fit and, apart from the fact that they were all rather large-breasted, might well have been trained dancers. Their legs, thighs, buttocks and shoulders all looked very well muscled, though not in the overstated way of female body builders, and such restricted movements as they did make during the process of being dressed were lithe, supple and graceful. Instantly, Sara found herself hating them.

As each girl was sealed to the neck inside her bright rubber skin, a leather corset, similar to the pony girth, was added. Despite the fact that not one of the half-dozen had a waist measurement exceeding twenty-four inches, it seemed that they were to be reduced even further. Margot, who had returned to Sara's side, threw some light on to this enigma.

'When they're laced really tightly,' she explained, 'it makes them breathe heavier, even when they first stop running. That means that the hunters can use their ears to pinpoint them in the darkness, in case they manage to find any cover thick enough to hide those colours behind.

'And see where their nipples just protrude through the openings? Before they're released, they'll have little bells clipped on to their rings, so when they are moving they'll be easy to hear. Of course, just like you ponies, their arms will rendered fairly useless, or at least their hands will. They'll need to use their arms a certain amount for balancing as they run and for breaking their fall if they trip. It would be far too dangerous to pouch their arms behind them as yours are.'

At least there was some consideration for physical wellbeing then, Sara thought, and might have smiled had the tight bit not already been holding her mouth in its fixed grimace.

'The hunt will take place out in the woods and across a couple of stretches of meadow you haven't yet seen,' Margot continued. 'By the time we start, there will be a

237

whole lot of lanterns hung at intervals in the trees, so it won't be completely dark. Of course, we keep the ponies and their carts to the actual tracks, but the hunters can dismount and follow in on foot when necessary.

'Ever go on one of those paint-balling days, Sassie? I expect all you executive types have had a try at it – supposed to be good for team building and bonding, or some such nonsense.' Sara nodded, for she had tried the sport several times and found it very exhilarating. As to whether it did build team spirit or not, she had never been able to decide, but her senior position in the company meant that she had to be seen to support it and she had done so quite willingly.

'Of course,' Margot was saying, 'the difference here is that the quarry can't fire back, plus there's no padding inside those suits, so the hits tend to sting a bit, especially from a close-range shot. That's the other purpose of the leather corset, to protect some of the more vulnerable organs, and the crotch straps they're putting on them now give some cover in the same way. A cunt shot on the unprotected flesh can be agony – or so I'm told.

'For the same reason, they give the stags protection for their male bits, as you'll see when they bring Plodder and Pascal through from the stables. Pascal is a sweet young thing, completely gay, though he pretends to be bisexual, and a dancer in some West End revue. Plodder, by the way, is the name I've given to your would-be master.

'We decided to see if he makes as good a stag as he does a pony. He was a bit more reluctant than you, of course, but he's done surprisingly well for his first experience. Trouble is, we've had to let him wear his pony hooves – his legs just aren't trained up to coping with the deer ones, any more than yours would be just yet, I'm afraid.'

The process of preparing the six does was continuing apace. Their arms were slipped into tight-laced leather sleeves, each of which ended in a blanked-off end. Once in place, they deprived the wearer of any dexterity, while leaving the actual arms unhindered for other purposes, as Margot had explained. This meant that, while their safety was uncompromised as far as possible, the chance of the girls removing their nipple bells, loosening their corsets or in any other way escaping from their costumes was reduced to nil.

The final touch was to put on their heads, beautifully sculpted creations in rubber, coloured to match each body suit, a variety of zips, straps and laces ensuring a snug fit over the stiff neck collars and reducing each doe to being recognisable only by that colour, regardless of whether she were blonde, brunette, redhead or, in the case of two of the girls, black- or brown-skinned.

Finally attired, all six looked remarkably alike and, as they milled about among the expectant crowd that was now gathering inside the barn, Sara quickly found that she could no longer remember which of them was which. In its own perverse way, she thought grimly, this system assured an equality unmatched in the outside world.

Except that all six of them here, though equal to each other, were equal only in that they were all to be victims, a fate, Sara presumed, they had quite willingly agreed to accept – as she had agreed to accept hers now.

'It will be better for you, in the short term as well as in the long term, to accept your fate, Tammy,' Amaarini said, as she reined the buggy to a halt at the side of the racing circuit. Far above them, the clouds had finally parted, so that the scene was now bathed in pale moonlight, the trees surrounding the long oval clearing standing like black sentinels against the eerie glow.

'You will find Rekoli a considerate master, if you fulfil your duties and obligations to him.'

'You mean have his baby?' Tammy snorted. 'The idea makes me want to vomit, or can't you understand that?'

'I can understand your reluctance, of course I can,' Amaarini replied, levelly, 'but the choice is not yours to make. The only choice you *can* make is whether to accept the inevitable gracefully, or to be simply strapped down and covered like a brood mare.'

'I'm surprised you don't just use some sort of artificial insemination,' Tammy snarled. 'That would be far more clinical.'

239

'Far *too* clinical,' Amaarini laughed. 'Whatever else you might think, we have certain protocols that we prefer to observe and your offspring will be the child of our leader, as well as potentially being the mother or father of an entire new line of male hosts. It would not be fitting for such an important new life to be brought about as if its mother were just some heifer on a croft farm.'

'So I'm supposed to just lie back and spread my legs for this Rekoli guy, is that it?'

'I think perhaps you may do a little more than that, my dear,' Amaarini retorted. 'You seem to be forgetting how that lovely body of yours is designed to work.' Before Tammy could react, she reached across and grasped her right nipple through the thin dress fabric, gripping it firmly, but massaging it at the same time. Immediately, Tammy felt a bolt of warmth shooting upwards from the region of her crotch and gasped in a mixture of alarm, shame and attempted denial.

'By the time Rekoli is ready to enter you,' Amaarini whispered, leaning with her mouth close to Tammy's ear, 'I guarantee you'll be wriggling around like a Glasgow tart in heat. Your head may still seek to deny it, but every other part of you will be screaming out for release in the only way that will satisfy your physical craving.'

'Never!' Tammy spat, but she knew her tormentress was speaking the truth, for already the continued manipulation of her swollen teat was making her squirm and pant.

The first mask he tried was useless, the openings for the eyes so small that Geordie's field of vision was restricted in all directions. He could not even see the floor in front of him without bending his neck and craning his head awkwardly. The smell of leather was also extremely claustrophobic and the second mask was little better in this regard. However, the eye apertures on this one were easily twice the size and, if he were to have any chance of moving about among these people without arousing suspicion, the aroma was something he would have to suffer or get used to.

With a sigh, he finished tightening the laces at the nape of his neck and looked about for a mirror, but it was almost a relief when he saw that there was not one in this room. He could imagine exactly how he now looked and he did not need his reflection to confirm just how stupid he now felt. The tight trousers, rubber shirt, heavy-soled boots and the wide, studded belt may have been *de rigueur* among the male members of this little club, but Geordie knew only too well that they were not him.

'The things I do,' he whispered, and the rows of black and red shiny garments seemed to rustle and mock him as he moved towards the door.

Twenty-Five

'You make a better pony than you do a stag, Plodder dear,' Celia Butler said, checking over Colin's outfit, as he stood mutely in the empty stall, his mouth, inside the rubber deer head with its hat-rack antlers, filled with the inflated gag.

'No,' Celia added, stepping back and looking him up and down critically, 'you just don't have the grace, do you? Never mind, though, it's just for the one hunt and the run will help get some of that flab off your rump, always assuming you aren't captured too quickly. I'm afraid that arse makes a very easy target.'

Especially with the silver and mauve Day-Glo rubber covering it, as well as every other inch of his sweating body, Colin thought. Had he been able to speak, he knew he would have begged her to release him now, agreed to sign the disclaimer that she had shown him earlier and promised not to take any further action when he returned to the real world outside. And he suspected Celia already knew as much, but she had contrived to leave his preparation to three totally disinterested handlers and, by the time she did return, he was once again unable to speak.

Celia reached down and patted his ramrod erection, now safely enclosed, together with his testicles, in a sheath of thick leather, enclosed, one of the handlers had told him, for his own good.

'Try not to point this in the direction of the guns,' she advised. 'Even with this much protection, a close-range

242

shot will bring tears to your eyes and some of our guests have rather unpleasant senses of humour, particularly the male ones.

'Your best bet will be to get yourself shot or captured by a female hunter,' she continued, grinning widely beneath the studded mask that once again covered the top half of her head and face. 'At least that way you'll be able to get some enjoyment at the *après*-hunt. Of course, some of the male hunters will just turn you over to one of the females anyway, but don't count on it. If one takes the trouble to bring you down, the likelihood is that it's because he wants you as his own trophy, and I'm sure I don't need to paint you any pictures in that regard.'

Out in the farmyard, Sara saw that there were now several buggies lined up, all of a much lighter construction than anything she had seen until now. By one end of the barn, a high-sided lorry stood with its tailboard down, and two men were carefully unloading yet another cart of the same design. Obviously, these racy little vehicles were kept elsewhere and brought in only for special occasions, probably because there was a limit to the storage space here, or possibly because they were too valuable to leave around in the outbuildings of a farm that presumably was deserted for much of the time.

One by one, the girl ponies and the one remaining male equine were led towards the line of carts and secured between the twin shafts. Couplings and traces were checked and double-checked, wheels examined, using powerful flashlights, and then the respective drivers began to climb up on to their seats.

Each carried a sinister-looking weapon slung over his or her shoulder and, if Sara had not been forewarned, she would have taken them for authentic rifles in the poor light, instead of the powerful paint-ball guns they actually were. She drew in a deep breath and looked across to where the small herd of brilliantly coloured does was being assembled near the gateway and was grateful that she was being hitched between the shafts and not waiting with them to be turned loose into the woods beyond, where the twinkling illumination from a hundred or more assorted gas and oil lanterns waited to light the way for the hunt.

'Terribly exciting, isn't it, Sassie?' Margot was standing next to her now, holding her bridle firmly, her other hand casually stroking Sara's breast. 'All these keen hunters and only eight poor animals to go around. We'll have to make sure we're on our toes tonight, Sassie dear.

'Have to catch at least one doe, preferably two. That way, I can offer an alternative to whoever it is might have taken a fancy to you. I really don't feel like giving you up just yet and I'm sure you feel the same way, so it's up to you as well, my little pony. Run well and go exactly where I indicate and we'll have ourselves a brace of beauties to barter with.

'Otherwise, I'm afraid you could spend the rest of the night and most of tomorrow squirming on the end of some sweaty beast's cock and neither of us want that, do we?'

With Celia's warning words still ringing in his ears, Colin began working his way into the deepest part of the woods the moment the handlers turned all the hunt quarry loose. In the back of his mind was the possibility that, if he got far enough away from the main action, he might well be able to escape capture altogether and eventually get completely away.

There was one problem with that plan, however. With his hands useless and dressed in such a bizarre fashion, wherever he went he would need some third-party assistance and he was far from keen on the idea of appearing like this in front of yet more people, especially people who would not find his current appearance as acceptable as did Celia's crowd.

Unable to speak and with his face hidden inside the deer mask, there was no way he could communicate with anyone he might happen upon and he could imagine the reaction a normal person might have to being confronted by anything that looked the way he currently did.

As he waded through tangles of undergrowth, he was finally forced to admit to himself that complete escape was

244

not a practical alternative. His only real option was to endure Celia's humiliations for another day or so and rely on her ultimately releasing him as she had stated she would. Meanwhile, his more immediate concern was to stay away from the farm area for as long as possible, evade capture on the night and return to the house after daybreak, when presumably the various guests and participants would be exhausted from their night's revelry.

The assorted lanterns and lamps had been set at random intervals, hanging just above head height from various convenient branches and set just back from the sides of the pathways that honeycombed the woods. Their light meant that there was seldom more than a few yards of darkness along any one track, but the pools of illumination rarely extended far into the trees and bushes themselves, leaving some sizable areas of almost total darkness.

It was safe to assume that the hunters would also carry flashlights with them – he had seen the powerful torches being used in the yard earlier – and the various deer costumes had plainly been designed to reflect even the minimum of light, but Colin reasoned that there would be only so many lanterns available and even these narrow paths had to peter out eventually. If he kept going, he could probably put himself beyond the main hunt sector, find the densest retreat he could and just lie low, literally.

Which was when he ran straight into the fence, bounced off the tightly strung wire mesh and landed on his back in the midst of a tangled thorn bush.

Margot's determination to make an early capture was plain to see and translated into a fierce tirade of exhortations, accompanied by frequent flicks of her driving whip. Eager to play her own part, Sara responded willingly, lurching along the uneven pathways, her bells and harness producing a surprisingly melodic accompaniment.

'Whoa, steady there, girl!' Margot hauled back on the reins, driving the bit painfully deeper inside Sara's mouth, as a flash of luminous pink crossed from one side to the other, barely twenty yards ahead of her. Behind Sara, the cart bounced and then Margot was running past, already unslinging the cumbersome rifle, the tangled net draped over her shoulder in readiness. She looked back over her shoulder and called out, excitedly.

'Come Sassie! Walk on up here!' she shouted and turned into the trees in pursuit of the fleeing figure. Uncertainly, Sara moved forward again, until she was level with the point where Margot had left the track, where she paused, waiting and listening. In the distance, she could hear other cries and shouts of encouragement, but the immediate vicinity seemed suddenly quiet and deserted.

Cautiously, Sara turned her head from left to right, but the bushes and trees remained undisturbed, black and sinister-looking, despite the nearby lanterns on both sides. Margot had not made her instructions totally clear, but Sara could see there was no way she could leave the pathway while still attached to the cart, so her only option was to stand and wait, trying hard not to shuffle her feet in frustration as she did so.

She was not left in suspense for long, however. Despite the barely fractured gloom, her keen eye caught a brief glimpse of pink again, this time about fifty yards further along the track. She froze, not wanting to let the girl know she had been seen, confident also that Margot would not expect her to move in any closer. The seconds ticked by.

Then, crouching low, the doe emerged completely, crossing the open space and ducking back into the woods on the opposite side from where she had come and melting into the cover there. Sara waited, expecting to see Margot appear in pursuit, but instead she heard a flat, dull report, followed by a high-pitched squeal from the direction in which she had seen the fugitive travelling.

Silently, she cursed, for the pink doe must have blundered straight into another hunter, depriving Margot of her 'kill', but to her astonishment, when the lurid figure finally reappeared a minute or two later, wrists strapped in front of her, it was Margot who held the leash that was now clipped about her neck and the identifying yellow paint splatter across her breasts was from Margot's weapon.

'Almost too easy, Sassie,' Margot grinned, as she led her captive up to the cart. 'I doubled back behind you and crossed over behind the last bend. I guessed she'd be watching you and expecting me to try to come up behind her. Then, when she thought I'd lost her trail, she crossed over too, and ran straight into me.' She laughed and jerked gently on the leash.

'C'mon, sexy buns,' she urged. 'Round the back here and let's hook you up to the buggy. And just you make sure you don't drag back. I don't want to wear my poor pony out unnecessarily.'

The fence was easily twelve feet high. Topped with a double strand of barbed wire and supported by angled steel posts, it appeared to run through the woods as far as Colin could see in either direction. Whether there were gaps, or even a gate in it, it was not worth even hazarding a guess, for following its meandering route was rendered impossible by the fact that the undergrowth seemed to grow even thicker along its base, thinning only where this narrow side track ran up to it.

Turning away and looking back along the way he had come, Colin knew he needed to rethink his strategy and rethink it rapidly. He knew he should have foreseen this, for Celia would have been aware of the dangers of determined ramblers stumbling across her property, as well as the possibility that one or more of her quarry might decide to try the same strategy as he had intended. The path also looked surprisingly clear of growth for a route that ended against a blank fence, so he had to presume that it was an area that was checked out frequently, and at any moment, if a hunter appeared on the path, he would find himself trapped in full view, with only two possible escape directions, as opposed to the multiple choices afforded in the middle of the woodland.

Panting from his exertions, he backtracked about a hundred yards, found an area to his left that was less densely overgrown, and ducked back into cover, pushing several yards further through the clawing branches until he felt he was far enough in not to be easily spotted from the path. Crouching down, he listened intently, but the rubber stretched over his ears was reducing his hearing efficiency drastically and he quickly realised that he would have to rely almost entirely upon his eyes.

Which was why, he realised later, he never heard the approaching stalker until it was too late and the ensnaring net was already falling over his head. As his feet were jerked from under him and he toppled headlong inside the tightening mesh, he caught a brief glimpse of the triumphant grin of his captor, and, as he saw the full-lipped mouth below the black mask that covered the top of her head, he said a silent prayer of thanks.

At least she was a female!

The rules of the hunt were quite simple, it seemed. Each hunter carried a paint gun and a net. If he or she netted a 'deer', then that 'animal' was his or her capture, or 'kill', and was simply secured by means of linking the leather arm sheaths together and hitched to the back of the appropriate pony cart.

In addition, the deer could be claimed by shooting at them with the paint guns. A hit in the head, chest or back was counted as a kill and the victim was supposed to surrender to the shooter immediately, with some quite drastic penalties for any who failed to do so. Hits to other parts of the anatomy were counted up only later, if the deer in question was not finally killed or netted.

Each hunter's gun contained paint projectiles of a different colour and points were awarded for hits, depending upon which parts of the body they were on. Margot registered a single point with a snap shot at the fleeing green doe, but the mechanism of her weapon jammed before she could fire again and the 'wounded' creature disappeared with a lurid yellow splash still dripping from her left arm.

'Bugger it!' Margot fumed, as she ejected the offending projectile and reprimed the rifle. 'Arm shot is only a single and someone's bound to hit her in the leg before the end.

Leg shot is worth three points, Sassie, with an extra point if it's in the actual arse.' She pointed her weapon at a nearby tree and fired off a test shot. This time the weapon operated perfectly and the trunk was splattered dead centre, just below a fading red paint stain that was evidently the legacy of a previous hunt.

'We'll have to double back,' Margot said, slinging the rifle over her shoulder. 'There's a clearing just ahead where you can turn, Sassie – the track's far too narrow here.'

Just how extensive the hunt area was, or how long it was likely to go on, Sara had no idea, but it already felt to her as if she had been running all night and there seemed little immediate likelihood of any respite. Wearily, she turned about in the clearing and set off back down the track, Margot's weight now becoming, so it seemed, greater and greater with every passing yard. Snorting and gasping, she began to pray for another sighting, but when it came, instead of heading immediately back into cover, the blue doe simply lengthened her stride and kept to the pathway, looking back over her shoulder every few seconds to ensure that her pursuers were not gaining on her.

Sara drove herself forward, hoping that Margot would recognise the futility of trying to run the girl down in this way, for the combined weight of cart and driver was too big a handicap and, if anything, the gap between herself and the fleeing doe was widening. Surely, she thought, Margot would have a far better chance of overhauling her on foot.

Eventually, it seemed, Margot did accept the futility and reined her to a halt, but, when she alighted from the buggy, instead of chasing off after her quarry, she simply came up to Sara and patted her on the shoulder.

'Nice effort, girl,' she grinned. 'It was worth a try, just in case she'd already run herself out, but obviously she's still fresh.' She sighed, reached up and unclipped one side of Sara's bit, removed it and offered her the neck of a small water bottle. Sara gulped several mouthfuls greedily.

'I – I'm sorry,' she gasped, when Margot finally took the bottle away from her lips. 'She was too fast for me. The weight –'

'Yes, I know,' Margot agreed, patting her consolingly. 'That's part of the game.'

'Couldn't you have chased after her yourself?' Sara suggested, as Margot raised the bit to her mouth once more. Margot smiled.

'Against the rules, old Sassie,' she said. 'Can't follow on foot unless they go to cover. If they stick to the tracks, we have to chase in the carts and they know that gives them the speed advantage. Also, it's a waste of time trying to shoot at them. Hitting a moving target from a bouncing buggy is impossible with these weapons, even at fairly close range.

'Of course, they have to be wary of staying in the open too long. Another cart coming up the other way and they'd be in big trouble, even if they ducked back into the trees again. Two hunters coming at them from different angles, you see.

'Mind you, some of these does are old stagers now and they know just how far to push it. Run the pony out of puff, open up a decent lead and the hunter won't bother trying to follow them to cover. I think that was Coral we were chasing then and she's one of the cutest.

'Not only does she manage to avoid an out-and-out kill nine times out of ten, she hasn't even taken a hit for the last four hunts.' Margot paused, clipping the bit back to its ring. 'Usually,' she said, 'I wouldn't bother trying to catch Coral, not while there are other, easier quarry still in the field, but I've already got this one here,' she said, jerking her head back to indicate the captured doe behind the buggy, 'and we've been out for a while, so I should think the field has been whittled down some by now.'

She took hold of Sara's bridle and gave a short tug, indicating she wanted Sara to start walking forward again.

'So,' she said, as she fell into step beside her, 'we'll just let you get your wind back again and think about this for a little while. It's considered unsporting to actually break the rules, but there's nothing says I can't bend them just a little bit.'

* * *

The upper floors of the house were completely deserted by the time Geordie finally emerged from the attic stockroom and a rapid search through the unoccupied rooms revealed little of interest, save a few names gleaned from various credit cards left in the clothing that had evidently been shed by the various guests who were now, apparently, devoted to apparel of a far less sensible nature.

Peering through the various bedroom windows, Geordie had watched as the curious crowd had first gathered in the yard below and then set off beyond the perimeter wall, some mounted on the high driving seats of the small buggies, others harnessed to draw them and the little group that had first gone out, mainly female and dressed in the most lurid outfits, each one wearing what appeared to be the head of an animal.

However, not everyone had abandoned the house. At the foot of the stairs, Geordie found himself confronted by what he could only describe as a housemaid, although her black, shiny uniform was hardly practical for serious work duties. He tensed himself, ready to grab her, but she did not seem at all worried by his sudden appearance.

'Would you like a drink, master?' she enquired, cocking her blonde head slightly to one side. 'Or would you prefer something else?' She licked her full red lips deliberately, her pale blue eyes twinkling. Geordie swallowed hard, trying to keep his eyes off both her deliciously enticing cleavage and her incredibly long legs, including the stocking tops that were in full view beneath the hem of her ridiculously brief skirt.

'Er, no – thank you,' he blurted. 'I really ought to be getting outside. Over to the barn?' he added. She smiled.

'I think they're all long gone now,' she said. 'You must have arrived very late.'

'Um, yes,' Geordie said. 'Car trouble. Now, if you don't mind, I really have to get a move on.'

'Of course, master,' the girl replied, coquettishly. 'Perhaps you'd like me to come with you. I'm sure there'll be a spare harness or two and I know there's always at least one buggy extra brought along. I don't usually, of course, but it would be a shame for you to miss out on the hunt fun.

'Mind you,' she added, pulling a face, 'by the time you get me ready, I expect it'll all be over. Of course, there's other ways of having fun.' She looked him up and down appreciatively and there was no mistaking her meaning. Geordie took a deep breath.

'What's your name, girl?' he demanded.

'Millie, master,' she smiled back.

'Well, Millie,' he said, trying to sound as authoritarian as he could manage, 'there is a small job you can do for me.'

'Yes, master?'

'Yes, Millie.' He hesitated. 'This is my first visit to this particular place, but Madame Celia is an old friend of mine. However, I don't really know my way around, so I need your help.'

'Anything you say, master,' Millie replied, demurely. 'It's my job to keep Madame's guests happy.' Geordie heaved a sigh of relief; at least he had got the terminology about right.

'Well, Millie,' he instructed her, 'I want you to fetch me . . .' He considered, briefly. 'I want you to fetch me sufficient equipment to secure and gag four females. I saw a few items up in the attic room that might be suitable.'

'There are plenty of things in the barn itself,' Millie replied, 'or would you prefer the things you saw upstairs?'

'No, the barn will do,' Geordie said. 'And remember, I want proper gags, not those bit things the pony girls wear – something that will keep the wearer quiet properly, understand?'

'Perfectly, master.' Millie curtseyed and turned towards the front door, but Geordie reached out and grabbed at her sleeve.

'One other thing,' he added. 'Have they left you here all by yourself?' She shook her head.

'No, master,' she said. 'Jemma and Pauline are in the kitchen, preparing supper.'

Geordie paused, considering this. 'In that case,' he said, at last, 'I think I shall come across to the barn with you.'

252

Twenty-Six

The only food Samba had so far found was a large, plastic bucket, filled with a sort of grain mash, the sort of thing usually fed to horses, although not usually in such a refined form as this and certainly not with the vague lemon smell and taste that this stuff had. She scooped up a handful, let the majority of it trickle through her fingers and brought the remnants up to her mouth, licking experimentally and running the tip of her tongue over the roof of her mouth.

It was fairly bland, apart from the citrus taste, but not unpleasant and, she reasoned, if they fed this stuff to their girl ponies, it had to contain a reasonable amount of nourishment. Samba knew nothing of proteins and minerals, but she did know, from bitter experience, that anything was better than an empty stomach. She also knew that the night air could grow extremely cold and saw no reason why this place should be any different from the foothills where she had grown up.

In the second stall, unoccupied like the first, she found a large, empty plastic bottle, wide-necked and with a screw cap. She opened it, sniffed and nodded. Whatever it had held previously, it had plainly been thoroughly washed out since and it would serve to carry away some of the food from the next-door chamber. All she now needed was some clothing, not just for herself, but for Gypsy, too, for if they hoped to get far in their escape bid, they would need some sort of protection from the elements.

She stood the bottle by the door and turned her attention to the rack on the back wall, examining the strange garments one by one, her nose again twitching at the unfamiliar, cloying aroma, seeing, in her mind's eye, that strange-looking pony woman as she had trotted stiffly out of sight along the pathway outside.

'I have delivered the bride to her groom,' Amaarini smirked. Alex peered through the wide lenses, trying to focus on her face, wondering just how much longer this torture would continue. She had long since lost track of time, but she had been left standing outside for at least an hour and felt certain that there could not be much left of the night. Surely, she thought, the woman would relent soon and let her rest, but Amaarini's next words dashed any hopes of an early respite.

'That leaves just us, horse face,' she said, 'and I am not feeling too sleepy just yet. The night is fine, if a little chilly, so you shall take me back down to the track. From there, I think a gentle ride along the shore way and then perhaps back up along the track that runs around the lower slopes of the hill.

'You will need to practise working on hill tracks.' She unhitched Alex's reins from the bush where she had previously tethered them. 'Where you'll be going soon, you'll see plenty of them. I shall miss you, of course,' she said, maliciously, 'but I shall think of you every day, hauling your little carts over those picturesque South American mountains, year after year!'

The black rubber cape covered most of the captured doe's pink outfit, leaving just her pointed snout peeping out from under the voluminous hood and her booted legs showing beneath the hem. Hefting her up into the driver's seat, Margot wound a length of cord about her waist, securing her to the back rest, and gave her instructions.

'You just sit there, slut, right?' The pink snout nodded. 'And you, my little Sassie, will just walk very steadily along this pathway. You don't stop unless you hear me tell you, OK?' This time Sara nodded.

'About two hundred yards or so further on, you'll come to another turning point. Turn right around and start back this way again. If you see the blue bitch in front of you, then make as if you are giving chase, but don't run flat out. Just stay in sight of her for as long as possible, right?' Again Sara nodded, this time in appreciation, as she began to understand Margot's plan. If Coral was still in this part of the woods and if she tried to repeat her earlier tactics, this was one hunt when she might not escape capture.

The maid, Millie, raised not the slightest protest when Geordie drew her arms behind her back and began fastening them into the long-sleeve affair, though she did seem surprised when he enquired to make sure he was not drawing the laces too tightly.

'Of course not, master,' she giggled. 'I can make my elbows touch, look!' And to prove it, she threw back her shoulders. The leather tube went slack about her upper limbs and Geordie barely managed to conceal his astonishment.

'Fair enough,' he grunted and tightened the restraint until her arms were held in the position into which she had put them. The extreme position didn't seem to worry her and he certainly did not want to arouse suspicions by doing a half-hearted job. 'That better?'

Millie nodded, smiling contentedly. 'Much better, thank you,' she sighed. 'But are you sure you don't want me to be your pony?'

'Quite sure,' Geordie replied, gruffly. 'Now, how do we get this thing on your head?'

'Just open the back and slide it over the front of my face, master,' Millie instructed, obligingly. 'The gag piece on the inside goes into my mouth. Have you never used one of these hoods before?'

'Er, not exactly one like this,' Geordie muttered, fumbling with the limp rubber. 'I'm what you might call a recent convert.'

Too bloody recent, he thought, grimly, as he struggled to fit the slippery hood over the all-too-willing blonde head and, as he tugged the rear zip down to the nape of her slim neck, he wondered just how authentic he ought to try to make this scenario.

* * *

Sara was surprised at the wave of elation she felt when the blue-skinned figure emerged from the trees some fifty yards ahead of her. The snout-faced head turned and its wearer hesitated, apparently making certain she had been seen, and then, the moment Sara began to accelerate into a loping canter, she herself began to run as before.

Counting as she ran, Sara estimated that the chase lasted three or four minutes, taking them back along the same route over which she and Margot had pursued the same quarry earlier, and then further on, through the next turning clearing and then left into the narrower of the two possible paths. By the time the running figure finally veered off and back into cover, Sara was again panting heavily and was grateful to be able to slow to a gentle walk once more.

Margot had been very clear in her instructions – Sara was not to stop until she reached the turning point after Coral had gone to ground again, but there she was to wait until her mistress returned, or until she sent someone else with instructions, depending upon circumstances.

As it happened, it was Margot herself who finally appeared, dragging a badly paint-splattered Coral in her wake and grinning triumphantly, from ear to ear.

'Well done, Sassie!' she cried, striding across the clearing. 'She ran almost straight into me, the silly slut. She did her usual thing, waited for the gap between her and the cart to be too great for me to have any reasonable chance of overhauling her, except that it wasn't actually me chasing her.

'And she can't complain, because I never chased her on foot out of cover. In fact,' Margot laughed, 'I didn't even have to chase her at all. I'd worked out she'd lead you up the narrower path from the fork, as it would tire you quicker, so all I had to do was wait for her. Got off two shots before she even realised I was there, look – one in the tits and another straight in her cunt. The head shot was just for fun and to teach her not to be so clever in future.'

She dragged the sorry-looking doe into the centre of the clearing and threw her down on to the grass. Coral, her arms linked uselessly in front of her, made no attempt to rise again.

'I think,' Margot said, silkily, 'that before we take this cunning little creature back to the farm, I deserve something of a reward for all my efforts. And so do you, Sassie dear,' she added. 'Under this pretty little blue head is a pretty little brown one, if I'm not mistaken, complete with a pretty little pink tongue.

'Let's see if she can make her tongue go as fast as these lovely long legs, shall we?'

If the leather and rubber costume, combined with the mask, had not served as sufficient camouflage on their own, it seemed to Geordie that the fact he was leading a bound and masked female slave on the end of a chain leash was more than enough to establish his credibility, and, as he moved through the knots of returning hunters, their ponies and their prey, hardly an eye was cast in his direction.

It all seemed so unreal and, despite the ease with which he had effected the deception, something was now troubling him deeply. For several minutes, as he paraded his captive around the yard, all the time looking out for any sign of either Colin or Sara, he could not quite fathom it, but finally the penny dropped.

'C'mon, Flossie,' he said to Millie, tugging the chain and turning her towards the gate. 'You and me have to talk some.'

He led the unresisting maid out into the meadow between the yard and the woods, guiding her towards the nearest trees and as far away from the flickering lanterns as was possible. Eventually, he found one small area that was in almost total darkness.

'Now listen here,' he said, tugging the hood clear of her head, 'and listen carefully.' Millie stared at him with huge eyes, a mask of innocence that was betrayed only by the slight quivering at the corners of her mouth.

'I'm listening, master,' she replied, dutifully and Geordie let out a loud sigh of total exasperation.

'Millie,' he said, carefully, 'I want to ask you a question.' She nodded, without speaking. 'And the question is this: what if I want to, well, you know, have sex with you?'

'Oh, master!' she sighed, rolling her eyes extravagantly. Geordie sighed again.

'For fuck's sake!' he stormed. 'Will you be serious?' Millie stared at him and even in the darkness there was no mistaking the look of hurt incomprehension in her eyes. Geordie shook his head and took her by the shoulders.

'Listen, hen,' he said, 'I think there's something you should know. I'm a policeman, right?' She smiled back at him, nodding like a puppet.

'Yes?'

'Yes,' he said. 'I'm a policeman and I'm here to find out what these crazies have been doing to a couple of my friends. There's an awful lot I don't understand about this set-up and I'm only telling you this because I can pop this hood thing back on you and I'll be finished and gone before you can blow the whistle on me. So, what I need are a few straight answers, OK?'

'OK.'

'To start with, how do these bastards force you into this in the first place?'

Millie regarded him seriously and suddenly the mask slipped away. 'Forced me?' she said. 'Oh, you poor, misguided man, you. I haven't been forced into this. I come here quite willingly, once or twice a month, because I enjoy it.'

'But why do you enjoy it?'

Millie sniggered and half turned away. 'That would take too long to explain,' she said, 'and if you need to even ask the question, the odds are that you'd never understand the explanation anyway.' All of a sudden, Geordie realised, her entire personality seemed to have changed. In place of the fluffy blonde doll had emerged a very confident and positive person.

'I don't know what you expected to find here,' she continued, 'but I can tell you that you're almost certainly missing the plot, OK? All of us here are here because we want to be and because we want to escape from the shit heap that passes for the real world out there. You asked me what would happen if you wanted to have sex with me, didn't you? Well, basically, provided you use a condom – and there's a couple in the pocket of this uniform, just in case you haven't come prepared, which I doubt you have – then there's no problem at all.

'I don't care what the fuck you are out there: policeman, fireman, taxi driver, it's all the same to me. I come here for one thing and, if you can give that to me, what does anything else matter? And, if you really do want me, then fine, and don't think you need to make any excuses. It needn't even compromise whatever it is you're up to here. Just stick the bloody mask back on me – before or after doesn't make any difference, either, in case you're wondering – and you can just carry on regardless.

'After all,' she said, grinning slyly, 'what difference does one dumb blonde, more or less, make to the equation?'

Wishing that his outfit had a pocket large enough to hold his cigarettes and lighter, Geordie slumped down on to the length of fallen tree trunk that lay at the clearing's edge.

'Tell me,' he said, staring morosely at the grass, 'what exactly are you in that outside world?'

Millie shuffled over and lowered herself down beside him. 'Between you and me,' she said, 'I'm a barrister. A junior counsel, as it happens, and my real name is Melinda. But, right now, I'm out of chambers and on my own time, so, Mr Policeman, are you going to fuck me, or frustrate me? Either way, I'll give you a free counsel's opinion!'

Twenty-Seven

The rubber skin suits had all appeared far too small, but, when Samba finally decided that they represented her only realistic chance of finding some protection against the elements and started to try one, she discovered that the slippery fabric had astonishing elastic properties and stretched to fit her rounded curves with no difficulty at all. Not only that, but for something so thin it felt surprisingly warm.

She peered down at herself and especially at her now black-clad feet, doubting that the material would last long on the rough ground outside. In the corner of the stall were several pairs of boots, but all had the same strange hoof-shaped soles, complete with steel horseshoes, and weighed far too much to be practical. Discarding them, she scooped up a dark-grey suit for Gypsy, tucked the food bottle under her arm and opened the door just wide enough to see out.

The main concourse beyond was still deserted, the overhead lights dimmed, and, crouching low, Samba slipped out again and made for the shadows afforded by the pony carts. As she paused to listen again, she saw that most of the carts had oblong storage boxes bolted behind the driver's seat and, on impulse, she opened the nearest one.

In the gloom, it was difficult to see the contents properly, but she quickly found a coiled whip, a set of steel manacles, an unpleasant-looking rubber hood and . . . a pair of knee-length boots. Her immediate elation quickly gave way to frustration, however, for as she took the boots out it was immediately apparent that they were both far too large for her small feet and, even had they fitted, the towering, spiked heels would have made walking a very precarious occupation.

She swore, silently, replaced everything as she had found it, and moved on to the next cart. The yield here was a little better, for the first item was a rubber cape, complete with a tight-fitting hood that left the face exposed. Grinning, Samba wriggled into it, but immediately tugged the hood down around her neck, for the close-fitting rubber impaired her hearing far too much and she knew she would need all her senses at their sharpest. Later, perhaps, the hood would serve a purpose and the swishing cape afforded an extra layer of potential warmth.

Again there was a whip, more manacles and another pair of boots, slightly smaller this time, but with the same impractical heels. The most interesting item apart from the cape was a pair of long gloves, again made from the rubbery fabric. Holding them up for inspection, Samba began to form an idea for their use; it did not include wearing them, but she knew, nonetheless, that they could serve a valuable purpose. She wrapped them inside the spare suit and moved further along the row of vehicles.

By the time she had reached the final cart, Samba was feeling quite pleased with her scavenging expedition. Her trophies did now include a pair of boots that looked like they might just fit her and, although they too had heels, they were much lower and not so slim as seemed to be the norm here.

She also had a plastic bottle containing water – stale, but still drinkable – a small flashlight, a coil of thin but strong cord, a second cape identical to the one she now wore and something that she eventually identified as one of the pouches that she had seen used to hold the pony girl's arms folded behind her back, but which now served as a bag in which to carry everything she had found.

Feeling more than satisfied with her haul, she made one last check that there was no one coming and slipped, like a dark shadow, towards the mouth of the exit tunnel.

* * *

'Where you're going to, horse face,' Amaarini sneered, 'will make you appreciate what you could have had here.' Alex was still harnessed between the shafts of the cart, but at least the big woman was now walking alongside her, albeit frequently jerking at her bridle to emphasise her words.

'Our South American friend assures us that you'll be working up to eighteen hours a day, hauling carts and packs over some of the worst terrain known to human kind. And, when you're not working as a mule, they'll find other uses for you, so you won't get much rest.' She laughed, harshly.

'And do you know, they weren't even fussy about taking your personal control unit along,' Amaarini continued. 'But then you won't have any need of a voice, will you? In fact, I shouldn't be at all surprised if they left your horse face on you for good.' She pulled on the shortened rein, turning Alex abruptly left and a few yards further on the path opened up into a small clearing.

At first, the combination of the semidarkness and the wide-spaced lenses made it difficult for Alex to make out the object set in the centre of the open space, but, as they drew nearer, there was little doubting its purpose.

Set on a heavy timber base, a tripod stand rose some two feet into the air, from where a single, circular steel pole projected further, topped with a slightly curved black extension that was unmistakable. Beside Alex, Amaarini laughed again.

'I had our workshops turn out three of these,' she said, 'all made to my own design. Very simple but very effective, and so much more aesthetically pleasing than an ordinary hitching rail. I'm sure you can work out the principle on which it is based.'

Indeed, Alex could and the efficiency of the device was quickly demonstrated. She was unhitched from the cart and Amaarini led her forward, pulling her over the vertical dildo and forcing her thighs apart. Once she was in position, the crotch strap was unbuckled and removed, the existing phallus withdrawn and then Amaarini manually raised the upright pole, pushing the stationary shaft up and deep within her and engaging a locking pin at the top of the tripod to prevent it dropping down again.

The effect was to keep Alex impaled over the stand, unable to raise her stance beyond the already elevated position forced on her by the hoof boots and thus unable to move in any direction. Until Amaarini or some third party intervened, Alex was therefore effectively immobilised.

'There you are, horse face,' Amaarini declared, triumphantly. 'A nice open-air stable for you. Actually, the workshop has just finished an improved model, motor driven, but if you get too bored you'll have to rely on your own efforts tonight, I'm afraid.' She stepped back, folding her arms.

'I promised you I'd teach you to appreciate when you were well off,' she said, 'and I had no intention of waiting until you're the other side of the ocean to prove a point. And,' she added, the crooked smirk widening, 'there is still sufficient time between now and when you're to be shipped for me to introduce you to a few other innovations.'

She turned and began walking back the way they had earlier come. 'I'll be back for you in a few hours,' she called, over her shoulder, 'unless something more important comes up, of course!'

Geordie was not certain which sections of the Police and Criminal Evidence Act he had just contravened, but he was certain that they were both several and potentially serious, though he somehow doubted whether Millie, or even Melinda the barrister, would ever bring a complaint against him.

Supporting himself on his elbows, he looked down into her contented face and gently ground his pelvic bone against hers. The action elicited a deep sigh, a small tremor and a low groan. She opened her eyes and smiled up at him.

'You really believe in giving everything to authenticity in your undercover jobs, don't you?' she snickered. She stuck out her bottom lip and blew away a strand of grass that had managed to come to rest against the side of her pert nose. 'And, in case you're wondering, I'm quite happy to be your personal slave maid for the rest of the night. Tomorrow, too, if you like.'

Carefully withdrawing from her, Geordie rolled on to his side and sat up. They were in the shadow of a clump of tall bushes on the very edge of the woods and no one seemed to have been paying any attention to their activities.

'I don't really fancy spending any more time here than I have to,' he said. 'This isn't really my scene at all.' Millie looked up again and grinned.

'You could have fooled me,' she said. Geordie felt himself reddening.

'That was, well . . .' He hesitated. 'Look, I shouldn't have done that. I'm sorry.'

'Well, don't be,' Millie retorted. 'I could easily have screamed out if I'd wanted to stop you. You didn't put the mask and gag back on me, after all.'

'And would anyone have taken any notice if you had screamed?'

She sniggered again. 'Depends what I'd screamed,' she said, 'but probably, no.'

'So,' Geordie said, quietly, 'where do we go from here?' Millie rolled her eyes.

'Don't let me down now,' she said. 'You're supposed to be the master, so that means you make the decisions.' She struggled into a sitting position, her arms still laced behind her back. 'However,' she went on, 'if you do want my advice, then this is it.

'You need to make sure your pals are OK, right? Well, if the girl is the one I saw with Margot earlier, then she's better than OK, believe me. As for your policeman friend, I'm assuming he's the one Celia calls Plodder; all the other men here tonight I've seen before.'

'And where is this . . . Plodder?' Millie nodded towards the woods.

'Out there, somewhere,' she said. 'He was the stag in the stripy body suit. Mind you, he may already have been captured by now and be back in the barn. I seem to have

264

been paying attention to more immediate concerns just lately!'

Samba stood over the unconscious figure of Amaarini, one of the rubber gloves, the fingers and hand part filled with several medium-sized stones, dangling from her right hand. It really had been too easy, she thought, for the arrogant bitch just had not expected anything to happen to her here.

Stooping down, she checked Amaarini's neck for a pulse and gave a long, low whistle. After a few moments, a second caped figure materialised from the darkness of the trees and padded across the grass to join her. Gypsy's huge eyes seemed even larger than usual, shining in the pale moonlight, and her taut features betrayed fear and unwillingness.

'Help,' Samba ordered and reached down to seize one of Amaarini's booted ankles. Gypsy hesitated, backing away, but quickly returned to take the other ankle when Samba straightened up and made to move towards her. Between the two of them, they dragged the big woman behind the nearest bushes, where Samba quickly utilised some of the cord from the bag to truss her hand and foot.

'Come,' she said, when they returned to the pathway. She stabbed a finger indicating the direction from which Amaarini had appeared and towards where they had watched her leading her hapless victim just a few minutes earlier. 'Come. Pony woman. We find.'

By the time his captor finally led Colin back into the barn, it seemed that the rest of the weekend party had already arrived ahead of them, for the main area was now quite crowded. However, seeing him stumbling in the wake of the tall female, they began backing away towards the walls, leaving a clear arena in their centre.

'What price my stag!' Colin's nemesis roared and there was a general ripple of amusement.

'Two hours with the fastest pony girl in England, Olive!' one male voice roared. 'And then two hours with me!'

The woman, Olive, turned in the direction of the voice, grinning. 'I'm told you're faster than that bloody filly of

265

yours,' she quipped. 'You'll need to do better than that, Glaze!'

'Swap you my doe for your stag!' This time the offer came from a female and, as the speaker pushed towards the front of the throng, Colin felt his stomach somersault, for she was the biggest woman he had ever set eyes on; not only was she at least six feet tall, without the aid of the spike-heeled boots she currently wore, but she was easily eighteen stone plus and not a single ounce of that appeared to be surplus fat.

Apart from the knee boots, she wore a tight pair of leather shorts, a brief leather halter that was fighting a losing battle with an impressive bosom and a curious mask that covered the top half of her head, together with an extension that jutted over her nose. About her neck was a broad, wickedly spiked collar and similar spikes adorned the wrists of the heavy gauntlets that covered her hands. Olive turned and regarded her, clearly considering the proposition.

'Which one did you bring in, Val?' she demanded. The muscular amazon reached behind her and hauled the sleek yellow doe into the ring.

'The one with the biggest tits, as you can see,' she said, and indeed, Colin had to admit, although the girl was slim-waisted, she was otherwise generously endowed. Leading him by the rope halter she had placed about his neck, Olive strolled slowly across to the girl and looked her up and down as casually as if she were examining stock at a cattle market.

'Not bad,' she said, eventually. 'You've got yourself a deal.' She slipped the noose over Colin's head and dropped it neatly on to her new acquisition. 'C'mon, my little melon,' she said, tugging gently, 'let's go peel you and see what the fruit is really like.'

'Why not do it here?' Val suggested. 'Give us all a bit of a show. After all, I'm going to mount the stag here after dinner and everyone's invited.'

Olive shook her head. 'No thanks,' she replied, firmly. 'You can give your usual public performance, if you like,

266

but I'm going to get to know this little treasure in private.'
Val shrugged her powerful shoulders.

'Suit yourself,' she retorted. 'But the after-dinner invite
still stands for everybody, you included.'

Olive smiled, pulling the yellow doe girl to her and
cupping one of her breasts. 'I wouldn't miss it for the
world,' she said.

'Who are you?' Alex gasped, when the hateful horse head
was finally pulled clear, dragging the gag with it. She stared
at the two small figures, for even in the moonlight she
could see that the colour of their faces was far darker than
anything she had seen on the island before now. They
stared back at her and the one on the left, the one who had
actually worked out how to lower the stand on which she
had been so cruelly mounted and then solved the intricacies of the pony-mask fastenings, said something to her
companion in a language that was unlike anything Alex
had ever heard. She took a deep breath and, wishing her
arms were free so that she could point at herself, tried the
simplest approach.

'Me, Alex,' she said and repeated her name once more
for good measure. She turned, wriggling her shoulders and
indicating for the girl to release her arms from the
restraining pouch. The girl, in turn, moved forward, but
her companion grabbed her wrist and jabbered something
completely incomprehensible. The first girl rolled her eyes,
shook off her grip and stepped up to examine the buckles
and clips.

'Idiot girl,' she grinned, pointing at her scared-looking
companion. 'Fucking slut.' Alex almost wept with relief as
the pouch fell away, but instead she groaned as she
straightened her arms for the first time in what seemed like
eternity. She turned to the first girl, who was shaking out
the pouch and adjusting the loose straps.

'Thank you!' she gasped. Her hands were still balled into
virtually useless fists, but she could not wait until her
saviour was ready to try to release them too, and rubbed
each upper arm in turn, wincing as the circulation began

to restore itself to something approaching a normal level. Meanwhile, the first girl had succeeded in converting the restraining pouch into something approximating a shoulder bag. She handed it to the second girl and muttered something in the strange language again. The second girl hesitated and then turned and padded off into the darkness.

'Me, Alex.' Alex tried again, this time using her right fist to point to herself. The remaining girl nodded and smiled, pointing at her own chest.

'Me, Samba,' she said. She pointed away, extending her arm back in the direction the other girl had taken, along the path leading back, ultimately, to the stables. 'She Gypsy – stupid slut. Simple.' She made a rotary motion next to her temple with the forefinger of her other hand. 'Silly bitch,' she added, her white teeth gleaming.

'What are you doing here?' Alex began, but immediately gave up on that question, for it was clear enough that Samba's English vocabulary was very limited, to say the least. She looked around the clearing, expecting Amaarini to reappear at any moment, for this could easily be that bitch's idea of a joke.

'Big woman,' she tried, raising her hand to indicate someone of Amaarini's impressive height. 'Big woman.' She pointed at the abandoned pony cart and acted someone shaking out a set of reins. Samba's grin grew wider still.

'Big bitch!' she cried, jumping up and down excitedly. Again she pointed up the track. 'Big bitch,' she said again and this time made a sort of slashing motion with her right arm, as if she was wielding a club. Then she closed her eyes and pressed the palms of her hands together, next to her cheek. She held the pose for three or four seconds and then opened one eye, peering at Alex impishly.

'Big bitch,' she said again. 'Well fucked.'

They stripped Colin naked, apart from a pair of pony boots, the stag's head and the protective sheath about his genitalia, but then quickly laced his hands into what he at first took to be boxing gloves, except that they were

268

padded with a very spongy substance that gave his fists the appearance of two small footballs.

Then, with a male groom on his left and a tall, slim, masked female on his right, he was escorted back into the main area of the barn. The guests had evidently finished their late dinner, for most of them were already gathered and awaiting his arrival. He was led out into the centre of the clear area and the female stooped down and began releasing the sheath, revealing his erection to the watching eyes. There were several ribald comments at this and one woman, dressed in an almost transparent toga-like garment, even stepped forward and reached out a hand to touch it.

'Hands off my property, you drunken slag!' The roared command preceded Val's entrance by several seconds and, when she finally emerged from the small throng nearest the entrance, Colin felt his knees go weak.

Like him, she was stripped now, save for her mask and boots, her impressive body glistening beneath a sheen of oil, her massive breasts rising and falling in slow majesty. She pointed a talon-like fingernail towards him and then beckoned. Colin hesitated and then took a backward pace. Val's response was to throw back her head and roar with laughter.

'Look's like he could be a runner,' she said, when her mirth finally subsided. 'Someone put some ankle shackles on him. I don't want to spend all night chasing round in circles.'

Willing hands grabbed him, pinning his arms, while more eager helpers produced the ankle cuffs and locked them into place. Miserably, Colin stared down at the short length of chain between them and realised that further flight was pointless. He looked up again, squared his shoulders and waited.

'Much better,' Val thundered. 'Now get your worthless arse over here. And somebody get that stupid head off him. The sort of head I've got planned needs a clear mouth.

'Now, Plodder, or whatever you're called,' she whispered, when he finally confronted her without the stag mask, 'let's see if you were worth the trade. Get down on your knees and crawl over here.'

Twenty-Eight

The sun had already been up for more than two hours by the time Geordie collected his room key from the reception at the hotel, but the girl behind the desk handed it to him without so much as a raised eyebrow. Inside the room, he threw the grip bag into the bottom of the wardrobe, stripped off his jacket, kicked off his shoes and collapsed on to the bed. Within two minutes, he was sound asleep.

He was awakened by an insistent bleeping sound and it took several seconds before he realised that it was coming from the telephone receiver on the bedside cabinet. Blearily, he scooped up the receiver.

'Mr Walker?' He recognised the receptionist's voice and struggled to sit up. 'I have a Miss Harvey-Johnson in reception for you.'

Geordie blinked and stifled a yawn. 'Who?' And then he remembered. 'Oh, yes. Sorry,' he mumbled. 'Could you send her up?'

The girl agreed that she would, but in a tone that suggested she did not quite approve, and a few minutes later there was a light tap on the door. Tossing aside the hand towel with which he had been wiping the cold water from his face, Geordie closed the bathroom door behind him and went to answer the knock.

'I wasn't sure you'd come,' he said.

Melinda Harvey-Johnson smiled sweetly at him. 'I never break a promise,' she said, peering past him into the room. 'And you promised me coffee and dinner. Aren't you going to invite me in?'

'Dinner?' Geordie looked confused. 'What the hell time is it?' Automatically, he checked his wrist, but the watch was still in the pocket of his discarded jacket.

'Just after five o'clock,' Melinda/Millie replied, stepping past him as he stood aside. 'And, from the look of you, I'd say you've been asleep since you got back.'

'Do I look that bad?'

'You looked better in your mask,' she tittered, as he closed the door. 'But a hot bath and a shave will work wonders. Why don't you ring down for coffee and I'll go through and start the water running. I might even wash your back.'

'But I can't just hang around here!' Geordie protested. 'Colin's still back there.'

'And we talked about that before you left,' Melinda reminded him. 'And yes, I did make a few discreet enquiries. They'll be letting him go soon, probably tomorrow morning.'

'But are you sure about that?'

'As near certain as I can be. I managed to have a little chat with Margot, just before I left. She didn't say he was a policeman – they wouldn't want to scare any of us off, as you can imagine – but she did say he was some sort of snooper and that he just needed teaching a lesson. They won't hurt him, believe me.'

Only his pride, Geordie thought to himself, as he picked up the phone to order a large pot of coffee, for that final image of Colin with the massive Val – Millie had told him that was only short for Valkyrie, her nickname – would remain imprinted on his memory for ever and he doubted Colin would ever forget the experience, either.

'Bugger it!' he swore, not quite under his breath. 'What a complete waste of time and effort.'

'I'm glad you've decided to stay, Sassie.' Margot closed the bedroom door and let Sara's lead rein drop from her hand. Smiling, she reached out and carefully detached her bit, removing it slowly. She tapped it gently on the tip of Sara's nose.

271

'Of course,' she said, 'I realise that you'll probably want more than just another woman – sadly most of you do, eventually. But, for the moment, I think we can be quite happy together, you and I. We have another place – yes, Mumsie is pretty wealthy – in the real wilds of Wales, miles and miles from anywhere, with a big cottage and a lovely stable. I think maybe I'll take you there for a couple of weeks, before the weather breaks. I can trot you for hours there and no one will disturb us.'

'It sounds delightful . . . mistress,' Sara said, sombrely. 'When are you thinking of going?'

'As soon as possible, Sassie,' Margot replied. 'I presume you'll have to make a couple of phone calls to explain your absence.'

Sara nodded. 'There won't be any problems,' she promised. 'Everyone knows how upset I was when Andrew died and my doctor has been telling me to get away for weeks now. He said I needed a change.'

'Well, I can certainly promise you that,' Margot laughed. She tossed the spittle-sodden bit aside and reached out to cup Sara's breasts. 'And I think I can change you, too.'

Sara arched her spine and let out a deep breath. Her nipples already felt as if they must surely burst.

'I think . . . I think I've changed quite a lot already,' she sighed. Margot grasped her bridle with one hand and drew her face towards her own.

'I think so, too,' she agreed. Tenderly, she kissed Sara's willingly parting lips, her tongue flicking between them. 'And you look so pretty in your harness, as I'm sure you know.'

'Yes, mistress,' Sara whispered. 'I'm so glad you like me this way.'

'I like you that way so much,' Margot said, 'that I'd love to keep you in harness for ever, except it wouldn't be very practical, would it?'

Sara's eyelids fluttered. 'Why not?' she breathed. 'I don't really want to go back to my job, not now Andrew isn't there any more. The company will be taken over by chinless wonders, parts of it sold off – things will change, as they always do.'

Carefully, Margot steered her backwards towards the bed and pushed her backwards on to it, her legs dangling with the heavy hoof boots now clear of the floor. She knelt down, her fingers busy with the crotch-strap buckles, and presently withdrew the dildo that the strap had been holding in place for so long. She held it to her mouth and slowly ran her tongue along its glistening length.

'Yes,' she said, dreamily, 'things do change.' She carefully placed the rubber phallus beside Sara and leaned forward, her tongue seeking the warm crevice that gaped so invitingly before her. 'So sweet, Sassie,' she sighed.

'So very, very sweet.'

Millie had excused herself to the ladies', but Geordie waited until the waiter had brought the coffees before voicing his thoughts.

'That bloody Sara has put us right in it,' he snapped. 'The fact that she's decided to stay with that cow Margot really shoots holes through any case we might have had.'

Colin, who seemed remarkably well recovered from his ordeal, stirred his coffee almost absently.

'Maybe,' he said, 'but I doubt it. Apart from the fact there's no way I want anyone else seeing pictures of what happened to me back there, we don't really have a case. Sara and I both went to Celia's first place of our own accord and I couldn't prove a bloody thing, apart from the fact that I seemed – and I stress the word "seemed" – to be a willing participant.'

'But we both know different,' Geordie persisted.

Colin shook his head. ''Tain't proof, old bean,' he retorted. 'I doubt even any of the early pictures you took would hold up in court and nothing you got afterwards would be even admissible. You were trespassing at the very least and probably guilty of breaking and entering.'

'Don't forget theft,' Geordie added. 'I've still got that bloody mask and outfit upstairs in my room. I just grabbed my own clothes and changed once I was back at the car. Didn't want to hang around.'

'At least you had a choice,' Colin muttered. 'And to think it was all for nothing.'

'I still don't buy that.'

'Well, you heard what your new lady friend said just now and she does work for the CPS. Like she told it, they wouldn't touch this with a bargepole. Besides, any action would just be against Celia and her daughter, not Health-glow.'

'But at least we know there's a definite link now,' Geordie said. He drew out a cigarette and twiddled it idly in his fingers. 'That's got to be something.'

'Oh, yeah, really something. We *already* had a link established, that's why I stuck my neck out like I did. What we don't have is evidence of any criminal activity.'

'So we just give up, is that it?'

'If we had any sense, yes,' Colin confirmed. 'However, as policemen, we aren't expected to be too strong on sense, are we?'

'Well, I'm just a thick lad from bloody Tyneside,' Geordie said. 'We hit our heads against brick walls because it's nice when we stop.'

'But you don't intend to stop just yet.' Colin said. It wasn't a question and they both knew it.

Geordie shook his head, lit his cigarette and exhaled a cloud of smoke. 'Not till I find out who killed Alex Gregory,' he said. 'Somehow, I'll find a way of getting on that bloody island, even if it takes me the next five years. Now, let's change the subject, shall we? My lady friend, as you call her, is coming back.'

Twenty-Nine

It had taken Samba an hour to find the tiny cave. It was well hidden in the rocks above one of the island's several small coves, but Alex doubted that its location was unknown to Amaarini and her cronies. However, it was better than remaining in the open and its difficult approach afforded some defensive possibilities, at least until Boolik and his guards decided to use those weird weapons she had seen put to such efficient use on the night she had first arrived here.

She sat in the narrow entrance, looking out over the misleadingly calm surface of the sea, toying with the second glove Samba had given her, weighing the collection of pebbles that now filled one end of it. Samba's glove, similarly weighted, had made short work of Amaarini, it was true, but against the sort of firepower these people could bring to bear, it was a pathetic token.

On the horizon, beyond and to the left of Carigillie, Alex identified two of the blue smudges of the inner islands – less than twenty miles away, but as good as in a different universe. Even without the weighted boots – their best efforts had failed to crack the locks that held them in place – it would be suicide to try to reach them without a boat. The currents between the islands were strong and unpredictably treacherous and even a seasoned marathon swimmer would not last long in such waters.

'Cry-cry?'

Alex turned her head at the sound of Samba's voice. The little Indian girl was crouched behind her, her expression sorrowful. 'What?'

Samba pointed to her own face and made an even more mournful expression, her fingers drawing down on the corners of her mouth. 'Cry-cry,' she repeated.

Alex shook her head. 'No,' she said. 'Not cry-cry. Can't fucking cry-cry in this body. Just very sad.'

Samba looked at her, uncomprehendingly. 'Sad?' she echoed. She considered this for a moment and then nodded. 'Sad, yes,' she repeated. She held up her own weighted glove.

'Go fuck some more?' she suggested.

Despite the blackness of her mood, Alex laughed. 'No,' she said, shaking her head. 'No fuck any more. Men have guns.' She mimed pointing a rifle. 'Bang-bang!' Except their rifles, if that was what they were, didn't go bang-bang, but there was no point trying to explain that to the girl.

Samba raised her eyebrows, then pointed out towards the water. 'Long go,' she said.

Alex nodded. 'Bloody long go,' she agreed.

Samba dropped her glove and made a breast-stroke motion with her arms.

Again, Alex shook her head. 'No,' she said. 'Bad water.' Bad bloody news. These two strange little females had rescued her from Amaarini's immediate clutches, but to what effect and for how long? Without the means to get off the island, she had simply enlarged the walls of her prison and temporarily rid herself of the most restrictive of her bondage.

Samba peered west, towards the slowly setting sun, shielding her eyes with one hand. 'Bad water?' She sighed and shook her own head. 'No go?'

'No,' Alex said, mournfully. 'No go at all.' She snorted and patted the younger girl's arm.

'I think,' she said, as much to herself as to Samba, 'that your favourite expression seems to fit the bill only too accurately right now. Well fucked.'

One way or the other, she reflected, it was a fair summing up.

NEW BOOKS

Coming up from Nexus

Captive by Aishling Moran
4 January 2001   £5.99   ISBN 0 352 33585 8
Set in the same world of nubile girls, cruel men and rampant goblins as its prequel, *Maiden*, *Captive* follows the tribulations of the maid, Aisla, as she endeavours to free her mistress Sulitea from a life of drudgery and punishment, only to find her less than grateful. As she struggles to return home with Sulitea, they must overcome numerous men, trolls and yet worse beasts, and when Aisla is taken prisoner in foreign lands, it is her turn to escape, or else face a humiliating public execution.

Soldier Girls by Yolanda Celbridge
4 January 2001   £5.99   ISBN 0 352 33586 6
Stripped of her uniform for 'sexual outrage', soldier-nurse Lise Gallard is forced to endure corporal punishment in the Foreign legion women's prison. But she is spotted there by dominatrix Dr Crevasse, who engineers Lise's release from her own flagellant purposes. Can Lise hope to escape her cruel mistress? Or will she in turn learn to wield the can?

Eroticon 1 ed. J-P Spencer
4 January 2001   £5.99   ISBN 0 352 33593 9
A Nexus Classic unavailable for some time; a selection of a dozen of the most exhilerating excerpts from rare and once-forbidden works of erotic literature. They range from the work of the French poet Guillaume Apollinaire to the most explicit sexual confession of the Edwardian era – Walter's *My Secret Life*.

Angel by Lindsay Gordon
8 February 2001   £5.99   0 352 33590 4
Angel is a Companion. He has sold his freedom for access to a world inhabited by the most ambitious, beautiful – and sometimes cruel – women imaginable: an executive who demands to be handled by a stranger in uniform; a celebrity who adores rope and wet under-things; a doctor who lives her secret life inside tight rubber skins. And it's not Angel's place to refuse.

Tie and Tease by Penny Birch
8 February 2001   £5.99   0 352 33591 2
Caught by a total stranger, Beth, while playing the fox in a bizarre hunting game, Penny finds herself compromised by Beth's failure to understand her submissive sexuality. Penny is determined to seduce the girl, but her efforts get her into more and more difficulty, involving ever more frequent punishments and humiliations until, turned on a roasting spit, she is unsure how much more even she can take.

Eroticon 2 Ed. J-P Spencer
8 February 2001   £5.99   0 352 33594 7
Like its companion volumes, a sample of excerpts from rare and once-forbidden works of erotic literature. Spanning three centuries, it ranges from Andrea de Nericat's eighteenth century *The Pleasures of Lolotte* to the Edwardian tale *Maudie*.

NEXUS BACKLIST

All books are priced £5.99 unless another price is given. If a date is supplied, the book in question will not be available until that month in 2000.

CONTEMPORARY EROTICA

THE BLACK MASQUE	Lisette Ashton	
THE BLACK WIDOW	Lisette Ashton	
THE BOND	Lindsay Gordon	
BRAT	Penny Birch	
BROUGHT TO HEEL	Arabella Knight	July
DANCE OF SUBMISSION	Lisette Ashton	
DISCIPLES OF SHAME	Stephanie Calvin	
DISCIPLINE OF THE PRIVATE HOUSE	Esme Ombreux	
DISCIPLINED SKIN	Wendy Swanscombe	Nov
DISPLAYS OF EXPERIENCE	Lucy Golden	
AN EDUCATION IN THE PRIVATE HOUSE	Esme Ombreux	Aug
EMMA'S SECRET DOMINATION	Hilary James	
GISELLE	Jean Aveline	
GROOMING LUCY	Yvonne Marshall	Sept
HEART OF DESIRE	Maria del Rey	
HOUSE RULES	G.C. Scott	
IN FOR A PENNY	Penny Birch	
LESSONS OF OBEDIENCE	Lucy Golden	Dec
ONE WEEK IN THE PRIVATE HOUSE	Esme Ombreux	
THE ORDER	Nadine Somers	
THE PALACE OF EROS	Delver Maddingley	
PEEPING AT PAMELA	Yolanda Celbridge	Oct
PLAYTHING	Penny Birch	

THE PLEASURE CHAMBER	Brigitte Markham		
POLICE LADIES	Yolanda Celbridge		
THE RELUCTANT VIRGIN	Kendal Grahame		
SANDRA'S NEW SCHOOL	Yolanda Celbridge		
SKIN SLAVE	Yolanda Celbridge		June
THE SLAVE AUCTION	Lisette Ashton		
SLAVE EXODUS	Jennifer Jane Pope		Dec
SLAVE GENESIS	Jennifer Jane Pope		
SLAVE SENTENCE	Lisette Ashton		
THE SUBMISSION GALLERY	Lindsay Gordon		
SURRENDER	Laura Bowen		Aug
TAKING PAINS TO PLEASE	Arabella Knight		
TIGHT WHITE COTTON	Penny Birch		Oct
THE TORTURE CHAMBER	Lisette Ashton		Sept
THE TRAINING OF FALLEN ANGELS	Kendal Grahame		
THE YOUNG WIFE	Stephanie Calvin		May

ANCIENT & FANTASY SETTINGS

THE CASTLE OF MALDONA	Yolanda Celbridge		
NYMPHS OF DIONYSUS	Susan Tinoff	£4.99	
MAIDEN	Aishling Morgan		
TIGER, TIGER	Aishling Morgan		
THE WARRIOR QUEEN	Kendal Grahame		

EDWARDIAN, VICTORIAN & OLDER EROTICA

BEATRICE	Anonymous		
CONFESSION OF AN ENGLISH SLAVE	Yolanda Celbridge		
DEVON CREAM	Aishling Morgan		
THE GOVERNESS AT ST AGATHA'S	Yolanda Celbridge		
PURITY	Aishling Morgan		July
THE RAKE	Aishling Morgan		
THE TRAINING OF AN ENGLISH GENTLEMAN	Yolanda Celbridge		

SAMPLERS & COLLECTIONS

NEW EROTICA 3		
NEW EROTICA 5		Nov
A DOZEN STROKES	Various	

NEXUS CLASSICS

A new imprint dedicated to putting the finest works of erotic fiction back in print

AGONY AUNT	G. C. Scott	
THE HANDMAIDENS	Aran Ashe	
OBSESSION	Maria del Rey	
HIS MISTRESS'S VOICE	G.C. Scott	
CITADEL OF SERVITUDE	Aran Ashe	
BOUND TO SERVE	Amanda Ware	
SISTERHOOD OF THE INSTITUTE	Maria del Rey	
A MATTER OF POSSESSION	G.C. Scott	
THE PLEASURE PRINCIPLE	Maria del Rey	
CONDUCT UNBECOMING	Arabella Knight	
CANDY IN CAPTIVITY	Arabella Knight	
THE SLAVE OF LIDIR	Aran Ashe	
THE DUNGEONS OF LIDIR	Aran Ashe	
SERVING TIME	Sarah Veitch	July
THE TRAINING GROUNDS	Sarah Veitch	Aug
DIFFERENT STROKES	Sarah Veitch	Sept
LINGERING LESSONS	Sarah Veitch	Oct
EDEN UNVEILED	Maria del Rey	Nov
UNDERWORLD	Maria del Rey	Dec

Please send me the books I have ticked above.

Name ....

Address ....

....

....

.... Post code....................

Send to: **Cash Sales, Nexus Books, Thames Wharf Studios, Rainville Road, London W6 9HA**

US customers: for prices and details of how to order books for delivery by mail, call 1-800-805-1083.

Please enclose a cheque or postal order, made payable to **Nexus Books**, to the value of the books you have ordered plus postage and packing costs as follows:

UK and BFPO – £1.00 for the first book, 50p for the second book and 30p for each subsequent book to a maximum of £3.00;

Overseas (including Republic of Ireland) – £2.00 for the first book, £1.00 for the second book and 50p for each subsequent book.

We accept all major credit cards, including VISA, ACCESS/ MASTERCARD, AMEX, DINERS CLUB, SWITCH, SOLO, and DELTA. Please write your card number and expiry date here:

....

Please allow up to 28 days for delivery.

Signature ....